THE GIFT
OF GOD IS
ETERNAL LIFE

THE GIFT
OF GOD IS
ETERNAL LIFE

A Novel about Universalism

STEVEN H. PROPP

THE GIFT OF GOD IS ETERNAL LIFE
A NOVEL ABOUT UNIVERSALISM

iUniverse books may be ordered through booksellers or by contacting:

iUniverse
1663 Liberty Drive
Bloomington, IN 47403
www.iuniverse.com
1-800-Authors (1-800-288-4677)

ISBN: 978-1-5320-1423-9 (sc)
ISBN: 978-1-5320-1422-2 (hc)
ISBN: 978-1-5320-1421-5 (e)

Library of Congress Control Number: 2016921422

Print information available on the last page.

iUniverse rev. date: 12/28/2016

CONTENTS

"For the wages of sin is death; but **the gift of God is eternal life** through Jesus Christ our Lord." (Romans 6:23, KJV)

"God our Savior, who wants all people to be saved and to come to a knowledge of the truth. For there is one God and one mediator between God and mankind, the man Christ Jesus, who gave himself as a ransom for all people." (1 Timothy 2:3-6, NIV)

"For as in Adam all die, even so in Christ shall all be made alive." (1 Cor 15:22, KJV)

"Consequently, just as one trespass resulted in condemnation for all people, so also one righteous act resulted in justification and life for all people." (Romans 5:18, NIV)

DEDICATION

To those who are willing to seriously ponder "difficult" and even "uncomfortable" questions...

ACKNOWLEDGEMENTS

As always, this book is offered with deep love, and continuing gratitude, for the help, encouragement, and support of:

My friends and readers everywhere;

Our six wonderful grandkids: Devonte, Joseph, Dominic, Kayla, Mariah, and Brea;

My brother-in-law Darrel Buzynski;

My fantastic big sister Susan;

My niece Jennifer and her husband Brade—and their daughters Madison and Leila;

My "favorite" nephew Jason;

And all the rest of our diverse, evolving, and always loving family.

But most of all: To my beautiful, wonderful wife, Nancy—the light and love of my life, forever and always—whose love has sustained and inspired me for thirty years… and whose loving heart is continually being passed on to the next generations…

NOTE TO READERS

The sermon preached by John Murray in Chapter 2 is based on a number of his sermon outlines, which are available in his three volumes of *Letters and Sketches of Sermons* (particularly the first volume).

The arguments used in the 19th century debate (Chapters 4 & 5) are those used in actual debates from this period; see the "Discussions, Debates" section in the Bibliography, for examples.

PART ONE

THE SEVENTEENTH CENTURY (ENGLAND)

CHAPTER 1

New Doctrines, and A New Land (1661)

The nicely-dressed middle-aged man reached out, and took hold of the metal handle, then pulled it to open the well-worn door of the tavern. He stepped inside the darkened room, then waited a moment while his eyes adjusted to the darkness.

The newcomer began to search the room, ignoring the various groups of men, who were loudly conversing with each other. Then he noticed a younger man (in his mid-20s) sitting at a back corner table by himself, with a pint of ale in front of him; the younger man saw him, and smiled. After nodding slightly to the seated man, the newcomer walked over to the bar, and waited for the proprietor to approach him.

"What'll ye be havin', mate?" the proprietor of the inn said, in a friendly voice.

"A pint of ale," he replied. The proprietor nodded, then picked up a mug from a stack on the bar, and headed over to a large wooden keg. In the meantime, the newcomer took out several coins from his pocket, and placed them on the thick wooden counter.

"Thank you," he said, as the proprietor handed him the mug—spilling it slightly, as they made the exchange.

"Sorry, mate," the proprietor said apologetically. "Lemme fill that back up for you…"

The newcomer shook his head, and said, "That's not necessary; thank you, anyway." He moved the coins he had placed on the counter over to the proprietor, who promptly swept them into a pocket of his apron, and then returned to wait on his other customers.

The newcomer walked with his mug toward the younger man in the corner, while discreetly avoiding making eye contact with all others in the room—although several of them looked at the newcomer with curiosity (his clothes seemed rather "finer" than those the others were wearing), but then they simply resumed their own animated conversations.

The younger man in the corner motioned for the newcomer to take the seat at the table opposite him, which he did.

Once they were seated, the older man smiled, then extended his hand and said softly, "Good evening, Adam; it's good to see you."

"I'm very glad to see you, Walter," the younger man replied, as they shook hands warmly. The younger man ("Adam") motioned for the older man ("Walter") to take a drink of his beverage; Walter did so gratefully, and then breathed out a sigh of relaxed relief.

Adam looked at Walter expectantly, but the older man said nothing (although there was noticeably a small twinkle in his eye, as he took another leisurely swallow of his ale).

Finally, Adam could wait no longer, and whispered (with excitement mixed with agitation), "Well?" He looked anxiously at the older man, who seemingly enjoyed drawing out the moment.

Finally, Walter said with seeming casualness, "I bought it."

"You did?" Adam gasped, his enthusiasm causing his voice to rise. He quickly glanced around, to see if he had attracted the notice of anyone, but the others in the room remained absorbed in their own affairs, and paid the duo sitting in the back no mind.

"I did indeed," Walter confirmed, placing his hand on the younger man's forearm, as he said earnestly, "And I read it in one sitting last night. It is a fine work, Adam; a fine work!"

A tremendous weight seemed to be lifted from Adam's shoulders, after hearing this. He took a large drink from his mug of ale, and then let out a long sigh of satisfaction.

But he quickly turned anxious again, and asked Walter, "Was it on display at the bookseller's? Or did you have to ask…"

"I had to ask for it, of course," Walter explained. "I simply gave the bookseller the pen name you used, and the title of the book, and asked if he had a copy I could purchase; he immediately nodded, and then pulled out a copy of it from right behind the counter, and handed it to me." He drank some more ale, and then said apologetically, "I could not see how many other copies he might have had behind the counter."

Adam thought for a moment, and then admitted, "It's good, I think, that the book is not on display; that way, there's fewer nosey 'churchmen' to take notice of it, and then take up their cudgels against me!" He smiled, then added, "I don't fancy myself as being the subject of critical sermons by Anglican or Romanist clerics, who view themselves as the defenders of the public morality!" He took a fast swallow from his mug, and then leaned back in his seat, seemingly deep in thought.

"The book was well-argued, I felt," Walter explained. "I enjoyed the early chapters, outlining the history of the new doctrines on the continent: beginning with Anabaptists like Balthasar Hubmaier and Michael Sattler in Germany, Menno Simons in the Low Countries, and leading up to the Socinians in Poland." He reflected for a moment, then said thoughtfully, "This historical material is very important, since so many of the writings of these persons and groups have been suppressed, or are not available in English translation."

Adam said, with uncharacteristic bitterness in his voice, "The self-righteous leaders of the 'established' churches have ruthlessly suppressed the Anabaptist publications... as well as their leaders! Hubmaier and Sattler were *executed* in Austria—as you know from my book."

"Indeed," Walter said gravely, taking a long draught from his ale.

An undercurrent of anger rose in Adam's voice, as he said acidly, "And all because they dared to challenge the 'characteristic' teaching of the Romanists and Reformed churchmen!"

"And particularly, because they dared to quote *Scripture* in defense of their unorthodox views," Walter said, then glancing around the room nervously as he spoke, to make sure that their words were not attracting the attention of any of the other patrons; but they remained unnoticed, so he relaxed a bit, and looked at the younger man sitting across from him once again with curiosity.

Adam (in a hushed, but passionate voice) said, "But the doctrine of 'soul sleep' is clearly taught in the Holy Bible! Martin Luther himself was a strong defender of it, in many of his voluminous writings." He

5

grimaced, then added, "But then John Calvin—when he was still strongly influenced by Romanism, it must be admitted—wrote that damnable book, *Psychopannychia,* condemning the biblical doctrine of the sleep of the soul; and he and Zwingli viciously persecuted the Anabaptists who taught the doctrine."

Walter nodded, and added, "Even as Calvin's condemnation of Michael Servetus's denial of the Trinity resulted in Servetus being burned at the stake." He leaned forward in his chair, and said fervently, "But that is why I continue to counsel you, my impetuous young friend, to remain *anonymous* in your writings on this subject. No one—save the printer, the bookseller, and those of us close friends in whom you choose to confide—need know that it is *you* who is expressing these radical ideas…"

Adam said indignantly, "You would have me hide the *truth?* Did not the Savior himself say that 'No man, when he hath lighted a candle, covereth it with a vessel, or putteth it under a bed; but setteth it on a candlestick, that they which enter in may see the light'?" [Lk 8:16]

Walter pointed out, "Remember that our Savior was *crucified.*" He added meaningfully, "And, by your own doctrines, *you* could not expect to be raised from the dead on the third day." Adam seemed chagrined by this statement, and Walter raised his hands defensively, and said consolingly, "I do not mean to silence you, my friend; I simply advise a measure of *prudence,* in your…"

Adam quickly grasped his friend's hands reassuringly, and said, "I apologize, my friend; I spoke out of turn. I assure you that my vitriol is not directed against you, but against those forces in the English and Romanist churches who dogmatically oppose all disagreements with their doctrines: not with arguments from Scripture or reason, but with the *stake,* and their many implements of torture."

Walter shivered involuntarily, and said, "Which is why I fear for you, my young friend. True, the printer and the bookseller are much in sympathy with your views, and would certainly shield you to the best of their ability. But if the local magistrate should take action to compel them to reveal your identity, I fear that their instincts of *self-preservation* would overrule their noble beliefs in the principle of freedom of thought, and…"

Adam drew himself up proudly, and said, "But why should the magistrate be interested in me? I am not denying the Trinity: I gladly affirm that Christ was both fully God, and fully Man, and that the Holy Spirit is the third Person in the Divine Godhead, along with the Father. I do not even deny the doctrine of the baptism of infants, as do the Anabaptists; and I fully and unhesitatingly accept the complete authority of the Holy Bible!" He shrugged, and added, "And if I merely point out that the Bible itself teaches that the soul 'sleeps' after death, while awaiting the general resurrection of the dead, what of it? As I said earlier, Luther himself taught this!"

Walter nodded, and said cautiously, "That is true; but you also affirm, in your book, some more *controversial* doctrines—in particular, your strong and fervent rejection of the doctrine of the eternal fiery torment of the damned in Hell."

"The illustrious Samuel Richardson has recently expressed his own rejection of the theory of eternal torment; I cannot do otherwise," Adam replied, with deep conviction in his voice. "The Scriptures tell us clearly that 'God is *love*'; yet churchmen in their pulpits arrogantly assert that this loving Father has arbitrarily chosen some souls for eternal bliss in Heaven, while just as arbitrarily condemning other souls to eternal flames!" He shook his head, and said vigorously, "Our Savior assuredly taught no such doctrine; and it is a near-*blasphemy* of God to suggest that He is the author of such a travesty! The gates of the New Jerusalem 'shall not be shut at all,' says the Apostle in the Book of the Revelation, chapter 21, verse 25."

"Those in ecclesiastical authority say otherwise," Walter advised, his voice calm and steady. He patted Adam's hand reassuringly, then said softly, "You know that I unhesitatingly agree with you on this point, and feel as strongly as you that the doctrine of eternal torment in a fiery Hell is an abomination; and, like you, I hope and pray for the day when those of us who realize this truth, can persuade those in authority to agree with us." He then looked directly into the younger man's eyes, and said with deep feeling, "But at the present time, my friend, you and I do not live in the New Jerusalem: we live in England! True, some 'ivory tower' philosophers at Cambridge University—such as Ralph Cudworth, and Henry More— may feel themselves able freely to speculate about such matters; but you and I are but ordinary men, not academics."

Adam snorted contemptuously, and replied, "So you are saying that non-professors have no right to think, and to reason?"

Walter smiled slightly, and replied. "You know that I am not saying that." They both drank from their mugs. Then Walter noted, "And, I beg you, please remember that our country has an 'established' Church, which is fully supported by the crown, and paid for by taxes imposed on all of us; and all those who do not subscribe to this church are pilloried as 'Dissenters,' and become subject to various forms of persecution. And, although Romanism has now been vastly reduced in terms of its influence in our homeland, it has not been that long since 'Bloody Mary' was on the throne, and wrought her terrible vengeance upon those who would not conform to the Roman Church!"

"Which is why I shall shortly be leaving these shores," Adam said, with seeming indifference.

Walter was nearly struck dumb by this unexpected revelation. When he finally regained his presence of mind and voice, he asked, "You are leaving England?"

"Yes," Adam replied, his mouth in a tight smile. "I have already booked passage on a ship; I shall be leaving for the colonies next month." Seeing the look of astonishment on Walter's face, he shrugged, and asked, "And why not? I am a strong and intelligent young man; stodgy Olde England can have but little attraction for me."

Still nonplussed, Walter asked, "But isn't your father counting on your taking up his trade, after he…"

"I have not the patience to wait that long… nor any deep desire to assume the trade of a common shoemaker," Adam replied. He added proudly, "My calling is to the world of books, and ideas."

With a slight smile, Walter added, "But books and ideas do not provide the *income* needed to support even a bright and industrious young man; much less a family." Adam remained silent, so Walter simply sighed, took a long drink of his ale, and then asked, "Where will you go?"

Eagerly, Adam explained, "Initially, to New England, in the northeastern area; but I plan to make my way down to an area called 'Providence,' where the former Puritan Roger Williams has established a colony, which has as its fundamental idea, that of *religious freedom!*"

Walter frowned, and asked doubtfully, "Was Roger Williams not *expelled* from the Massachusetts Bay Colony, on the grounds of heresy?"

Adam shrugged, and replied, "What if he was? His new colony allows both Baptists and Dissenters the freedom to worship as they please."

Still dubious, Walter commented, "If you were a Reformed Baptist, I should simply wish you 'Godspeed.'" He again looked Adam directly in the eyes, and then said soberly, "But the doctrines you seemingly espouse go far beyond the rejection of the Predestinarian heresies of John Calvin, and the denial of a Hell of eternal misery for the unrepentant. And, while I respect your powerful Scriptural arguments in favor of your new ideas, I must say that I part company with you with respect to your espousal of *Origenism*."

Adam shrugged again and took a long drink of his ale, before replying calmly, "The Romanist Church suppressed the writings of Origen for hundreds of years. Now that these books have finally seen the light of day again and been reprinted, so that all those of us with a scholarly bent can read them, we are able to see the truths which he so powerfully advocated."

"Origen was condemned as a heretic at the Second Council of Constantinople!" Walter hissed—but then immediately looked cautiously about the room, to see if his outburst had attracted any attention. (Two men at a nearby table briefly glanced over at him, but then just as quickly returned to their own ale and conversations.) Relieved, he turned his attention back to his younger friend.

Adam explained patiently, "Origen was 'condemned' by the Roman Church nearly three hundred years after his death; so he had no opportunity to defend himself against these Romanist attacks. Furthermore, many of his writings were destroyed after this condemnation, so that we of later generations cannot fairly assess whether he indeed taught any 'heresies.'"

Walter said bluntly, "He taught the *pre-existence* of the human soul; he denied the ultimate and final resurrection of the body. And, as you well know, he advocated the heretical doctrine of the *ultimate reconciliation* of all men—perhaps even of the Devil!"

Adam chuckled lightly, and observed, "If by the sin of Adam condemnation came upon all—as the Apostle Paul in his letter to the Romans tells us [5:18]—then, as he added, 'even so by the righteousness of one the free gift came upon *all men* unto justification of life.'" He added, in a hushed tone, "If we were all *condemned* through Adam, then does it not follow logically that, through Christ, we are all *redeemed*?"

Walter just shook his head sadly, and said, "I am not a Scripture scholar, my friend; but *none* of the official branches of the Christian Church— Roman, Greek, Lutheran, Reformed, Anglican, or even Anabaptist—have ever formally taught such a doctrine. And the Romanist Church strongly repudiated it as heresy!"

Adam shrugged his shoulders again, then gazed into his mug of ale for a long moment. Finally, he said, "I have not said here, nor did I say in my short book, that I was yet fully *persuaded* of the Origenist position. I simply suggest that it is a position that seems to have some considerable Scriptural support; and I believe it should be possible to freely discuss it, without fear of reprisals from hostile churchmen. But I would also note that Gerrard Winstanley—one of the 'True Levellers'—has recently openly advocated the Origenist doctrine of universal salvation." Walter did not reply, so Adam added hopefully, "You could even *join* me, in the New World; your wife passed on years ago, and you could just as easily ply your trade there, as here."

Walter looked long at the face and eyes of his younger friend, and then observed, "Yes, I believe that the New World is *indeed* an appropriate place for a lively-minded young man such as yourself." He took another drink from his mug, but then admitted, "For myself, I am an older man; the notion of pulling myself up by the roots, and leaving the country of my heritage and birth at this late date would be … far more than I could tolerate, I am afraid."

Adam smiled, and said gently, "You are not so old, my friend." He patted Walter's hand reassuringly.

Walter shrugged, and replied, "Too old for an adventure such as you propose, I fear." He raised his mug, and said, "But wherever you may venture, Adam McGavin, I pray that the Lord's blessing will be upon you. You are a good, an earnest, and an honest man; you deserve nothing but the best: in this life, and in the life to come."

Adam raised his own mug, and they clacked them together, then drank a toast.

Placing his mug back down on the table, Walter asked, "So will the bookseller continue to carry your book, after your departure?"

Adam nodded, and replied, "Of the hundred copies I paid the printer for, I will be keeping seventy for myself; they shall be the most important component of my baggage, when I travel abroad." He said with a grin, "I shall be packing more books than clothes!" and they both laughed. He added, in a serious tone, "And I profoundly hope to discover that, in the New World, one can openly publish such sincere books, without the necessity of using a *pseudonym!*" and they both laughed heartily.

Having finished their drinks, they both rose from the table. As they shook hands across the table once again, Adam pledged, "I will regularly write to you, my friend, to let you know how my adventure is progressing."

"I shall await your letters eagerly," Walter replied. The two men began to head to the exit.

As they passed by one table, one of the men sitting there (whose breath reeked of cheap gin) reached out a hand to stop Walter, and he said gruffly, "I thought I heard you two discussin' religion; you ain't no damned *Anabaptists,* are ye?"

Walter drew himself up, and said with genuine indignity, "Certainly not! I was baptized into the Church of England at birth, as was my friend."

The gruff man removed his hand from Walter's arm and nodded his head, then said, "That's good, that's good. Them damned Anabaptists need a good *beating,* they do—imagine 'em sayin' that we wasn't really baptized!" He downed the last of his gin, then barked, "Bloody 'ell! My Mum and Dad had me baptized when I was a week old; and there ain't nothin' no Anabaptists can do, to take that away!"

Walter just nodded silently, and then subtly motioned with his head for Adam to follow him to the door.

Once they were safely outside the establishment, the two men shook hands a final time. Walter said, "We surely must get together again, before you depart."

Adam smiled, and agreed: "And so we shall. Goodbye for now, my friend." He waved, and then set off on foot.

Walter began walking in the opposite direction.

PART TWO

THE EIGHTEENTH CENTURY (RHODE ISLAND)

CHAPTER 2

A Preacher of the Gospel
(Fall, 1773)

Joseph Strong was a farmer in his early 30s. Although he had once been a rather jovial, outgoing man, he was now considered by nearly all in the area to be taciturn and moody—not desiring the company of others. He seemed content to simply work hard, raising and harvesting his crops all by himself—since he had no wife, nor any offspring. But his fall crop had recently been fully harvested, so he sat down on a stump in the late afternoon, and picked up a stray stalk of wheat, which he turned about idly in his hand, as he looked out over his vacant fields.

A man on a horse emerged from the thick trees, and rode into the clearing; the horse was walking slowly, as if exhausted. The stranger spied Joseph sitting down, and then pulled the reins gently, to move his steed to head in that direction.

As he approached Joseph, the stranger said in a warm tone, "Good day, friend. My horse and I have traveled quite some time, and both of us are assailed by thirst. I wonder if we might trouble you for some water?" Joseph noted that the man spoke with an English accent.

"Certainly," Joseph replied quickly, dropping his stalk of wheat, and getting up from the stump. He motioned for the stranger to follow him to the nearby well; the stranger dismounted, and led his horse following Joseph.

Joseph turned the handle to lower, and then raise the wooden bucket in the well. When it reached the top of the well, he removed the wooden dipper from the bucket, and handed it to the stranger, being careful not to spill it. The stranger drank from it thirstily, then handed it back to Joseph, saying, "Thank you, kind Sir; your charity is much appreciated."

Joseph then poured the rest of the bucket of water into a larger trough in front of the well, and began lowering the bucket into the well again. The stranger's horse immediately began lapping up the water. Once Joseph had raised the bucket again, he once more poured its contents into the trough.

When the horse had satisfied its thirst, Joseph lowered the bucket back down into the well. Then he turned to examine the stranger more carefully: his visitor was about the same age as himself, although his hair was much longer in the back and sides; the stranger's clothes seemed more appropriate to a cultured gentleman, than to one riding alone in the wilderness.

"You're English?" Joseph asked the stranger.

"I am," admitted the newcomer.

Joseph shrugged, and said, "My grandparents were English; but my father and I were born in this country."

The stranger nodded, and said, "I've been here for but two years, myself; but already, I am quite taken with this land."

Joseph asked, "Where are you coming from?"

"Connecticut," the stranger replied. "I am intending to visit several towns in Rhode Island; I spent some time in Providence, shortly after I arrived in this country. I greatly enjoyed my time there."

Joseph nodded, then inquired, "So what business draws you here?"

The stranger looked Joseph in the eyes, and replied evenly, "I am a preacher of the Gospel."

Joseph immediately turned rigid, and he looked at the stranger with hard eyes filled with great suspicion. He said in a cold, flat tone, "I have no use for religion, myself." Remembering his manners, he added, "But the town has a number of churches in it; I'm sure you will find welcome someplace therein." He began to turn away, intending to head back to his tree stump.

The stranger asked gently, "Might I first inquire of you, dear Sir, why does the mere mention of my calling seem to so displease you? I assure you that I had no designs upon you, other than to ask for some water for myself and my horse."

Joseph stopped, and turned around to face the stranger. With a sharp edge in his voice, he said, "My wife and I used to belong to one of the churches in the town; the one my grandfather and father helped establish."

"I see," the stranger replied. "So are you no longer a parishioner there? And is your wife…"

"My wife is dead," Joseph replied, his tone flat, and lifeless. With bitterness in his voice, he added, "And your God seemingly has no use for her."

The stranger seemed puzzled. With the expression on his face conveying genuine sympathy, he asked gently, "But the Gospel I preach asserts firmly that, one day, you will be reunited with your wife, and…"

Joseph cut him off, saying, "That's not what the 'learned minister' of our church said of her, after she died; he said that she had clearly shown herself to be *not* one of the 'Elect'!"

The stranger looked shocked, and then said with feeling, "I can hardly believe that a minister, of whatever persuasion, would say such a thing! What a shocking misstatement of the 'good news' of the Gospel message!" His voice softened, and he added, "But please be assured, my grieving friend, that I feel deep, profound, and *personal* sympathy for you. My own beloved wife passed on, shortly before I decided to come to this country."

Joseph looked at the stranger with newfound respect and appreciation, and he said in a gentler tone, "You are also a widower, then?"

The stranger said softly, "I am." Drawing himself up, he said to Joseph in an encouraging tone, "But the Gospel of which I am a messenger assures me that your wife is now safely in the loving hands of her Creator; and that one day, you and she will again be…"

Joseph said harshly, "The minister of the church of my father and grandfather charged that her actions proved that she had no 'calling' of God, as one of His Elect. So if his 'God' has no use for my beloved Regina, then I have no use for his God!" This harsh, bitter statement hung starkly in the air, as both men remained silent for a long moment.

Finally, the stranger shook his head sympathetically, and observed, "That is indeed shocking, my friend." He thought for a moment, and then asked, "May I inquire of what church your grandfather comes from?"

"He was of Puritan stock," Joseph replied. "He was a strong admirer of Jonathan Edwards of Massachusetts, as was my father."

"I see," the stranger said, nodding his head with understanding. "Followers of the doctrines of John Calvin, I see. But please accept my assurance that my own doctrines bear no resemblance to those of Calvin— whose teachings I frankly find abhorrent, and in complete contradiction to the 'good news' of the Gospel of Jesus Christ!" He thought for a moment, then asked quietly, "You said that this minister raised objection to some 'actions' of your wife. Might I inquire of what nature those were?"

Joseph hesitated, and then replied, "Regina became friendly with some women in town of German extraction. They were members of no formal church, but met periodically to read the Scriptures, and pray. They also read aloud works by authors such as Jakob Böhme and Johann Arndt. They believed that the formal Church was in error, and that there needed to be a revival of true, *devout* Christianity."

The stranger nodded again, and asked, "Your wife was a Christian, then?"

Joseph replied passionately, "In all my life, I have never known a finer Christian!" With tears coming to his eyes, he recalled, "Her entire life was one of the utmost piety; she read her Bible, and prayed, and served her Lord with her every deed." A slight smile came to his lips, as he remembered, "She would even come and read the Scriptures to me, as I worked in the field. Although I was not a particularly devout churchgoer, something in her spirit simply... found a resonance, within me." He said wistfully, "At times... I could nearly *believe,* in the God of whom she spoke."

The stranger said firmly, "Your testimony has quite persuaded me; your dear wife was indeed a fine, Christian woman." He touched Joseph's shoulder gently, and said, "I feel quite as strongly about my own dear Eliza, my grieving friend."

Joseph firmly clasped the stranger's hand in his own, and noted, "We appear to be brothers in profound *loss,* then." Then they let their hands fall back down to their sides.

The stranger sighed, and said, "I have heard much of the doctrines of this Jonathan Edwards; and I have even read a reprint of one of his sermons, entitled, 'Sinners in the Hands of an Angry God.'" He shivered involuntarily, and then added, "Such doctrines seem to me to be a gross *slander* of our loving Creator." He shook his head, and said in a firm tone, "If I should likewise preach the terrors of a future world, what would be the consequence of this? Would my hearers *love* God the better? True, they might *fear* God the more—but is there any fear in love? The Apostle John told us that 'perfect love casteth out fear.'" [1 Jn 4:18]

Joseph said with enthusiasm, "That passage was one of Regina's favorites, from the Scriptures! She would quote it to me frequently!"

The stranger observed, "There are those—unfortunately bearing ministerial credentials, in most cases—who believe that the redemption of Christ our Redeemer is confined to a very few; with these few having been chosen before the foundation of the world. Yet they also teach that those of this 'Elect' possess no peculiar excellence, which would grant them the favor of the Almighty." He shook his head, and said proudly, "My own doctrine, however, is firmly set against such 'partialists'; but I am afraid that my way represents the *narrow* way spoken of by the Saviour—while the *broad* way is thronged by persons of every description."

Becoming interested (in spite of himself), Joseph asked, "What is your doctrine, then?"

"It is not mine, only," the stranger explained. "It is the great doctrine of the final salvation of the entire family of man. The name 'Universalist' has been applied to our doctrines. We believe that we have nothing to fear, but everything to hope; and we live in the expectation of living with our common Saviour, for all of eternity."

Fascinated with this statement, Joseph said earnestly, "I would gladly hear more of your doctrine, Sir. Have you any pressing engagements—or can you perhaps sup with me this evening?"

The stranger smiled, and replied, "I have no engagements; I simply enter a town, and seek to find some empathic souls."

Joseph said warmly, "Then let us take your horse to my barn, and find him some food, whilst you and I discuss these weightier matters." He held out his hand to the stranger, and said, "My name is Strong; Joseph Strong."

As they shook hands, the stranger replied, "And I am Murray: John Murray."

Joseph then led Murray's horse to the barn.

***

After dinner, as they sat before the fire enjoying a cup of wine, Joseph asked Murray, "So please tell me more, of how you happened to arrive in this country."

Murray nodded, took a sip of his wine, then replied, "I was once a fervent supporter of the traditional doctrines; of Methodism, in my case. I was an earnest advocate of this way, and was actually viewed as a lay 'leader' in my home congregation; in this capacity, I was not infrequently asked to present our version of the gospel to those we deemed 'unconverted.'" He recalled for a moment, and then added, "But one day, I was asked to lead a small group of my younger and less experienced religious brethren: to approach a young lady, who we felt had strayed from the path of truth. I was fully expected to convert her, back to what we deemed the true path."

He leaned back in his chair (with a contented smile on his face, over this memory), and explained, "But this lady remained firm. She asked me, 'Pray, sir; what is the unbeliever damned for not believing?' I was surprised by her question, but I finally replied that he must believe that Jesus Christ is his complete Saviour. But then she pointed out that, since Jesus Christ is not the Saviour of unbelievers, this would be calling upon him to believe a *lie!* She then asked me, 'Why should any unbeliever believe that Jesus Christ is his Saviour, if he be *not* his Saviour?'"

"Hmm," Joseph murmured, genuinely surprised by this question.

Murray continued, "She then stated that 'Jesus is the complete Saviour of unbelievers,' and that unbelievers are therefore called upon to believe the truth; and that, by believing, they are saved, in their own apprehension, from 'all those dreadful fears which are consequent upon a state of conscious condemnation.' I was left stumbling for an answer, and she next asked me about the circumstances of my own salvation, perplexing me with the inquiry, 'Did Jesus never *die* for you, till you believed, sir?' I was left mortified and speechless by this unexpected question."

Joseph took a swallow of his wine, and admitted, "As I would have been."

Murray went on, "The young lady had clearly bested me in the argument, but she was gracious enough not to press her advantage; she simply bade us well, and my colleagues and I departed—with my companions clearly disappointed, and resentful of what they deemed was my poor performance." He thought for a moment, and then added, "But, as I reflected over the incident, I soon came to see that the young lady was quite correct: and that if the Redeemer did *not* taste death for all; if He has *not* purchased all, then those for whom He has *not* tasted death, and whom He has *not* purchased, have no right to believe that He has! And, were they so to believe, they must indubitably believe a lie!"

"That is indeed a most striking point," Joseph admitted, looking with ever-deepening respect at his guest.

Murray continued his narrative: "At this same time, I had heard of a James Relly—whom my Methodist colleagues considered to be but little separated from Satan himself! But I chanced upon a copy of his book, *Union: or a Treatise on the Consanguinity and Affinity between Christ and His Church,* in my father-in-law's library, and he loaned it to me. This marvelous book introduced me to many passages of Scripture which had previously quite escaped my observation. Soon, my wife and I quietly went to hear Relly preach in one of the Quakers' meeting-houses."

With near-awe in his eyes, he recalled, "I was absolutely captivated by his sermon—I felt I had never before heard such unadulterated truth; it was the first truly *consistent* sermon I had ever heard! Indeed, I wondered how it was possible that discoveries so important should never, until now, have been made; and now, only by this one man. It was Relly who wholly removed the final vestiges of the Calvinist doctrine from me; I was humbled by my new knowledge that there was no such body as 'the Elect.' I now began my dedicated and diligent re-reading of the Scriptures, and found that the Bible was indeed a *new book* to me."

"Indeed," Joseph observed, captivated by Murray's story.

Murray added, "Thus, I became what Relly called a 'Universalist.' In due course, my Methodist society brethren could no longer abide my changed beliefs, and they duly voted me out of their society. It was, sadly, at this same time that my dear wife passed on, as well. So, after a chance encounter with an American, I became intrigued by the possibilities of life over here; so, on the advice and encouragement of friends, two years ago last July—with only my Bible, my wife's letters, and a volume of Relly's sermon outlines, which he gave me as a parting gift—I set out for the New World. The ship I traveled on ran aground, so I disembarked in New Jersey: intent upon boldly promulgating the Gospel of God, our Saviour."

He smiled in a self-deprecating manner, and then explained, "I decidedly possessed no 'credentials' whatsoever to preach; not even a letter of introduction. But providentially, I soon encountered a fine senior gentleman named Thomas Potter, who had sympathies with the Universalist cause; he had built a meeting-house on his property, which he allowed various itinerant preachers to use; it was in this setting that I preached my first Universalist sermon. Mr. Potter persuaded me to stay on there for a while, since he considered me to be 'God's appointed messenger'—a role I firmly disclaimed, of course."

Joseph smiled, and said, "I am glad to hear that; I do not fancy the idea of having invited a 'messenger of God' into my humble home," and they both laughed.

Joseph looked at his visitor, and said in a warm manner, "I find myself surprisingly interested in your ideas, John; had I heard someone espousing them after my wife's tragic death, it might have kept me from stopping my attendance at church services on the Sabbath. But still, I can see where your ideas might be considered quite controversial—even as the ideas discussed in my wife's prayer and study group were. Have you... encountered any such controversies or difficulties, in this regard?"

Murray smiled wryly, and admitted, "I have been pelted by stones while engaged in the pulpit, more than once. One time, a stone weighing a pound-and-a-half was thrown violently in through a window at me, but it fortunately missed. So, with the congregation watching in amazed attention, I lifted this stone up, and waved it in the view of the parishioners, and then observed, 'This argument is *solid* and *weighty;* but is it neither *rational,* nor *convincing,*'" and they both laughed heartily.

An idea occurred to Joseph, and he said, "Today is Friday; have you any scheduled engagements for the coming Sabbath?"

Murray shook his head, and said, "No; but I have been to Rhode Island before, so I supposed that I would just follow my usual practice: enter town, and begin to talk to some congenial folks about religion, and..."

Joseph interrupted, saying enthusiastically, "My neighbor to the south is a Congregationalist; but he tells me that their regular pastor will be away for several weeks, visiting other parishes. I could speak to him, if you might fancy the notion of staying with me for a few days, and preaching in his church this Sunday."

Murray thought for a moment, and then said, "I would be agreeable to that; but I do not wish to put you out, and impose on your gracious hospitality. Is there not a lodging-house nearby, where I might..."

"Please, I would not tolerate that," Joseph said firmly. He raised his glass of wine, and then said, "In the morrow, we will go and speak with my neighbor. I think you will find that most—many, anyway—members of his congregation are quite open-minded, and rational, about matters of religion..."

***

That Sunday morning, Murray stepped up to the simple, unadorned wooden pulpit, which was situated at one end of the equally simple one-room meeting house. As the weather had turned unseasonably warm, the windows of the room were fully opened, to allow the late morning breeze to freely enter.

Murray opened his well-worn Bible and laid it down on the pulpit, then announced, "My text this morning is taken from the twenty-fifth chapter of the Gospel according to Matthew, verses 31-46." Looking down at his Bible, he proceeded to read in a calm, unhurried voice:

> When the Son of man shall come in his glory, and all the holy angels with him, then shall he sit upon the throne of his glory: And before him shall be gathered all nations: and he shall separate them one from another, as a shepherd divideth his sheep from the goats: And he shall set the sheep on his right hand, but the goats on the left. Then shall the King say unto them on his right hand, Come, ye blessed of my Father, inherit the kingdom prepared for you from the foundation of the world: For I was hungry, and ye gave me meat: I was thirsty, and ye gave me drink: I was a stranger, and ye took me in: Naked, and ye clothed me: I was sick, and ye visited me: I was in prison, and ye came unto me. Then shall the righteous answer him, saying, Lord, when saw we thee hungry, and fed thee? or thirsty, and gave thee drink? When saw we thee a stranger, and took thee in? or naked, and clothed thee? Or when saw we thee sick, or in prison, and came unto thee? And the King shall answer and say unto them, Verily I say unto you, Inasmuch

as ye have done it unto one of the least of these my brethren, ye have done it unto me.

Then shall he say also unto them on the left hand, Depart from me, ye cursed, into everlasting fire, prepared for the devil and his angels: For I was hungry, and ye gave me no meat: I was thirsty, and ye gave me no drink: I was a stranger, and ye took me not in: naked, and ye clothed me not: sick, and in prison, and ye visited me not. Then shall they also answer him, saying, Lord, when saw we thee hungry, or athirst, or a stranger, or naked, or sick, or in prison, and did not minister unto thee? Then shall he answer them, saying, Verily I say unto you, Inasmuch as ye did it not to one of the least of these, ye did it not to me. And these shall go away into everlasting punishment: but the righteous into life eternal.

He left his Bible open, as he addressed the congregation, "Who were those he spake to, and who were those he spake of? The Apostle Jude informs us in verse 6 of his book that they were the angels, who 'kept not their first estate'; who are 'reserved in everlasting chains under darkness, unto the judgment of the great day.' In the parable I just read, Christ is describing this scene of judgment.

"Let us remember that Satan, the arch-fiend, was *cursed* by God in the garden of Eden; and since Christ, the Saviour of men, had not been made a curse to redeem *angels* [Gal 3:13], but only men, those rebellious angels are still cursed. Matthew 25 thus describes how our faithful Creator will separate the *deceivers* from the *deceived*—even as a shepherd divides his sheep from his goats, putting one on his right hand, and the other on his left. And, turning to the other subjects of this general judgment, he shall say, 'Depart … ye cursed into everlasting fire, prepared for the Devil and his angels.' Kindly notice that this fire **was *prepared for the Devil and his angels***, and *not* for the purpose of punishing *men*."

He looked out over the congregation, and said, "Perhaps you wonder, 'But when did the Devil and his angels fail to feed the hungry, or neglect to visit the sick?' But have you not heard of individuals being *instigated* by the Devil? Does not Luke 22:3 tell us that the Devil 'entered into' Judas? Can you not conceive of evil spirits, so powerfully operating upon the hearts of the children of disobedience, as to *prevent* their feeding the hungry, giving drink to the thirsty, sheltering the stranger, clothing the naked, or visiting the sick and the imprisoned?" He let this question hang over his listeners, for a long moment.

He went on, "What about those on the Saviour's right hand? These include every individual of the human family; but now, they are no longer operated upon by evil spirits, who have all been imprisoned! In this period, they will all be recovered and restored to the true shepherd and bishop of souls. These are the ransomed of the Lord: ascending with God who made them, with the God-man who redeemed them, and saved them from their sins. The whole posterity of Adam complete, shall inherit the kingdom, and shall enter into life eternal."

Seeing discomfort coming over the faces of some of his listeners, he turned to another page in his Bible, and said, "In Matthew 5:19, in the Sermon on the Mount, Christ tells us, 'Whosoever therefore shall break one of these least commandments, and shall teach men so, he shall be called the least in the kingdom of heaven: but whosoever shall do and teach them, the same shall be called great in the kingdom of heaven.' But kindly notice, my friends, that, although some had lesser, and some higher status, Christ said that they were *all* in the kingdom of heaven! Both commandment-breakers, and commandment-keepers."

He looked directly into the eyes of those among the congregation who had hostile expressions on their faces, and said, "But here in the parable that is my text, where the whole world shall be assembled before the judgment seat of Christ, is there not to be a further distinction between those on the right hand? Revelation 20:12 tells us that 'the dead were judged out of those things which were written in the books, according to their works.' The Scripture here is clear. But when the searching eye of Deity shall examine our works—when it is divine justice that operates the scale—do you think that *any* man's work will abide? Romans 3:10 tells us that 'There is none righteous, no, not one.' Verily, there is none good but God; surely, *every* man's works will be weighed in the balance, and be found wanting." He looked out over the congregation, who sat in somber silence.

He continued, "John the Baptist said in Matthew 3:12 that Christ will 'thoroughly purge his floor, and gather his wheat into the garner; but he will burn up the chaff with unquenchable fire.' In this statement, the wheat is undoubtedly a figure of the human race; but what is this 'chaff' a figure of? How are we to understand it? Chaff, of course, is the dry, inedible protective casings of the seeds of grain. In this instance, it represents all those impurities which cleave to humanity, from which every individual must eventually be purged, at the hands of its great Proprietor!"

His eyes roved over the congregation, meeting every pair of eyes he could, and he added, "In this passage, the chaff does not represent *weeds,* such as in Christ's parable of the tares in Matthew 13:24-30; the weeds in Matthew 13 came from *separate seeds,* which had been sown by the householder's enemy: Satan, in other words. Weeds may certainly be separated from wheat, and destroyed—as was described in the passage I used as my text this morning; where the Devil and his demons were to be cast into 'everlasting fire.'

"But the chaff to which John the Baptist referred is *part of the wheat—* it springs up from the same seed! The chaff does *not* represent a separate class of men, who are to be burned in everlasting fire! No, the chaff here represents our own sins, our own impurities; the destruction of the chaff is, in truth, the *salvation* of the wheat! The wheat could never separate itself from its own chaff, having neither will, nor power thus to do. But the omnipotent proprietor of the harvest has appointed a day, in which he would gather all things into one, and then thoroughly purge his wheat of this chaff. He would then gather his wheat—thus purified—into his garner; and then he will burn up the chaff—our own impurities—with unquenchable fire. Is this not what the Apostle Paul refers to, when he told us that 'If any man's work shall be burned, he shall suffer loss: but he himself shall be saved; yet so as by fire'? [1 Cor 3:15] God shall burn our impurities, and rid us of them; and thus, we shall yet be saved!" (A number of members of the congregation seemed to be in surprised agreement with this point.)

He went on, "To quote Revelation 20:12 again, 'And I saw the dead, small and great, stand before God; and the books were opened: and another book was opened, which is the book of life.' In this book of God, the names of *all* members are written. Christ is the head, and the people are the members of his mystical body; in this consummation, Christ will not be rendered imperfect—not a member shall in that day be disunited from his sacred, mystical body. Then, will the angel preach the everlasting gospel [Rev 14:6]; then, will the veil be taken from every heart [2 Cor 3:16]. And finally, as the Apostle Paul said in Romans 14:11 and Philippians 2:11, 'every knee shall bow to me,' and 'every tongue should confess that Jesus Christ is Lord, to the glory of God the Father.'" (Several members of the congregation voiced agreement with this summation; but other members were becoming increasingly upset with this unorthodox manner of preaching.)

In an even, grave voice, Murray acknowledged, "However, we must admit that we do not see all men confess Jesus *here;* but is that what the apostle promised us? No! All men here in this present world do not have faith, but neither can they: for is not faith the gift of God? The Apostle told us in Ephesians 2:8, 'For by grace are ye saved through faith; and *that not of yourselves*: it is the gift of God.' Still others may object, 'Do not the scriptures say that all unbelievers; all murderers; all whoremongers, sorcerers, idolaters and liars shall have their part in the lake that burns with fire and brimstone—forever, and ever?'" He dramatically allowed this question to hang over his listeners for a long moment.

Then, he answered his own question: "The scriptures indeed say in Revelation 21:8 that such characters shall have their portion in the lake that burns with fire and brimstone; but the Scripture does not say they shall have this portion 'forever and ever.' Indeed, it refers to this experience as 'the second death.' Yes, there are individuals of the human family who shall be 'punished with everlasting destruction from the presence of the Lord' [2 Thess 1:9]. But it is one thing to be 'punished with everlasting *destruction,*' and yet another to be *everlastingly punished* with destruction. If a candle were to burn for endless ages, and you put your finger into that candle but for a moment, you would suffer—in that moment—the pain of 'everlasting fire'; but your own pain would not be 'everlasting.'"

He paused for a moment, and then explained, "I once had a conversation with a friend, in which he cited against my views Daniel 12:2, in which the prophet spoke of some awakening 'to shame and everlasting contempt.' I endeavored to make him conceive the difference between 'rising to everlasting shame and contempt,' and *enduring* this shame and contempt *everlastingly!* I may certainly be cast into a lake of everlasting, inextinguishable fire; but I myself may yet not be everlastingly *detained* in this fire. Certainly, open violators of the law, and hardened transgressors of it, shall be tried; and thus every mouth will be stopped, and all the world become guilty before God. Doubtless such persons will shrink appalled from the face of him who sitteth upon the throne, and from that *wrath* which they suppose existing in the Lamb of God. Who can describe their sufferings, in this condition? While at the judgment seat of Christ, they have not seen the Lord who bought them; therefore, they are subjected to the most terrifying apprehensions."

He continued, "We know that Jesus Christ 'gave himself a ransom for all, to be testified in due time' [1 Tim 2:6]; but we know not *when* this due time will be. Many, no doubt, will arise to the resurrection of condemnation; what may be their sufferings in such a state of separation from the body, no tongue can tell, and no heart conceive. But mistake me not: they will not suffer *to atone for their sins*—by no means! The Lamb of God has paid the forfeit; he has made the atonement, he has taken away the sin of the world. Thus, as such sinners did not see Jesus, they laid down in that darkness which engenders fear; even that fear which produces torment.

"It is in this sense that we should understand the Saviour's parable of the rich man and Lazarus in Luke 16:19-31. The parabolic nature of this passage is demonstrated by the language of its beginning: 'a certain rich man...' Furthermore, it would be absurd to suppose that individual angels of the celestial hierarchy had left the abodes of blessedness to pick up a deceased beggar, and deliver him to 'Abraham's bosom'; or that there exists a *material* gulf between Abraham and the rich man! One might as well suppose that our Saviour is literally a door; a vine; a piece of bread, and similar examples. The rich man in this story is symbolic of the Jewish nation, who were blessed with a land 'flowing with milk and honey,' which symbolizes the Law. The angels carrying Lazarus suggests the bringing of Gentiles into that faith by which the mind of Abraham was illumined, when he believed that in his seed—of which the Apostle Paul told us in Galatians 3:29, Abraham's seed is Christ—*all the nations of the earth* shall be blessed!"

He began speaking more rapidly and forcefully, saying, "Now if it be true that God is unchangeable, then it will always be *His will* that all men 'be saved, and ... come unto the knowledge of the truth.' [1 Tim 2:4]

But if, as some would have it, any man should remain forever in a state of damnation, and so be eternally lost; then our God must remain eternally *unsatisfied*—while the devilish adversary of mankind will obtain a most signal *victory* over the will of his and our Creator!" He added passionately, "Will you ignore the explicitly declared will of God? Will you make God a liar out of his own mouth? Is there any who possesses sufficient force, to prevent Omnipotence from achieving *all* of His pleasure?" He shook his head negatively, and concluded, "Let the worshipper of Omnipotence determine how these questions should be answered." (Some heads in the congregation were nodding their agreement; while others just sat in stony silence.)

He went on, returning to his normal speaking voice, "We have long since learned that Jesus Christ is the Saviour of believers, and that all who believed, should be delivered from death hereafter. But perhaps we have never fully considered that our Saviour—by destroying him who had the power of death—also delivered those who had not the power given them to believe, and who therefore remained in a state of bondage, for all their lifetimes. We have not duly considered what Romans 11:32 says of Israel: 'For God hath concluded them all in unbelief, that he might have mercy upon all.' Persons of this description—who never attained in this life that knowledge which is life eternal—are nevertheless His children; and Jesus, their elder brother, took part in this same flesh and blood, that he might destroy the Devil, and so deliver not only those who had power given them to believe, but those also who were lifetime slaves to unbelief and fear, and consequently subjected to bondage. Jesus, by tasting death for every man, delivered even those unbelievers." (He ignored several murmurs of disagreement coming from some of his hearers.)

Calmly, he continued, "I know that both God and man each have a will. Both God and man will make every effort in their power to obtain their respective wishes; and if the power of God should be found greater than the power of devils and men united, then God will obtain the object of his will; who, indeed, can doubt this? The consequence will be that every heart in heaven and on earth, shall with cheerful, willing hearts, ascribe glory to the Lamb. Hence, we see the absurdity of those who are forever exclaiming, 'What—will God save people, whether they will, or not?' The fact is that *all* hearts are in the hands of God; and he can fashion our will to his own irreversible purposes.

"Therefore: either Jesus Christ was delivered up for my offenses, and raised again for my justification, or he was not. If he was, then I am saved in Jesus Christ with an everlasting salvation; if he was not, I am doomed to everlasting misery. For if he were not delivered up for my offenses, then he never can be; for, having died once, he can die no more—and the Bible tells us that without the shedding of blood, there can be no remission of sins. It is thus of the first importance for us to determine whether Christ was delivered up for us, or not." (He paused, to allow these statements to be absorbed by the congregation.)

He continued, "The sum and substance of the Old and New Testament results in two eminently consolatory facts: 'The wages of sin is death, but the gift of God is eternal life' [Rom 6:23], and 'the gifts and calling of God are without repentance' [Rom 11:29]. God will never repent, or call back again, either of these two facts. Jesus is the Saviour of *all men* [1 Tim 4:10]; he gave himself a ransom *for all* [1 Tim 2:6]; he is the propitiation for the sins of, not just believers, but 'for the sins of the *whole world*' [1 Jn 2:2]. All these testimonies prove that God takes no pleasure in the death of the sinner; that He wills that none should perish, but that all should be saved, and come unto the knowledge of the truth." He shook his head sadly, and added, "But we do not see that all are saved; we do not see that all are cleansed. Many go out of this world, ignorant of the Lord who brought them into it. But if God hath said it in His Word, shall He not do it?"

At this point, perhaps seven or eight of his listeners suddenly stood up in their seats, and indignantly walked as a group to the exit. When the last of them (one who was a young man, with unkempt beard) reached the door, he turned and shook his hand at Murray, and shouted, "You damned heretic!" Then he loudly closed the door to the meeting house behind him.

A shocked hush fell over the rest of the listeners (about eighty souls), and they looked with scandalized anticipation at Murray, to see what his reaction would be to this disruption.

Murray simply flipped to another page in his Bible, and continued speaking in his same, matter-of-fact manner: "Jesus *is* a complete Saviour; he came to save his people from their sins. And, as all souls are his, he will therefore save all people from their sins. God has told us in His Word, that he 'sent not his Son into the world to condemn the world; but that *the world* through him might be saved.'" [Jn 3:17]

Murray looked out at the congregation, and acknowledged, "But, perhaps you are thinking, such passages apply only to the *believing* 'world,' and not to the world in general. But, sir, consider this: in the Bible, those in 'the world' are never called *believers*; nor are *believers* ever called 'the world.' You might also ask me, how one can be made alive in Christ, without believing? I reply, just as well as they could *die in Adam,* without believing. It is the same word of God which says, 'as in Adam *all* die, even so in Christ shall *all* be made alive' [1 Cor 15:22]; and yet, you say that it is only those who believe, that shall be made alive!"

His voice became animated—even fiery—as he stated, "Was it our *believing* that saved us from the curse of the law? No, it was Christ redeeming us 'from the curse of the law, being made a curse for us.' [Gal 3:13] Was it our *believing* that saved us from that death which was the wages of sin? No, it was the death of Jesus. Was it our *believing* that reconciled us to God? No, it was God in Christ reconciling the world unto himself.' [2 Cor 5:19] Is it our *believing* that presents us faultless before God? No, it is the blood of Jesus that 'cleanseth from all sin.' [1 Jn 1:7] Is it our *believing* that presents us before God without spot or blemish? No, it is our being *one* with his human nature, as he was *one* with the divine nature."

He looked down at another page in his Bible, and then said vehemently, "In the second chapter of Luke's gospel, the angel told the shepherds that 'I bring you good tidings of great joy, which shall be to all people.' What were these 'good tidings,' which were to be to *all people*? Was it that they might be saved, *if they would?* Was it that there was a Saviour born *only* unto believers? Can you not see, my beloved brethren, that such was *not* the language of this celestial messenger?"

He continued, "I would indeed call upon every sinner to believe on the Lord Jesus; but I certainly would not tell them that Christ was their Saviour *if* they believe—for how absurd is such an idea! Under this supposition, before the foundation of the world, a great, sublime plan was laid, and is executed by an omnipotent Being; and yet, in the end, its *veracity* or *effect* rests wholly upon the reception given to it by the human creature—which creature has neither the will, nor the power, to do any such thing for himself. I will therefore, rather, tell the world that Christ died for them; that he died to save them from their sins; and that, having died for them, they are bound to live, not for themselves, but unto him who died for them, and rose again. The Gospel is a divine declaration of this consolatory truth, and is therefore 'good tidings.' If the Redeemer died only for a few, then a few only can be saved; but if he rather died for *all men*, then all men will be saved! To every human creature, then, this word of salvation is sent. But in no instance does the truth of this message rest upon the *reception* it meets with, from those to whom it is delivered." (A number of persons listening vocally affirmed their agreement with these sentiments.)

He summarized, "If then *all* souls belonged unto the Father, and all that the Father had he gave to the Son, who is the head of every man; and if none can pluck them out of his hand, then assuredly they who are kept by the power of God until salvation must include every individual of mankind; all of mankind must constitute the fullness of Jew and Gentile, the *'every man'* for whom Jesus tasted death. Thus, from a cloud of witnesses it becomes plain that the whole human race belongs unto him who created them, who redeemed their lost nature, and who preserves the creatures he has made. 'All souls,' says God in Ezekiel 18:4, 'are mine.'" With an expression of sorrow on his face, he added, "It is true that we have sold ourselves for nought; and we have made a covenant with death, and with hell we are at agreement. But, says God by the prophet Isaiah [28:18], 'Your covenant with death shall be disannulled, and your agreement with hell shall not stand.'" (A few of those listening applauded this statement.)

He asks, "But what of our sanctification? Does not our redemption await our complete sanctification? Errant nonsense! We are no more *sanctified* in part, than we are *justified* in part. The Apostle James said that 'For whosoever shall keep the whole law, and yet offend in one point, he is guilty of all.' [2:10] But in fact, as I said, our Saviour Jesus Christ is a *complete* Saviour; that is why the Apostle Paul spoke of 'Christ Jesus, who of God is made unto us wisdom, and righteousness, and *sanctification*, and redemption.' [1 Cor 1:30] And how is this salvation effected? Certainly not by any works of righteousness performed by us. As 'there is none righteous, no, not one' [Rom 3:10], it is plain that our righteousness can have nothing to do with this salvation. Again, 'For by grace ye are saved through faith, and that not of yourselves, it is the *gift of God.*'"

He looked out upon some of the faces in the congregation which were showing disagreement with his words, and said, "You may think, 'But do not many souls leave this life in a state of rebellion against God, and our Saviour? How could they be saved?' Let me cite Psalm 16:31, wherein David said, 'Thou wilt not leave my soul in hell; neither wilt thou suffer thine Holy One to see corruption.' The Hebrew word translated as 'hell' is *Sheol*. The Apostle Peter quotes this Psalm in Acts 2:31, and tells us that this speaks 'of the resurrection of Christ, that his soul was not left in hell, neither his flesh did see corruption.' Thus, it is evident that the soul of the Redeemer himself was in Hell, although it was not *left there*. It was in this 'hell' that the spirits of those Antediluvians—those who lived until the Flood of Noah—were imprisoned; those of whom the apostle Peter speaks, 'he went and preached unto the spirits in prison,' and 'for this cause was the gospel preached also to them that are dead.' [1 Pet 3:18, 4:6] Into this hell, the wicked, and all the nations that forget God, shall be turned. Does it not, then, include every *unbeliever*? And what is a believer, but one who was once an unbeliever?

"Thus, assuredly Jesus *is* the Saviour of all men, and assuredly all the nations of the earth will one day *remember* the God who made them. To assert that God cannot manifest himself, and his redeeming grace, to the soul which has departed from this earthly state of things, is indeed most arrogantly to limit the Holy One of Israel. Is God obliged to speak to us only in this sphere, and nowhere else? Can we not hear his voice, except we are encrusted in this earthly tenement? Cannot the children understand the sovereign goodness of paternal Deity somewhere else? If they cannot, then what must become of those *infants*, who pass away before they reach the age of..."

At this point he suddenly stopped, because a rock came hurtling through one of the open windows, and violently struck the front of the pulpit from which Murray was speaking. He stepped back—rather calmly—to see whether any other such missiles were forthcoming; but none came.

Several of the elders of the congregation leaped up, and quickly closed all the windows of the meeting house. One of them called out to Murray, "Reverend Murray, we thank you for your inspired preaching this morning;

but I think we need to bring this service to an end!" Murray nodded, and stepped back from the pulpit.

Another of the elders (one who had helped close the windows) said to him, "Those who threw the rock are standing outside the front door; but we can slip you out by the back door; your horse, and the other horses are out there, as well, so you can… well, you can make your safe departure." Embarrassed, he added, "I am truly mortified by the conduct of some of our parishioners; but… well, we have not heard such doctrines as yours before, and…"

Murray held up his hand, and said graciously, "I have been treated with respect and kindness by most in your congregation; as for the others, I hold it not against them: my own reactions when I first heard this doctrine of Universal Reconciliation were not unlike theirs."

The elder nodded, and then led the way to the back door, saying softly, "This way, please…" and Murray began to follow him to this exit.

But Joseph quickly strode forward, and gently placed his hand on Murray's arm, saying, "Please, Reverend Murray; come back to my home, and stay with us longer." He indicated with his hand a half-dozen men standing behind him, and said, "There are a number of us who would gladly welcome your message; and I am sure that there are many others in our community, who would likewise hear it with gratitude. We pledge that we will forthwith build you a fine meeting house, and pay for your support, if you will but consent to stay, and preach this new message to us." The men standing behind Joseph nodded their fervent support for this statement.

Murray smiled, but then replied warmly, "I thank you most sincerely for your flattering offer. But I believe that I was sent out by God to preach the Gospel throughout the 'highways and hedges'; and, as a servant of God, I must neither loiter by the way, nor seek to evade the spirit of my commission." Joseph and the other men looked greatly disappointed, so Murray told them consolingly, "I thank you again for your hospitality, Joseph; if you are willing, I shall communicate with you often by letter. The next time my travels take me to this area, perhaps I can again be welcomed to your house; and, mayhap, I may even preach, if a suitable setting can be found." He smiled, and then added, "Perhaps the other residents of this area will be more receptive to the Gospel message I preach, by then!" And the others reluctantly laughed.

Murray shook the hands of all the men, and then followed the elder outside, and walked swiftly to his own horse. After he had mounted it, he tipped his hat to the growing group of well-wishers watching his departure; then, he began to turn his horse around.

Just then, one of the young men who had left the meeting house in protest came racing around the corner, and shouted, "Here he is! I thought he might have slipped out the back way!" He shook his fist at Murray, and said, "You damned heretic! You think that rogues, whores, and such as you will ever go to Heaven?"

Murray smiled, and replied calmly, "As the Saviour said to his own opponents, 'Verily I say unto you, that the *publicans* and the *harlots* go into the kingdom of God before you.'" [Mt 21:31]

He then spurred his horse, and swiftly departed.

PART THREE

THE NINETEENTH CENTURY (IOWA)

CHAPTER 3

THE SOUL THAT SLEEPS?
(February, 1861)

It was a pleasant, sunny day; quite warm for a day in February. Thomas Claudville was sitting on a grassy hill located just outside of town, and quietly reading a book, when a man with a long beard approached him.

"Good morning, friend," the man said, genially.

"Good morning," Thomas replied, looking up from his book, to take in the man: he had graying hair, was wearing a neat dark gray suit, and appeared to be in his 50s; Thomas himself was clean-shaven, in his mid-30s, and wearing casual clothes (such as was appropriate for sitting on the grass on a warm afternoon).

The newcomer pointed at the book Thomas was reading, and said, "I'm a man who likes to read, myself. May I enquire what book you are reading?"

Thomas replied, "It's called, *The Second Death and the Restitution of All Things;* it was written by an English clergyman named Andrew John Jukes."

The man seemed to be deep in thought for a moment, and then said, "I've never heard of it; but I've read rather widely in biblical and theological books."

"The book was published in England," Thomas explained. "I just received this copy, which was given to me as a gift by a friend, who was visiting this country from England."

"Interesting," the man replied. He pointed at the grass next to Thomas, and asked, "Mind if I sit down for a bit? I've been walking for quite some time."

"I don't mind at all," Thomas said warmly, motioning for the man to sit down. The man did so, gratefully slipping a heavy canvas bag off his shoulder, and laying it on the ground.

The man held out his hand to shake, saying, "My name is Arthur Douglass."

"Thomas Claudville," came the reply, as the men shook hands.

Arthur observed, "You don't have an English accent; so you are not English?"

"I'm a native-born American," Thomas said proudly. "But I'm new to this state; my wife and I just moved here a year ago."

Arthur nodded, then said, "I'm from Michigan, myself; I was born and raised there."

Thomas asked with curiosity, "Then what brings you to Iowa? Your line of work, perhaps?"

The man smiled, and replied, "Yes, you might say that; although I would prefer to call it, 'The *Lord's* work.'"

"Ah," Thomas said, nodding his head, and smiling slightly. "You are a man of spiritual purposes."

"I am," Arthur acknowledged.

"As am I," Thomas admitted. "I am a minister; I preside over a congregation, here in town."

"I see," Arthur said, now looking at Thomas more carefully. Cautiously, he asked, "Might I inquire, which denomination you represent?"

Thomas replied easily, "I am a minister of the Universalist Church."

"The Universalist Church?" Arthur repeated, puzzled. "I'm not sure that I've ever heard of that one."

"We've been in this country for nearly one hundred years," Thomas explained. "We preach the doctrine of 'Universal Reconciliation'; that is, the eventual Restoration and Restitution of all souls to eternal communion with God."

"Hmm,' Arthur said, frowning as he thought about this puzzling response. He looked over at Thomas, and asked, "Is your doctrine Scriptural?"

Thomas nodded firmly, saying, "The Bible, aided by human reason, is our only source of authority."

This reply encouraged Arthur, who then asked, "You said that book you were reading was, in part, about the 'second death'; by this the author meant the second death as revealed in the Book of the Revelation, I presume?"

"That is correct," Thomas agreed.

Arthur asked quietly, "Does the author endorse the popular view: namely, that the 'second' death' represents hopeless, endless torment?"

"He does not," Thomas replied firmly. "I have not yet finished the book, but Parson Jukes seemingly agrees with me—that what is called the 'second death' in the Scriptures is but God's way to *free* those who are yet bound up within the dark world of disobedience and sin."

Arthur again looked confused by this response, and asked, "What do you mean by 'freeing' those who are yet sinners?"

"Simply what God's Word says," Thomas replied immediately. "As Paul said in First Timothy 2:4, God 'will have *all men* to be saved, and to come unto the knowledge of the truth.'"

Arthur frowned, and asked, "So you believe that *all men*—even those who remain in wickedness—are to be saved?"

"They will not be saved *while* they are yet sinners," Thomas clarified. "But, in the will and purposes of God, they will be changed and transformed by processes such as the 'second death,' so that they are *no longer* sinners." Arthur remained silent, mulling over this response. Thomas added, "How else would the apostle Peter's words in Acts 3:21, 'until the times of restitution of all things, which God hath spoken by the mouth of all his holy prophets since the world began,' be fulfilled?"

A crafty look came into Arthur's eyes, and he said noncommittally, "My friend, I can tell that you are a man who takes the Scriptures seriously."

"Of course," Thomas replied.

Arthur said slyly, "But if I can prove to you otherwise from the Holy Scriptures, will you accept this proof?"

Thomas smiled slightly, and said, "I am rather doubtful that such a 'proof' could be given; however, if you were to prove my doctrine to be incorrect from the Scriptures, I would gladly accept and welcome this correction."

Arthur smiled with satisfaction, and reached into his bag, pulling out a well-worn Bible, which he placed on the grass between them. He then said, with practiced ease, "The popular philosophers and theologians would have us believe that man has a mysterious 'dual' nature: part material, and part immaterial; one part a body, which perishes at death, and another part an immortal 'soul' or 'spirit,' which lives on beyond the man's death."

"That is correct," Thomas agreed. "And that is what I myself believe."

With a gleam in his eye, Arthur asked, "Now, if this is what man is, would we not expect to find revelation within the pages of God's Word on this point? Would not such revelatory passages be, in fact, prolific, in the Scriptures?"

Thomas looked at Arthur warily, and said, "Yes, we would expect that; yet I believe that is exactly what we find in the Holy Script..."

Arthur interrupted, "Of what was man made? Does not the book of Genesis tell us that man was made out of the dust of the ground?" He opened his Bible, placing his finger on the passage.

"Yes, it does," Thomas admitted. "Genesis 2:7 tells us that the Lord God 'breathed into his nostrils the breath of life; and man became a living soul.' And the apostle Paul quotes this in First Corinthians 15:45, adding that the 'last Adam,' or Christ, was made a 'quickening spirit'..."

Arthur interrupted, "But does the book of Genesis give any hint of such a 'double nature' of man, as he was originally created by God? Was it not the man himself, who was made out of *dust,* who constituted the 'living soul'?"

"Not until God breathed into his nostrils the breath of life," Thomas countered.

Arthur said, "Now, my friend, are you aware that not only man, but the lower *beasts* as well, have a 'spirit'—according to Solomon in Ecclesiastes 3:21?"

Thomas hesitated, but then replied, "That may be true; but one must be very cautious in quoting from the book of Ecclesiastes, since much in that book is not the positive revelation of God, but contains only Solomon's *earthly* philosophical musings..."

Arthur went on, "The term, 'living soul,' in the Scriptures, is applied indiscriminately with reference to every beast, bird, insect and reptile—as well as to man. Revelation 16:3, for instance, refers to 'every living soul' in the sea dying! So if being a 'living soul' means that man is immortal, then the very *beasts* as well are in full possession of such a nature!"

Thomas frowned, and objected, "I cannot agree with your opinion about the term 'living soul.' The Bible says in Genesis 1:27 that 'God created man in his own image.' Now, since God is immortal, it follows that…"

Arthur shot back, "If man's being made in the image of God is supposed to 'prove' that man is immortal, then why are we not like God in being omniscient and omnipotent? And if Adam in the Garden of Eden had an 'immortal soul,' why then did the Lord expel him from it, 'lest he put forth his hand, and take also of the tree of life, and eat, and live for ever'? If Adam had an 'immortal soul,' why would he have *needed* this tree of life?"

Thomas thought for a long moment, and then acknowledged, "You speak about matters under the *Old* Dispensation. But in the *New* Dispensation, Paul advised us in Romans 2:7 to 'seek for glory and honour and *immortality, eternal life.*' Paul further advises us in First Corinthians 15:53-54 that 'this mortal must put on immortality'; and he said in Second Timothy 1:10 that Jesus 'hath abolished death, and hath brought life and *immortality* to light through the gospel.' So these verses indicate that…"

Arthur cut him off again, saying, "But Paul said in First Timothy 6:16 that God is He 'who *only* hath immortality.' You cannot find the term 'immortal soul' in the Bible; not one single text declares the human soul to be 'immortal,' or the spirit of man to be 'deathless.' God alone is immortal; and God has given this life to his Son, Jesus Christ. And God will also bestow this gift as a reward, to those who patiently serve him here on earth. So, as Paul said in that passage you just quoted, 'this mortal must *put on* immortality.'"

Thomas had a puzzled look on his face, and stated, "If you agree that men are *given* immortality by God, then I do not see a major difference with my belief that we are *already* immortal, and…"

Arthur smiled, and said, "Ah, but that is where you are wrong, my friend. Adam in the Garden of Eden was placed on 'trial,' as it were, to see if he was *worthy* of immortality; but since he disobeyed God, he remained mortal, and thus was subject to eventual death. But this 'death' was not simply a transition from one form of conscious existence to another; no, death resulted in the complete *deprivation* of man's conscious existence."

"What?" Thomas gasped, genuinely surprised. "But there are many passages in the Bible that speak of man's continuing conscious awareness after death, such as..."

Arthur held up one hand, as he flipped to another page in his Bible, and said confidently, "Let us see what David had to say on the subject. In Psalm 146:4, he says of man that 'he returneth to his earth; in that very day his thoughts perish.'" He looked directly at Thomas, then asked, "Can a man be 'conscious' if he has no thoughts? Furthermore, in Psalm 115:17, David noted that 'The dead praise not the Lord, neither any that go down into silence.' Would not the righteous *continue* to praise the Lord after death, if they were able?"

Thomas replied impatiently, "One cannot simply quote isolated verses of Scripture to prove a point; the very words of *Satan* are sometimes included in the Bible, but they certainly cannot be cited to prove any point of doctrine! And as I said earlier about the words of Solomon in Ecclesiastes, not all words in the Bible represent the actual *revelation* from God, and..."

Arthur interjected, "Then let us turn to the words of Peter in Acts 2:29-34, where he testified, 'Men and brethren, let me freely speak unto you of the patriarch David, that he is both dead and buried, and his sepulchre is with us unto this day... For David is *not* ascended into the heavens.' Now, who more than David would have gone to heaven, if God took the righteous there at time of death?"

Growing frustrated, Thomas argued, "After His resurrection, Jesus *ascended* into the heavens, to sit at the right hand of God the Father; now, although I believe that David remained in a temporary or 'intermediate' state of conscious existence, he did not *ascend* to Heaven after his death, in the same sense that Christ did."

Arthur said firmly, "Then let us look at the words of the Saviour Himself. In the 11th chapter of John, Jesus said plainly to his disciples, 'Lazarus is *dead*.' But then after Christ raised Lazarus, the text does not say that Lazarus 'came down from heaven, and returned to his body'; no, it says instead that 'he that was dead came forth.'"

Thomas frowned, and said, "The Biblical text tells us nothing about the condition of Lazarus from the time after his death, until the time when he was raised by Christ; so you attempt to make an argument from *silence*."

Before Arthur could reply, he quickly added, "How do you interpret the appearance of Moses and Elijah on the mount of Transfiguration, in Matthew 17? Since Moses was dead and buried, does not his appearance to both Christ and three of the disciples indicate that Moses was in fact *alive,* after his death?"

Arthur shrugged, and replied, "It is possible, of course, that Moses was individually raised from the dead for this occasion; but since Elijah had been 'taken away' alive and *bodily,* he was perhaps simply brought to the scene from his place of abode on earth…"

Thomas interrupted, "Second Kings 2:11 tells us, 'Elijah went up by a whirlwind into *heaven.*' So he was certainly not simply concealed somewhere on the earth!"

Arthur shrugged again, and suggested, "The purpose of this incident was to give Peter, James, and John a glimpse of the power, majesty, and glory of the Kingdom. There was no need for Moses or Elijah to be actually present in a *physical form*; and in fact Christ himself, in verse 9, describes this event as a 'vision.'

The expression on Thomas's face showed his strong disagreement with this explanation. He then asked Arthur, "What do you say of Jesus' statement to the Sadducees in Luke 20:37-38: how that Moses 'calleth the Lord the God of Abraham, and the God of Isaac, and the God of Jacob. For he is not a God of the dead, but of the living: for all live unto him.' Do not the Saviour's words clearly refute the doctrine of the Sadducees, who said that there was no resurrection?" [Lk 20:27, Acts 23:8]

Arthur replied simply, "Certainly, all live 'unto God'; God, in His omniscience, knows all who have died, from the creation of the world. But Jesus was certainly not contradicting the clear statements throughout the Bible, that the dead are *not* in conscious existence."

Thomas just frowned, and then asked, "So tell me in plain words: what do you think is the condition of a man, after death?"

Arthur replied confidently, "The dead *sleep;* they rest unconsciously in the grave. But, in the providence of God, they *may* one day be raised from the dead!"

Thomas nodded, and noted, "Ah; so you *do* believe in the doctrine of the resurrection from the dead."

Arthur replied indignantly, "My friend, I believe in every doctrine which is plainly taught in Holy Scripture. The resurrection from the dead was the patriarch Job's only hope; it was King David's only hope; it was the great theme and hope of the apostle Paul's preaching; and it was the time identified by Christ Himself, when the virtuous were to receive their reward."

Thomas acknowledged, "I agree with much of what you now say; but…"

Arthur continued, "Paul argued in First Corinthians 15:17-18, 'if Christ be not raised… Then they also which are fallen asleep in Christ are *perished*.' But, in your interpretation, the 'immortal souls' of the dead had been in *glory*; so, could they not as well enjoy life and bliss *without* a resurrection, as *with* one? When Paul wanted to comfort the brethren in Thessalonica in chapter 4:13-18 of his first letter, why did he say that 'the dead in Christ shall rise first'? Why didn't he comfort them with the knowledge that 'the dead still exist in some heavenly realm; and they are now enjoying bliss and glory there'?"

Thomas spent a moment pondering this response, before he finally replied, "Although the dead remain in a state of conscious existence after death, they are not in a full, final, *bodily* state of existence; which is why they must await the resurrection from the dead. Christ himself was in such a condition prior to his bodily resurrection, which is why he was able to assure the thief on the cross, that 'Today shalt thou be with me in paradise.'"

Arthur shook his head firmly, and said, "That statement by Christ is mistranslated in our common Bible. Let us remember that the original Greek Scriptures did not contain punctuation marks; and thus, the comma in that statement should be placed after the word 'today,' so that it correctly reads, 'Verily I say unto thee today, thou shalt be with me in paradise.'"

Thomas shook his head emphatically, and said, "I trust the translators here, over your speculative *interpretation* of the sacred text." He added, "As I said earlier, there are many biblical texts that clearly indicate that the believer is 'with Christ' immediately after death, such as Philippians 1:23, where Paul expresses his 'desire to depart, and to be with Christ,' and…"

Arthur countered, "Paul expresses a desire to 'be with Christ,' to be sure; but how did he expect to get there, or to be with him? Simply by dying? No, he knew that he would be with Christ *as a living man,* by departing to meet Christ in the heavens—as First Thessalonians 4:16 says."

Thomas shook his head again, and said, "Paul said in verse 21, 'For to me to live is Christ, and to die is gain'; so, clearly, he *was* talking about *dying,* as bringing him into Christ's presence."

Arthur said dismissively, "You probably believe that the story of the rich man and Lazarus in Luke 16:19-31 'proves' the conscious existence of men after death; but this story is only a *parable,* and not a true event…"

"I agree with you that the story is a parable," Thomas said, nodding his head, in rare agreement with the stranger.

Arthur looked pleased, and said, "If this parable is supposed to teach the consciousness of man after death, then it clearly contradicts the words of Job, David, Solomon, Daniel, Paul, as well as Jesus himself, in many other passages in the Scriptures!"

Thomas just shrugged, and said, "I believe that you and I will simply have to disagree about that matter."

Arthur looked at Thomas with curiosity, and asked, "So do you accept the common opinion of men, that the parable of the rich man teaches *eternal torment* in an afterlife?"

Thomas shook his head emphatically, and explained, "Absolutely not! The principal teaching of my denomination is a firm and resolute *rejection* of the notion of endless misery in Sheol, Hades, Gehenna, or any other sort of 'Hell'!"

"I am delighted to hear you say that!" Arthur said enthusiastically. "The idea of 'eternal misery' makes God into a cruel tyrant!"

"I very much agree," Thomas replied. He thought for a moment, and then asked, "I am curious: how would you interpret Jesus' words in Matthew 25—the parable of the sheep and the goats? I know my own interpretation of the passage, of course; but I would be very interested to hear your views on it."

Arthur replied confidently, "In that parable, 'eternal punishment' is contrasted with 'eternal life'; Christ did *not* contrast 'eternal *misery*' with 'eternal *happiness.*' He threatened the unregenerate with an 'eternal' punishment, but he did not describe the *nature* of this punishment. All that this passage can prove, is that the 'punishment' is eternal; but the punishment might be—rather than an eternal existence in misery—eternal *destruction;* the eternal deprivation of life!"

Thomas thought about this response for a long moment, and then admitted, "I do not agree, but at least I can understand your rationale."

Arthur said with a satisfied smile, "It is those who assert 'punishment' and *pain* to be synonymous, who are going far beyond what the text says—while an eternity of *destruction* is fully in agreement with the biblical statement."

Thomas nodded, and asked, "What do you say of Mark 9:43-48, where Christ says repeatedly of hell that 'the worm dieth not, and the fire is not quenched'?"

Arthur laughed mockingly, then replied, "Those of the common view must believe, not merely in an 'immortal soul,' but in immortal *worms*—who are somehow able to feed upon the bodies of these nonphysical 'souls' for all of eternity!" He shook his head forcefully, then concluded, "Clearly, Christ was teaching in this passage the *destruction* of the bodies of the dead."

Thomas explained, "In my denomination, we view the punishment described in this verse as *limited* in time—as lasting for an 'age'; a distinct 'period of time.' But you did not give your interpretation of the fire that is not quenched...?"

Arthur said dismissively, "When the bodies are consumed, what would this devouring fire *consume,* for all the untold cycles of eternity? Certainly not a disembodied, eternal 'soul'! The purpose of the fire is to accomplish the complete *destruction* of everything upon which it is loosed; in this case, of the whole man or his *being,* to contrast with its eternal preservation in the fiery torments of Hell, such as the common interpretation would have it." He sniffed, then added, "The situation is comparable to Revelation 14, which says of those who worship the beast or receive his mark, that 'the smoke of their torment ascendeth up for ever and ever: and they have no rest day nor night.' It is the *smoke* that rises forever and ever; and if they are consumed by this fire, they certainly will never experience any 'rest.' Revelation 11:18 clearly indicates that God will ultimately '*destroy* them which destroy the earth'; and Revelation 20:14 tells us that death and hell are cast into the metaphorical *fire;* and this is the 'second death.'"

Thomas nodded, and said, "My own interpretation is not markedly dissimilar from yours, of those passages."

Arthur smiled again, and said, "The plain truth, my friend, is that the common doctrines of 'eternal misery,' and the 'immortal soul,' are not found in the Holy Bible. As Ezekiel 18 tells us, 'The soul that sinneth, it shall *die*.' Immortality is a gift of God, which is at the consummation given *only* to those who obey the Gospel; but all of us *now* are completely mortal—and those who are disobedient, will not be made immortal. They shall perish, and be destroyed forever." He concluded with a satisfied smile, "Our position is sometimes called 'Annihilationism'; or other times, 'Conditional Immortality.'"

Thomas said, "I understand your position much more clearly, now. Thank you for discussing these points with me, in a congenial manner."

"I enjoyed our discussion," Arthur replied. He then brought a canteen out of his bag, and took a long drink from it.

Thomas asked, "Have you arrived at these conclusions simply from your own reading and interpretation of the Scriptures? Or are there any books you have found useful?"

Arthur took a book out of his bag, and handed it to Thomas; the book was *Man Not Immortal: The Only Shield Against the Seductions of Modern Spiritualism;* it had been written by one 'D.P. Hall.' Thomas made a mental note of the book's author, title, and publisher, then handed it back to Arthur, saying, "I shall have to order a copy of it; there is a store owner in town from whom I can place orders for any books in which I have an interest."

Arthur said confidently, "You will be greatly pleased and enlightened by the book, I assure you." With sudden excitement coming into his voice, he added, "But I *am* also affiliated with an organization, which teaches the doctrines that I hold."

Thomas was surprised, and asked with interest, "Is it a church? Or even an entire denomination, perhaps?"

Arthur replied, "We refer to ourselves as 'Seventh Day Adventists'; this name indicates both our firm belief that Christians *are* required to observe the Biblical Sabbath—since it has never been repealed in the Bible, and was clearly stated in the Scriptures to be an 'eternal' ordinance—as well as our belief that the Second Coming of Christ will occur after a 'time of trouble'… which might happen very *soon!*"

Thomas thought for a moment, and then said, "I have heard of 'Seventh Day *Baptists*,' who believe that the Biblical Sabbath is still a requirement; but I have never heard of your denomination."

Arthur said breathlessly, "Many of us came from the 'Millerite' movement, in the 1840s; yet the errors of that movement were apparent, by 1844. But then, a most remarkable woman appeared: Ellen Gould White. Her writings cast an unparalleled light upon the Scriptures!"

Thomas said cautiously, "I have never heard of her. Has she received any theological training, or…"

Arthur said proudly, "She receives her inspiration directly from *God!* She is a true *prophetess!*"

Thomas was genuinely shocked by this bold statement, and said cautiously, "My church, as well as nearly every other Christian church, believes that, with the publication of the Holy Scriptures, there is no longer any need for direct 'prophecy' in the Church, and…"

Arthur said reassuringly, "My friend, you must read her works for yourself; and then you will surely see that the hand of the Lord is upon her."

Thomas looked at Arthur for a long moment, and finally concluded, "I believe that this is simply another matter upon which you and I will need to remain in disagreement." He removed the watch from his shirt pocket, then looked at it and said apologetically, "I am afraid that I must be heading back to my home; my wife will be serving supper, and she dislikes it when I am late."

Both men stood up, and Thomas held out his hand, and said, "It was good to meet you, Arthur. I enjoyed our conversation. Are you staying here in town, or…"

Arthur shook his head negatively, while he shook Thomas's hand. He explained, "I am simply a 'sojourner'; I travel from town to town, spreading the Gospel message, wherever I have the opportunity."

"Then allow me to wish you the very best, in your future endeavors," Thomas said, with a warm smile.

And the two men went off, in their respective ways.

CHAPTER 4

An Answer to Every Man
(Early March, 1861)

Thomas was just leaving the town's General Store after placing another book order, when a somewhat younger man approached him, and said, "I beg your pardon, Sir; are you Thomas Claudville?"

"I am," Thomas admitted, looking at the younger man with curiosity. The younger man was wearing relatively casual attire.

The younger man asked, "I understand that you are a minister?"

"Yes, I am," Thomas replied, his concern immediately piqued, and he asked quickly, "Is there some service I can render to you?"

But the other man simply asked another question, "And are you the minister of the *Universalist* church here in town?"

"Yes," Thomas replied, starting to become more cautious about his inquirer.

The younger man noted, "You have a large congregation."

Thomas (beginning to become irritated by the younger man's noncommittal manner) said, "Since you evidently know who I am, might I ask who you are?"

The other man then extended his hand, and said, "My apologies; my name is Wesley Richardson. I am the newly-appointed Pastor of the Evangelical Church. I arrived in town only a few days ago."

"Aha," Thomas said, smiling as he shook the man's hand. "It's always a pleasure to meet a fellow Christian minister. You have a lively and growing congregation, I understand." He thought for a moment, and then explained, "We have a variety of churches here in town: Presbyterian,

Methodist, two Baptist, one Congregational, and an Episcopalian parish; we once even had a small Quaker group, but I believe that they disbanded, after two of their member families moved out of the…"

Wesley interrupted, "Actually, it is *you* with whom I am interested." Thomas looked at him warily, as Wesley said, "When you introduced yourself to me, you referred to yourself as a 'fellow Christian minister.' Pardon my presumption, but I must ask you such an important question quite plainly: *are* you a Christian minister?"

"Of course," Thomas replied, by now exasperated by the man's manner. He started to turn away, saying, "I'm afraid that I must return to my home. to finish preparing my sermon for this Sunday's service…"

Wesley blurted out, "What, sir, do you *mean* by the term, 'Christian'?"

Thomas sighed, and then replied, "One who is a follower of Jesus Christ. Now, if you will excuse me…"

Wesley interjected, "What think you of the Holy Bible, sir?"

Thomas replied without hesitation, "It is God's revelation to us."

Wesley pressed on, "And do you accept the 1803 Winchester Profession of Faith, promulgated by the Universalist churches?"

"I do," Thomas replied.

Wesley said firmly, "Then you cannot believe the Holy Bible to be God's revelation."

Genuinely irritated, Thomas asked, "And why is that, sir?"

Wesley replied confidently, "Does not the Second Article of this Profession state that God 'will finally restore the whole family of mankind to holiness and happiness'?"

"It does," Thomas replied, adding, "And the First Article also states that 'We believe that the Holy Scriptures of the Old and New Testament contain a revelation of…"

Wesley interrupted again, "Would you be interested in discussing this matter?"

Thomas replied sharply, "Are we not discussing this matter now?"

Wesley said with exaggerated deference, "No, no; I mean in a *public forum*; in a formal debate, perhaps." He smiled confidently.

Thomas exhaled loudly, and said, "The Apostle Paul wisely advised us in Second Timothy 2:23 and Titus 3:9 to avoid 'foolish questions,' which produce 'strifes, contentions, and strivings,' and are 'unprofitable and vain.' So I have no…"

Wesley asked bluntly, "But the final destination of man is surely not a 'foolish question,' is it? Is not 'Universal Salvation' the entire focus of your 'church'?"

Thomas said calmly, "If it is disputation you are interested in, sir, I might suggest the Presbyterian and Baptist churches; they have held public debates here in town on several occasions, and might…"

Wesley replied, "I have no interest in disputing with legitimate, Bible-affirming, Christian brethren. But the teachings of your 'church' are, I must conclude, a grave *heresy!*"

"Good day to you, sir," Thomas said curtly, turning to walk away; but he stopped when the younger man put his hand on Thomas's shoulder. Reluctantly, Thomas turned back to face the younger man.

Wesley said haughtily, "As the new Pastor of my flock, it is my sacred responsibility to guide them in the ways of truth. But I must also steer them away from false and harmful doctrines, which could imperil their eternal souls."

Thomas said brusquely, "For the flock in your church, I am sure you will endeavor to lead them soundly. But you might, in the meantime, show some Christian *courtesy* toward those in other churches…"

Wesley said in a more aggressive tone, "If you do not wish to participate in a public debate, then I must inform you that I would, then, plan to hold a series of public meetings, in which I shall rightfully denounce the heresy of Universalism, as well as other false and satanic doctrines."

"You are free to do as you please, sir," Thomas replied brusquely. He began to turn away again.

Wesley asked sharply after him, "Does not First Peter 3:15 instruct us, 'be ready always to give an answer to *every man* that asketh you a reason of the hope that is in you'?"

Thomas stopped, turned around, and then nodded and added, "Yes, it does; but it adds, 'with meekness and fear.' But I cannot see any good that could come from such a public disputation…"

Wesley cut in again, "Your Universalist brethren in other localities apparently do not share your sentiments. I am aware of at least half-a-dozen such debates in which they have willingly participated. And the transcripts of these debates have often been published in the Universalist newspapers!" Thomas remained silent.

Realizing that he was having little impact upon Thomas, Wesley changed tactics, and said in a softer tone, "You have my word of honor, sir, that the debate would be conducted in accordance with strict rules of formal procedures, and with all proper decorum. I certainly harbor no ill-will toward you; my intention is simply to clarify the differences between your position, and the Evangelical one." Thomas remained silent, but he appeared to be thinking about this last statement.

Wesley saw that his conciliatory manner had some impact upon Thomas, so he quickly added, "And who knows? If given such an opportunity to formally present your case to the community at large, perhaps you would turn some hearts toward your own views...?"

Thomas sighed once again, and finally asked, "When would you propose that such a debate take place...?"

Wesley smiled, then put his arm around Thomas's shoulder in a friendly manner, and said enthusiastically, "Why don't you let me follow you to your home, and we can discuss the details there?" So the two men headed over to Thomas's carriage, which was parked nearby.

***

It was the evening of the first day of the two-day debate.

Thomas came up onto the stage (where two tables had been placed, on opposite sides of the podium), then walked over and shook hands with the Moderator (who was a prominent landowner in town, and owned several businesses), and then with his Evangelical minister opponent, before taking his seat behind one of the tables. Reverend Richardson then took his seat at the opposite table, with his thick Bible proudly placed directly on the table in front of him, next to a number of pages of handwritten notes. (By contrast, Thomas had nothing besides his own Bible on the table he sat down at.)

Looking about the hall (which was normally used for town meetings, or other assemblages of large groups of citizens), he noticed that the room was filled to capacity; in fact, there were even a fair number of standees at the back of the hall. His own congregation was well-represented in the room—as was the congregation of Reverend Richardson—but Thomas noted with interest that the majority in the audience were persons whom he did not recognize; also in the audience were even some well-known "unchurched" citizens. He mused, *Perhaps a modicum of good may come of this affair, after all. If some hear the gospel of Universal Reconciliation for the first time, perhaps it will soften their hearts, to listen to the message of the Lord.*

The Moderator asked Thomas softly, "Reverend Claudville, are you ready to begin?" Thomas nodded to him. The Moderator next posed the same question to Reverend Richardson, who replied "Yes!" eagerly. The Moderator then took his position at the podium, and waited for the crowd to fall quiet; a sense of excited anticipation came over the room.

The Moderator said, "Good evening, ladies and gentlemen; my name is Elwin Habermas. I would like to welcome you to the first evening of this two-evening discussion. The question to be considered is, 'Do the Holy Scriptures and Reason Teach the Ultimate Salvation of All Mankind, or Do They Teach That Some Must Spend Eternity in Torment in Hell?' To discuss this important question, we have two distinguished local ministers: Reverend Wesley Richardson, the newly-installed Pastor of the Evangelical Church; Reverend Richardson will be presenting the view of Hell as eternal torment. On the other side, we have the Reverend Thomas Claudville, minister of the local Universalist Church; Reverend Claudville will be presenting the viewpoint of 'Universal Reconciliation,' as he calls it. Each speaker will make an opening speech, in turn; then, they will offer a second speech, which is their opportunity to present rebuttal of any points made by their opponent—or, they may introduce new material, as they wish. By mutual consent of the speakers, Reverend Claudville will speak first. I invite your attention to Reverend Claudville." Polite applause came from the audience, as Thomas picked up his Bible, stood up, and headed to the podium.

Thomas placed his Bible on the podium, as he breathed a silent prayer. Then he looked out on his audience, smiled, and began speaking: "Thank you, Mr. Moderator; and thank you to Reverend Richardson, my friend and fellow participant on the Evangelical side. I welcome all members of the audience to this discussion, which I believe will be conducted in a friendly, and nonpartisan manner."

He took a deep breath, then began his presentation, "I submit that whatever may be our faith, and whatever may be the truth: no human—and, most of all, no Christian soul—can ever be truly satisfied by a salvation that is less than *universal*. The fact is that the relation that God bears to man is that of the father to the child. No matter how far down the path of crime a man or woman may have gone—no matter how far they may have wandered in the wilderness of sin, no matter what may be our moral condition—we are, still, legitimately, children of God, and an object of his paternal solicitude. The fact that a portion of our race are alienated from him by disobedience, does not prove that we are not his by creation, and the objects of his love and protection. Even while God chastens and punishes men for their sins, still he calls them his 'children'! If you were to place the eternal interests of all our race in a *mother's* hands, all people would certainly be saved—for a mother has love enough to save a world, if she only had the power; and is not God as good as that mother? Will God cast off his children forever, and abandon them to a state of endless wretchedness? No, no! Strong as is the mother's love, God's love is yet stronger, and more enduring."

He paused for a moment, then looked down at his Bible, saying, "I read First Timothy 2:4-6: 'Who will have *all men* to be saved, and to come unto the knowledge of the truth. For there is one God, and one mediator between God and men, the man Christ Jesus; Who gave himself a ransom *for all*, to be testified in due time.' It would be impossible for me to select any words more expressive of the idea of 'universality'! The language is not difficult, or metaphorical; it can be comprehended by even the weakest intellect. God, having willed the salvation of all men, must necessarily have willed all the means and agencies necessary to secure this result. Would Christ have undertaken his divine work, had he supposed that he would fail of bringing *all* to the knowledge of the truth? God's will is that all shall be saved; therefore, Christ came to do that will, and to finish His work!

"When the Saviour said to the leper in Mark 8:3, 'I will—be thou clean,' Christ did not express a mere *desire*, but a determinate *will*. And this is the will of Almighty God: for universal salvation! If not: if this be merely a desire, and all will not ultimately be saved, then I would like to know if this does not mean that God will have an *ungratified desire* for all of eternity!" He shook his head, and added, "But that God cannot be disappointed in any of his intentions, we are bound to believe, by every enlightened conception of our perfect Creator. Now, as it was God's deliberate purpose to finally make all mankind holy and happy—and as he does all according to his purpose, and none can *thwart* him—it is impossible to arrive at any other conclusion, than that the entire human race will ultimately be brought to repentance, purity, and Heaven!" He paused, to allow this statement to be considered by the audience.

He continued, "To say that God *can* save all men, but *will* not, is to say that he is bad. To say that he *desires* to save all men but cannot, is to say that he is weak. To say that he cannot *plan* in such a way as to achieve what he wishes, is to say he is not wise. The Arminian has a weak God, but a good one; the Calvinist has a strong God, but a bad one. The Universalist, on the other hand, takes the goodness of Arminianism, and the strength of Calvinism, and combines them, to form one perfect system. We Universalists believe that Christ is both able and willing to save the world, and to complete the mission on which his Father sent him.

"The very punishments and chastisements which God inflicts on mankind, so far from being designed to injure, are especially designed for our benefit: to humble, subdue, correct and amend; and therefore, they are not in contravention of His numerous promises of universal salvation. What are the true goals of God's punishment? They are: First, the reformation of the punished; and Second, the benefit of those who witness the punishment. Whatever the amount of chastisement is necessary to reform the guilty, will operate as an example to deter others from doing wrong. I firmly repudiate the idea of God punishing men, with no aim or desire whatever for their good! It violates all reasonable conceptions of a wise, just, and perfect government by God. Surely, we are able to conceive how good may result from some temporary evils; in fact, we have often *witnessed* good resulting from many of them. But why are these evils often seen to result in good? For the very reason that they are *temporary,* and *limited,* in nature. But endless punishment with no possibility of reformation is a final evil; a limitless, boundless evil, beyond which no good can result—for it will never end."

He turned to another page in his Bible, then said, "The biblical declaration in John 4:42 and First John 4:14 is that Christ is actually and absolutely the Saviour of the world. Christ said in John 12:32, 'And I, if I be lifted up from the earth, will draw *all men* unto me.' This was a conditional promise, the condition of which was fulfilled in his resurrection. Now, if the Saviour died to save all men, then all must be saved—because nothing is clearer than the declarations of the Bible to the effect that what Jesus undertook, he will accomplish. He cannot be the 'Saviour of the world' if only a *part* of the world is ever saved. Reverend Richardson may argue that the expression 'all men' in the gospel does not really mean *all men*. But we know from the Scriptures that Christ gave himself as a ransom for all, as the 'propitiation for our sins, and not for ours only, but also for the sins of the whole world.' [1 Jn 2:2]. What possible reason is there why the term 'all' should be limited to only a few? Why should not the word be taken in its common and proper sense?" He paused for a moment, to emphasize this question.

He went on, "Perhaps the most objectionable aspect of the doctrine of eternal torment is its contention that the whole work of man's redemption is confined to this short and momentary life. Look at the facts: Untold millions: whole nations, empires even, have lived and died in utter ignorance of Christ; and he supposedly cannot save *any* of all these—and yet he is called the Saviour of the world! I would like to know why we should limit the mercy and grace of God to this one short life? Have men ever sought to enter into the *Church*, yet were not able, because the Lord had closed the door? I think not. The Lord said in Revelation 3:8, 'I have set before thee an open door, and no man can shut it.' He says to all, 'Come.' And the time will come when the righteous 'shall come from the east, and from the west, and from the north, and from the south, and shall sit down in the kingdom of God.'" [Lk 13:29]

He looked up from his Bible, and said fervently, "Are not *all* the 'lost sheep,' the 'lost coin,' that Christ seeks to save? If the parable of the Prodigal Son in Luke 15:11-32 taught the traditional doctrine of a fiery Hell of torment, the parable would read: 'A man had five or six sons and lost three, then hunted around and found two of them; and he thought that if the other one wanted to wander off—why, he would just let him go.'" He shook his head vehemently, and added, "The language is the same in all of Jesus' parables; no matter how many were lost, the Bible indicates that *all* the lost were to be sought out, and saved. God will subdue all things to himself, in Christ. First Corinthians 15:24-28 says, 'And when all things shall be subdued unto him, then shall the Son also, himself, be subject unto him that put all things under him; that God may be all in all.' As all are to be subdued to Christ, thereby receiving spiritual life, all will ultimately be holy and saved."

He held up his Bible, and stated, "In fact, the doctrine of Eternal Torment is not found anywhere in the Old Testament: which is a most remarkable fact! The Jews—the only people who had oral communication with the Creator, for many ages—were not instructed in that doctrine. Among all the richly detailed doctrines, laws, and precepts that were communicated to his ancient people by their Creator, 'Eternal Torment' and 'Endless Punishment' are not to be found. The Ancient Patriarchs make no mention of it; Solomon, the wisest of men, gives no indication that he ever heard of it! The long line of Prophets—who spake as God gave them utterance—revealed no such sentiment. How can this profound silence be accounted for, if that doctrine is true?

"I firmly believe in all the 'hell' of which the Bible speaks; but I am not able to accept the view of it held by my friend at the other table. Even David was in hell, according to Psalm 86:13; and yet, he was delivered from it! David uses the word in a figurative sense, when he says, 'The pains of Hell got hold upon me.' [Ps 116:3] Jonah, the prophet, says, 'Out of the belly of Hell cried I; and thou heardst my voice.' [2:2] Of Jesus Christ, it is said in Acts 2:27 and 31 that 'his soul was not left in hell.' Therefore, Christ himself was in hell—the literal hell! Nowhere do we read of an endless hell. The Greek word most often translated 'hell' in the New Testament is *hades*. Hades, in its original and primitive signification, means not a state of torment, but the grave, the state of death in general—without regard to the goodness or badness of persons, or their happiness or misery!

"If the doctrine of eternal torment is true, why did neither Christ nor his Apostles ever teach it? Why did none of the Apostles, whose preaching is recorded for us in the Book of Acts, ever threaten their hearers with Hell torments, in even one solitary instance? Why did Paul, the great Apostle to the Gentiles, never use any word that is translated as 'hell'—such as 'Gehenna,' or 'Tartarus'—with the sole exception of his one use of 'hades' in First Corinthians 15:55… which he only mentions to show its *destruction*? If the doctrine of endless Hell torments is true, why have we no account of its ever having been preached in the Christian church before the days of Tertullian, in the third century?" He looked over the silent crowd, as they pondered these statements.

He continued, "God being infinitely wise, good, and holy, would not have created his offspring, unless he knew they would be 'gainers' thereby, and not 'losers.' God's infinite benevolence must prompt him to seek not only the collective good of the whole, but the individual good of each; and that not for *time* merely, but for *eternity*. The greatest amount of good for the whole, must consist in the consummation of the perfect and eternal beatitude of each individual intelligence.

"If God foresaw that any number of beings would, if ushered into existence, become doomed to endless blasphemy and woe, why would he persist in creating them? There was no power above God, compelling him to form his creatures for such a dreadful fate! If it was foreseen that their existence must terminate in endless agony, then why not simply allow them to remain in the unconscious and harmless sleep of non-entity? Surely, they can injure none there; they cannot infringe on the happiness of God, nor affect the felicity of angels. No principle but that of *infinite hatred* could have produced a single being, while knowing that such a being would ultimately be endlessly miserable. If God made the wicked, while having a perfect knowledge that they would be lost, then did he not make them for the purpose of being lost? Could he create men, absolutely knowing they would be damned, and yet not make them to be damned? Can they help being damned, as was foreseen? This is the doctrine of Calvinism, which reasonable men and women everywhere now reject!"

He saw that the Moderator was signaling that his time was coming to an end, so he concluded, speaking more passionately, "According to my friend's creed, God made a world—He proposed an end, He introduced all the means necessary—and yet, in the end, He is about to fail in it! My friend must strive to prove that God's government is imperfect; that his law will remain forever unfulfilled; that his beneficent purposes in man's existence are ultimately frustrated; and that Jesus Christ was ultimately defeated in the great object of his mission! That countless millions of intelligent beings—who are capable, under favorable influences, of arising to an equality with the angels, in holiness and love—are instead thrust down to the companionship of devils; to roll in agony, and blaspheme the name of their Father throughout eternity!

"Most of the Evangelical faith say that a majority of the world have died as unbelievers; in fact, that even a majority of those who have *heard* the gospel have rejected it—and we know that only a small portion of mankind have ever heard it at all. And thus are apparently consigned to endless torments all those who have never heard the gospel, and thus were not capable of exercising faith in its life-giving precepts. If this life is a 'state of probation,' then is there no hope for the entire Pagan world! They must die as sinners; and, if there is no change possible after death, they must remain sinners eternally—so that the whole Pagan world is to be eternally lost! Pagans, my friend might argue, will be judged according to the light they have. True, but that is not the point; this is the question: Shall the whole Pagan world be lost endlessly, because they had not the light of the Gospel here? They are brought into existence under the Providence of God, in a circumstance where they cannot have the light necessary for salvation. Thus, the Pagans supposedly have light enough to *damn* them, but not enough to *save* them!" He saw a number of heads in the audience nodding their agreement with him.

He finished, "If this short life affords our only chance of avoiding eternal doom, or of securing endless bliss, then the chances of damnation for mankind generally—when compared to the chances of salvation—are certainly as great as ten to one *against* salvation; especially when we consider the millions and millions of Pagans who live and die without ever hearing that one and only name given under heaven among men, whereby we may be saved. Can it be possible that God has created a world of intelligences under such unfavorable terms to human salvation? Surely not, if he is a just Creator. Before I turn over this podium to my friend, I would wonder: does he believe in his soul that only a *few* are to be finally saved, and that the *many* are to be damned endlessly? This was a popular doctrine a century ago, when the theology of John Calvin was dominant in this country. I would be glad to hear my friend's opinion on this important subject. I thank you all for your kind attention."

He picked up his Bible, and sat back down at his table.

Reverend Richardson practically leaped up from his table and headed swiftly to the podium, eager to begin his own presentation. He placed his Bible carefully down, opened it to his desired page, and then said forcefully, "My opponent apparently accuses me of inconsistency, in preaching that a part of mankind *will* be lost, while I desire and believe that all *may* be saved. In fact, I believe that a great many—including some Pagans—will secure heaven, through Jesus Christ. Revelation 7:9 tells us that 'a great multitude, which no man could number, of all nations, and kindreds, and people, and tongues, stood before the throne.' Yet, while I maintain there is sufficient evidence for believing that many or most will be lost, I also maintain and believe that none *need* be lost. There is no *necessity* imposed on any human being, requiring them to forfeit heaven and eternal happiness; but, on the contrary, many advantages are furnished to them, with the direct view of securing their salvation; and the whole responsibility of a failure—where a failure occurs—rests on man, not on God.

"Since my opponent just posed a question to me, let me in turn pose a question to him, and to all of you: What would be my fate, if it should happen that Universalism is correct? Suppose that I persist in opposing this doctrine all my life, yet find in the end that it is true—what will be the consequences?" He stopped speaking to allow the audience to consider this, and then calmly answered his own question, "None: in fact, I shall be made holy and happy in Heaven; I am, therefore, in no danger, let the matter turn out as it may—my error cannot inflict lasting misfortune or misery upon my soul.

"If Universalism is true, then all men will be saved: whether they believe it or not, and whether they oppose it or not; in the future state, we shall all be quite as happy as the Universalists themselves. What great practical advantage, then, would be gained by my converting to the Universalist faith? Should my opponent's doctrine prove true, it is of but little importance whether we debate it or not, or whether anybody believes it or not." He paused, and then continued in an urgent tone, "But suppose Universalism turns out to be false? Why, those who embrace it are eternally ruined! If my opponent is mistaken, it is of *incalculable* importance that all men should know this, as soon as possible. If he is wrong, then the spreading of that false doctrine—insofar as it disposes some to be indifferent, in this crucial lifetime—may result in their condemnation to undying agonies!" (Several persons in the audience—perhaps members of his congregation—openly applauded this statement.)

He went on, "The authority of God emanates from his infinite goodness. If the government of God was organized and administered for the purpose of *destroying* the happiness of a part of his creatures, then those creatures would be under no moral obligation to obey him. But every moral being *is* under obligation to obey God, because in fact His government is organized and administered to *secure* the happiness of each and all. It is a perfect government: perfect in its organization, in its laws, and in its administration; accomplishing all its objects, according to the prompting of this infinite goodness and wisdom. God's government will secure the greatest possible good, at the least possible expense of evil. But evil, moral and physical, is an unavoidable accompaniment to our rational moral agency; and if God had not permitted, controlled, or punished it in some instances, and pardoned it in others, His justice, holiness, wrath, and mercy could not have been known at all—and none of His other perfections could have been so fully developed and glorified. Consequently, God could never have been enjoyed by any creature.

"Here is the broad difference between Orthodoxy and Universalism. Universalism claims that God cannot be a God of love, and let any man be lost. We, on the other hand, claim that while God is a God of love, he has done all that he could do for man's salvation, consistent with man's free agency—leaving it wholly optional with man to resist God and die, or to serve Him and live forever. It is not true that God *causes* the misery of sinful men; they cause their own misery, by assuming such an attitude to the law and government of God, as to make their own unhappiness a natural and necessary consequence. And, continuing their attitude of hostility and rebellion in utter rejection of the terms of reconciliation, they alone are responsible for the consequences to themselves—even though it be endless perdition.

"My opponent has a one-idea doctrine: He takes one of God's perfections, Love, and ignores all the rest: which are just as important, and just as essential to the divine character. He sees God's love, but ignores His holiness and justice. God cannot love holiness, without hating sin, in just the same proportion that he loves holiness. We know from observation that the more holy and like God a *man* becomes in this life, the more he hates sin; it follows, then, that God—having infinite love for holiness—has an infinite hatred for sin. If God is opposed to sin in an *infinite* degree, corresponding to the infinite holiness of the character of God, then he will also punish sin accordingly."

He turned to another page in his Bible, then continued, "The Bible says in Psalm 7:11, 'God is angry with the wicked every day.' Oh, yes: God has wrath; He has anger. We read in Psalm 2:12, 'Kiss the Son, lest He be angry, and ye perish from the way.' What would this mean, if God has no wrath; if He never is angry? We are poor judges of the gravity of sin. We know that it is committed by free moral agents, against a God infinitely worthy to be loved and obeyed: as our Creator, Preserver, and Redeemer. What sin committed against such a Being deserves, we are not capable of judging; but we *do* know that the disposition of men is such as to look with excess *softness* upon their own sins—and that men deserve far *greater* punishment than they themselves suppose. But surely, we can agree that the magnitude of a crime is increased by the dignity of the being imposed against; thus, a violent act against a judge, or an elected official, is of greater import, than the same act committed against an ordinary citizen. And thus, sin against a God of *infinite goodness* is far more heinous than sin against a fellow-being: reaching even the level of *infinite evil*—and thus requiring an *infinite sacrifice*, for its atonement.

"My opponent asks, 'Can the plan of the infinitely wise and powerful God fail?' Of course not; it is certain that whatever God does, He does according to His will. And so God willed that all men should be infinitely happy; but, notwithstanding His intent, that which He commanded is not done—and His law is broken, and His purpose trampled on. Thus, to say that because such was His desire, or such what 'He would have' men to do, therefore must happen—is to deny our experience, and to abrogate our reason."

He also held up his Bible, and said, "In contrast to my opponent, I firmly contend that the Old Testament *does* teach the doctrine of eternal punishment. I would refer you to Isaiah 66:20-24, where the Lord commands the prophet to 'look upon the carcasses of the men that have transgressed against me: for their worm shall not die, neither shall their fire be quenched; and they shall be an abhorring unto all flesh.' Then again in Daniel 12:1-3, the prophet gives his vision of the resurrection, and the subsequent everlasting punishment of the wicked. Says Daniel, they 'shall come forth, some to everlasting life, some to shame and everlasting contempt.'

"The Scriptures clearly teach that the souls of men *do* exist in a state of happiness or of misery after death, and before the resurrection. In Matthew 22:31-32, we read: 'But as touching the resurrection of the dead, have ye not read that which was spoken unto you by God, saying, I am the God of Abraham, and the God of Isaac, and the God of Jacob? God is not the God of the dead, but of the living.' The Saviour here certainly teaches that Abraham, Isaac, and Jacob—though their bodies were dead—were at that time still living. In Matthew 17:3, we read that when Christ and his disciples were on the mount where he was transfigured, 'there appeared unto them Moses and Elias, talking with him.' Moses and Elias were clearly still living, though their bodies were dead.

"This is further confirmed by our Saviour's statement to the penitent thief, where he said: 'Today shalt thou be with me in paradise.' [Lk 23:43] Stephen, the first Christian martyr, prayed while dying, 'Lord Jesus, receive my spirit.' [Acts 7:51] Evidently, he expected his soul to pass immediately into the presence of Jesus in Heaven. Paul likewise uses the following language: 'For I am in a strait betwixt two, having a desire to depart, and to be with Christ; which is far better.' [Phil 1:22] Certainly, Paul expected to go immediately to Heaven upon his death—and hence he desired to die. And this same doctrine is most clearly taught by the account of the rich man and Lazarus: 'And it came to pass, that the beggar died, and was carried by the angels into Abraham's bosom. The rich man also died; and in hell he lifted up his eyes, being in torment.' [Luke 16:19-23] These portions of Scripture teach that the righteous go, immediately after death, into a state of happiness, and the wicked into a state of misery."

He lifted his eyes up from his Bible, and said fervently, "My opponent claims that God so loves his enemies that he will save them—though these enemies, throughout life, refuse to be reconciled to Him! It is indeed true that God loves his enemies; but our Saviour also says: 'For God so loved the world that he gave his only begotten Son, that whosoever believeth in him should not *perish*, but have everlasting life.' [Jn 3:16] Thus, we are taught by Christ himself—not that God determined to save all men, regardless of their will, or moral character—but that those who *believe* in Christ should not perish, but will have everlasting life. And I would ask, what does the word 'perish' mean in this passage, if not the opposite of 'everlasting life'? Therefore, those who do *not* believe will perish, and will *not* have everlasting life.

"That life implies death; that *eternal* life implies *eternal* death; is as great a contrast as reason or language knows. In the preaching of Jesus, to be 'cast into hell,' or consigned 'into everlasting fire' clearly means endless punishment, as certainly as to 'enter into life' or 'into the kingdom of God' means endless bliss. It is true that the terms 'eternal,' 'endless,' and 'everlasting,' like all other words, are sometimes used figuratively; I may sometimes speak of my 'everlasting solace,' my 'endless labors,' and so on. But who infers from such statements that these words may have no higher signification with me? Or that, when applied to things after death and beyond time, that they mean a *limited* time, or a *short* duration? These are not words that belong to time in a figurative sense; in their literal sense, they are only applicable to God, and to that world which is itself eternal. Hence God, in both Testaments, is called the everlasting and the eternal God."

He referred to his Bible again, saying, "The future state of the righteous is called by Jesus 'eternal life,' and the future state of the wicked is called 'everlasting punishment.' Jesus uses the terms 'hell fire,' 'unquenchable fire,' and 'everlasting fire' either as substitutes for Hell, or as equivalent to one another. Hell is, by Jesus, contrasted with life: to 'go into hell' is opposed to 'entering into life.' But to 'enter into life' is equivalent to entering into Heaven after death; therefore, to go into Hell is the opposite of going into Heaven. If Heaven is everlasting bliss, Hell is everlasting misery.

"Of the abundant scriptural evidence for the doctrine of eternal torment, perhaps the clearest is the story of the rich man and Lazarus, in Luke 16. What did our Lord intend to teach, when he shared this story? He represents a rich man permitting a poor but righteous man to lie at his door, and to feed on the crumbs that fall from the rich man's table. 'The rich man died, and in hell he lifted up his eyes, being in torment.' The rich man dies, and immediately is punished; tormented for his sins. This passage most impressively teaches two important truths: 1. That immediately after death, the righteous are perfectly happy, and the wicked are miserable and in torment, because of their deeds done in the body; and, 2. That the happiness of the one, and the misery of the other, will be eternal; this truth is taught by the impassable gulf—represented as existing between the righteous and the wicked, so that there can be no passing from the one side, to the other.

"Christ warned in Matthew 10:28, 'fear not them which kill the body, but are not able to kill the soul, but rather fear him which is able to destroy both soul and body in hell.' Now, what does Jesus teach here? First, that the body may be killed, and the soul live on; second, that the body and soul may both be destroyed in Hell; and thirdly, it teaches that Hell is a place in which souls and bodies may be destroyed. The Greek word translated 'soul' in this passage is constantly used for the *immortal soul*; there can be no doubt concerning its meaning. If the word does not mean the immortal soul, then why cannot men kill it?

"Equally persuasive is Matthew 25:31-46, where the Saviour said, 'When the Son of man shall come in his glory... before him shall be gathered all nations: and he shall separate them one from another, as a shepherd divideth his sheep from the goats: And he shall set the sheep on his right hand, but the goats on the left. Then shall the King say unto them on his right hand, Come, ye blessed of my Father, inherit the kingdom prepared for you from the foundation of the world ... Then shall he say also unto them on the left hand, Depart from me, ye cursed, into everlasting fire, prepared for the devil and his angels ... And these shall go away into everlasting punishment: but the righteous into life eternal.'" He looked up from his Bible, and added solemnly, "These words, surely, require no commentary from me."

He noticed the Moderator signaling to him that his time was almost up, so he quickly looked over at Thomas, and then turned back to the audience, and stated, "A large class of Universalists—those following 'Father' Hosea Ballou—have rejected all concepts of punishment for sin, except those that occur in this present life. How, then, is such punishment to be inflicted in this life? Why, purely by mental anguish! But does an *adequate* punishment for all sins committed in this life take place before death? Every man of reason is bound to say *no!* Suppose a man has committed the most aggravated murder; and while his hands are yet stained with blood, he is stricken with a bolt of lightning, and thus taken out of the world—without feeling even the first pang of remorse! In such cases, clearly, no adequate punishment is inflicted in this life; thus, he surely must be punished after death!

"My opponent claims that there is no good effect to be achieved from punishment, or from threats of eternal punishment; but even he seems to admit that such threats may restrain men from vice. Yet more importantly, punishment also serves to vindicate the injured majesty of God's law—and is God's law not to be vindicated? When a man is an incorrigible disturber of the peace, and commits a heinous crime, we in civil society may imprison him for life. Shall not God have the same power—during the immortal *spiritual* life—as human judges do, during the *natural* life?"

He concluded, "My opponent boldly claims to know what God could, and couldn't do. I humbly say that I am not able to measure, and compare, and decide upon what must be the attributes of God, or their workings; shall I attempt to say that such-and-such result must accrue from the attributes of the infinite God of Eternity? All we know about His attributes is contained here in the Bible. But I would suggest, that if the attributes of God can obviously harmonize with the *brief* misery of some of his creatures in this present world, then the misery of a week should likewise be consistent with them; and so the misery of a year, or of an age—therefore, so may the misery of *eternity* be consistent with the moral attributes of God. And if the six thousand years' misery on this planet of some of His creatures is consistent with His attributes, I know not why their *continued* misery and sinfulness may not be."

He closed his Bible, and said, "I thank you for your kind attention, and your prayers." He left the podium, and returned to his table.

Thomas returned with his Bible to the podium, then looked out at the audience again, and began, "My friend asks, 'Do not the Scriptures speak of God as a God of wrath? Do they not represent Him as being angry?' Yes, they do. But the same Scriptures also speak of God as a being who has arms, and eyes, and a mouth; that is, they speak of Him *after the manner of men*. But when Jesus Christ speaks of God, he speaks of Him as the Eternal Father; as a Being of Infinite Love—whose goodness is greater than we have yet imagined. What the Scriptures mean by God's 'wrath' is his temporal punishments; but even these arise out of His goodness and love. They are not vindictive, they are not intended to destroy; their object is not to make men miserable, but to teach them, to instruct them, to make them understand their duty, to lead them into the way of life. They are *reformatory* in their character.

"Reverend Richardson might well ask, 'If there is no danger of eternal damnation, why did Christ threaten it?' There was indeed a 'damnation' which Christ threatened; but it was not one that was *endless*. My friend admits that terms such as 'eternal,' 'endless,' 'everlasting,' and 'forever,' are equivocal; they may be, and are, applied in the Scriptures to all different degrees of duration: from short periods, to much longer ones. For example, the prophet Jonah says [2:6]: 'The earth with her bars was about me *for ever.*' when he had been inside the fish but three days; thus, the term 'for ever' clearly needs not signify an endless duration. But if my friend thus admits that words like 'everlasting' may be used in such a limited sense, how does he know that they are not used in such a limited sense in the very passages he relies upon to support his doctrine?" He paused, noting with satisfaction some nods of agreement in the audience.

He went on, "If he interprets 'everlasting' in Matthew 25:41 & 46 as meaning an endless duration, I would remind him that the Levitical priesthood is called an 'everlasting priesthood' in Exodus 40:15 and Numbers 25:13; does that prove that this priesthood is yet in force now, and will be for all eternity? If not, then if 'everlasting' means a limited duration when applied to that priesthood, it should bear the same signification when applied to *punishment* in Matthew 25. The yearly atonement for sin made in the Jewish Temple was called an 'everlasting statute' in Leviticus 16:34; but was it 'everlasting'? No; again, the meaning is one of long continuance. Thus, the punishment into which the children of Israel fell, and in which they now continue, is called 'endless' in both the Old and New Testaments.

"My friend thinks that because the Bible speaks of the *everlasting* Father, 'everlasting' therefore always signifies endless duration. But although it does bear that meaning when referring to *God*, it does not follow that it means 'endless' when applied to *punishment*. If you were to find such terms 6,000 times in the Old and New Testaments—and out of that number, 5,900 times they applied to God and his perfections—nevertheless, if in the other hundred instances, they were applied to a variety of objects of shorter duration, which by their nature could *not* be 'endless,' you would not have gained even one step towards establishing the doctrine of 'eternal torment.'"

He held up his hands, as if to indicate uncertainty, and asked, "How, then, do we judge the meaning of such words? We should not rely on ambiguous, single words; we should depend upon expressions which admit of no such limitation, such as Psalm 102:27, which says of God: 'thou art the same, and thy years shall have no end.' By such definite language do the Scriptures teach the endless existence of God. Neither should we rely on ambiguous words to prove the endless existence of the soul; the Bible employs other terms to teach that glorious truth. But nowhere do the sacred writers assert that the life of the damned in hell will continue forever in such state, or that their miseries will never end.

"My friend apparently *assumes* that the term 'perish' is synonymous with endless torment. But the 'perishing' in John 3:16 was a state of *moral* death, darkness, and depravity—the very opposite of the 'everlasting life' enjoyed by the believer. My friend called our attention to Revelation 20, and he may yet cite Revelation 19:3, 'her smoke rose up for ever and ever.' But let us refer to Isaiah 34:10, where the prophet speaks of the destruction of Idumea, thus representing only *temporal* calamities. What form of expression does Isaiah use? 'the smoke thereof shall go up for ever'—the same as we find in Revelation 19. Here, the very same expressions are applied to the *temporal* desolation and destruction of a single country and people, that my opponent thinks apply to the *endless* torment of men in the immortal world. But let us read on in Isaiah: 'From generation to generation it shall lie waste: none shall pass through it for ever and ever.' Thus, is it again demonstrated that such language does not necessarily mean *eternity*.

"The language of Isaiah 66:24—'Their worm shall not die, neither shall their fire be quenched'—is quite as strong as the expression, 'their worm dieth not, and the fire is not quenched' in Mark 9:44-48; substantially the same thing is meant in both passages. Isaiah 66:23 also says: 'And it shall come to pass, that from one new moon to another, and from one sabbath to another, shall all flesh come to worship before me, saith the Lord. And they shall go forth, and look upon the carcasses of the men that have transgressed against me.' This fire that was not to be quenched was in a place where there are new moons and Sabbaths! Are there to be new moons and Sabbaths in eternity?" (A number of persons in the audience voiced their agreement with the statement, only to be signaled to remain silent by the Moderator.)

THOMAS TURNED IN HIS BIBLE, AND THEN ARGUED, "My friend thinks highly of the parable of the rich man and Lazarus in Luke 16; but how he expects to derive detailed doctrine from a *parable*, is not clear to me. As a parable, its language must be figurative; it cannot refer to the natural death of all men, and any punishment immediately following it. This parable of

the rich nan and Lazarus was intended to convey real truth in the form
of fiction; the story is fictitious, but its truth is real. It was intended to
represent a condition of moral blindness, darkness, and suffering in *this*
life—not in the future life.

"But simply taking the parable as it is, does it support my friend's
doctrine? I would point out that there is no indication in the text of the
duration of the rich man's punishment; so why should my friend assume
that this punishment is 'endless'? The rich man is also represented as being
in *Hades*, not *Gehenna;* and most eminent commentators—including those
of the Evangelical faith—assert that it is Gehenna, and not Hades, which
is the place of future endless torment; and significantly, the punishment in
Gehenna does not take place until *after* the resurrection of the dead! Yet in
this parable, we have the rich man in 'hell,' and suffering torment, without
ever having been raised from the dead! And even if we supposed that this
Hades is indeed a place of punishment, it exists in a time *intermediate*
between the man's death, and the final resurrection—therefore, it certainly
cannot be 'endless' in its duration." (He noted with satisfaction that
a number of his hearers appeared to be positively impressed by these
statements.)

He continued, "I now turn to Matthew 10:28: 'fear him which is able
to destroy both soul and body in hell.' Understood literally, this passage
proves only the *power* of God to bring about the destruction of the soul and
body—the same as he had the power to raise up children to Abraham from
the literal stones of the field. But let us suppose God not only to possess
the power, but to exercise it literally to destroy both soul and body in this
hell—what follows from this? Not eternal torment, but the *destruction* of
the soul, and the annihilation of the material body in hell! How, then, can
they suffer? Therefore, the text in this interpretation would *disprove* endless
misery; it would actually support the views of those who call themselves
'Annihilationists,' and support a doctrine called 'Conditional Immortality.'
But it certainly does not support my friend's perspective."

He turned to another page in his Bible, and said, "Next, we will
consider Matthew 25. In the beginning of this parable—verses 31-32—
we find a 'gathering of all nations' spoken of, and a separation: not of
individuals, but of *nations*! We are not told that the individuals specified
in the parable were to inherit the kingdom because they had been 'born

again,' or because they 'had faith in the gospel,' but solely as a result of their *good deeds*. But does my friend believe that our future salvation is the result of *works*? If so, what becomes of his doctrine of grace?

"I contend that neither the 'everlasting punishment' nor the 'life eternal' of Matthew 25:46 expresses the ultimate condition of the sinner or the saint; the parable in Matthew 25 prefigures the separation which took place between the true and false professors of Christ's religion in that age, when Christ should come in judgment upon that nation. The 'everlasting punishment' is synonymous with those judgments so frequently predicted in the Old Testament using the symbol of fire. Thus, the language of Daniel and the Savior were to be literally fulfilled—but even this punishment is not to be *endless!*

"My friend has several times cited the Book of Revelation—a book universally acknowledged to be highly figurative—and he has *assumed* that the passages he has quoted are to be interpreted in a literal manner; but this I vigorously deny. Has my friend given us any evidence that the 'second death' in Revelation 20:14 signifies a state of endless suffering? To take the metaphorical expressions of such a symbolic book, and apply them literally to the support of any doctrine, is to insult good sense. The 'second death' is a figurative form of speech, used in reference to God's dealings with the Jews: it was a *national* death."

He turned to another page in his Bible, and continued, "My friend also quoted Daniel 12, and its reference to a resurrection. I want to distinguish between this *first* resurrection of which Daniel is writing, and the *final* resurrection. Daniel 12 refers to the first resurrection mentioned in Revelation 20:5, which took place before the generation in which Jesus lived passed away, namely: at that dreadful time when the people of Jerusalem were overwhelmed. This is explicitly taught in the words of our Saviour in Matthew 24:15-16: 'When ye, therefore, shall see the abomination of desolation, spoken of by Daniel, the prophet, stand in the holy place… Then let them which be in Judea flee into the mountains.' Clearly, this must have been a local, temporary affair; after all, what would be the use of running into the mountains, if this was the final judgment? You cannot escape such a *worldwide* judgment in that way!

"I must also ask my friend, what would be the *purpose* of a judgment at the end of time? The man that goes to hell or hades must already have been judged; and so with the man who goes to paradise or heaven. But my friend still believes in *another*, future judgment: when all Hell is to be disembodied of its contents, and Heaven depopulated, to attend this great trial. I ask again, what is the use of this second judgment? Is it to rectify mistakes made in the first judgment? My friend may tell us that the object of the final judgment will be to 'pass sentence on all,' but has not everyone already been judged and sentenced as soon as they die, and consigned to hell or heaven? Why, then, re-judge them?" (He observed furrowed eyebrows on many of his listeners, as they pondered this question.)

He turned back to his Bible, and said, "My friend speaks forcefully of the anger of God; but he forgets what God himself said of his anger: 'I shall not contend forever, nor be always wroth, for the spirit would fail before me.' [Isa 57:16] Therefore, God will not be always angry; Psalm 30:5 says, 'His anger endureth but a moment'—a moment indeed, when compared with the eternity of peace, and joy, and love, which he has provided for all the intelligent creatures made by his hand. God is said to be angry with the wicked, but he retains not his wrath for eternity; nor is the term of man's woe without limit.

"Consider the case of Cain the murderer; not one word is said in Genesis 4:10-12 about 'eternal torment' being imposed for this great offence. Consider those destroyed in the Flood of Noah: in Genesis 6:5-6 and 7:21-23 is found all we know of the punishment pronounced upon the antediluvians; yet there is not one word of any misery to come in the eternal world. Consider the destruction of Sodom and Gomorrah: again, not one word is said in Genesis 19:24-25 about any 'endless punishment' in the eternal world. Adam received the retribution God threatened; Cain was punished by God himself; the antediluvians were swept from the face of the earth; Sodom and Gomorrah and the cities of the plain were overthrown and destroyed; and in Exodus 9 we read of the Lord's tenfold vengeance upon sinful Egypt. Yet not in all this is there even the most distant allusion to 'eternal torment.' How is this to be accounted for, if this doctrine is supposedly the truth of God's Word?"

He continued, "The doctrine of Eternal Torment violates that fundamental biblical rule in Romans 2:6, that God 'will render to every man according to his deeds.' The doctrine of eternal torment consigns the wicked of every age, of every grade, of every different degree of crime, to the same eternity of woe! It punishes the young sinner of eighteen years of age—who had but just fallen into the slightest transgressions—and casts him into the same place, and for the same length of time, as the hardened wretch of three score and ten, who has trampled on God's law throughout his life! Endless punishment does not propose to reform men; neither, notwithstanding the suggestion of my friend, does it propose to benefit others by the influence of example—because, unfortunately, this example is not provided until *after* the entire period of mortal probation is ended! What, then, is the object of endless punishment? Are we, then, to believe in a doctrine for which we can assign no adequate or rational reason?

"I ask any man to sit down a moment and reflect on this: a universe to be filled with misery, and eternal torment, and a God supporting the everlasting pains of his own children throughout eternity! If this be love, tell me: what would be *hatred?* If this be God, tell me what *Satan* himself could do that would be any worse, than God determining to punish a being forever, and giving him an immortal nature that will enable him to endure such endless misery? Let us not mock the character of God thus, and believe Him capable of such cruelty and injustice!" (A number of members of the audience applauded this statement.)

Seeing the Moderator signaling again that his time was almost up, Thomas went on forcefully, "Suppose that a man is guilty of almost every crime known. According to the doctrine of the Evangelicals, this man may have spent nearly his entire life in the grossest wickedness, without receiving any 'punishment'; yet, by repentance just before his death, this man will go immediately to heaven, to enjoy an eternity of bliss! So where, I ask, does he receive any punishment for his crimes of half a century? He gets no punishment at all! Therefore, under this doctrine, it would not be true that such a man receives recompense in the future world 'according to his works'! According to Reverend Richardson's doctrine, I might even slay this entire assembled group—killing men, women, and children—yet I could be screened from every future punishment, simply by becoming converted a single moment before I died!

"If so awful a doctrine as endless punishment be true, then the whole world ought to know it, that they might have a chance to avoid it. But the fact that only a small portion of the world know anything about this doctrine, is good evidence that it is false. Furthermore, if the doctrine of endless torment is true, it should not be difficult to find in the Bible; the Bible would utter it from the first verse of Genesis, to the last verse of Revelation—and in terms so plainly told that no man could fail to see it. Yet there are many thousands of Christians who cannot see it at all, though they have examined the Bible most carefully.

He concluded, "If God designed this doctrine to be revealed in his Gospel to man, it should be uttered in thunderous, unmistakable voices: **ETERNAL TORMENT FOR THE WICKED!** And the people who believe this doctrine ought to give neither sleep to their eyes, nor slumber to their eyelids, until they succeed in impressing this fearful news on the ears of all men. And the ministers of the Gospel, instead of good-naturedly enjoying their dinner, and their conversations and jokes afterward—happy and contented, in spite of this fearsome doctrine—ought to incessantly thunder it in the ears of their fellow-men!" He smiled, and then added with a smile, "But I give the Evangelicals credit... for not really *believing* what they preach!" and a number of individuals in the audience laughed.

He returned to his seat at the table (giving a long, relieved sigh).

Reverend Richardson swiftly took his place at the podium again; his face was flushed, with anger and emotion. He said sharply, "My opponent suggests that an evil man might deliberately plan to convert just prior to death, in order to achieve Heaven. But the deliberate calculation which such a sinner supposed he might make beforehand—in regard to repentance, and escape from punishment—would itself constitute a *forfeiture* of the grace of repentance and salvation! No man who forms a plan in his own mind to go and commit a crime—on the supposition that he will be able afterwards to repent and obtain divine pardon—will be able to carry out his plan; he may indeed commit the crime, but the very fact that he had calculated upon this way of escape beforehand, would deprive him of the power of *repentance*. The grant of pardon under such circumstances would, and must be, withheld by God.

He went on, "Let us critically examine my opponent's use of Scripture. Jesus Christ does not call the story of the rich man and Lazarus a 'parable,' even though he often identifies his parables as such; read Matthew 13, for example. Furthermore, the Jews to whom Jesus Christ uttered this story *believed* in an endless, future punishment. Let me ask my opponent this question: would this language of Christ in Luke 16 *strengthen* such a belief in future punishment, or would it *weaken* it? If the doctrine of future punishment were an error, would Christ not instead have spoken words to rebuke this error? Yet we are plainly told that this rich man was in *torment*—and to one like myself who believes the Bible, that settles the question.

"We have recorded in Luke 13:23 an interesting conversation between one of the disciples and the Saviour. The disciple asks, 'Lord, are there few that be saved?' If Christ had been a Universalist, he would have replied, 'Oh, you mistake the whole matter; *every* individual of the human family will be saved.' But mark instead the emphatic words of Jesus: 'Strive to enter in at the straight gate; for many, I say unto you, will seek to enter in and shall not be able'! Again, Christ says in Matthew 7:13-14: 'Enter ye in at the strait gate; for wide is the gate and broad is the way, that leadeth to destruction, and many there be which go in thereat: Because strait is the gate, and narrow is the way that leadeth unto life, and few there be that find it.' The Saviour earnestly exhorted those whom he addressed to labor to enter in at the strait gate, lest they should fail to find salvation. But Universalism argues, 'All shall enter into life, whether they strive or not'—thus directly contradicting the very words of Christ."

He looked over at Thomas sitting down at his table, then turned back to the audience, and said, "My opponent seems to regard it as a problem that, since the Pagan heathen did not *ask* of God to be created, they should have been brought forth into their present condition. But is God to be held responsible for the sins they commit? Paul teaches us in Romans 1:18-21: 'that which may be known of God is manifest in them; for God hath shewed it unto them... when they knew God, they glorified him not as God, neither were thankful; but became vain in their imaginations, and their foolish heart was darkened.' In the second chapter, the apostle teaches us that all will be judged by the light they have: 'For as many as have sinned without law'—that is, without the revealed law of God—'shall perish without law: and as many as have sinned in the law, shall be judged by the law.' If, then, as the apostle declares, they are without excuse, where is the 'cruelty' of punishing them for their own sins? If they are responsible only for sinning against the amount of light they have, where is the 'injustice'?"

He added in a sharp, sarcastic tone, "My opponent asked how Satan could be more cruel than his own twisted perception of God; but I immediately thought of the apostle's words in Romans 9:19-22, 'Nay but, O man, who are thou that repliest against God? Shall the thing formed say to him that formed it, "Why hast thou made me thus?" Hath not the potter power over the clay, of the same lump to make one vessel unto honor, and another unto dishonor?'" He shook his head, and added solemnly, "Men have been given free moral agency—the freedom to act well, or ill—and they make their choice; I cannot explain this any better, or more plainly."

He took a deep breath, and then said in his normal tone of voice, "My opponent apparently thinks it is curious that, if the doctrines of 'endless punishment' and 'eternal torment' are really true, that these terms do not occur specifically within the pages of the Bible; he is evidently not satisfied with my reference to 'everlasting punishment' in Matthew 25:46. But let us note that there is likewise nothing in the Bible about 'endless bliss,' 'everlasting joy,' 'eternal happiness,' or *endless* anything else being promised to men. The term 'endless life' occurs but once—in Hebrews 7:16—and then it is neither predicated of man, nor promised to him. But does this lack suggest to my opponent that God has *not* promised such happiness to those who are saved?"

He turned a page in his Bible, and then explained, "In Matthew 25:46, the same Greek word, *aionios*—which is translated as both 'everlasting' and 'eternal,' in the same sentence—is used to express the duration both of the *life*, and of the *punishment*. That this word must mean the same in both places in this single sentence, is beyond all reasonable dispute. And just so certain that the duration of the life mentioned in this passage is endless, so the punishment is likewise endless; for the very same word that describes the life of the righteous also expresses the punishment of the wicked. I would thus like to ask my opponent, what other language could the Almighty have used that would express the concept of endless punishment, if the language I have already cited does not? If men may be in 'danger of eternal damnation,' 'go into everlasting punishment,' and be 'tormented day and night forever and ever' in a place 'where the worm dieth not and the fire is not quenched,' without this referring to their suffering 'endless torment,' then there is no language on earth that can do so!

"My opponent attempted to make a point about the use of the word 'nations' in Matthew 25:32. This is a mere quibble; what difference does it make, whether they were nations, or individuals? Those who were wicked were sentenced to *everlasting punishment*—that is very sure! He may call them 'nations,' or 'individuals,' just as he pleases—but the final result will be the same. My opponent also seemingly made the amazing claim that the apocalyptic imagery in Matthew 24 and 25 took place in the 1st century A.D. Let me ask him, when in that century did Christ 'sit upon the throne of his glory' [Mt 19:28]? Were there 'before him … gathered all nations' [Mt 25:32]? Did he 'separate … his sheep from the goats' [Mt 25:32]? I also ask, how 'the world' was judged? The world was not judged at the destruction of Jerusalem, for the *world* was not there present! And as the 'man of sin' of 2 Thessalonians 2:3-8 was to be destroyed when Christ would come, how does it happen that he is not now destroyed?" He shook his head and added, "The idea that such passages refer to anything but a future final judgment of the entire human race is too preposterous to deserve an answer!

"I would call his attention to Luke 21:24: 'And they shall fall by the edge of the sword, and shall be led away captive into all nations; and Jerusalem shall be trodden down of the gentiles until the time of the gentiles be fulfilled.' The expression, 'they shall fall by the edge of the sword,' refers to the destruction of Jerusalem, I will admit; but the expression, 'they shall be led away captive into all nations,' certainly extends a long way beyond that ancient event. And the words, 'Jerusalem shall be trodden down of the gentiles until the times of the gentiles shall be fulfilled,' certainly extends up to the present time."

He looked out at the audience, which was attentively listening to him, then continued, "My opponent also suggests that God would not have created any of his intelligent creatures if He had known that they were to be endlessly punished. But the *Devil* is likewise one of God's intelligent creatures; so tell me—when is Satan to get out of Hell? Let us follow my opponent's notion, and see where it leads: According to the Universalist, the Devil and his rebellious angels are apparently to be brought to heaven along with all the rest of God's intelligent creatures; are we thus to kiss and make up with the *Devil*, who has given us all the trouble we have ever had in this world? After all, the angels are above man—according to Psalm 8:5 and Hebrews 2:7—and if God loves man well enough to save him, does He not love well enough those who were nearer his throne than man, to do the same thing for them? May it never be! My opponent's argument fails, because if God would create an angel such as the Devil—knowing full well that this angel would fall, and would ultimately be forever punished with the most horrible torments of Hell—why would God not also create, and sometimes punish, human creatures whom He created a 'little *lower* than the angels'?

"My opponent may wonder why does God not withhold existence from those whom He foresees will ultimately be damned, and provide existence only to such beings as would be saved: but I answer, this would be to violate the principles of God's own government, and contravene the divine impartiality. My opponent might just as well ask, 'Why did God create men, knowing they would suffer *at all?*' But the sufferings we experience in this lifetime are indeed often reformatory in their character. The difference between my opponent and myself is that I firmly believe the statement of Hebrews 9:27: 'it is appointed unto men once to die, but after this the judgment.' No opportunity is mentioned in this passage of any chance to repent, or change one's mind, after this sole physical death."

He noticed the Moderator motioning that his time was coming to an end, so he quickly added, "We all believe that God *does* desire that 'all men shall be saved,' and that God used every method consistent with man's moral freedom to the end that men *shall* be saved. Nevertheless, we also believe that when Jesus said to one and all, 'Come unto me that ye may have life,' he sought to persuade men to avail themselves of the means that were provided for their salvation. But here is the whole point at issue: Shall the *rejecter* of Christ and his Gospel be saved? Can men be saved who deliberately, willfully, and persistently will not believe? Certainly, they cannot. Jesus Christ, having suffered and died, cannot save men who will not come to him by their own volition, accept of his atonement, be washed in his blood, and be cleansed and purified by the grace which he imparts."

He said in a passionate voice. "God beseeches men, and prays for them to be reconciled to him. And this shows clearly that God's purpose to reconcile all things to himself depends for its accomplishment upon the *persons* to be reconciled. It is not an 'absolute' purpose, depending only upon *God* for its accomplishment; as my opponent must assume, in order to make his argument. Some men *refuse* to be reconciled to God and saved; and thus, God does not reconcile and save such men. Will God ever change? No; a thousand times, no! Then who can hope to prove from the desire of God, that all *will* ultimately be reconciled to God, and saved? No one! Those who die in sin will not be sanctified in the hereafter. They will, therefore, continue to rebel and sin against God, forever. The punishment of the wicked will be eternal because of their sins committed in this world, but also because they will *continue* to sin hereafter. They who have formed habits of sinning will not suddenly *become* holy, simply because they have passed into the eternal state."

He concluded in a fiery tone, "To prove his doctrine, my opponent must prove that the sinner will *eternally* have the power to will; and that the sinner will, at some future date, exercise that power. But my opponent cannot prove this; no man can do so. Many sinners greatly impair, if not entirely destroy, their own will power—even in this brief lifetime. God will always be love, goodness, and mercy; but *we* may not always be just what we are now: having the power of loving, willing, and doing. I would therefore fervently admonish the sinner that 'now is the accepted time... now is the day of salvation.' [2 Cor 6:2] *This* is the time for him to will, and love, and obey; as it will one day be too late."

He closed his Bible, and then returned to his seat.

The Moderator then took to the podium again, saying to the audience, "And that will conclude this evening's discussion. We hope that you will join us again tomorrow evening, for the conclusion. Until then, I thank you for your attendance; good night to all, and may God Bless." The crowd began standing up, and heading to the exits; the room was immediately filled with the loud buzz of excited conversations.

Thomas stood up, and was about to go over and thank the Moderator, when Reverend Richardson came up to him, saying hotly, "We need to extend this debate; two days is simply not enough time to adequately address all of the biblical texts, and other issues!"

Thomas said quietly, "You might recall that I was not in favor of any debate lasting more than one day; I agreed to the second day only as an attempt to compromise with your own strong wishes." He added, "And I am greatly unhappy with this apparent 'debate' format: wherein we are expected to argue against the views of the other, publicly. We are both Christians, and Christians should be able to resolve their differences amicably—or at least, to not let them be the public cause of discord between us." He said in a conciliatory tone, "Suppose that for tomorrow's program, we both sat at the same table, and simply responded to questions submitted to us by the audience; and each of us gave his own response to the questioner in turn, and…"

"You are no Christian!" Rev. Richardson hissed. "I suspected as much, knowing you were a Universalist; but hearing your near-blasphemous statements tonight has removed any shadow of doubt from my mind! To sit at the same table as you, would imply an *equality* in our respective positions—a mutual respect, and a mutual consideration, which can never exist, between God and evil!" After saying this, he abruptly turned away, and went over to speak to the Moderator.

Thomas's face flushed with surprise and shock at this unexpected outburst; but he simply picked up his Bible, and left the stage… to join some members of his own congregation, who were waiting with his wife to congratulate him on his performance.

CHAPTER 5

The Great Debate, Continued (The next evening)

The Moderator stepped up to the podium, and then said to the assembled crowd (which was even larger than on the previous evening), "Good evening, ladies and gentlemen; my name is Elwin Habermas. I would like to welcome you to the second and final evening of this two-part discussion. I would remind you that the question to be discussed is, 'Do the Holy Scriptures and Reason Teach the Ultimate Salvation of All Mankind, or Do They Teach That Some Must Spend Eternity in Torment in Hell?' Returning to discuss this important question are local ministers Reverend Wesley Richardson, of the Evangelical Church; and Reverend Thomas Claudville, representing the Universalist Church. As was true yesterday, each speaker will have two separate speeches in which to present his case, or refute the case presented by the other speaker. And again, by mutual consent of the speakers, Reverend Claudville will speak first; and thus, Reverend Richardson will have the final word. I invite your attention to Reverend Claudville." He then left the podium, to return to his seat in the front row.

Thomas stepped back up to the podium, placed his Bible down on it, and then said, "Thank you, Mr. Moderator; ladies and gentlemen, I am glad to have this second opportunity to present the biblical evidence, as well as the evidence from reason, supporting the doctrine of Universal Reconciliation, or Universalism.

"Reverend Richardson asked us last evening whether there is any 'injustice' done to Pagans who have never heard of Jesus Christ, by punishing them for their own sins. But the question is not whether Pagans are justly *punished*; the question is whether they are consigned to endless torment—when God has, according to the Evangelical doctrine, given them no possible means by which they can be saved! Universalists do not deny that Pagans are punished for their own sins, and that the punishment will be balanced against the degree of light that they have; but we do deny that—not having had light enough to *save* them, under the Evangelical's conditions of salvation—they are justly sent to endless damnation! Some may contend that the terms of salvation are offered to all; but in fact, they are clearly *not* offered to all. Millions of men live and die, to whom the Gospel is never offered. Yet the Bible says in Titus 2:11 that 'the grace of God that bringeth salvation hath appeared to all men,' and it is the proclamation of this salvation that shall come to all which is the *Gospel*, the 'good news.' Those who hear, and receive that Gospel, will certainly experience a special, *present* salvation in this life; but that does not imply that all *others* are therefore doomed to perdition.

"My opponent maintains that in the future world, we can never change our character, or condition; we can do it here, he agrees, but he believes *never* in the future world. But when he takes that position, he thereby gives up his doctrine of 'moral freedom.' In his interpretation, moral freedom exists down here, but only for a little while; it is a sort of snare, or trap—cunningly placed by God, in order to secure the damnation of some of His creatures. God gives them moral freedom only long enough to expose them to temptation, and thus to sin. But I would ask you to consider this: if we are moral beings here, having the freedom to return to God, why should it not be the same after our deaths? Would our loving Father somehow *remove* our freedom, in the next world? In my opponent's interpretation, God will not even allow the lost the favor of being *annihilated*—but He will instead compel them to live forever, that He may always have the opportunity of tormenting them!" He paused after this passionate statement, to allow the audience to consider it fully.

He went on, "We have a perfect right to reason and derive principles from the parental character of the Deity, as revealed to us in the Scriptures. A wise and good earthly father will at any time allow his disobedient children to repent, reform, and return to obedience and happiness; he will adopt no measure which he foresees will result in fixing his children in disobedience. Much less would he, after a season, place them where they should have no opportunity to reform. We are, I would suggest, compelled to reason in the same manner about our Heavenly Father. Why should He set a fixed and very limited time, and insist that if His blind and erring children do not repent during that brief time, He will somehow deny them forever the privilege of repenting? And that He would then place them in a location where they would become eternally fixed in wickedness, and blaspheme His name forever? No! Whenever the sinner would repent—in any life, in any world—God allows it. And why should He not? Who would be injured by it? Is reconciliation with God not the ultimate goal of all?

"It is claimed by Evangelicals and some others that God forces men into this world in a condition where they are 'sinful' and 'greatly depraved,' due to the sin of Adam; and then God forces most of them to remain in Hell in torment, forever and ever—that is called 'sound, gospel preaching,' by many. But if we Universalists suggest that the grace of God will ultimately regenerate all souls, a howl loud and long goes up from ten thousand pulpits, and we are charged with teaching that God will 'force' men into Heaven! We are even accused of being Predestinarians, such as the Calvinists! But it would surely be more godlike to force men into *heaven*, than into *hell*—even as it is better to force men into the right direction, than the wrong direction. My opponent admits that God's mercy extends to all sinners now, and that he wills and *desires* the salvation of all; thus, life and salvation are free to all sinners now. We Universalists simply take the logical next step, and assert that life and salvation will be free to all eternally, for exactly the same reasons that they are free to all now. Salvation is now free to the 'lost,' the 'dead,' and to 'the chief of sinners'; and it will remain free, as long as there are souls who are in those conditions."

He looked out over the audience, and then continued, "My opponent also notes that some refuse to be saved now, and he asks, 'Why may not some remain unsaved for all eternity?' But the reason that all—even the vilest of the vile—*can* be saved now is because there is a God who is good; and since there always will be a God of such goodness, all can forever be saved. That is our position; and that is exactly what my opponent denies. Let him try to *prove* from the Bible that the God of love wills the conversion of sinners now, but as soon as the other world opens to those who pass the grave unconverted, their damnation is permanently sealed by the divine will. Even if a man leaves this world sinful—as all do, more or less—why cannot he later be enlightened by divine wisdom, and sanctified by divine grace? He will be the same man he was before his body was dropped in the grave; he will still be made in the image of God, and will still be a child of God. As he will have intellect, what will prevent him from believing in God, and believing in Jesus? And as he will possess moral qualities, what will prevent his loving and obeying the truth?"

He thought for a moment, and then suggested, "In fact, I cannot but see that regeneration would be accomplished infinitely *easier* on the golden shore than in this world, if the opportunity was given. Here, we are chained to bodily appetites and passions—but there, we will be freed from them; here, there are not only temptations within, but without—there, we shall be removed from them; here, we stand near the grave—there, nearer God's throne. With all those advantages, how would it happen that a man will not become *better* able to be saved in the eternal world?" He paused, to allow the audience to ponder these ideas.

He continued, "I would ask my opponent, what about infants? As well as the mentally retarded? They are not fit to enjoy a state of perfect purity, and holiness, and happiness in heaven as they are, if they are subject to the sin of Adam—as we all are, according to Romans 5:12-14; therefore, they must be changed *after death!* Evangelicals believe in infant *depravity,* yet they do not believe in infant *baptism* as the Romanists do, so there is no other option. And what of the great masses of children that die before they are old enough to be deemed 'accountable' for their actions?" He allowed this question to hang in the air, for a long moment.

Then he shrugged his shoulders, and added, "But perhaps I judge my opponent's doctrine wrongly, and he *does* allow for the salvation of infants. Yet how is the salvation of those dying in infancy to be achieved, under his doctrine? He believes that in the future world, there can be no change of one's character or condition. But children are born in sin, and depraved; if he believes that all are to be saved who happen to die in infancy, how is this to be brought about, if there is no change allowed after this world? We know that children are not 'Christians' in this world: they have neither knowledge, faith, virtue, nor goodness. My opponent says that faith is essential to salvation; but if all infants are to be saved, then apparently he does *not* believe that faith is *always* essential to salvation."

Looking very directly into the eyes of members of the audience, he added in a grave tone, "Another question: if all infants are saved; and if, after growing to adulthood, all have the serious risk of eternal damnation—would it not be much better for all to die in infancy, under this doctrine? Under my opponent's doctrine, should parents pray that their children may be removed from this world by death, *before* they cross the dangerous threshold line into 'moral responsibility'?" (This remark produced a brief "buzz" of whispered comments, from the audience.)

He went on, "My opponent surely holds that all men are sinners, till the very day they die. Thus, even the most pious saints require a change *after death*, to properly fit them for heaven. Some require a greater change, and some a lesser; yet all, without exception, require *some* change after death, to make them fit for the perfect purity of the immortal world. Furthermore, let us consider the condition of the entire Christian world: divided into sects, full of differences with one another; yet, in many respects walking uprightly before God—people who rightly expect to go to heaven when they die. But even the best Christians now on earth must be changed after death, to ensure perfect unity of feeling among them. Yet if there is no growth allowed after death, even the best of us will never be perfectly saved, or reconciled to God.

"Does Paul say that Jesus Christ came to save the righteous? No, he says that Jesus came 'to save sinners; of whom I am the chief.' [1 Tim 1:15] David, Peter and Saul of Tarsus were great sinners; and yet God saved them. Why not, then, save others? And why not save *all* others? David was called a murderer; Peter denied his master; and Saul persecuted the Christian church—yet all these were saved. In like manner, I say that all sinners may be saved, by being made righteous. They are not saved *in* their sins, and they are not taken *in* their corruption up to heaven; but they are first purified, and reconciled to God. Can there be any objection to this sentiment, in view of all the light thrown upon it by the Scriptures? My difference with my opponent is that he refuses to allow any change of heart after a person's death. Notice, however, that I do not speculate about precisely *how*, or *when*, this ultimate reconciliation is to be effected; only that all who leave this world sinful will finally be reconciled to God, and saved. But I would suggest that perhaps in the resurrection of the dead, all men are so changed, as to be introduced into a state of holiness, happiness, and immortality. Further growth and change may also be effected in the future world, as well."

He explained, "If all are ultimately to be holy and happy, will this be by 'compulsion'? No: all are not going to be 'compelled.' We Universalists believe that when all beings realize God's love, and appreciate his goodness, they will believe without compulsion. That God could have prevented the existence of sin by withholding man's moral agency, there can be no doubt. But the fact that he gave his creatures such free agency, should convince us that he clearly foresaw he could save them from the temporary sin into which they would fall, by exercise of their will. It should satisfy us also that he well knew he could, through this very agency, finally bring them all into that state of free and voluntary obedience to his government, which is alone pleasant or acceptable unto him. This redemption from sin the Creator can accomplish, without resort to physical compulsion, or force of any description.

"Universalists do not reject the Atonement; we believe in the Atonement precisely as it is taught in the Bible; but we firmly reject the old Heathen dogma of a sacrifice offered to placate the wrath of a god. According to my opponent's doctrine, God punishes an innocent being—Jesus Christ—in place of the offender, and then forgives the latter, and allows him to go. Under this doctrine, God does not forgive until he punishes somebody— either the guilty party, or a substitute—and then his justice is satisfied. The difference between my opponent's doctrine and mine, is that while his represents God as not willing to forgive until the *innocent* has been punished, and the *guilty* go free, my doctrine insists that God does not forgive until the guilty themselves are punished! I ask, which of the two is the most consistent, and which exerts the best moral influence? We Universalists believe in an Atonement made for all men. We believe the object of Christ's mission was to bring the creature into unity with the Creator—and to reconcile man to God."

He paused for a moment, and then admitted, "My opponent is aware that there is a difference of opinion among Universalists, as to whether there will be punishment for our sins beyond this life. My own position, as well as most modern Universalists, is that there *is* punishment beyond this life; Hosea Ballou and some others thought differently. But in fairness to Ballou's view, we should note there are numerous ways in which God chastises the guilty in this life, such as through the power of conscience. Those who have been addicted to immoral practices, when they speak the honest convictions of their hearts, will often acknowledge that they found no true happiness in sin; but that there was always a worm of guilt constantly gnawing within them, that destroyed all real peace of mind.

"There are a great many Bible passages that speak of punishment. I do not deny punishment; punishment is consonant with the government of God, and righteous punishment will be executed, wherever it is required. I believe as firmly as does my opponent in all the punishment that God has threatened in his holy Word—except that I maintain it is not *endless*; for if it were, it would be pointless. Punishment is not an end in itself; it is only a means which God employs, to achieve an end. The question is not, 'Will God punish mankind for the transgression of his laws?' The question is, 'What *amount* of punishment will God's love sanction?' Will it render the sinner a hopeless, miserable, ruined outcast forever and ever? Will it place him beyond the reach of love, where it can never reclaim him? Can God, as a being of love, seal the fate of millions of his own offspring in endless woe and wretchedness? Certainly, every sinner deserves to be punished, and some time must elapse before the sinner receives all the punishment he deserves; this time may be long or short, according to the degree of the sinner's crimes. But for my part, I would greatly prefer taking the amount of punishment that *God* would deem it right to inflict on me, than the amount which my *enemies* would award me!" A number of persons in the audience laughed at this statement.

He went on, "The evils of this world have an end, and are quite reconcilable with the goodness of God; but the evils of an endless hell have no end, and cannot be reconciled with goodness. I asked last evening, 'Would God create men, knowing they would be eternally lost?' My opponent answered by asking, 'Why did God create men knowing they would suffer at all?' He can apparently see no difference between suffering for a few days, and suffering for all eternity! We are, to be sure, able to see how good may result from some *temporary* evils; in fact, we have often witnessed good resulting from them. But why are these evils sometimes seen to result in good? For the very reason that they are temporary, and limited. But endless punishment is a final evil: a limitless, boundless evil, beyond which no good can result, for it will never end."

The Moderator began signaling him that his time was running out, so he said quickly, "But, my opponent may again argue that punishment is set forth to warn others away from rebellion and apostasy; and such is often the case in this world. But if the *saints in glory* cannot be restrained from rebellion and apostasy without the threat of endless damnation before their eyes, it is certain they cannot be very 'holy'—nor much in love with God and heaven. And I, for one, could never covet either their society, or their condition. My opponent ignores the remarkable difference between limited punishment—which eventuates in good—and endless torture, which has no ending. A God of love cannot inflict an endless curse upon any of his offspring; but he can punish them, and do it in love, for this punishment will result in good. But I firmly deny that a God of love can inflict endless punishment upon any of his creatures! These two sentiments are in direct opposition to each other—and either the one, or the other, must be false."

He looked out at the audience again, and said fervently, "I must conclude my remarks at this time. But I would remind my hearers that the issue now before us is in regard to the final holiness and happiness of all mankind. It is not about whether all men go directly to heaven; or whether a thousand years, or millions of ages shall elapse, before they are permitted to enter that glory above—their final holiness and happiness is the only question involved!" He picked up his Bible, and concluded, "Again, I thank you for your attention," and he returned to his seat at his table.

Reverend Richardson again took the podium quickly, and immediately began speaking: "My opponent suggests that in the resurrection of the dead a change is to be effected, which will introduce all men into a state of holiness and salvation. But this proposition leaves us perfectly in the dark concerning the state of the soul between death and the resurrection; what becomes of their souls during that long period?" He shook his head vehemently, and added, "He quoted from First Corinthians 15; but I want him to answer this one plain question: does not all that is said there, relate to change of the *body?* Is there a word said in this whole chapter about any change taking place in the *soul,* at the resurrection? By his almighty energy God will raise the bodies of men from the dead and change them, so that they will become spiritual and immortal. But is it true that the mind and the spirit are to be made holy by physical power exerted on the *body?* Sin belongs not to matter, but to mind; and I know not how a change in the former, can impart holiness to the latter. The body will certainly be changed; but the soul, the moral being, will remain in the same state precisely that it was at the moment of its separation from the body.

"In John 5:25 the Saviour speaks first of the spiritual resurrection: 'the hour is coming, and now is, when the dead shall hear the voice of the Son of God, and they that hear, shall live.' Then he proceeds to speak of the literal or physical resurrection: 'the hour is coming, in the which all that are in the graves shall hear his voice, and shall come forth; they that have done good, unto the resurrection of life, and they that have done evil, to the resurrection of damnation.' [v. 28-29] According to the Universalists, all will be raised to life and glory; but here in the gospel we are taught that some shall be raised to life, and others to damnation. Here we have an irrefutable argument proving future punishment—not only after death, but also after the general resurrection of the dead.

"My opponent asks, 'If faith is necessary to salvation, how can infants be saved?' I answer: God works through means, when means can be used; but when they cannot, he is free to work without them. In the nature of the case, infants cannot understand and believe the Gospel, and thus cannot be saved by faith; therefore, if God in his wisdom calls them into eternity in infancy, he can save them without means. But what has this to do with the argument concerning the salvation of *adults?* Will my opponent argue that because infants cannot be saved by faith, therefore, adults are not required to believe in order to achieve salvation? Is there any biblical evidence that adults are saved in just the same way as infants are? May not God save infants by means through which adults cannot be saved?"

He said in a fiery voice, "We Evangelicals hold, it is true, that even the thief on the cross may be pardoned, if properly penitent; but we assure all men that the longer they persevere in sin, the less hope there is that they will break their evil habits, and turn to God. But Universalism says to the most ungodly—to the drunkard, the debauchee, the liar, the oppressor, the murderer—'Fear not, it shall be well with you. In the resurrection you shall stand amongst prophets, apostles, martyrs, and saints, and wear a crown as bright as theirs!' Paul fought the good fight, finished his course, and kept the faith; but Universalism says all this shall be of no advantage to him in the next world; the greatest villain shall be in a condition fully as desirable as Paul's! Thus, instead of calling on men to love God and lay up their treasures in heaven, Universalism actually *discourages* the righteous—by informing them that all their labor, toil and suffering in the cause of truth and righteousness is in vain, so far as eternity is concerned. It encourages the wicked man to persevere in sin, by assuring him that wickedness will take him fully as far towards heaven and eternal happiness, as will obedience to God's law!

"My opponent argues that if Christ died for all, then all must be saved. But the Scriptures say that God gave his Son, not that all might be saved, but 'that whosoever *believeth* in him should not perish, but have everlasting life.' [Jn 3:16] Salvation is, indeed, *offered* to all; but it is *bestowed* only on those who receive Christ by faith. My opponent asserts that the resurrection will save all men, whether they believe or not! Romans 5:1 flatly contradicts this: 'Being justified by faith, we have peace with God through our Lord Jesus Christ, by whom we have access by faith into this grace wherein we stand and rejoice in the hope of the glory of God.' By *faith*, the Apostle says, men are justified, and rejoice in the hope of the glory of God. But my opponent says that all are justified, made righteous, and may hope for the glory of God—whether they have faith or not! Everywhere the Scriptures make faith essential to salvation; and this fact alone proves Universalism untrue." (This remark generated applause from some members of the audience.)

He went on, "Not only does the Bible give no hint that a man can change his character and condition in hell, but it teaches the very opposite. Hear the words of the Saviour: 'ye ... shall seek me, and shall die in your sins: whither I go, ye cannot come.' [Jn 8:21] Does this sound like a man changing his character, condition, and life in Hell during any period of eternity, and ascending into heaven? If, with the influence of the Holy Spirit, the sinner cannot be prevailed upon to repent and believe in Christ in this world, what hope is there that the sinner would be inclined to repent, when shut up in the prison of Hell—where none of these means of grace exist? Where in the Bible is even a single passage which teaches that any will ever come to Christ after death? Can he find even one? And yet, if we are to believe him, it is the great design of the Scriptures to teach Universalism. Moreover, he has admitted that many *do* die in their sins. Is it not most marvelous, then, that neither Christ nor any one of the inspired writers ever said that any will come to Christ after death? How shall we account for this, if Universalism is true?

"Let us consider John 6:39: 'of all which he hath given me I should lose nothing, but should raise it up again at the last day.' We must ask, 'Whom has the Father given Christ?' and 'What is meant by the word "given"'? Did Christ mean that *all mankind* was 'given to him'? And that they were all to be raised up and glorified in the last day? If such is its meaning, John 17:12 must be sadly at fault: 'none of them is lost, but the son of perdition.' Christ would then be convicted of the folly of selecting a person as a disciple whom God knew was to be *lost!* Under my opponent's doctrine, even Judas is saved! He who betrayed our Saviour is exalted to stand abreast with all the apostles who devoted their lives, and died as witnesses to the faith that Jesus had sent them to declare! By contrast, I hold that the persons who were 'given to him' in this passage are exclusively *Christians*.

"Nowhere did Jesus ever utter a prayer for the salvation of the whole world. He said of Judas in Mark 14:21 that it would be better for him if he had never been born. Were Judas to suffer during as many millions of years as my opponent can conceive, but eventually be restored to holiness and happiness and have an eternity of blessedness before him, it could not be said that it would have been better for him had he never been born. Why, then, did Christ say this of Judas? Because he was *lost;* a son of perdition, a child of the devil, and doomed to endure eternal punishment."

He turned and looked at Thomas contemptuously, then turned back to the audience, and said, "Among the various factions of Universalism, my opponent is apparently a 'Restorationist'—that is, one who contends that after death, wicked men are punished for a time, in some place. This I would quite naturally call 'Purgatory'—a true and proper Purgatory, even as the Romanists hold. 'Purgatory' is an appropriate name for it, because my opponent alleges that the punishment in his Purgatory ultimately ends in holiness, and the perfect love of God." He looked over at Thomas again, then said, "Now, sir, I would ask you: if the wrath of God in your Purgatory ultimately creates such love in the human heart, why has not God tried this method in the present world? Please explain to us, how those who are hardened by the *love* of God here, are to be softened by the *wrath* of God hereafter!"

He continued, "The Universalist continually asks us, 'What good can punishment after death can do?' I answer that it will maintain the government of God throughout the universe; and especially, it will help to restrain evil spirits in this world. The utility of punishment is not to be estimated by the reformation of the subject of it—for this but seldom happens—the punishment of sinners is to 'set forth for an example' [Jude 7], and to secure others from rebellion or apostasy. But can he tell us what possible good such a *limited* punishment as he speaks of will do? Will it restrain sinners to tell them that their judgment may be entirely in the past—as the renowned Universalist Hosea Ballou claimed?"

He looked over at Thomas again, and said in a mocking tone, "My opponent insists that 'no good can result' from endless punishment. Now, sir, if I thought that you knew the whole universe; had lived through eternity; and knew what was good for every creature in every part of it, then indeed your assertion would merit our serious consideration. But in the absence of this knowledge and experience, your claim is of no more authority than that of the *child,* who says that volcanoes in the ocean; icy mountains in the polar regions; lions, tigers, and hyenas among the beasts; as well as vegetable and mineral poisons among plants and metals, are all useless things. Everything is useless to him that does not know the utility of it: And seeing that there are a multitude of things called 'evils' against which we are daily fighting—the utility of which we know not—how is it proper to claim that future and eternal evils are useless, simply because we cannot presently explain them, to my opponent's satisfaction?

"I ask my opponent, if God does not, in his great and infinite love, prevent suffering here, how do you know he will do so hereafter? You admit that God changes not. Thus, since he punishes men in this life, how do you know he will not punish them in the life to come, for violations of his divine law? You say that in the next world, God's love will be so overwhelming, that the sinner will be constrained to accept salvation. How do you know that? If God designs to overwhelm men in that manner, why does he not overwhelm them here in the same manner, and bring them while here to accept the offer of salvation? Surely he can do it as well here, as in the next world.

"I suggest in reference to my opponent's 'Purgatory,' his reformatory school, that anything which can have the effect to hasten the departure of the sinners of this world into that place of 'reform' would seemingly be a helpful thing in the sight of Almighty God, and of all sensible people. My opponent should, therefore, carry out his teachings to their logical sequence—and take his revolver in hand, and *kill* all those who are doing the work of evil, to speed them off to this 'school of reformation' that awaits them in the world to come."

The Moderator signaled to Reverend Richardson, so he began speaking even more vigorously, "All my opponent's arguments—based on the power, goodness, justice, and mercy of God as implying an ultimate termination of sin and suffering—would equally have forbid the possibility of sin and suffering at all; for if the Divine perfections must bring it to an end, they ought never to have allowed it to begin, in the first place. His hypothetical speculations are perfectly refuted by the fact that moral evil and physical pain are as old as this creation; and if God is immutable in all his perfections, it is clearly compatible with the Divine perfections to permit the continuance of evil and pain for a period as long as eternity itself. It is therefore preposterous to argue from any such speculative views of the Divine perfections, against what the Scriptures clearly affirm about what God may or may not do, in reference to sin and sinners.

"My opponent poses questions that are commonly asked, such as: 'Why did God create men, knowing that they would be eternally lost?' and 'Why did God allow evil to come into the universe?' These are questions that perhaps no one can answer—not even to his own satisfaction. But this fact is not at all favorable to Universalism; Universalists can no more satisfactorily solve these great questions than can other people. God created; this we know. Evil and misery are in the world; we know this also. But the reasons for these troublesome facts, lie too deep for the reasonings of frail mortals, such as we are."

He concluded, "Finally, if Universalism is true, and is in fact the great Gospel truth the Bible was designed to teach, should it not to be taught there with very great clarity? But even if, as my opponent suggests, Universalism *is* clearly taught in the Scriptures, how can he account for the indisputable fact that during the previous eighteen hundred years, extremely few readers of the Bible ever saw this doctrine in it? How can we account for the amazing *stupidity* of all Christendom for so long a period, if Universalism is true?"

The Moderator signaled to him again, so he picked up his Bible, and said curtly to the audience, "I thank you again." He headed back to the seat at his table.

Thomas calmly took his place at the podium once more, then explained, "I will deal with my opponent's final argument first: namely, why the doctrine of Universalism was not prevalent in the early Church. We Universalists firmly believe that the Scriptures teach the future life to be one of happiness, holiness and bliss for all men; but we also acknowledge that, even in apostolic times, errors began to creep into the church. For example, we see in the 15th chapter of First Corinthians—which my opponent just finished discussing at some length—that some of those who were 'Christ's at his coming' denied the resurrection of the dead. Paul said in Second Thessalonians 2:7 that the 'mystery of iniquity doth already work,' even in his day. The early Pagan converts to Christianity also brought into the church many of their old Pagan notions, such as that of 'atoning sacrifices.' Still, the sublime idea of the ultimate holiness and salvation of all mankind was not wholly lost for several centuries after the death of the apostles: Clement of Alexandria, Origen, Gregory of Nyssa, and others, had not lost that great sentiment of the Gospel. It was held in the Christian church until the 6th century, when it was lost sight of, until the Reformation.

"My opponent criticizes me for making some judgments based on the Divine attributes as revealed to us in Scripture; yet he is not afraid to 'judge' that some men will go to hell forever, while he prohibits Universalists from 'judging' that all will go to heaven. I certainly do not think that we can see all things, but we can see some things—and we can surely see that *infinite goodness* requires something other than the *infinite torments* of hell; and we can also see that infinite goodness can ultimately be satisfied only with good results. If we cannot 'judge' here, I do not know where we can judge at all.

"In regard to salvation from sin, the major difference between the two of us is that, while he believes that a part of mankind will be saved from sin in the future world, I believe that all will be. All are not brought to obey God in this life: but does it follow that they *never* will be brought to obey and love him? Are we to infer that man can go beyond the reach of God's love? What could there be in the nature of the soul that will prevent

God's love from reaching it in and beyond the resurrection? I would ask my opponent, why do Evangelicals find it so difficult to convert sinners now? Is it not the unfavorable circumstances by which they are surrounded? Here, they are constantly exposed to a thousand temptations and trials, which are the offspring of our earthly condition. Why, then, may not the soul be even more readily changed after death, when it shall be freed from all these mortal encumbrances? Jesus can certainly have no less access to the heart of the sinner in eternity, than he has here."

He thought for a moment, then proceeded, "I admit that, to a certain degree, the magnitude of a crime is increased by the dignity of the being sinned against; and I also allow that sin against a God of infinite goodness is more heinous than sin against a fellow human creature. But this falls far short of establishing the conclusion that sin against God is an 'infinite evil'! The magnitude of acts committed must also be measured by the power and capabilities of their *authors*. An effect cannot exceed its cause; and as Man is finite, so all his acts must necessarily be finite. Following my opponent's logic, if all our sinful deeds are 'infinite' in scope because they are committed against an infinite God, so our good deeds must also be 'infinite'—because they are performed *in favor of* an infinite God.

"I also acknowledge the moral free agency of man; but I am not prepared to accept my opponent's conclusion that our final destiny is made entirely contingent upon that moral agency. It is mere assumption to contend that the final destiny of man is based solely upon the deeds of this life. To assert that finite beings can, by the deeds of a few years of transitory existence, eternally damn their immortal souls, is at variance with the plainest teachings of reason and revelation. In the administration of his government, God has enacted certain laws for the benefit of his children: Obedience to those laws is productive of happiness, while disobedience results in misery and wretchedness; but in neither case, is the reward endless happiness, or eternal misery! Man's acts involve finite consequences alone; further than this, our moral agency cannot go; the issues of eternal life and eternal death have not been committed into our hands.

"My opponent states that the Bible does not say that any may come to Christ after death. True, it does not state this in so many words; but the Bible does say that *all* will certainly be drawn to Christ. Yesterday, I pointed out that Christ said in John 12:32, 'If I be lifted up from the earth, I will draw all men unto me'; and certainly, Christ *was* lifted up from the earth. My opponent also asks where Scripture says that all men will be reconciled to God or saved, after death. Again, it is not said in that precise form of expression. Yet we do expect to die, and we also know that God's promises will positively be accomplished; thus, we expect that if they are not fulfilled in this life—as they certainly are not—then they absolutely will be after death; for God's word cannot fail, nor his will ever be frustrated."

Turning the pages in his Bible, he said, "But let us not leave the matter there; let us go further into the Scriptures. Note the expression in Matthew 12:31-32, 'All manner of sin and blasphemy shall be forgiven unto men: but the blasphemy against the Holy Ghost shall not be forgiven unto men. And whosoever speaketh a word against the Son of man, it shall be forgiven him: but whosoever speaketh against the Holy Ghost, it shall not be forgiven him, neither in this world, neither in the world to come.' The Greek word *aion*—which is translated here as 'world'—simply means 'age'; it has no reference to the eternal world!

"Inasmuch as Jesus said, '*All* manner of sin and blasphemy shall be forgiven,' it follows that the blasphemy against the Holy Ghost shall also be forgiven, only not in that age—the Jewish age—nor in that age which was to come: the Christian age. But the great truth was also stated by Christ that 'all manner of sin and blasphemy shall be forgiven unto men.' To this end, the apostle Paul said in Ephesians 2:7, that God 'hath raised us up together, and made us sit together in heavenly places in Christ Jesus: That in the ages—(the Greek word is *aion*)—to come he might shew the exceeding riches of his grace in his kindness toward us through Christ Jesus.' Therefore, might not we be forgiven in the *ages* to come?

"Let us consider once again my opponent's assertion that there is no possibility of repentance, and no possibility of salvation beyond the present life; that the whole work of the Redeemer is to be accomplished here, and nowhere else. My opponent should remember that Christ, after being crucified, descended into hell, according to Acts 2:27 & 31; and according to First Peter 3:18-20, he 'went and preached unto the spirits in prison; Which sometime were disobedient.' The Greek word *kerusso* in this passage is the same word that is used for 'preached' throughout the New Testament. If Christ could do this for those who 'were disobedient … in the days of Noah,' could he not do the same for others, whose wickedness was not nearly so great as to merit the destruction of all life on the face of the earth?" He smiled slightly, noting with satisfaction the thoughtful looks this argument produced on the faces of many listeners.

He said confidently, "I shall now take up the case of Judas, which seems to trouble my opponent so greatly. The saying, 'it had been good for that man if he had not been born' in Matthew 26:24 proves nothing in regard to the doctrine of *eternal torment*. You will note that in John 17:12, which my opponent quoted, the use of the present tense indicates that Judas was then lost as an apostle; but this language makes no reference whatever to his *future* condition, much less to his eternal fate. I would also point out that when Judas saw that the Saviour was condemned, he repented—according to Matthew 27:3—and carried back the thirty pieces of silver, and threw them down in the Temple, declaring that he had sinned, in that he had betrayed innocent blood!

"In that judgment hall, Judas alone, of all the disciples, declared the innocence of the Son of God! Where were James, and John, and Peter? Turn to Matthew 26:6: 'all the disciples forsook him and fled'! Even Peter thrice denied Jesus, and cursed and swore that he knew him not! I would suggest that the repentance of Judas was both thorough, and sincere; and that you will not find an instance of more sincere repentance in the Scriptures. Where else will you find a person having $500, who will come forward as boldly and manfully as Judas did, repent of the course he had pursued, and throw away his ill-gotten money? This, I think, is godly sorrow." (His defense of Judas generated an excited buzz of whispered comments from the audience.)

He continued, "In First Timothy 4:10 we read, 'we trust in the living God, who is the Saviour of all men'; here is the great fact proclaimed, that God 'is the Saviour of *all men*.' Paul means not in this life—for all are not saved here—rather, Paul speaks of the final, universal salvation. But there is another clause to this passage: 'we trust in the living God who is the Saviour of all men; *especially of those that believe*.' Now, it is true that here, only a part of all men believe; and consequently, only a part have the special, present salvation that is enjoyed by Christians in this life. But beyond this, is the future salvation of all men in the life to come—a deliverance from present sin, evil, and death.

"The apostle Paul quoted Hosea 13:14 in First Corinthians 15:55: 'O death, where is thy sting? O grave, where is thy victory?' The Greek word here translated as 'grave' is *Hades*; Hades is, of course, the place in which the rich man of Luke 16 is now supposedly suffering—with all therein later being raised to the incorruptible, immortal state. But death itself is to be no more: 'The last enemy that shall be destroyed is death.' [15:26] And so it is said that 'Death is swallowed up in victory.' [15:54] Note that death is to be destroyed at the resurrection! There can be no death, no sin, and no Hell in the immortal world, because death is the last enemy, and it shall be destroyed. Paul is here quoting Isaiah 25:8, where the Prophet says, 'He will swallow up death in victory; and the Lord God will wipe tears from off all faces; and the rebuke of his people shall he take away from off all the earth: for the Lord hath spoken it.' I ask you, in view of all this testimony, is it not clearly established that there is to be an ultimate deliverance of man from all his enemies, introducing all men into a state of liberty and blessedness?"

Thomas then turned to look directly at Reverend Richardson, before saying to the audience, "My opponent has several times appeared to address his questions directly to me—rather than to our audience, as is customary in a discussion such as this. Therefore, I should like to ask him directly, whether he has ever prayed that an unrepentant sinner might go down to Hell?" He paused, to let this challenging question register among the listeners, and then added sharply, "My opponent would probably deny that he has ever prayed such a prayer; but I would ask him, why not? If there is a place of endless torment established by God, and if it is 'just' and 'right' for the wicked to go there—which is what my opponent professes to believe—why should he *not* pray for such an awful event to take place? The answer is, because there is not a professing Christian in the world, having the slightest regard for his reputation, who would *dare* admit in public to making such a prayer! Indeed, there is no true Christian who would have the slightest inclination to put up such a prayer to our God, who is sitting on the Throne of Infinite Love."

Referring to a page of notes he had placed in his Bible, he said, "And yet Jonathan Edwards said in his sermon, *The End of the Wicked Contemplated by the Righteous*, that the damnation of the wicked would be 'an occasion for rejoicing' by the righteous: 'They will rejoice in seeing the justice of God glorified in the sufferings of the damned... It will occasion rejoicing in them, as they will have the greater sense of their own happiness, by seeing the contrary misery... When they shall see how miserable others of their fellow-creatures are, who were naturally in the same circumstances with themselves; when they shall see the smoke of their torment, and the raging of the flames of their burning, and hear their dolorous shrieks and cries, and consider that they in the meantime are in the most blissful state, and shall surely be in it to all eternity; how will they rejoice!'" There were some muttered expressions of surprise and shock from the audience, and Thomas added gravely, "This is the doctrine we are asked to hold. in opposition to the glorious and sublime sentiment of Universal Reconciliation and happiness!

"Yet Parson Edwards was not the only one to make such outrageous and unchristian statements. The Scottish theologian Thomas Boston wrote in his book, *Human Nature in Its Fourfold State,* that 'the godly husband will say Amen to the damnation of her who lay in his bosom! and the godly wife shall applaud the justice of the judge in the condemnation of her ungodly husband! The godly parents shall say *hallelujah!* at the passing of the sentence against their ungodly child! and the godly child shall, from his heart, approve the damnation of his wicked parents, the father who begot him, and the mother who bore him!'" He shook his head firmly, and said passionately, "Can this truly be the attitude of a genuine Christian? When a son or a daughter goes to heaven, is the familial tie severed for eternity, that connected the dear one with the parents? It seems to me, that much of the happiness of heaven will result from *whole families* being there—and with not a member lost. Yes, the relation of family, kindred, will survive death; and the blessed promise of Acts 3:25 is that all *kindreds* of the earth shall be blessed in Christ.

"My opponent's doctrine asserts that there are thousands of parents who have lost children that had reached the 'years of discretion,' or 'age of accountability,' who will never meet them again. He strives to make children believe that they have beloved parents residing in an endless Hell; that the father and mother who watched over them in their infant years, and who trained them with care and affection, are now shrieking in endless despair and anguish; that they are calling on God for even the slightest display of mercy, and the smallest mitigation of their torture;

but alas!—they are calling in vain. My opponent seeks to prove that vast numbers of parents who may arrive in Heaven will be childless there, and that thousands of children there will be orphans—that when the redeemed in Heaven shall strike their golden harps in praise of the Majesty of Heaven, the sweet melody of their songs will be combined with sorrow, at the absence of the dearest objects of their affection, who are suffering an infinite torment!

"Let us not forget the words of our heavenly Parent in Isaiah 49:15, 'Can a woman forget her sucking child, that she should not have compassion on the son of her womb? yea, they may forget, yet will I not forget thee.' It is but barely possible for a mother to forget her own child; but it is *impossible* for God to forget his! The good mother punishes her erring child because she loves him, and for his own good. So too, our heavenly Parent punishes his erring children because he loves them, and for their ultimate good. But God forbid that we should entertain the dreadful thought that the Father of our spirits will fill Hell with his own children, and that all heaven will say 'Amen!' to this dreadful deed!" This remark produced some scattered applause from his audience.

He went on, "My opponent suggested tonight that the notion of Hell may 'help restrain evil spirits in this world.' Some craven spirits, perhaps, may be prevented from doing evil by the fear of Hell. But I wish the religious world would become wiser, and understand that all *true* religion and religious piety is to spring from *love*, and from love alone. I say to all my hearers who so accept this doctrine of endless torture: you may fear God, and you may tremble in dread of his anger, and you may repent and pray—but you cannot truly *love* him! There is no 'loveliness' in a Being who can deal thusly with his creatures; it would be impossible to love him. I could not love such a Being, and I would not if I could. The character which this endless torment doctrine ascribes to the Almighty renders him unworthy the love of a single intelligent creature!" This bold remark produced both applause, and murmurs of strong disagreement, from his listeners.

Seeing the Moderator signal him, he said, "As I conclude my presentation, let me make a point somewhat opposite to that made by my opponent at the beginning of his own presentation. If we Universalists should happen to be wrong—even if innocently—he believes that his God would condemn us all to endless torment. I have, however, a better opinion of our heavenly Father than that. I am quite happy holding this opinion, because this world has more than trials and troubles enough, without my feeling that there is looking over me a malignant power, from whose awful grasp I cannot wrench myself—and who may, in a moment of his anger, crush me. I thank God that Universalist views differ so widely from what my opponent and his religious brethren hold. Their views I find revolting, and unworthy of the great Being who made this marvelous universe, and who placed us so wisely and beneficently in it."

He looked over the entire crowd, and then added in a softer tone, "Ladies and gentlemen, you may make Hell as mild as you please; but if it is *endless* in duration, its horrors are beyond imagination. A billion years would be not even one second of an endless Hell—and all this for the sins of this sole, brief life! My God, what a creed; I could not believe such a monstrosity as this fathomless, boundless eternity of wretchedness, serving no possible good end. I simply ask my hearers to try and realize the awful, revolting nature of the doctrine of endless misery; and to consider the dark, unholy imputations it casts on the character of the upholder of the Universe.

"Endless misery! Think of it for a moment: Days, months, years will pass away; ages on ages will roll past the sinners in hell, multiplied ten thousand *millions* of times into itself; yet even then, you would not even begin to form an idea of the doctrine of endless, unceasing, interminable misery. Did Jesus Christ believe and preach that millions, made in the image of God, would be damned by that God whose very name is Love, for all eternity? Did Jesus Christ believe and preach that millions of the precious souls for whom he was about to die would be cursed by his God, and cursed by himself, endlessly? I say to you, no! A thousand times, no!"

He ceased speaking, picked up his Bible, and returned to his table.

Reverend Richardson began speaking enthusiastically as soon as he reached the podium: "My opponent has asked us to believe that the Word of God supports the belief that God will make all persons both holy and happy throughout eternity. He claims this is the only reasonable deduction from the characteristics of God, as revealed in the Scriptures. But I would again ask my hearers, does the goodness of God make all men happy now? Does the goodness of God make them all religious now? Does it unite them all to Christ now? Thus, if the goodness of God does not *now* require Him to make all men holy or happy, where is the evidence that God will make them holy and happy through eternity? If God is unchangeable, and if all men are not holy and happy now, then it must be evident that God cannot in the nature of things make all men holy and happy—unless there is a change in the individuals themselves, to make them so. If the doctrine which my opponent affirms is true, all we ask him to do is to show us the *unequivocal texts* in which the Bible teaches this doctrine." He glared at Thomas, as if daring him to reply.

He continued, "Let us consider my opponent's assertion—which, of course, he has not proved—that Jesus went and preached to the spirits in prison after he was put to death, so that there is what we might call a 'post-mortem gospel' now being preached to the dead; does the truth of my opponent's proposition follow? By no means. Do we know that all, or even *any*, of the spirits in prison would accept the Gospel? Certainly not. Do you think that the wicked men of Noah's day would repent? Even if it was granted that the Gospel is preached to the dead—to those who heard it, as well as to those who never heard it, here on earth—it cannot be proved that they will all accept it. And even if it were granted that the gospel is preached to those who died without hearing it here, it does not follow that it will be preached again to those who heard it while in the flesh! There is, therefore, nothing in the few passages of Scripture my opponent has cited that proves that *all* who leave this world sinful will finally be reconciled to God, and saved.

"Certainly First Peter 3:18-20 proves no such thing, as it says nothing about God's mercy extending to spirits in prison in the *future* world. The passage, it is true, speaks of 'spirits in prison'; and therefore, I believe that there are 'spirits in prison,' awaiting the Judgment day—'reserved unto the day of Judgment to be punished,' as Peter taught in Second Peter 2:9. But Peter did not say that this preaching was done in *prison*; the preaching he speaks of was done 'in the days of Noah,' while the ark was being prepared! My opponent quoted John 12:32: 'And I, if I be lifted up from the earth, will draw all men unto me.' But how does Christ draw all men? By the gracious invitations of the Gospel. But what was, and is, more common, is that those invitations—given by Christ, by the apostles, as well as by the ministers of the present day—were, instead of being accepted, rejected and spurned, and the career of sin still persevered in.

"I believe that every man is a free moral agent, and that in consequence of man's deep depravity—his great aversion to God's character, His law, and His Gospel—some men will not accept God's offered salvation. The doctrine of election is this: God, in his infinite mercy, determined to incline and help a vast multitude of sinners to come to Christ and be saved. Such is the opposition of the human heart to God and His service, that, but for this purpose of God to incline them to come to Christ, the whole human race would reject the Gospel and perish. Is there anything wrong in a purpose to save a *multitude* of sinners? As to those sometimes called the 'non-elect,' the worst that can be said about God's dealings with them, is that He simply lets them alone—He leaves them to choose their own course, and punishes them for those sins in which they choose to persevere."

He flipped a page in his Bible, then went on, "Universalists claim that after death—or at least, after the Final Judgment—all men will be made holy and righteous. But the last sayings of the revealing angel in the Apocalypse flatly and directly contradict this: for after the Final Judgment, this angel will say, 'He that is unjust, let him be unjust still: and he which is filthy, let him be filthy still: and he that is righteous, let him be righteous still: and he that is holy, let him be holy still.' [Rev 22:11] Where now is this 'universal holiness' my opponent suggests? There are still some unjust, filthy, unrighteous, and unholy persons after the final adjudication, according to the Revelation of John; they are, then, *not* all holy.

"The scripture does not say that 'Christ must reign till all yield obedience; and then, he will deliver up the kingdom to God, who shall be all in all.' No, it says, 'He must reign, till he hath put all enemies under his feet.' [1 Cor 15:25] Then Christ will deliver up the kingdom to God, who will be all in all in the kingdom. Then, it will be too late for the enemies of the cross of Christ to be saved, even if they would. Then, the Spirit and the bride will cease to say, 'Come.' Then, the terrible sentence will be pronounced: 'He that is filthy, let him be filthy still.' Then, some who have despised the love and mercy of God—who would not love righteousness, virtue, salvation, life, and heaven for their own sakes—in their terrible fright 'will seek to enter in, and shall not be able' [Lk 13:24], because it takes more than fright to fit a man for Heaven. Then those who have spurned, and scoffed, and sneered, and jeered, and scowled at the Savior, may take up the doleful lamentation, 'The harvest is past, the summer is ended, and we are not saved' [Jer 8:20], and so sink forever down under their now irremediable depravity."

He looked over at Thomas, then commented sarcastically, "We Evangelicals are certainly not Calvinists—such as were Thomas Boston and Jonathan Edwards—so we have no need to defend their erroneous interpretations of Predestination and Election. But I feel impelled to ask my opponent, who charges those excellent men with 'gloating' over the damnation of the wicked? Edwards and Boston say not that the righteous will rejoice because the wicked *suffer*, but that they rejoice because the *justice of God* is vindicated; and because they will be grateful to God, who, in His infinite mercy, saved them from a similar doom!" There was some scattered applause from the audience, after this statement.

He looked over at Thomas again, saying, "How far you and the heavenly hosts differ on the subject of divine punishment for sins, and how differently you and they conceive of suitable judgment, may be clearly seen from the beginning of the 19th chapter of Revelation, where we read: 'I heard a great voice of much people in heaven, saying, Alleluia; Salvation, and glory, and honour, and power, unto the Lord our God: For true and righteous are his judgments: for he hath judged the great whore, which did corrupt the earth with her fornication, and hath avenged the blood of his servants at her hand. And again they said, Alleluia, and the smoke of her torment rose up for ever and ever.'"

He added in a fiery tone, "My opponent would teach that you can go on, if you choose, in your course of sin—which Christ sternly warned the people against, of course—and that you can continue in this course of sin until you die, after which there will be some mysterious process by which Christ will somehow bring about your 'final holiness and happiness,' in this 'final resurrection' of which my opponent has spoken. In his doctrine, the sins of the soul are dissolved into trifling foibles; and every sinner—however vile and base he may be in this life—can enter Heaven beside the best of earth's saints; just as truly and certainly as if his course had been one of uprightness and purity, such as the Scriptures command us to follow.

"Universalism tells the sinner that if he does not choose to turn to God now, he can do so when he finds a more 'convenient' time: if not today, he can tomorrow; or if not in this 'age,' then in the next age; or, if not in the next age, he can do so at his eternal leisure—in any of the coming ages of eternity!" He shook his head firmly, then added, "Under the influence of such teaching, the habit-bound sinner may feel he can afford to sit down, and sin away his whole lifetime! But the Scriptures tell us that he will do so at the cost of the loss of his immortal soul!"

He flipped to another passage in his Bible, then said, "I say to my opponent, you never seem to have read these words from Luke 16:10: 'he that is unjust in the least is unjust also in much.' You think that it is just, merciful, and benevolent to punish a defaulter for ten thousand years, but unjust and cruel to punish him forever! Your philosophy has now become clear: It is that punishment cures sin; that punishment is the means, and holiness the end. Christ has then died in vain; the Devil is getting better; the Jews are more holy now than they were 2000 years ago; and penitentiaries—if they have punishment severe enough, and long enough—cannot fail to sanctify all the murderers and miscreants within their walls! A few years in your post-mortem 'Purgatory' will supposedly save more souls than the actual sacrifice of Christ. If the Creator, then, would just occasionally rain fire and brimstone on all the cities—instead of giving them blessed rain from heaven, and fruitful seasons—He would have acted more wisely than by showing forth His goodness and love; for, according to your reasoning, it is the *wrath* of God, rather than His love, that leads men to reformation."

In a strong voice, he continued, "If Universalism is true, then indeed Paul labored in vain; and so does everyone labor in vain who works for the Lord, for their work amounts to nothing—men are to be saved anyway; it is impossible to perish! Why would Paul bear his forty stripes, save one? Or his shipwreck, imprisonment, and final martyrdom? Why would he have endured all this, if he believed that, in the end, the whole race of men was to be swept into Heaven, and made finally and eternally holy and happy?

"My opponent boldly demands that the government of God must fit into his own canons of 'reasonableness.' Yet, must *we* have a reason for everything God does in His universe? Let us try to think for a moment of the magnitude of this boundless universe; could my opponent govern it? If not, then how shall he dictate to Almighty God a moral philosophy for the government of the universe, and demand of Him a 'reason' for everything He does? For my part, I can think of nothing more supremely ridiculous. I see many things in the Bible, as well as in nature, the 'reason' of which lies too deep for me. If the specific purpose of a final 'day of judgment' is the only reality my opponent has ever come across for which he could not grasp the 'reason,' he has either gone blind through the world, or is vastly more far-seeing than most of his fellow creatures."

The Moderator was signaling him, so he turned the pages in his Bible again, and said, "In conclusion, let me simply read the 7th and 8th verses of Revelation 21: 'He that overcometh shall inherit all things; and I will be his God, and he shall be my son. But the fearful, and unbelieving, and the abominable, and murderers, and whoremongers, sorcerers, and idolaters, and all liars, shall have their part in the lake which burneth with fire and brimstone; which is the second death.' My opponent may shamelessly appeal to the *emotions* of our audience, and pronounce the doctrine of eternal punishment 'cruel' and 'pointless'; but here in the final book of the Bible, the doctrine of everlasting, eternal, endless, conscious punishment and torment is quite clearly and impressively taught."

He closed his Bible, picked it up, then looked at Thomas one last time, before saying gravely, "I might respect the candor of a Freethinker or a Deist, who would openly renounce the Bible because he dislikes its doctrines; but I cannot say as much for those who *profess* to believe it is true, while they pervert even its plainest declarations—and represent it as teaching doctrines which are precisely the opposite of those it most obviously teaches!"

He turned back to the audience, and concluded, "I thank you again for your kind attention. Please pray for me; but especially pray for all the Universalists—pray earnestly that they may realize the error of their ways, and repent, and truly *believe* the Gospel!"

He then returned to his seat.

The Moderator walked up to the podium, and said, "Thank you to both Reverend Wesley Richardson, and Reverend Thomas Claudville, for a most stimulating two evenings of theological discussion. I trust that all of us have been given a great deal of material to mull over and digest. If you wish to learn more from either of these two gentlemen, I would remind you that Reverend Richardson is the Pastor of the Evangelical Church just outside town, while Reverend Claudville ministers to the local Universalist congregation. Thanks to all of you in the audience for your patience, and courtesy to our two speakers, during this two-day discussion. May God watch over you, as you journey safely back to your homes. Good evening, and may God Bless."

The audience began rising from their seats, as the hall was instantly filled with excited talk and discussion.

Thomas had barely risen from his seat, when he saw that Reverend Richardson had strode briskly across the stage, and was standing in front of him, saying sharply, "This forum simply was not long enough to allow for a profitable discussion of these doctrines! We should have continued for at least *three* hours each night, and for a minimum of *six* nights of discussion…"

Smiling slightly, Thomas said, "I think we need to be more mindful than that of the *endurance* of our audience; the present forum length was clearly taxing enough for them…"

Reverend Richardson interrupted in a cutting tone, "As you know, our congregation paid for the attendance of two professional transcribers, so that we shall have an official transcript of our statements. I will give you the opportunity to review the transcript, of course; but we shall then print it in the newspaper which our congregation publishes. After that, I would strongly advise that we should continue this discussion in the pages of that paper, since you seem to have little stomach for personal discussions of more than merely *superficial* length…"

Thomas interrupted, "I have little appetite for discussions such as these, because, while they may greatly stir the passions, they produce but little in the way of positive *results!*"

"Only when their length is insufficient to encompass the gravity and importance of the subject," Reverend Richardson replied, sniffing haughtily. "You previously raised no objection to the publication of the transcript of this debate; is that still the case, or have you now…"

"You may publish the transcript in your newspaper," Thomas said with a weary sigh. "*After* I have had an opportunity to review it, and correct any transcriptional errors. I will not take long in such a task, I assure you."

Reverend Richardson looked pleased, and then said soberly, "And will you consent, then, to continuing our discussion in the pages of that journal, and…"

Thomas shook his head vehemently, and said, "I have no interest in further debates with you: whether written, or oral. I felt myself under duress even during these two days of discussion; and I certainly have no desire to extend my agitation."

Reverend Richardson warned gravely, "In that case, I shall have to publish my own detailed views on Universalism in our newspaper, unaccompanied by any contradictory views…"

Thomas replied calmly, "You are, of course, free to do that."

Richardson sniffed again, and said, "I assure you that we shall. Good evening to you, sir."

"And to you," Thomas said. Reverend Richardson turned away, without offering his hand to shake. He left the stage, and joined a crowd of his pleased and enthusiastic parishioners.

Thomas went over to the Moderator, to thank him for his work; and then he went to join his wife, along with his own parishioners and well-wishers.

CHAPTER 6

IS THERE SALVATION OUTSIDE...?
(Late March, 1861)

Thomas was riding in his horse-drawn wagon along the dirt road leading into town, when he saw a man wearing a black hat and a long black garment walking alongside the same road.

As he drew up next to the man, he called out in an inviting tone, "Good morning, friend; are you headed into town?"

"Yes, I am," the man replied. (He seemed somewhat out of breath, and his brow was covered in sweat. Thomas noted that he spoke with a distinct Irish accent.)

Realizing that the man was wearing a clerical collar, Thomas said helpfully, "I'm on my way into town; can I give you a ride?"

The other man hesitated briefly, then said, "Well, if it wouldn't be putting you out of your way..."

"Not at all," Thomas replied, motioning for the man to approach the wagon; he held out his hand for the man to grasp, and then he helped pull him up, and into the adjoining seat in the wagon. Thomas shook the reins lightly, and the horse again began pulling the wagon forward.

The man in black explained, "My own wagon is having a wheel repaired in town; it should be finished by now, so I was just going to pick it up."

Thomas looked more closely at the man's curious black garment, and then said genially, "I take it that you're a 'man of the cloth' like I am. My name is Thomas Claudville; I'm a minister of the Universalist Church in town." He held out his hand to shake.

As the two shook hands, the man in black replied, "I'm Father Patrick O'Reilly."

"'Father'?" Thomas repeated, his brow furrowing with concentration. "Are you Episcopalian?"

"I'm a Catholic priest," came the reply.

"Catholic?" Thomas said, genuinely surprised. "I didn't think we had a Roman Catholic church here."

"We're just getting started," the priest replied. "We have nearly four dozen souls; most of whom are, like myself, recent immigrants from the old country." Seeing the lack of understanding on Thomas's face, he added, "Ireland."

"Ah! Yes, I see," Thomas said, nodding. He smiled, and added, "I should have guessed that from your accent."

"To be sure," Father O'Reilly replied, with a smile. After a moment, he stated, "The men of our parish have just finished building our church; it's about two miles southeast of where you picked me up."

Thomas nodded, and said, "I suppose I don't get out in that area very often."

Father O'Reilly explained, "That's where most of the members of our parish live; most of them are farmers—which is what they also were back home." He shook his head sadly, and said, "But the dreadful potato blight back home ravaged so many of our crops, that hundreds of thousands died back in the 1840s and '50s. That's why so many have come here—hoping to get a new start."

Thomas nodded again, and remarked, "America is definitely a land to come to, for such purpose." He thought for a moment, then asked, "So is that why you came, as well?"

Father O'Reilly shook his head, and said, "The Church asked me to come; but I was more than willing to accept the assignment." He sighed, then added, "There are so many of my countrymen who have come to this country; yet there are so few priests serving this vast area, that most members of my parish have been entirely without the sacraments for several years!"

Thomas said, "My church doesn't really practice the administration of 'sacraments,' as such. Oh, I'll baptize a child, if its parents so wish; but we only observe the Lord's Supper on Easter and Christmas."

The priest looked at Thomas with genuine surprise, then asked, "What did you say the name of your church was, again?"

"The Universalist Church," Thomas replied proudly.

Father O'Reilly thought for a long moment, and then admitted, "I'm afraid that I've never heard of that one. Is it a *Protestant* church?"

Thomas hesitated, then said, "Well… not exactly. I suppose we are 'Protestant' in the sense that our doctrines are based solely upon the Bible, and on human reason; but we are also strongly opposed to the doctrines of men of the Reformation like John Calvin—whose doctrine of Predestination we strongly reject!"

"I see," the priest replied, appearing to be deep in thought, considering this matter.

Thomas chuckled, and said, "I recently participated in a two-day debate with an Evangelical minister—who treated me almost as if I were an infidel! But, interestingly, he also said that my doctrine was somewhat similar to the Roman Catholic doctrine of Purgatory!" He shrugged, and acknowledged, "I must admit that I really don't know much about Roman Catholic doctrines, including Purgatory; so I can't attest as to whether his charge was true or not…"

The priest interrupted, saying with practiced ease, "Purgatory is a place of temporal punishment, for souls who die in a state of grace, but who are still guilty of venial sins, and are not pure enough to enter Heaven."

Thomas looked over at his riding companion, and asked with genuine curiosity, "What do you mean by, 'venial' sins?"

Father O'Reilly replied, "Venial sins are those that do not result in a complete separation from God. *Mortal* sins, on the other hand, are those which bring everlasting death and damnation upon the soul."

"I see," Thomas said noncommittally. Then he asked, "So you believe in a Hell of 'everlasting' death?" The priest nodded, and Thomas next asked, "Now, by 'death,' do you mean some kind of *punishment*, or even of 'torment'?"

The priest replied without hesitation, "Of course; the Church and the Bible have always taught that Hell is a place of everlasting torment, for those who die out of a state of grace."

Thomas smiled slightly, then said, "That was largely the issue that the Evangelical Minister and I contended over." He thought for a moment, and then asked, "So for you, is Hell a place of *endless* torment? Or does its torment have a purpose of reform, and purification—so that its torments may one day end, when this purification has been achieved?"

Father O'Reilly said solemnly, "Hell is not a place of repentance; at a man's death, his time to be able to earn merit, or receive mercy, is over."

"Precisely what my Evangelical opponent believes," Thomas observed, with a shrug. He looked over at the priest, and asked, "So is that true for Purgatory, as well? I thought that Purgatory was supposed to be a place for 'purging' oneself of sins, and …"

Father O'Reilly interjected, "The Beatific Vision of God is delayed, for those in Purgatory. But yes, although the torments of Purgatory are indeed terrible—more so than even the greatest sufferings of this life—the souls in Purgatory know that they are destined for Heaven, once they have been completely purified, and made worthy to be in the presence of God for eternity."

"Ah!" Thomas said, interested. "I believe that I now see why my Evangelical opponent thought that my doctrine was similar to yours. You see, we Universalists believe that, after death, some souls may have to endure a period of punishment—but one that is *reformatory* in nature." His companion said nothing, so Thomas asked, "So who is in Purgatory? And how long are they there?"

The priest shrugged, and replied, "We don't know for sure *which* souls are in Purgatory; and the actual *duration* of the pains of Purgatory is likewise unknown, but varies according to the remaining sins of the individual. Consequently, we must continue to pray for those who have died, and were apparently in a state of grace at the time of death."

Thomas frowned, and asked with surprise, "You pray for the dead?" The priest nodded, and Thomas queried, "Why? What good will that do?"

Father O'Reilly explained patiently, "Indulgences can ease the sufferings of those in Purgatory." Seeing the look of puzzlement on Thomas's face, he added, "An indulgence is a remission of the *temporal punishment* due to sins whose guilt has already been forgiven."

Thomas frowned, and said, "And just how does the dead person *receive* such an 'indulgence'?"

The priest replied without hesitation, "Having Masses said for the deceased—as well as the giving of offerings and alms; and works of piety, such as prayers and fasts, performed by the living—can minimize the time the dead person must spend in Purgatory."

"I see," Thomas replied. He shook his head, and observed, "Well, that's not at all what we believe, in my church." The two men rode in silence for a minute, and then Thomas asked, "Is Purgatory simply a dogmatic teaching of your church? Or is there any basis for it in the Scriptures?"

"Of course Purgatory is in the Bible," Father O'Reilly replied confidently. "Judas Maccabee offered sacrifice for those who had died in their sins; as it says in the Scriptures, 'For if he had not hoped that they that were slain should rise again, it would have seemed superfluous and vain to pray for the dead. And because he considered that they who had fallen asleep with godliness, had great grace laid up for them. It is therefore a holy and wholesome thought to pray for the dead, that they may be loosed from sins.'"

Thomas looked bewildered, and asked, "Where is that in the Bible? I've read my Bible from cover to cover many times, but I can't recall ever reading that particular…"

The priest explained, "That passage is found in Second Maccabees 12:44-46."

"Second Maccabees?" Thomas said, still roundly confused. "I've still never heard of…" but then he stopped short, snapped his fingers, and said, "Wait: don't Roman Catholic Bibles include some books called… what are they called… oh, the *Apocrypha?*"

Father O'Reilly said curtly, "Second Maccabees *is* part of the Holy Bible. It is *deuterocanonical,* or part of the 'second canon,' to be sure; but it has always been an accepted part of the Holy Scriptures in the Church."

Thomas started to reply, but then just shrugged, and asked, "Are there any passages in the *regular* Bible—not a 'deuterocanonical' part of it—that mention Purgatory?"

"Certainly," the priest said without hesitation. "First Corinthians 3:13-15 says, 'Every man's work shall be manifest; for the day of the Lord shall declare it, because it shall be revealed in fire; and the fire shall try every man's work, of what sort it is. If any man's work abide, which he hath built thereupon, he shall receive a reward. If any man's work burn, he shall suffer loss; but he himself shall be saved, yet so as by fire.'"

"Interesting," Thomas replied, with some appreciation. "We Universalists use that passage to support our notion of a *limited* punishment after death." He turned to his companion, and asked with genuine interest, "What else?"

"The Gospels," Father O'Reilly replied immediately. "Matthew 5:26 says, '...and thou be cast into prison. Amen I say to thee, thou shalt not go out from thence til thou repay the last farthing.' And Matthew 12:32 says, 'whosoever shall speak a word against the Son of man, it shall be forgiven him; but he that shall speak against the Holy Ghost, it shall not be forgiven him, neither in this world, nor in the world to come.' These passages from the Saviour indicate that there is an end to *some* kinds of torment in the afterlife, and that *some* sins—venial ones, of course—can be forgiven in the next life."

"We use both of those passages, as well," Thomas acknowledged.

Father O'Reilly said, "And finally, there is Zechariah 13:9, which says, 'And I will bring the third part through the fire, and will refine them as silver is refined: and I will try them as gold is tried.'"

"Hmm; I had never really thought of using that passage," Thomas observed. He reflected for a moment, and then asked, "So is this Purgatory sitting right next to Heaven? Or..."

Father O'Reilly replied, "Purgatory is within the Earth." Noticing the look of genuine surprise this produced on Thomas's face, he quickly added, "Jesus said in Matthew 12:40, 'so shall the Son of man be in the heart of the earth three days and three nights.' After His death, Christ was preaching to the souls of the righteous, who were waiting for the gates of Heaven to be opened to them; and these 'righteous' would have included those in Purgatory. Furthermore, most Doctors and Fathers of the Church also locate Purgatory within the Earth."

"Uhh... I see; thank you for the explanation," Thomas said hesitantly. There was another moment of silence, and then he asked, "Don't Roman Catholics also believe in another place called 'Limbo'?"

The priest nodded, and explained, "The word 'limbo' is actually of Teutonic origin, and means 'hem' or 'border,' such as the border of a garment. The Church distinguishes between what in Latin is called the *Limbus Patrum*—the Limbo of the Fathers—and the *Limbus Infantium*, or Limbo of the Children and Infants. When the word 'Hell' is used in the Apostles' Creed, this is referring to the Limbo of the Fathers."

Seeing the look of complete incomprehension on Thomas's face, he clarified, "The *Limbus Patrum* is not the same as Purgatory, because it is a place of happiness, not punishment. It is called 'Abraham's bosom' in Luke 16, and was called 'Paradise' by Jesus in his promise to the thief on the cross. Jesus also often referred to it as a 'banquet,' or a 'marriage feast.'"

"But it's not Heaven?" Thomas asked, frowning with concentration.

Father O'Reilly shook his head, and continued, "Since the Fall of Adam and Eve, Heaven had been closed to men, until after the redemption accomplished by Christ, and His Ascension into Heaven. But after His crucifixion, as First Peter 3:19 tells us, 'he preached to those spirits that were in prison.' You see, under the Old Dispensation, prior to the time of Christ, there were always some good and just men—such as Abraham, Isaac, Jacob, Moses, David, and others, who died as 'friends of God'—who served God to the best of their knowledge, keeping the laws that had been given to them, and believing in the coming of the future Messiah. When such men died, they certainly could not go to Hell, because they were good men; they also could not go to Purgatory, which was a place of suffering. So God provided a place of happiness for them, where they remained, until they were taken to Heaven with Christ at His Ascension."

Thomas nodded, and asked, "So you think that the Old Testament patriarchs are now in Heaven, right?"

"That's correct," the priest agreed. Seeing that Thomas had no further questions, he went on, "But now that Heaven is opened, and Purgatory prepares souls for Heaven, the *Limbus Patrum* is no longer needed. But the *Limbus Infantium* still exists, and is a place of perfect natural happiness for those infants and children who, having not been properly baptized, are still in their birth condition of Original Sin, at time of death."

Thomas said (with an expression of genuine surprise on his face), "So you think that unbaptized babies *don't* go to Heaven? That they will never know God?" The priest nodded, so Thomas shook his head, and added, "Not even my Evangelical opponent thought that!"

Father O'Reilly replied patiently, "Christ was very clear in John 3:5 about the *absolute necessity* of being 'born again of water and the Holy Ghost,' to enter into Heaven."

Thomas objected, "Yes, but he was also very clear in Matthew 19:14 about little children: 'for of such is the kingdom of heaven'; and in Mark 10:15, he said, 'Whosoever shall not receive the kingdom of God *as a little child*, he shall not enter therein'..."

The priest interrupted, "Paul told us in Romans 5 that we are all born into a state of sin; baptism removes the stain of Original Sin, but the means of regeneration through the sacraments are not available to infants and very young children, so they cannot enter Heaven." He looked directly at Thomas, and added sympathetically, "But those in the *Limbus Infantium* are in a state of 'perfect natural happiness'; so, even though they are excluded from the Beatific Vision of God, they still are in a state much superior to this life..."

Thomas asked (with genuine incredulity in his voice), "And they remain perpetual infants *forever?* And they will never grow up, or directly experience God?"

"That is why the sacrament of Baptism is so essential!" Father O'Reilly replied firmly. He added gravely, "Among the members of my new parish, a number of them had children who had not yet been baptized; so that was among my very first tasks, upon my arrival."

"I see," Thomas said. He thought for a moment, and then asked, "So you don't think there is any kind of opportunity provided by God *after death* for any unregenerate person to achieve salvation?"

The priest shook his head firmly, and replied, "The means of regeneration that are provided for our benefit in this lifetime, do not remain available after death; thus, those who die in an unregenerate condition are eternally excluded from Heaven, and the sight of God. In Hell, they must endure the most dreadful torments—*forever!*"

Thomas said passionately, "Well, that's precisely the point that my own church strongly rejects! How could anyone possibly enjoy Heaven, if they knew that many millions of others were forced to endure horrible torments forever and ever? Unless God somehow blotted out all of their memories, and..."

Father O'Reilly said gravely, "In fact, Saint Thomas Aquinas told us—in the Supplement to the Third Part of his *Summa Theologica;* Question 94, Article 1—that 'in order that the happiness of the saints may be more delightful to them and that they may render more copious thanks to God for it, they are allowed to see perfectly the sufferings of the damned.'"

Thomas's mouth fell open in shock, and he stammered, "So you believe that a mother who son or daughter died without being a Christian, is going to *watch* that child being *tormented* for all of eternity? And this will make them *happier?*" The priest remained silent, but he nodded his head slightly in response. Thomas said, with genuine horror in his voice, "Well, then I am profoundly glad that my wife—who was raised Roman Catholic, but converted to Universalism after she came to this country—doesn't believe that doctrine!"

Father O'Reilly suddenly snapped to full attention, and asked sharply, "Your wife was raised Catholic?"

Thomas nodded, then explained, "She told me that she went through Confirmation in the Roman church; but her family moved here from England shortly after that, and she…"

The priest said urgently, with deadly seriousness, "Please listen to me carefully, my friend: a non-Catholic such as yourself—who was validly baptized, and who truly believes that the church to which he belongs is the true church, and who was doing all he could to serve God—*may* in the end be saved; as Pope Pius IX said in his Apostolic Letter *Singulari Quadam,* 'Far be it from us … to presume on the limits of divine mercy which is infinite… [and] to wish to scrutinize the hidden counsel and "judgments of God" which are "a great abyss."' He added, "[T]hey who labor in ignorance of the true religion, if this ignorance is invincible, will not be held guilty of this in the eyes of God." Looking Thomas directly in the eyes, he added soberly, "But for a Catholic such as your wife, who *knows* that the Catholic Church is the only true Church, to separate herself from it is to forfeit her eternal salvation!"

"What?" Thomas exclaimed, indignantly. "I told you that my wife converted to Universalism after coming to this country, and…"

"That doesn't matter," the priest explained patiently. "If she went through Confirmation in the Church, then she has confessed her knowledge of the divine establishment of the Catholic Church by Christ. By willfully separating herself from it, she is committing a sin that is… unforgivable. In Latin, this doctrine is expressed by saying, *extra Ecclesiam nulla salus;* which in English is, 'Outside the Church there is no salvation.'"

"That is completely absurd!" Thomas spat out, sharply pulling the horse's reins, and bringing the wagon to a sudden halt. "My wife has a beautiful, and radiant Christian spirit! Even my Evangelical opponent would not presume to deny her salvation, when she..."

Father O'Reilly said calmly, "It is my duty to inform you of the inspired teachings of the Church; I am only bringing this to your attention because of my grave concern for you, but particularly for your wife." He put his hand gently on Thomas's shoulder, and said urgently, "I need to meet with her as soon as possible, so that I may..."

"My wife will have no interest whatsoever in meeting with you," Thomas replied sharply. "She has told me on many occasions how grateful she is for the Universalist message, and how she loves it far more than the rigid, authoritarian Roman church which she was raised in."

The priest continued, "My friend, the Catholic Church is the only ark of salvation; and he or she that has not entered therein will perish in the 'flood'..."

Thomas shook the reins, to make the horse start pulling the wagon again. The two men remained silent during the remainder of the ride into town.

As they entered the main street of the town, Thomas pointed to one large building, and said, "That's the Livery, and the Saddlery is right next door to it. I presume that's where you left your wagon to be repaired."

"My horse is being kept in the Livery, and one of their workers was repairing my wagon," the priest replied. He said helpfully, "You can let me off; I'll walk from here." Thomas stopped the wagon, and the priest climbed down to the ground.

Father O'Reilly said, "I'm very grateful to you, for your generous ride into town. And I regret that my words have clearly offended you." Thomas remained silent, and the priest added with genuine feeling, "But I have pledged my life to the Lord, and to deliver His truth—without compromise, and regardless of the consequences."

Thomas took a deep breath, and then said (in a more conciliatory tone), "I can respect the strength of your convictions, sir. Still, our conversation has simply made me even *more* grateful to God for having led me into the truth of Universal Salvation."

The priest frowned, and then said with dawning alarm, "'Universal Salvation,' you said? If you mean by that what I have heard that term means, it is a most serious form of *infidelity,* that will…"

Thomas interrupted, "The God I serve is a God of *love;* and the 'ark of salvation' he provides is wide enough to encompass all—including yourself!" He nodded, and said, "Good day to you, sir."

"Good day," the priest replied, and he began walking toward the Livery, as Thomas cued the horse to begin walking again.

PART FOUR

THE TWENTIETH CENTURY
(CALIFORNIA)

CHAPTER 7

Is Heaven Our Destiny?
(1961)

Clement (a studious-looking man in his late 30s) was sitting at the desk in his study in the mid-afternoon, flipping through various reference books and taking notes, when the doorbell rang.

Renee is out shopping, Clement remembered, placing his pen on the table, and getting up from his chair. He went out into the hall, and began quickly walking to the front door, as the doorbell rang again.

When he finally reached the door, he hurriedly opened it and looked outside, to see two men wearing neat, dark suits standing on his porch. One of the men was carrying a large, canvas briefcase.

The two men smiled, and one of them said warmly, "Good afternoon, sir; we're sorry to disturb you. But we're going around the neighborhood, and sharing with people an interesting article." He held out to Clement a booklet (entitled *The Watchtower*), which had the bold statement on its cover, ***Death Will Be No More***. Clement took the booklet from the outstretched hand, and glanced at its cover, with some interest.

The man continued, "Many people are touched by death; death is a very formidable enemy, and it leaves painful scars upon the hearts of the living…"

Clement interrupted, saying perfunctorily, "You're Jehovah's Witnesses."

The two men were momentarily taken aback, but then the speaker confidently replied, "Yes, we are."

The other man said, "We are representatives of the Watch Tower Society, who are calling upon people to encourage Bible study in the home…"

Clement interrupted again, saying, "I study the Bible diligently every day; I'm a minister."

"A minister?" the first man said, now looking at Clement warily. He asked suspiciously, "Of what denomination?"

"I'm a Universalist," Clement replied. The two men facing him looked at each other, exchanging blank expressions.

The second man shrugged, and then pointed at the booklet Clement was holding, and said, "Many have mistakenly been taught that at death, some persons will go to a burning 'hell,' forever. But the Bible plainly shows that this is not true."

Clement was immediately interested, and asked, "What? Are you saying that you don't believe in a 'fiery' Hell?"

The second man shook his head, and replied confidently, "No, sir. The Bible teaches no such thing." The three men stood facing each other silently, for a long moment.

"I guess I don't really know much of anything about your beliefs. Would you like to come inside for a little while, to discuss this?" Clement invited, but then he cautioned, "Just until my wife comes home from shopping, though; she hates having 'theological' discussions in our house!" and they all laughed.

"Thank you," the first man said, as Clement stepped back from the door, to invite them inside.

The two men sat down on the couch, while Clement sat on the footstool in front of a recliner chair, so he could face them. The first visitor pulled several books and some other publications from his large briefcase.

The first man then smiled, and said, "My name is Richard, and my companion is Ramón."

Clement rose, and came forward with his hand extended, and said, "My name is Clement; it's nice to meet you." He shook hands with the two visitors, then return to sit on his footstool.

Richard looked around the simple, plainly-furnished living room, and said, "You have a nice home."

"Thanks," Clement replied.

Ramón pointed to a nearby bookshelf, and said, "I see that you have a copy of the Bible on that top shelf."

Clement replied, "Several copies, in fact. I've got several different editions of the King James Version, of course, but also the American Standard Version, and the Revised Standard Version." After saying this, he went to the shelf, took down one of the copies of the Bible, and returned with it in hand to sit on his footstool.

Richard said eagerly, "The Watch Tower Society has just published this beautiful edition of the Bible; it's by far the most accurate English translation of the Bible that's ever been published!" He held out for Clement's inspection a book whose cover read, *New World Translation of the Holy Scriptures.*

Ramón said helpfully, "If you'd like a copy of it, you can have one for a small contribution…"

Clement looked back and forth from one visitor to the other, and then finally replied, "Uhh, no thanks; I'm happy with the Bibles that I've got." Ramón looked disappointed, but Richard calmly placed the Bible next to him on the couch.

Richard asked, "You said that you were a minister. What was that denomination, again?"

"I'm a Universalist," Clement repeated.

Ramón asked, "Is that Protestant, or Roman Catholic?"

Clement smiled, and replied, "Neither." Smiling at the puzzled look on their faces, he explained, "Our church was formed in the last part of the eighteenth century; we're neither Roman Catholic nor Protestant, but I suppose that we have more *cultural* affinity with Protestants. But one of our most important beliefs is the firm rejection of the notion that God will eternally torment *anyone* in a 'Hell,' 'Hades,' or any other place—which is why I was so interested when you mentioned that you don't believe in Hell. That *is* what you said, right?"

"That is correct," Richard replied. He explained, "The Hebrew word that is translated as 'hell' in the King James translation of the Bible, for example, is *Sheol.* This word is translated as *Hades* in the Christian Greek Scriptures. This can be proved because the word 'Sheol' in Psalm 16:10—'For you will not leave my soul in Sheol. You will not allow your loved one to see the pit'—is quoted in Acts 2:27 & 31, where it is translated as 'Hades.'"

"Agreed," Clement said, nodding his head.

Richard looked pleased, and went on, "Both 'good' and 'bad' persons go to Sheol after they die, because Sheol or Hades is simply the *common grave* of all mankind. Jesus himself was in Hades or 'hell' after he died, according to Acts 2:31-32."

"I agree," Clement said.

Richard continued, with growing confidence, "But deliverance is possible for those in Hades; we are delivered from this state by being resurrected! Everyone there will be resurrected. But then we are told in Revelation 20:12-14 that Hades is ultimately to be completely destroyed."

Clement nodded his agreement, then said, "But you don't think that anyone is *currently* being 'tormented' in Hades, do you?"

"Absolutely not," Richard replied confidently. He added, "We know this because those who are in Sheol are not simply 'separated' from God: they are actually *dead!*" (This remark puzzled Clement, so he remained silent, waiting for Richard's exposition to continue.)

Richard went on, "The Bible tells us that a person who is dead is actually unconscious, and inactive. Ecclesiastes 9:5 tells us that 'The living are conscious that they will die; but as for the dead, they are conscious of nothing at all.' Verse 10 adds, 'there is no work nor devising nor knowledge nor wisdom in Sheol, the place to which you are going.'"

Ramón added eagerly, "That's why the dead in Hades *cannot* be 'tormented'—because they are unconscious!"

Frowning, Clement said, "I think you need to be careful about trying to use the book of Ecclesiastes to establish any point of *doctrine!* That book just contains the musings of Solomon, which are often quite cynical. For example, he advises us to 'eat, drink, and be merry' in 8:15; in 4:3 he says that someone who has never been *born* is better off than the living; in 10:19 he says that 'money answers all things'; and in 12:8 he concludes that 'all is vanity.'"

Richard said confidently, "Psalm 146:4 also supports those quotations from Ecclesiastes, when it says that on our day of death, a man's spirit 'goes out, he goes back to his ground; In that day his thoughts do perish.'"

Clement said doubtfully, "So you think that our immortal souls just kind of ... well, *blank out* after we die, until we are eventually resurrected?"

Ramón said helpfully, "Jehovah God alone is immortal, as First Timothy 6:16 tells us. Jude 6 tells us that even the *angels* are not immortal!"

Clement started to object, but Richard stated smoothly, "Immortality is bestowed as a reward, only upon those whom Jehovah God designates as worthy of receiving it; it is not given as a *curse* on the wicked, so that they can be tormented everlastingly in some sort of 'hell'!"

Clement said, "It's true that in the Old Testament, life in Sheol was portrayed as being a kind of 'shadow' existence, where the dead were not fully 'alive.' But we're now in the New Testament era, when Jesus has been resurrected; and now we know that..."

Richard interrupted, "Jesus himself was *rewarded* by Jehovah God with immortality, at the time of his resurrection; as First Corinthians 15:20 tells us, he is the 'first fruits' of the resurrection—so now, he is no longer subject to death. And his resurrection opened the way for others to gain similar incorruptibility, as First Peter 1:3-4 tells us. And all those who are heirs of the heavenly kingdom receive immortality when they are raised from death, according to First Corinthians 15:50-54."

Clement was still frowning, as he said, "So basically, you deny that humans, who are made in the image of God, have an immortal soul."

Ramón said, "The Bible plainly shows that man *is* a soul, he doesn't *have* a soul; that's what Genesis 2:7 and First Corinthians 24:7 tell us. And when a man dies, he remains dead until the resurrection. That's why Ezekiel 18:4 says, 'The soul that is sinning—it itself will die.'"

Richard added, "Man is not superior to the animals when it comes to the spirit animating his body; the same invisible spirit or activating life-force is common to both, as Genesis 1:21 & 24 tell us. And Ecclesiastes 12:7 informs us that 'the dust returns to the earth... and the spirit itself returns to the [true] God who gave it.'"

Clement argued, "If for some reason you don't want to use the term 'soul,' that's fine. But right before Jesus died on the cross, he said to the Father, 'into thy hands I commend my *spirit*.' So his spirit—or his 'activating life-force,' or whatever it was that you called it—was still *alive;* and it was in his Father's care. And in Acts 7:59, as Stephen was being martyred, he saw Jesus, and called upon him to receive his own spirit..."

Richard interrupted, "The 'soul' is not the same as the 'spirit'; Hebrews 4:12 and First Thessalonians 5:23 clearly distinguish between the two. But when the spirit goes out, conscious life ceases, as Psalm 146:4 says." Clement was about to reply, but then he just shrugged, and let Richard continue his presentation.

Richard concluded confidently, "So no soul or spirit separates from the body at death, and continues conscious existence. Therefore, nothing survives that *can* be subjected to literal torment in any 'hell'!" With enthusiasm coming into his voice, he added, "But Jehovah God has promised deliverance of dead souls from Hades; Revelation 20:13 says that 'the sea gave up those dead in it, and death and Hades gave up those dead in them.' We are raised in incorruptible spirit bodies, according to First Corinthians 15."

Ramón said excitedly, "And the time when the resurrection will occur is getting very close! Judge Joseph Rutherford said of the year 1914 that…" but he stopped suddenly, as Richard slightly shook his head negatively at him. Ramón looked momentarily embarrassed, and he fell silent.

Clement took advantage of the momentary silence, to say, "I must disagree with your statements about the soul, and what happens to us after we die. For example, consider the story of the rich man and Lazarus in Luke 16…"

Richard objected, "The story in Luke 16 is a parable, or an illustration, and not literal reality. The purpose of the parable was to show us that money-loving, self-righteous religious leaders such as the chief priest, scribes, and Pharisees—even though they were physically 'alive'—were actually *dead,* in God's eyes. Whereas the beggar Lazarus represents those humble persons who were formerly despised, but who repented, and are now followers of Jesus and favored by God!"

Clement interrupted, "I basically agree with you; and I certainly don't accept the common view that it 'proves' the doctrine of *conscious torment* after death. But I mention it to make one point: namely, that if Jesus held the views you've been outlining to me, why in the world would he tell a parable that gives an entirely *misleading* view of continuing conscious life after a person's death?" His two listeners seemed surprised by this argument, and he continued, "Not only does the parable portray both the rich man and Lazarus as still *existing* after their deaths, but as capable of thought, feelings, and even *actions!* If Jesus didn't think that we remained consciously alive after our deaths, he could easily have developed another parable to make the same point about lovers of money, and…"

Richard said in a dogmatic tone, "Since we know from Genesis 25:8-10 that Abraham was dead and buried in the grave, Lazarus *couldn't* have been literally taken to his 'bosom,' as this parable suggests. Furthermore, Abraham couldn't have been in heaven, since Jesus told us in John 3:13 that 'no man has ascended into heaven but he that descended from heaven, the Son of man.' Therefore, we know that this parable is not intended to be taken literally."

Clement sighed, and then said, "Paul also indicated that *Christians*, at least, are with Jesus in Heaven after we die. He said in Philippians 1:23 that he desired 'to depart, and to be with Christ; which is far better'; and he said in Second Corinthians 5:6 that 'while we are at home in the body, we are absent from the Lord.'"

Richard flipped pages in his own copy of the Bible (he had placed 'tabs' on various pages, for easy reference), and then said easily, "That passage in Philippians actually says, 'what I do desire is the releasing and the being with Christ'; and the passage from Second Corinthians says, 'while we have our home in the body, we are absent from the Lord.' So neither of those passages suggest that Christians will go to heaven immediately after they die."

Clement rolled his eyes, and then said, "Then how about the thief on the cross? In Luke 23:43, Jesus told this thief, 'Today shalt thou be with me in paradise.' So on that very *day,* both Jesus and the thief would be in Paradise, or Heaven."

Richard calmly shook his head, and said, "The *punctuation* in modern translations of the Bible is added by the translators, and was not in the original Hebrew and Greek manuscripts."

Clement said impatiently, "I know that, of course; but…"

Richard went on, "Some translators incorrectly place the comma after the words 'tell you'; but the *accurate* translation places it after the word 'today,' so that the passage actually correctly reads, 'Truly I tell you *today,* you will be with me in Paradise.' So, on that day, Jesus was promising the thief that one day in the *future,* he would be with Jesus in an earthly paradise."

Ramón said to Clement helpfully, "That's why it's so important to be reading from an accurate translation of the Bible, such as our..."

"What?" Clement said indignantly. "That's absurd; Jesus used that expression, 'Verily I say unto thee,' numerous times, such as in Matthew 5:26, 6:2, and 26:34; John chapter 3, and 21:18—and he never uses the term 'today' to conclude the phrase! What would be the point? Obviously, he was speaking 'today'!"

Richard insisted, "There is nothing in the rest of the Scriptures to support the notion that the thief and Jesus both went to Heaven on the same day they were crucified."

Clement sighed, then said, "What about the Transfiguration? Peter, James and John saw Jesus with Moses and Elijah; do you think that God raised the two of them up just for this special meeting, and then put them back into 'sleep'?"

Ramón looked over for help to Richard, who calmly said to Clement, "In Matthew 17:8, Jesus told his disciples that this was a 'vision'; so Moses and Elijah were not literally *present* with Jesus—they were represented in a *vision*."

Frustration coming into his voice, Clement said, "The Greek word *horama* used in that statement of Jesus is translated as 'vision' throughout the Book of Acts—as in Chapter 9, when God told Ananias to meet with Saul of Tarsus—but it never means completely *fictional* 'representations' of real people!"

Richard insisted, "You have to interpret *all* of what the Bible says on a subject, so that it always speaks in harmony." (Clement just shook his head, in resignation.)

Clement then said, "Genesis 5:24 says, 'And Enoch walked with God: and he was not; for God took him.' Second Kings 2:11 says that Elijah 'went up by a whirlwind into heaven.' So you think that these two great prophets have been *unconscious* all this time? Or are they an exception?"

Richard replied, "Elijah did not die at that time; he was simply transferred to another prophetic assignment. And Elisha simply saw his master Elijah being carried up *toward* the heavens in a windstorm."

Ramón nodded his agreement, then added, "That's why Elisha didn't observe any period or 'mourning' for the death of his master: his master wasn't dead!"

Clement protested, "But verse 1 says the same thing: Elijah was taken 'into heaven'..."

Richard ignored him, saying, "Enoch, however, *did* die at the comparatively early age of 365, which is what the expression 'for God took him' means. But he and Elijah certainly didn't ascend into heaven, because, again, Jesus clearly told us in John 3:13 that 'no man has ascended into heaven' other than Jesus himself." (Clement sighed once more, and shook his head in disgust.)

Clement tried another tactic, saying, "What about the story of the Witch of Endor in First Samuel 28:7-20? Once the Witch summoned Samuel, he seemed to have been quite aware of what had transpired in Israel, and with Saul, since his death..."

Ramón said quickly, "Witchcraft is strongly condemned in the Bible! It warranted the death penalty in Leviticus 20:27; so Jehovah God certainly would not have answered Saul's inquiries by such a forbidden practice! Therefore, what this woman saw was obviously of demonic origin!"

Clement said, "In Matthew 22:31-32, Jesus said, 'But as touching the resurrection of the dead, have ye not read that which was spoken unto you by God, saying, I am the God of Abraham, and the God of Isaac, and the God of Jacob? God is not the God of the dead, but of the living.' So Jesus was certainly teaching that Abraham, Isaac, and Jacob—though their bodies were dead—were at that time still *living*."

Richard simply replied, "No, their spirits returned to God at their death; and they will one day be resurrected."

Refusing to give up, Clement said, "Let's take the Book of Revelation: both 6:9 and 20:4 say that John *saw* the 'souls' of those saints who had been slain; if these martyrs were simply 'in the grave' and awaiting resurrection, what was there for John to 'see'?"

Richard replied easily, "Remember that Revelation 9:17 tells us that this entire book was a *vision;* so again, you can't take such symbolic images *literally*."

Clement argued, "But at least those passages show that John conceived of these dead 'souls' as being *conscious;* in 6:10, for example, they cry out to the Lord, and they were even given white robes to wear..."

But Richard just shook his head, saying evenly, "Again, that's just what John was shown in the vision. But you have to harmonize such visionary experiences with the clear testimony of the *entire* Bible—which clearly shows us that the dead are unconscious, until the resurrection."

Clement exhaled wearily, placing his Bible fall back on the footstool next to him.

Ramón (trying to "smooth over" their disagreement on this issue) changed the subject, saying brightly, "Anyway, the Bible doesn't contrast 'life in happiness' with 'life in torment'; it contrasts *life* with *death!*"

Clement admitted, "Well, *that's* true, of course. But…"

Richard said with practiced ease, "The other Greek word that is translated as 'hell' in many Bible versions is *Gehenna.* Jesus used the word 'Gehenna' to represent the worst punishment that could befall a person—that is, complete destruction, with no hope of resurrection. The term 'Gehenna' is used in various places in the New Testament; but even when these passages associate 'fire' with Gehenna—such as in Matthew 5:22, Mark 9:43-48, and James 3:6—none of them speak of any *conscious suffering* after death. Instead, as Jesus pointed out in Matthew 10:28, God can 'destroy' not just the body, but the soul, the entire person, in Gehenna."

Clement said, "Well, I certainly agree that the Bible does not speak of *eternal* or *never-ending* conscious suffering after death. But there are various places in the Bible where it suggests that there will be, for some people, a *limited* period of punishment, before they are finally reconciled to God. Take Revelation 14:9-11, and Revelation 20:10 & 15, for example."

Richard replied, "Revelation 14:9-11 refers to a 'wild beast' and a 'Lamb,' which are obviously symbolic figures; therefore, the 'torment' in those verses is likewise symbolic. The 'Lake of Fire' in Revelation 20 is also symbolic, and in this case refers to those wicked persons who do not have the hope of ever being resurrected. They are eternally restrained from any conscious activity or existence; but they *do* experience some torment before they are plunged into complete, everlasting destruction. You see, total destruction, not torment, is the punishment for all who continue in disobedience. And Hades itself is not a 'lake of fire,' but will eventually be cast *into* a symbolic 'lake of fire'—meaning that it will be destroyed forever."

Ramón added, "But the 'torment' in the book of Revelation is not 'eternal torment in fire.' For example, the symbolic locusts in 9:5 tormented men only for *five months*, not forever!"

Clement replied, "Look, I'm glad to learn that we agree about the irrationality and unbiblical nature of 'eternal conscious torment' in Hell. But you still have the problem that traditional believers in Hell have, about people only having this short period of time on earth that is the sole basis for determining where they will spend *eternity!* So, for example, with young people who die in their teens..."

Ramón interrupted, "But *all* of the dead will be given the opportunity to live again, after the resurrection!" He added with genuine enthusiasm, "That is one of the most important truths that proved to me that the Watch Tower Society is the only organization teaching Jehovah's message!"

Richard nodded his agreement, and added, "The dead will have more than just the short lifespan that ended at their death; they will have the future opportunity to live according to Jehovah's law, here on earth."

"That's very interesting," Clement said, his interest stirred once again. "Now, is this for *all* the dead, or..."

"All the dead," Ramón replied immediately. "You see, here in our earthly existence, we all do not have equal opportunities to hear and obey Jehovah's righteous law. But when Jehovah's Kingdom is established on earth, under the rulership of Jesus Christ—along with 144,000 of the redeemed from earth functioning as 'kings and priests,' who have been raised to immortal life in the heavens—*all* people will have a fair chance to obey God's righteous commands, and thus to live forever in the earthly paradise."

Clement nodded, and summarized, "So you at least provide a 'second chance' after earthly death for everyone; I certainly agree with that concept. Of course, that's also one of the major objections that traditional believers in Hell raise against we Universalists."

Ramón had a puzzled look on his face, and asked, "What do you mean by that word, 'Universalists'?"

Clement explained, "It means that we believe that *all* persons will ultimately be saved, be reconciled with God, and spend eternity with Him in Heaven."

Richard and Ramón looked blankly at each other, and then Richard asked, "*All* persons will be saved? Even those who are disobedient to Jehovah's laws?"

"That's correct," Clement replied. With a slight smile, he added, "Now of course, for some people, it may take a considerably *longer* time to become reconciled to God, than for others. And remember that I said earlier that there will probably be for some people a *limited* period of punishment; but the difference between us, and believers in the traditional Hell, is that we see this punishment as having a *redemptive* purpose—that of *reforming* the individual."

Richard said soberly, "But what the Bible actually teaches is that those who are raised to life on earth, but prove ultimately unfaithful to God's law, will receive what Jesus called a 'resurrection of judgment'—which is the 'second death' spoken of in Revelation 20:14-15—a death from which no recovery is possible; an *eternal* death."

Clement shrugged, and conceded, "Well, I admit that I like your approach a lot more than what the 'traditional' people believe. But to Universalists like myself, there are just too many biblical passages that suggest that God's ultimate purpose wouldn't be fulfilled by having only *some* of his children—and perhaps, only a very small minority—reconciled to himself."

Richard remained silent, but Ramón impulsively asked, "What Bible passages are those?"

Clement replied with ease, "Romans 5:18: 'as by the offence of one judgment came upon all men to condemnation; even so by the righteousness of one the free gift came upon *all men* unto justification of life'; Romans 11:32: 'God hath concluded them all in unbelief, that he might have *mercy upon all*'; First Corinthians 15:22: 'For as in Adam all die, even so in Christ shall *all be made alive*'; Philippians 2:11: 'that *every tongue* should confess that Jesus Christ is Lord, to the glory of God the Father'; Colossians 1:20: 'having made peace through the blood of his cross, by him to *reconcile all things* unto himself'; First Timothy 2:4: God 'will *have all men to be saved*, and to come unto the knowledge of the truth.'" He smiled, and said "I can go on, if you'd like."

"That's not necessary," Richard said curtly.

Ramón asked with curiosity, "So do you think that *Satan* will be reconciled to God?"

Clement chuckled, and replied, "Well, I'm not personally all that sure that there even *is* such a being, as Satan is popularly pictured; you know, the all-red guy with horns and a pitchfork, who rules over the souls who are being tormented in the Lake of Fire..."

Richard interjected, "We agree that such images of Satan are nonsensical. Job 1:6-7 tells us that Satan was one of the 'sons of God,' and that he had been freely roving about in the earth, until the time that the Kingdom was established in Heaven in 1914, as described in Revelation 12:7-10. But Satan will not be cast into the 'lake of fire' until *after* the 1,000-year reign of Christ, according to Revelation 20:7-10. And Satan's 'torment' will be his 'confinement' in Everlasting Death. And similarly, as Jude 6 and Second Peter 2:4 say, the angels that rebelled with him will also be destroyed."

Clement shrugged, and said, "Well, if there actually *is* such a being as Satan, who is wandering around the earth and encouraging people to sin, it wouldn't particularly bother me if he was ultimately destroyed, as you think. But since the book of Job says that he was once one of the 'sons of God,' it's not clear to me why such a being should necessarily be 'beyond redemption.'"

Richard said perfunctorily, "But that's what the Bible says." There was a moment of silence, as no one seemed to have anything further to say.

Clement asked, "So are you two ministers in your Church?"

With a look of distaste on his face, Richard said proudly, "We followers of Jehovah aren't a 'church'; that is a term that is used by *Christendom!* In the Bible, the Greek word *ekklesia* refers to a group of believers—not to an eternal organization, or the building they meet in! The first Christians simply met in each other's *houses,* as Acts 2:46, 5:42, and 20:20—as well as Romans 16:5, First Corinthians 16:19, Colossians 4:15, and Philemon 2—make clear."

Ramón said, "Our places for meeting are called 'Kingdom Halls,' because that is where we proclaim the truths of Jehovah's coming Kingdom. And *all* of us baptized Christians who preach God's Word are 'ministers,' as Second Timothy 4:2 & 5 indicate. And all of us—including our wives—share in our public, house-to-house ministry."

Richard said proudly, "What is needed to be qualified as a 'minister' is a thorough knowledge of the Bible, and the spirit of Jehovah God—and not any specialized 'training' in some theological school or seminary, where a 'diploma' is awarded, and 'ordination' is conveyed at the conclusion."

Clement shrugged, and said, "That's fine for you; but personally, I found my education at Crane Theological School back in Massachusetts to be profoundly *useful* to me; I can't imagine having been prepared to begin a regular pulpit ministry without it."

At that point, the sound of a car horn came from outside. Clement quickly got up, explaining, "Uh, oh; that's my wife Renee—she's back from grocery shopping. I need to help her get the groceries put away."

Richard and Ramón both immediately rose to their feet, and Richard quickly put his books back into his briefcase.

Clement started to hand back the *Watchtower* booklet to Richard, but Richard just shook his head, and said, "You may keep that copy; I think you'll find it very interesting reading."

Ramón said warmly, "We'd like to come back again, and discuss these matters further. We also hold Bible Study classes in private homes, at no cost. Your wife would probably be very interested in this, as well as…"

"No thanks," Clement said brusquely. Seeing the disappointment on the faces of the two men, he added in a conciliatory tone, "Look, I enjoyed our conversation today; and I learned a great deal about your organization that I didn't know. But while we have a *few* beliefs in common, I just don't think we're going to be able to agree on some very fundamental matters."

The car horn outside sounded again, and the three men headed quickly to the front door. Richard opened the door, and the three of them went outside.

Richard spotted a woman standing next to a car that was filled with bags of groceries, She looked at the two visitors with curiosity.

"Good afternoon, ma'am," Richard said politely to Clement's wife, as he and Ramón walked past her.

"Hello," she replied, looking over at Clement with curiosity.

Clement smiled, then opened the car door, and picked up two bags of groceries. As she walked next to him while they headed to the house, he explained, "Those two gentlemen are Jehovah's Witnesses; they knocked on the door as I was preparing my sermon for tomorrow morning."

"Jehovah's Witnesses?" she said, looking at him with disapproval, as they entered the house. "Aren't they supposed to be some kind of *cult?*"

Richard chuckled, as he set the two bags down on the kitchen counter. Then he said with an ironic smile, "Well, some people think that *we* are a 'cult'!"

"Don't be ridiculous," she said, sitting down at the kitchen table and removing her high-heeled pumps; she sighed wearily, then asked, "So you want dinner at the usual time?"

"Maybe a little later than usual," Clement replied, turning back to the front door, to go retrieve the other bags of groceries. He added cheerily, "I just got some new *ideas,* for my sermon!"

CHAPTER 8

An End, and A Beginning (1961)

Clement was standing just inside the door of the small storefront church, and greeting his few parishioners as they arrived.

"Good morning, Dale," he said gently to an elderly lady, who was arriving by herself. He helped her to find a seat. (He had previously rearranged the two dozen folding chairs into a circle, so that the church members could all see each other. He had also placed the lectern from which he habitually preached off in a corner of the room.)

He addressed the nineteen people (including his wife Renee) who were seated, and said, "Well, as I told you, Roger and Stephanie called me this morning to say that they won't be joining us. And our son Todd is at his grandma's. So we may as well get started." With a forced smile, he said, "I'd like to welcome you to our final meeting; the last meeting of the River City Universalist Church."

Dale removed her glasses, and then raised a handkerchief to her eyes, as she began openly sobbing; the two elderly women sitting on either side of her moved quickly to comfort her. A depressed silence fell upon the rest of the group; and even Clement was unable to say anything.

When Dale was finally able to speak, she said in a voice choked with emotion, "I've been a proud member of the Universalist Church for all my life; I just can't believe it's coming to an end..."

Clement said gently, "It's a *new beginning*, Dale; not an 'ending.' Our church will continue..."

The woman sitting on Dale's right said bitterly, "We're being *swallowed up* by the Unitarians! How can that not be our 'ending'?"

The woman on Dale's other side nodded, then added, "I've never liked the Unitarians! They're snooty, and think they're so much better than we are." A number of the others sitting in the circle quickly voiced their agreement with this sentiment.

With a wan smile, Clement said, "The 19th century Unitarian minister Thomas Starr King said that the difference between Universalists and Unitarians was that Universalists think that *God* is too good to damn them forever; while Unitarians think that *they* are too good to be damned forever," and the group exploded with laughter—which somewhat eased the sense of heaviness in the room.

One of the men in the group observed, "Well, it was bound to happen; the writing has been on the wall for some time. In the ten years that I've been a member of this church, we've dropped off to only one-third what our size used to be." He shook his head sadly, and said resignedly, "That's just not a large enough congregation to be able to support a minister; that's why both Clem and Renee had to take on part-time jobs, years ago."

Dale said sarcastically, "People these days are just too tied up with their TV, their newspapers, and their bestsellers, to take the time out to go to church, anymore." Most of the people in the group nodded their agreement with this statement.

Clement suggested, "Well, I think a big part of our denomination's problem is that we haven't been able to attract the *younger* crowd. I'm 38—which actually makes me one of the 'young turks' in this group," and this generated more laughter from the group. He continued, "But seriously, the fact is that young people like to be around *other* young people. That's why they're mostly attracted to churches that have a vibrant youth program."

Renee recalled, "We had a small youth group when Clem and I were first called to this church; but little by little, all of the kids in our group quit coming. So Todd was by himself."

Clement nodded, and added ruefully, "And I have to take the blame for that, since I should have been trying much harder than I did to reach the younger generation, and…" but he stopped speaking, as impassioned denials immediately came forth from the group.

"It's not your fault, Clem," an older man said. "These young folks today are just too attached to their 'Rock-and-Roll' records, and their dances and parties, to give God a moment's thought."

"The whole *world's* going to the dogs; and the youngsters are the cause of most of it," another man said cynically.

Renee smiled, and then said to this man with a smile, "Well, I think you'd better be careful, Ronald; because, as Universalists, we're probably going to be spending *eternity* with those very same young people!" and the group exploded with laughter, again.

One of the younger women in the group said, "As long as they don't play their music too loud, they're fine with me." Several members of the group chuckled at this statement.

One of the women said in a hushed voice, "Stephanie told me that she and Roger are now going to start attending a *Presbyterian* church!" This remark produced several exclamations (almost gasps!) of surprise, and even indignation.

One of the oldest men in the group said bitterly, "The Presbyterians are *Calvinists!* They think that God just arbitrarily picks some people to *damn* them to Hell, for all eternity!" This produced many responses of agreement from the group.

Clement said in a conciliatory tone, "Roger told me about his plans; he said that a number of his coworkers go to that particular church, and they've recommended it to him and Stephanie." He shrugged, and added, "That church is affiliated with the Presbyterian Church USA, which is a pretty 'mainstream' denomination. To be sure, back in the days of the mid-17th century, when the Reformation clerics drew up the Westminster Confession of Faith and the other 'Westminster Standards,' Presbyterians were very conservative, and strongly taught the so-called 'Double Predestination' doctrine—that is, the notion that God foreordains people to *both* Heaven, and to Hell. But modern Presbyterians in the PCUSA don't hold to such outlandish doctrines; in fact, I believe they're fairly 'liberal' in their theology."

Renee said, "Stephanie told me that the church's minister *never* preaches about Hell, or Predestination, of anything like that. His sermons are always about Jesus, and the love of God, and other 'positive' topics like that. And he never suggests that people go anywhere except to Heaven, after they die."

A man observed cynically, "Well, I think that a lot of the reason why attendance at Universalist churches has dropped off so much is that people think, 'If everyone is going to be saved anyway, why should I bother to go to church?' And since most 'mainstream' churches today practically preach Universalism anyway, people like Roger and Stephanie figure, 'Why not just go there, instead of to a tiny little storefront church like this one?'" Many persons in the group murmured their reluctant agreement with this thought.

Clement smiled slightly, and pointed out, "Some people think that our denomination losing its independent identity means that Universalism has *failed* as a movement; but it's really more the case that the so-called 'mainstream' churches have just quietly *adopted* many of our doctrines, over the years. So our *influence* has actually spread rather widely, through our entire religious culture." He thought for a moment, and then added, "Remember that the Puritans were some of most influential among our country's 'Founding Fathers,' and the Puritans were all strong Calvinists. And early Universalism was very strongly opposed to the kind of Calvinism that was being preached in the 17th and 18th centuries, such as was exemplified by Jonathan Edwards' infamous sermon, *Sinners in the Hands of an Angry God*." Most persons in the group muttered negative comments, in response to hearing Edwards' name, and his most well-known sermon.

Clement continued, "But by the time Universalism reached its peak in the mid- to late 19th century, that kind of rigorous Calvinism was passé. In fact, today, some modern Presbyterian and Reformed ministers are practically on the 'cutting edge,' in terms of their acceptance and utilization of the innovations in the modern world. For example, down in Garden Grove there's a Reformed minister named Robert Schuller, who actually holds his church services in a *drive-in movie theater!*" The others laughed heartily at this.

"I've heard of Robert Schuller," one of the women acknowledged.

Renee nodded, and said, "He probably represents the *future* of his denomination," and the others generally agreed with this observation.

One woman asked, "I wonder if things will ever change in the Catholic Church? I was raised Catholic, but as soon as I graduated from high school,

I ran away from it, and never looked back; thank God, that I soon found this Church!" She shivered involuntarily, and added, "I had to listen to so many sermons on 'Hell Fire' and 'the torments of Purgatory' when I was growing up, that I almost never thought of God as a *loving* God!"

Another woman nodded her agreement, and said, "My sister, and her husband and children are Catholic, so I've gone to a number of Catholic funerals over the years. And they *still* believe that most people—even those they call 'good Catholics'—will go to Purgatory for hundreds or even *thousands* of years, before they finally make it to Heaven!"

Clement suggested, "But things may someday change even for the stodgy old Roman Catholic church. You might have read that in 1959, their leader, Pope John XXIII, called for a general Council of the Catholic church—their first one since the late 19th century, which declared that bizarre doctrine of 'papal infallibility.' But I've read that John XXIII is a lot more 'liberal' than those reactionary curialists in the 19th century were; so it's possible that even *Catholics* may start to moderate their own doctrines, when they start to meet and discuss things next year."

The first woman said with distaste, "They can't possibly change enough, or fast enough, to suit me!"

One of the men asked, "Say, Clement; when did the Universalist Church start, anyway?"

Clement smiled (glad to have a rare and attentive audience for this topic), and replied, "Opposition to the doctrine of eternal misery in Hell really began to rise in various countries in the sixteenth century. But figures such as George de Benneville brought the doctrine known as 'Universal Restoration' to this country in the mid-18th century. Then John Murray, who came from England to America, was very influential in starting a formal 'Universalist Church' in this country; that's why he's often called 'the Father of American Universalism.' This new Universalist Church attracted important figures such as Elhanan Winchester and Hosea Ballou to it. Ballou, in particular, was so well-thought of by Universalists of his era that he was affectionately known as 'Father' Ballou. In terms of the numbers of members we had, and our level of influence in the larger American culture, Universalism probably peaked in about 1860-1870; at that time, we were one of the largest denominations in the country, and were many times larger than the 'Unitarian' church."

"I was born in the wrong century," one of the women half-joked, and the group laughed along with her.

Clement continued, "Whereas now, the situation is almost exactly reversed. The Universalist Church is down to about 35,000 members, nationwide; a lot of other denominations have far more members than that in individual *cities!* And the Unitarians are now four or five times larger than we are." He added in a sad tone, "It's really impossible for us to try and maintain our three Universalist colleges, much less seminarian training, with such small and diminishing numbers of members. And with fewer young people in the denomination, no one is growing up wanting to enter the Universalist ministry any more. So, I'm afraid it was practically inevitable, that we would finally either have to merge with the Unitarians, or else simply die out."

Dale said stubbornly, "I would vote for, 'die out'!" Several of the others in the group agreed with her.

Clement said hopefully, "But I want all of us to give this merger with the Unitarians a fair chance. We will now be known as the 'Unitarian Universalist Association'; we will now be part of a group that is almost five times larger than us, and has much greater national and financial resources."

One of the men said bitterly, "It figures that they'd give the *Unitarians* the 'top billing' in the new name!" and many others agreed.

One woman said despondently, "We're going to be *lost,* in this larger group. Our unique emphasis on the love and reconciling nature of God, will be completely forgotten, in no time at all."

One of the men suggested tentatively, "I think that the Unitarians believe in Universal Salvation, just as we do…"

The same woman countered, "But they don't *emphasize* it, like we do! Their major doctrine is the one that their denomination was named for: namely, the idea that Jesus is not 'God'—at least, not in the sense that God *the Father* is. Whereas *we* were always the ones standing up to oppose the Calvinist doctrine of Predestination, and rejecting the idea of Hell!"

Another man asked Clement, "Clem, are you even going to ever get a chance to ever *preach,* in this new 'merged' congregation?" All eyes in the group turned to Clement, eager to hear his reaction.

Clement (somewhat sheepishly) replied, "I'm going to be called an 'Associate Pastor' in the new congregation; current plans are for me to preach the Sunday sermon about… oh, maybe every four or six weeks, or so." This remark produced a chorus of groans from the group.

One of the women exclaimed passionately, "Just as I thought! I'm not joining this 'new' congregation, then!" A number of members of the group muttered their fervent agreement with her.

A man said half-jokingly, "Maybe I'll just start staying at home—and read the newspaper, or play golf, on Sunday mornings." A number of others voiced humorous agreement with this sentiment.

Clement raised his hands to quiet the group, and said firmly, 'Now, come on, folks; we've all got to give this merger a fair chance." Most of the faces remained stony and unconvinced, and he went on, "I've visited their church facility several times, and it's really a lovely setting. The property was bequeathed to them, and the church building is surrounded by shade trees, bushes, and flowers. Without us, they have nearly two hundred members; and they even have a Youth Group! And their minister, Jacob Castle, is very much involved in the social issues of our day; he's gone down to the Deep South several times, to participate in Freedom rides, and other Civil Rights actions, for example."

One of the men said with a cynical sneer, "Great, just what we need: a preacher who's going to be *locked up* half the time!" and the group laughed heartily.

Clement pointed out, "Well, another very positive thing about their congregation is that they have about a dozen members who are Negroes! As well as some members who are Mexican, or Puerto Rican." He shook his head, and admitted with regret, "That's one thing I've always been dissatisfied with about our congregation: we're 100% Caucasian." Several reluctant voices of agreement came from the group, and he continued, "Of course, it's not that we wouldn't very warmly *welcome* any other people who came to our services; but in the section of town that we're located in, there just aren't any Negro or Hispanic people living in the neighborhood. Whereas the new merged congregation is located much closer to the downtown area, so they consequently have a lot more members who belong to minority groups." The group remained silent.

Finally, Dale spoke up (her sentiments clearly shared by many in the group), saying in a voice trembling with emotion, "Clement, do we *have* to go along with this merger? Couldn't we just continue meeting here, as we are?" Several people in the group uttered enthusiastic agreement with this proposal.

One man said, "There are a number of very small churches downtown, that aren't affiliated with any 'denomination'! Maybe we could be like one of them...!" and a sudden surge of excitement and hope came over the group.

But Clement just shook his head, and said in a sad voice, "I'm afraid that we've just gotten too small for that. Renee and I have been paying part of the rent, and all of the utility bills from our own funds, for several months. The plain fact is that we just don't take in enough in our offerings, to support a congregation..."

One of the women said tentatively, "You... you could have *asked* us all to contribute more..."

Clement shook his head firmly, and said, "All of you are already contributing as much as you can possibly afford. No, what's happened here has been happening all over the country, in our churches; they've been closing their doors, or else merging with other congregations. I'm afraid that if we don't accept this merger, our days as a legitimate 'denomination' are numbered." There was an awkward silence, followed by gloom, that slowly descended over the room.

One of the men said acidly, "Then to *hell* with our personal convictions! Let's just do what Roger and Stephanie did, and *conform!* Let's all become Presbyterians, or Episcopalians, or Southern Baptists, or even Roman Catholics! Let's just forget all about the fact that 'God is Love,' and pretend that we believe in a fiery Hell, just like everyone else!" Several of those in the group agreed with his bitter sentiments.

With a slight smile, Clement suggested, "If you did join any of those other groups, I think you'd find that most of *them* no longer believe in a 'fiery Hell'; or if they do, they certainly never *mention* it, in their weekly sermons. For example, the Congregationalists—who themselves went through a merger a few years back, becoming the 'United Church of Christ'—have mostly been tacit Universalists for some time, going all the way back to the 19th century. Universalists often shared pulpits with Congregationalists, for example."

One of the women observed, "It's like you said earlier, Clement: these 'mainstream' churches *stole our idea,* without giving us any of the credit for it!' Several in the group fervently applauded this statement.

Clement said with a degree of pride, "Well, I for one am far from 'embarrassed' to be a Universalist minister, because I think that we've done a great deal for the Christian message, and for the world! Remember that it was as Universalists that the first two women—Lydia Ann Jenkins, and Olympia Brown—achieved full ministerial status in any denomination in the United States! Furthermore, we were always a movement of the *people,* of laymen and laywomen, and not a movement of the 'upper' social classes. Our ministers were originally men and women who felt themselves *called of God* to preach this message; they weren't 'ordained' by religious institutions, in the traditional sense. So if this merger with the Unitarians is the end of Universalism as a distinct religious denomination, so be it." He shrugged, then added, "But I'm definitely going to enter into this next step with an open mind, and an open heart; and let's just see where it leads us."

He looked around the group, making eye contact with as many as possible, and said, "Anyway, so I hope to see all of you—or at least *most* of you—next Sunday at 10:30 in our new home.' But if you choose to go elsewhere, or even to just stay home, I still want you to know how much your support and encouragement have meant to me in the past thirteen years that I've been privileged to be your minister. And may the Lord richly bless you, and your families and loved ones, in everything you do."

Dale said fervently, "And we want to thank *you,* Clement. We couldn't have asked for a better, more knowledgeable, or more *loving* person to be our minister." This sentiment was greeted by warm and loving applause, coming from the entire group.

Clement (struggling to control his emotions) finally said, "Well, I don't want to keep you here too long; I know you've all got other things to do today. Shall we stand, and close with a final word of prayer?" The group immediately agreed. They all stood up, and linked hands.

Clement turned to his wife, and said, "Renee, would you like to lead us?"

She nodded, then bowed her head and said, "Lord Jesus, we want to thank you for having brought this congregation together, and for having sustained us over the years. May we continue to share your love, as we return to our homes, as we go out into the world, and perhaps… as we go our separate ways. But we look forward eagerly to the day when we will *all* be together, in your loving presence: *forever!* We ask this in the name of the Father, and of the Son, and of the Holy Ghost; Amen."

"Amen!" said the congregation fervently.

Then they all gathered together, to exchange a final round of hugs, kisses, and well wishes…

PART FIVE

THE TWENTY-FIRST CENTURY (CALIFORNIA)

CHAPTER 9

Some Common Ground (August, 2016)

Eric Swenson (a young-looking man in his late 30s, with light brown hair, and a carefully trimmed beard) was finishing his Saturday morning jog in the park, and had just come to a halt, when two smiling young men (wearing short-sleeved white shirts with black ties, and black slacks and shoes) rode up to him on bicycles.

Eric abruptly stopped, facing them; and then quickly raised his hands up, saying (in mock fear), "Sorry, guys; you'll have to shoot me—I left my wallet at home!"

The two young men (neither of whom seemed any older than nineteen or twenty) looked dismayed, and one of them said apologetically, "No, no! We didn't mean to startle you. We're...

Eric smiled and dropped his hands, then said good-naturedly, "I was just kidding; you're Mormons, right?"

One of them (with evident relief) replied, "We are missionaries of the Church of Jesus Christ of Latter-Day Saints; but you can call us 'Mormons,' if you prefer."

The other one held out his hand, and said, "I'm Elder Whitson." As they shook hands, the other missionary said, "And I'm Elder Richards," and then he and Eric shook hands.

Eric said, "I'm Eric Swenson."

"It's nice to meet you," Elder Richards said pleasantly. "So are you out for a morning jog?"

Eric nodded, and said, "I'm a minister; so I like to go over in my head the sermon I'm planning for the next day, so I can make any last-minute changes; for some reason, jogging seems to stimulate my thought processes."

The two missionaries looked at each other, and then Elder Whitson said hesitantly, "You're a minister?" They both looked at him warily (almost as if expecting to be attacked by him, at any moment).

"I am," Eric admitted. Seeing their discomfiture, he added quickly, "But don't worry: I'm not one of those Evangelicals who thinks that Mormons are 'cultists,' and are well on their way to eternal damnation. I'm actually a Universalist."

"That's good," Elder Richards said (but still looking at Eric with reserve).

Elder Whitson frowned, and then asked, "You're a what?"

Eric explained, "Technically, I'm a minister in the *Unitarian* Universalist Association; but Universalism is a crucial part of my own theology."

"Oh; okay," Elder Whitson said, still looking confused. He turned to his fellow missionary, who whispered to him, "Universalists were covered in the MTC, remember? They're *really* 'liberal'; they don't believe that Jesus is God, for example." (Eric suppressed a smile, as he watched them whispering back and forth.)

When they turned their attention back to him, Eric asked, "So you two are missionaries?"

Both young men nodded, and Elder Whitson said, "Our mission lasts two years. Elder Richards has been out longer than I have; I'm still kind of a 'newbie.'" Elder Richards gave his companion a sharp look, and Elder Whitson blushed, and fell immediately silent.

Eric asked, "Just out of curiosity, why are you doing your 'missionary' work here, in the United States? I'll admit that the percentage of our population who identify themselves as 'Christian' has been diminishing in recent decades; but still, information about Christianity is readily available in this country: on TV, radio, print media, the Internet, and even social media. So aren't there places in, say, Africa or Asia, or even China and India, where you would find a relatively 'unreached' population?"

Elder Richards replied, "Our missionaries have a very *strong* presence in Africa and Asia, as well as everywhere else in the world."

Elder Whitson said proudly, "We have 75,000 active, full-time missionaries, serving in countries all around the world!"

"75,000?" Eric repeated, genuinely impressed. "My word: you folks have one-third as many *missionaries,* as we have *members* in my entire denomination!" and they all laughed.

Elder Richards said, "How much do you know about the LDS Church?"

"LDS Church?" Eric repeated, puzzled. "What's that?"

"Latter-Day Saints," Elder Richards explained. "The Mormon Church, as you called it."

Eric thought for a moment, then said, "Very little. Your church began in the 19th century, I believe; and it was founded by, let's see… Joseph Smith, right? William James mentioned him in his book, *Varieties of Religious Experience,* as I recall." The two missionaries nodded, and he continued, "What else? Let's see: your church is supposed to own a lot of properties and have pretty vast material wealth, which it often uses to support politically conservative causes, such as opposition to abortion, and to marriage equality; right?"

Elder Richards hesitated, then finally replied, "Uhh… yes; that's … uhh, pretty close."

Elder Whitson held out a blue paperback book to Eric, and asked, "Have you ever heard of the Book or Mormon? Or read any of it?"

Eric replied, "I've *heard* of it, of course; but I haven't read any of it."

Elder Whitson handed the book to Eric, saying, "Then please accept that book, with our compliments."

"Oh," Eric said, awkwardly accepting the book, but then realizing that he had no pockets into which the book would fit; so he just held on to it.

Elder Whitson looked directly into Eric's eyes, and said earnestly, "But before you read it, it's *very important* that you *pray* about it, and ask God to reveal the truth of the book to you."

Eric frowned, and then asked, "*Pray* before reading it? What for?"

Elder Whitson said eagerly, "Do you see that page I have marked, in your Book of Mormon?" Eric noticed that a small red tab was sticking out of the book, and he nodded. Elder Whitson continued, "Then do you see the passage that I highlighted?" Eric noticed that one particular verse was marked with a yellow highlighter, and he nodded again.

Elder Whitson said (quoting from memory), "That passage says, 'I would exhort you that ye would ask God, the Eternal Father, in the name of Christ, if these things are not true; and if ye shall ask with a sincere heart, with real intent, having faith in Christ, he will manifest the truth of it unto you, by the power of the Holy Ghost.'" Eric didn't say anything, but just continued looking skeptically at the two missionaries.

Elder Richards asked, "Do you believe the Bible?"

Surprised by the directness of this question, Eric replied, "Well, yes; although, perhaps, not in the same way that *you* might…"

Elder Richards continued, "When Joseph Smith was a young man, he was very confused about the large number of churches there were, and he wanted to find the truth. He read the Bible, and found in James 1:5 a principle that was very helpful. This verse reads: 'If any of you lack wisdom, let him ask of God, that giveth to all men liberally, and upbraideth not; and it shall be given him.' And he received the *answer* to his sincere and humble prayers!"

Elder Whitson pointed to the Book of Mormon that Eric was holding, and said breathlessly, "And that book was *revealed* to Joseph Smith, through the power of the Holy Ghost! It tells the story of Jesus Christ, appearing on this very continent?"

"What?" Eric replied, genuinely surprised. Looking at the two missionaries, he asked doubtfully, "You're saying that Jesus appeared here, in North America?"

Elder Richards clarified, "Well… here, and also perhaps South America. But definitely in the American continents!"

Frowning with obvious disbelief, Eric said, "When is this supposed to have taken place?"

"Right after his resurrection," Elder Whitson replied, with complete assurance. "The whole story is told right there, in the Book of Mormon." (Eric remained silent, looking at the two sincere young men facing him, realizing that they were completely serious.)

Finally, he said, "Well, that's a pretty important claim. But is there any *evidence* that Jesus appeared on this continent? Other than in your book, of course?"

Elder Richards said confidently, "There is a *lot* of evidence that Jesus appeared on this continent. Are you familiar with the Mesoamerican story of Quetzalcoatl, for example?"

"Sure," Eric replied. "I studied Native American religions and literature back in college." Seeing the earnest expression on the faces of the two missionaries, he said, "Wait a minute: are you trying to tell me that you think that Quetzalcoatl, the 'Feathered Serpent,' was Jesus?"

Elder Whitson was about to reply, when Elder Richards touched his arm, as if signaling for him to be silent. Then Elder Richards said in a matter-of-fact manner, "We're just saying that there is a lot of very interesting archaeological information, which strongly confirms the story in the Book of Mormon. But you need to read the book for yourself, to find out."

Elder Whitson added quickly, "And make sure that you *pray,* before you read it. Just go back to that page I have marked."

"Uhh… well, I'll… umm, take that under advisement," Eric replied noncommittally. He thought for a moment, then said, "This conversation is getting too heavy to be carried on out on the streets like this. After I finish my run, I usually head to the Coffee House across the street; can I buy you gentlemen a cup of coffee?"

"We don't drink coffee," Elder Richards said (somewhat self-righteously). He added, "That would violate the Word of Wisdom, given to us by the Lord through the Prophet Joseph Smith."

"Oh; right," Eric said, nodding his head. "Mormons don't smoke, drink alcohol, or drink coffee or tea." He thought for a moment, and then asked, "What about decaf? That's what I usually drink. Or how about a decaffeinated soda?"

Elder Whitson shook his head negatively, but Elder Richards hesitated for a moment, before explaining, "The Church announced a few years ago that caffeinated sodas *could* be drunk by members of the Church. But most of us—particularly those of us out on the mission field—feel that, for health reasons, caffeinated beverages are still off limits."

Elder Whitson said helpfully, "But if your usual routine is to go to that coffee shop after your jog, we're certainly willing to come with you, so that we can continue our conversation."

"Sounds good, then," Eric said, and he motioned for the two missionaries to follow after him, and the two of them began walking their bikes behind Eric, toward the nearest crosswalk.

While they were waiting for the light to change, Elder Whitson admitted, "I'm afraid that I don't know much about the Universalist denomination. Is that a Protestant denomination, like a Presbyterian, or a Baptist?"

The light changed, and they began walking across the street, as Eric tried to suppress his smile, then replied, "Not really." Elder Whitson looked puzzled by this answer, but interested; but Eric did not elaborate any further. The two missionaries then busied themselves locking up their bikes in the shop's large bike rack. Then the three of them entered the shop.

After he ordered his coffee, Eric said to the two missionaries, "So what can I get you guys? My treat."

"Nothing, thanks," Elder Richards said primly. Eric Whitson looked as if he wanted to say something, but he looked cautiously over at the senior missionary, and then remained silent.

"Oh, come on," Eric encouraged. "We've got some serious theological discussion ahead of us, and you guys just gave me a free book; I need to give you *something,* in return."

Elder Richards shrugged, and then said, "A bottle of water, then." Elder Whitson nodded his agreement, so Eric placed the order, and received back two bottles of water, which he handed to the missionaries.

They located an empty wooden table to sit at, and took their seats. But no sooner had they sat down, when the cashier announced, "Eric?" so he got up, and went to get his black decaf coffee.

As he returned to the table, he noticed that a number of other patrons of the shop were staring at the two missionaries, with very "negative" expressions on their faces. Eric smiled to himself, and thought, *So I guess Universalists and Mormons have got something in common, after all: **social ostracism.***

He sat back down at the table, and noticed Elder Whitson looking around the shop, and frowning.

"Coffee's got a really strong odor," the younger missionary observed, wrinkling his nose with distaste.

"I always liked the smell of hot coffee brewing when I was young; especially on cold winter mornings," Eric said, adding, "And I couldn't wait until I grew up, and could drink it." He chuckled, and then admitted, "But then I grew up and found out that coffee has a somewhat *bitter* taste; which is why a lot of people drown their coffee in cream and sugar."

"Why drink it, then?" Elder Whitson asked, with genuine curiosity.

Eric shrugged, and then replied, "At some times of day—such as early morning, mid-morning, afternoon, and early evening—a warm beverage like coffee or tea just seems... well, *appropriate* to the situation." He took a very small sip from his hot coffee, then looked at both missionaries and said with a slight smile, "Okay, back to business. You two are 'missionaries'; so does that mean that you view those of us in America as 'heathens' who need to 'repent and believe the Gospel,' or else we'll spend eternity in fiery torment?"

"No, not at all," Elder Richards said, shaking his head negatively.

Eric nodded, and said with a smile, "I'm glad to hear that."

"You see, we know that there are three 'Kingdoms of Glory,' after this life," Elder Whitson eagerly explained. Seeing the look of disapproval he was receiving from his older companion, he whispered to him apologetically, "Remember that he's a *minister!* So we should be able to 'skip ahead' in the Lessons, a little bit. Besides, we already told him a little about Joseph Smith, the Book of Mormon, and modern revelation, right?" Elder Richards sighed, but reluctantly nodded at his companion, to indicate that he should continue.

Elder Whitson told Eric, "You see, the Apostle Paul told us in First Corinthians 15:40-41 that there were three levels of glory in the afterlife."

Eric looked puzzled, and then asked, "Three levels? Are you talking about the passage where Paul said that in the resurrection there were 'celestial bodies,' and 'terrestrial bodies'?"

"That's right! You know your Scriptures well, sir!" Elder Whitson complimented, "So there are three levels of glory: the *Telestial,* or lowest realm; the *Terrestrial,* or second level; and the third and highest realm is the *Celestial* realm! These correspond to the three levels of glory that Paul mentioned in that passage."

Genuinely confused, Eric asked, "You mean the glory he mentioned of the sun, the moon, and the stars? I really don't think that Paul had in mind *three separate levels* in the afterlife, or..."

Elder Whitson continued, "Paul also said in Second Corinthians 12:2 that he was once 'caught up to the third heaven.' Modern-day revelation has really clarified this for us, in Section 76 of the Doctrine and Covenants—which is another one of our Sacred Scriptures." But seeing another sharp look he received from his senior companion, he stopped speaking immediately, looking embarrassed again.

Eric drank some of his coffee as he thought for a moment, and then said, "So I take it that the lowest of these three levels is kind of a 'hellish' environment, where people are in endless misery?"

"Not at all," Elder Richards replied. He explained, "As my companion said, the lowest level of glory is called the 'Telestial'; the people in this level are those who continued in their sins, and did not repent in this life."

Eric looked closely at the missionary, as he asked, "But are these people *punished,* or *tormented,* in any way?"

Elder Richards shook his head, and said, "Compared to our earthly experience, the 'glory of the telestial... surpasses all understanding.'" [D&C 76:89]

"Really?" Eric said, both surprised and pleased. "And this is the *lowest* level, right?"

"That's right," Elder Richards agreed.

Now genuinely interested, Eric asked, "So what are the other two levels?"

The missionary continued, "The second level is known as the 'Terrestrial.' This level is for people who do not accept the 'fulness' of the gospel of Jesus Christ, but nevertheless live honorable lives."

Eric nodded, and said, "So this level is even better than the 'Telestial' level, right?" The two missionaries nodded. Eric smiled slightly, and added, "And I presume that you're now going to tell me just what you mean by the 'fulness of the gospel,' right?" and the two missionaries grinned, and nodded.

He asked, "So: what's the highest level?"

Elder Whitson said eagerly, "That is the *Celestial* level! This level is for those who have repented of their sins, *and* received the ordinances of the gospel, *and* kept the associated covenants." He looked directly into Eric's eyes, and said fervently, "You see, that's why it's so important for us to do our mission work in *this* country, as well as in other countries."

Eric was puzzled, and asked, "Then what do you mean by 'the ordinances of the gospel,' and 'associated covenants'? Are you referring to baptism, or confirmation? Or maybe the Lord's Supper?"

"Baptism is the first covenant," Elder Whitson confirmed.

Eric said, "Well, most Christians in this country have already been baptized. So what is the next..."

Elder Richards said firmly, "Baptism must be administered by one holding the proper *authority.*"

Not understanding this remark, Eric replied casually, "Well, I'm sure they were baptized by someone in the priesthood, or the ministry. So..." But both missionaries shook their heads negatively.

Genuinely surprised, Eric asked the missionaries, "So you think that baptism has to be administered by someone from *your* church?" They immediately nodded their agreement. Eric shook his head in amazement, and then observed, "Not even the Roman Catholic church is *that* 'picky' about baptism!"

"It's more than just that," Elder Whitson explained. "The investigators being baptized must have developed faith in Christ, have repented of their transgressions, and committed themselves to live lives of moral worthiness."

Elder Richards added, "They must also vow to obey the Word of Wisdom, and pay tithing."

Eric suppressed a smile, and asked, "So you don't believe in *infant baptism,* huh?"

Elder Whitson shook his head again, and said, "Children less than eight years of age do not need to be baptized; they are redeemed through the mercy of Christ."

"I see," Eric replied. He thought for a moment, took another swallow of his coffee, and then said, "But that's quite a bit of responsibility to impose on someone being baptized. Suppose you had someone was *wasn't* baptized; does that mean they couldn't go to one of your Heavens? Or do you have some kind of 'Hell,' where people are sent who didn't meet all of your requirements, and..."

Elder Whitson said soberly, "Those who have lived wickedly will go to Spirit Prison, rather than Paradise."

Before Eric could comment, Elder Richards added, "But in Spirit Prison, they *will* have the opportunity to hear the Gospel; and if they accept it, they will join the righteous in Paradise."

"Really?" Eric said, once again pleasantly surprised. "So you believe in a form of post-mortem or 'after death' opportunity for salvation?" The two elders nodded their heads, and Eric said, "That's *very* interesting. But how do they get around the requirement of baptism, and that other stuff?"

Elder Whitson impulsively blurted out, "We can perform the ordinance of baptism *for them*—just as the Apostle Paul said in First Corinthians 15:29!"

Eric thought about this for a long moment, and then asked, "That's the 'baptism for the dead' passage, right?" The missionaries nodded their agreement again. Eric pondered this information, and then finally observed, "But there must be *billions* of people who haven't been baptized by a member of your church. Every one of you would have to be baptized for literally *thousands* of people! That would be completely unworkable." But both Elders just looked at Eric calmly, seemingly undaunted by this task.

Eric shrugged, and then asked, "Now, what happens if someone ultimately *refuses* to accept your version of the Gospel? Do they still go to one of your heavens, or..."

"There is a place called 'Perdition,' or 'Outer Darkness'," Elder Richards explained. "Those who finally refuse to accept the Gospel will go there forever."

Elder Whitson added quickly, "But hardly anyone goes there—only beings like Satan, or others who *absolutely* refuse to accept the Gospel! Nearly everyone else goes to one of the three levels of Heaven—and most go to either the Terrestrial, or the Celestial realm!"

Eric nodded, and said, "So if I died, I could hope to go to the Celestial realm?"

The two Elders looked at each other for a moment, and Elder Richards finally said, "You could... *if* you followed all of the commandments and ordinances of the Gospel."

Eric smiled slightly, and observed, "If I became a *Mormon,* in other words."

Elder Richards hesitated, then admitted, "Well, yes." Energetically, he added, "But we would be more than happy to *teach* the Gospel to you! We have a series of Lessons that are carefully prepared by the Church for all Investigators, and…"

Eric interrupted, "I'm quite satisfied with my own church; but thanks anyway." He took a large swallow of his coffee.

The two Elders looked disappointed, so Eric added in a conciliatory tone, "But I'm glad to have had this conversation. I understand your beliefs much better, now. And I'm glad to see that we have some 'common ground.'"

"Common ground?" Elder Whitson repeated, and then added hopefully, "What are those things?"

Eric said, "Basically, you folks *are* Universalists. You basically think that nearly everyone goes to Heaven—except for those very few who are unrepentant to the end, and wind up in Outer Darkness." He shrugged, and then added, "And even though I'm a Universalist minister, I frankly wouldn't object *too* loudly if a select few individuals—the Hitlers, and Stalins; or the virulent atheists like the Marquis de Sade, who simply refuse to even *consider* God and religion—didn't actually make it to Heaven, or even were ultimately annihilated. And I also wouldn't mind not making it to your *highest* level of Heaven—because you told me that even the *lowest* level is still pretty good, right?"

Elder Whitson said passionately, "But the Celestial realm is so far beyond the other realms, that you should be satisfied with nothing less! In the Celestial realm, our earthly marriages continue, and we can have children throughout eternity! And… eventually, by the power and gift of God, we can become *like* our Heavenly Father! This is the glorious doctrine of *Exaltation!*" Elder Richards looked sharply at Elder Whitson, who again looked chagrined, and fell silent.

Eric said quietly, "So I could become a *God,* right?" The two Elders nodded their heads slightly. Eric said, "You know, I saw some program on PBS a while back that made that point; but I really thought they must have gotten it wrong." He looked the two young men in the eyes, and then asked soberly, "So you *really* believe that you can become Gods? Become like the

Creator of the universe?" The two young men nodded affirmatively. Eric smiled, and then said lightly, "Well, I think that you and I will just have to *agree to disagree* on that particular point! I really don't think that I'm ever going to be able to measure up to the high intellectual standards of the job; I'd be a poor designer of the Genetic Code, for example!"

Elder Richards said quickly, "But this is no more than what the Bible says in Romans 8:16-17" that we are 'children of God… heirs of God, and joint-heirs with Christ.' Latter-Day Saints see us as God's 'children' in a full and complete sense. By following the teachings of Jesus, we can become partakers of the divine nature,' as Second Peter 1:4 says. We each possess seeds of divinity, and can progress toward perfection…"

Eric held up his hand to stop him, then looked at his watch, and said, "Anyway, I need to get back and finalize my sermon for tomorrow. But I thank you two gentlemen for a very stimulating and enlightening conversation." They all stood up and shook hands, and then headed to the exit. (Eric noted that a number of people glanced in their direction as they left—with the expressions on their faces ranging from curiosity, to humor, to outright contempt.)

As they reached the sidewalk outside, Elder Whitson held up his bottle, and said. "Thanks for the water."

"You're welcome," Eric replied. They all shook hands again, and Eric jogged off.

As the two missionaries returned to their work… as did Eric.

CHAPTER 10

THE TIMES THEY ARE A-CHANGIN' (September 2016)

As he neared the end of his Monday morning jog, Eric thought, *I'll cut across the park, so I can stop at the Natural Foods Store before I head home.* He turned off from the cement walkway that surrounded the park, and headed in a diagonal direction, toward the shopping center directly across from the park.

He jogged past the basketball court, which had only one person playing on it; a tall silver-haired man with glasses who was wearing Levis, who put up a long shot just as Eric was moving past. The ball bounced off the side of the rim, and right toward Eric; he stopped to catch the ball, then gently bounce-passed the ball back to the older man.

"Thanks," the silver-haired man called out, as he pulled up for another long-range shot—which dropped cleanly through the basket this time, without even touching the rim.

"Nice shot," Eric complimented, taking advantage of this brief pause to take a swallow from the water bottle that was clipped to his belt.

The older man chuckled, and then said, "I'm just waiting for my brother to get here; we chase down each other's missed shots."

"That's helpful," Eric observed, capping his water bottle again. "So are both you guys retired, and this is your weekly workout?"

"We're not retired," the older man replied. He added with a smile, "Both of us are in professions where the 'normal retirement age' is… well, somewhat higher than average."

Intrigued, Eric asked, "So what professions are those?"

"My brother is a psychologist," came the reply. The older man looked Eric over for a long moment, and then said in a friendly tone, "So do you think you can guard an old 'retired' guy like me?"

Embarrassed, Eric said apologetically, "Uhh… I didn't mean to imply…"

The older man laughed easily, then bounced the ball to Eric, and said, "Come on; you can have the ball to start; first one to ten wins, two points a basket; make it, take it?"

"Uhh, sure," Eric replied (not exactly sure what the man meant, by this last reference). He dribbled the ball a few times tentatively, then joined the older man on the court. He thought, *I'd better go easy on him; I wouldn't want him to have a heart attack, or throw out his knee, while I was playing against him…*

The older man came up to guard Eric, but Eric hurriedly put up a shot, that clanged harmlessly off the rim.

The older man jogged over a few steps to collect the rebound, then took the ball back behind the free throw circle, and waited for Eric to come guard him.

Eric approached him tentatively, extending his hands, thinking, *I'll let him get past me and take his shot, and…* but the older man swiftly spun around and deftly dribbled past a surprised Eric, laying the ball up for an easy basket.

The older man passed the ball back to Eric, saying, "Check!" and then headed to the half-court line; he turned, and waited for Eric to pass him back the ball.

Eric passed the ball to him, then came up to guard the older man, with serious intent, thinking, *Okay, old dude; you got me that time. But this time I'm ready for you, and…* but the older man smoothly rolled around and past Eric in the opposite direction, then raced to the basket, where he spun around underneath it, and put up a scoop shot that fell cleanly through the hoop.

"Dang," Eric whistled, with growing admiration. *He might have to 'go easy' on me,* he thought. Within the space of two minutes, the score was 10-0, and the game was over.

The older man grinned as he came over to shake Eric's hand. "Good game," he said.

Eric chuckled good-naturedly as they shook hands, and said, "I'm just glad I didn't have any *money* on the game!" and they both laughed easily.

The older man said, "I take it basketball's not exactly 'your game.'"

Eric replied, "I used to run cross-country in high school, but team sports were not really my thing." Apologetically, he said, "And I really am sorry for what I said earlier; I didn't mean to imply that you were…"

The older man raised his hand to stop Eric, and said with a smile, "No offense taken, I assure you. Most people my age *are* retired, these days."

Eric asked tentatively, "You said your brother was a psychologist; is that what you…"

The older man said softly, "I'm a Catholic priest." He looked closely at Eric, waiting to see his reaction.

Eric was surprised, and it took him a moment to recover. "A priest? That's… uhh, I mean… I guess I'm surprised that you…"

"It's Monday; my day off," the older man explained. "Although usually I only get the mornings off; I typically go visit members of our congregation who are hospitalized or in seniors' homes, in the afternoon." He held out his hand to shake, and said, "My name's Matthew O'Sullivan; but please call me 'Matt.'"

"Eric Swenson," Eric replied warmly, as they shook hands again.

Matt smiled and noted, "Well, I'm relieved that you didn't run away after I told you the line of work I was in. Sometimes, people—especially inactive Catholics—look at Catholic priests as if we were Satan himself…!" and Eric laughed heartily.

Eric had a wry smile on his face, as he said, "Actually, I'm a minister myself; of the Unitarian Universalist congregation over on Wayfield Avenue." This time, it was Eric's turn to carefully watch and gauge the other man's reaction.

Matt frowned as he studied Eric's face closely, and then said, "Wait: I've seen you before; last June, weren't you one of us up on stage at the interfaith gathering supporting local Muslims, after Omar Mateen had shot some fifty people in that gay nightclub in Orlando, a few weeks before that?"

"I was," Eric admitted. Looking more closely at Matt, he admitted, "I should have recognized you; but you look different without… umm, you know…"

Matt laughed easily, and explained, "I have to wear my 'working clothes' to an event like that; it seems to make a bigger impression on both the public and the mass media if someone wearing a 'Roman collar' is acknowledging that gays and lesbians have a perfect right to socialize, and that Muslims aren't responsible for the violent acts of a few crazed individuals who *call* themselves 'Muslim.'"

"I know the feeling," Eric admitted, adding with a chuckle, "Unfortunately, I don't even *have* a 'clerical collar'; a suit and tie are my usual 'work clothes.'" He looked over at Matt, and asked, "So do you participate in political activism very often?"

Matt smiled ruefully, and replied, "Not like I did when I was younger. I fancied myself as one of those 'fighting young priests' during the seventies and eighties; and then after I got married, my wife and I participated in political activism quite a bit, and..."

"Your *wife?*" Eric interrupted, his face perplexed. "I thought that..."

Matt chuckled lightly, and explained, "I fell in love with an ex-Nun, and received a release from my priestly vows, so that we could be married." He paused for a moment, and then added softly, "But after my wife passed, thirteen years ago—she contracted ovarian cancer—I eventually applied for reinstatement to the active priesthood; and was accepted."

"I'm so sorry about your wife," Eric said, gently squeezing Matt's shoulder sympathetically. "That's horrible."

"At the time, it was completely devastating to me," Matt admitted. He shrugged his shoulders, and then added, "But as Tennyson said in his poem, *In Memoriam: A.H.H,* 'Tis better to have loved and lost, than never to have loved at all.'"

"That's very true," Eric agreed. He was about to ask another question, but he stopped when Matt's cell phone in his jeans hip pocket rang.

Pulling out his phone, Matt winked at Eric and said with a sigh, "Cell phones are the bane of our modern existence; they represent the end of privacy, and uninterrupted conversations," but then he looked at the Caller I.D., and said into the phone genially, "So where are you? Tired of having me kick your butt?"

Eric could just barely overhear the reply: "You wish! No, I have to cancel this week. I just got a call: one of my long-time clients got dumped by her lover last night, and she insisted that she had to see me this morning, or 'I just don't know *what* I might do!' She called my emergency number, and she's meeting me at the office in two minutes. I sent you a text about this, earlier."

Matt said, "Oh, right; I always forget to check for those," and he pressed a few buttons on his phone, and then said, "Aha; I see it now."

"Want to have our game later?" the voice from the phone said. "I should be done in an hour or two."

Matt replied, "Can't make it; I'm due at the Marian Home for the Elderly. Mrs. Martinelli wants the sacrament, again; she's convinced that she's 'going' this week."

"Ahh, she's been saying that for nearly two years," the voice replied with a laugh, then added, "I think she's just got the 'hots' for you!"

"*You* wish," Matt replied, laughing. Changing the subject, he said, "You and Brahmvir still 'on' for dinner this Thursday?"

"Absolutely," replied the unseen voice. "This means I'll just have to kick your ass twice as badly on the court next Monday."

In a deadpan tone, Matt said, "As an experienced psychologist, Mr. O'Sullivan, you should be aware of the nefarious effect of such *delusions...*"

The voice chuckled, and said, "See ya, Matt. Take care, bro."

"Later," Matt replied, and he ended the phone call. Turning to Eric, he said, "That was my brother; our basketball game's off this week."

"That's too bad," Eric said. "Do you get to see him often, or..."

"We see each other all the time," Matt replied. "I'm having dinner with him and his husband this Thursday."

"His *husband?*" Eric said, genuinely confused.

Matt laughed, and explained, "My brother Mark is gay; he and his partner Brahmvir got married last year, as soon as it was legal. I even said a blessing for them, after their civil ceremony." He looked at Eric quizzically, then asked, "So is your denomination opposed to same-sex marriage, or..."

Eric shook his head vigorously, and said, "No, far from it; we UUAs strongly advocate equal rights for lesbians, gays, bisexuals, and all transgender persons—and *definitely* including the right to marry. I'm just... well, surprised that *you,* a Catholic priest, are ... umm, apparently okay with it."

With a slight smile, Matt acknowledged, "Well, I have to admit that I'm a bit on the *liberal* or 'progressive' side among Catholic priests," and they both laughed. Turning serious again, Matt explained, "But things are gradually changing, in the Catholic Church—particularly under our new Pope, Francis I."

Eric nodded, and noted, "Yes, I remember reading that the new Pope apparently isn't *quite* as homophobic as his predecessor was."

Matt grimaced, then observed, "His predecessor was Benedict XVI— or 'Ratzinger,' to those of us who weren't exactly *fans* of his—who wrote in 2005 wrote that homosexuality was 'an intrinsic moral evil' and an 'objective disorder.' Whereas Francis, shortly after he was elected pope, told an interviewer who asked him about gays and lesbians, 'If they accept the Lord and have good will, who am I to judge them? They shouldn't be marginalized. The tendency is not the problem… they're our brothers.' He even used the English word 'gay,' although his interview was conducted in Italian."

"That's interesting," Eric said, nodding respectfully.

Matt added, "The gay magazine *The Advocate* even named Francis their 'Person of the Year' in 2013."

Eric asked with interest, "So does that mean that gay, lesbian, and transgender folks will be given 'equal rights' in the Catholic church, before long?"

With a rueful smile, Matt admitted, "I'm afraid that's far too optimistic; but at least, I think that we're finally moving in the *right direction.* For example, in his April 2016 document *Amoris Laetitia*—'The Joy of Love'—Francis said that the Church should welcome both gay people and unmarried straight couples who are living together, although he still opposed same-sex *marriages.* But more recently, he reportedly has privately suggested that the Catholic church might be accepting of 'civil unions'—although not 'marriages'—for same-sex partners, so that they can get the medical care benefits and property rights that are available to heterosexual couples." He shrugged, and then added, "On the other hand, Francis was also critical last August of schools that he claimed were teaching schoolchildren that they can simply 'choose their gender'—which is, to be sure, a ludicrous idea. So Francis obviously is still 'learning on the job,'" and Eric laughed.

Matt suddenly turned serious, and asked anxiously, "Say, I'm probably keeping you from something important; am I?"

Eric shook his head, and replied, "Actually, I was just taking a short-cut across the park, on my way to the Natural Foods Store."

Matt brightened, and said, "That's where I go after our game every week, to get my 'Health Shake'! Mind if I accompany you? I can jog along, if you're still jogging…"

Eric shook his head and said, "My run is over for the day; so I'd love to go there with you—this is a fascinating conversation!" So Matt picked up his basketball and put it back into his gym bag, and the two men began walking to the side of the park that was just across the street from the shopping center.

Matt asked Eric, "So you said that you were a Unitarian Universalist minister?"

"That's right," Eric replied. He added sheepishly, "You probably don't know anything about us; we're a pretty small…"

Matt interjected, "Your denomination resulted from a merger of the older Unitarian church, with the Universalist church, right?"

Surprised, Matt said, "That's right; we merged the two groups back in 1961." He thought for a moment, and then said, "I guess being a UU is kind of 'in my blood'; my grandfather Clement was a minister in the old Universalist Church, and he was actually still ministering when they had the 1961 merger. He became a minister in the new UUA organization, but I've heard from my Dad that Granddad said he always felt that the 'Universalist' branch got kind of 'lost' after the merger; but since the Universalists were only about one-fifth the size of the Unitarians at the time, however, that's not surprising." He looked over at Matt, and then said cautiously, "Of course, a lot of 'Christian' churches don't consider us to be their religious 'brothers and sisters'; we're not members of the World Council of Churches, for example."

"Neither is my Church," Matt said with a smile.

Surprised, Eric asked, "The Catholic Church isn't in the WCC? I … well, I guess I just assumed that you were."

Matt chuckled, and explained, "Oh, we've started participating in some of the WCC's committees, and we attend all their major meetings as 'outside observers'; but we're not 'members,' and perhaps never will be." He sighed, and admitted, "Some of the 'hardliners' in our Church still feel that joining an organization such as the WCC would be lowering our *status*—reducing us from being **THE** 'Church established by Christ,' to just being **A** 'Church established by Christ.'" He shook his head, and added sarcastically, "Those dinosaurs don't seem to remember a little thing called *Vatican II*, back in the '60s."

Eric nodded, and said, "Well, I doubt that your church would feel very warmly toward us, either. Since my denomination firmly repudiates the doctrine of a 'Hell' of eternal conscious torment, a lot of so-called 'Christians' felt that our old Universalist branch wasn't 'Christian'—even though the Bible, and human reason, were their only standards for their doctrines. And we UUAs firmly believe in the ultimate reconciliation of all persons with God, and..."

Matt interrupted, "Actually, I have a *lot* of sympathy with that viewpoint, myself. I've never preached a sermon about Hell in my entire life, and whenever I perform a funeral Mass, I usually suggest to the grieving family and friends that the deceased is now in Christ's presence— rather than just at the beginning of some thousands of years in *Purgatory*, or something like that."

"Really?" Eric replied, genuinely surprised. "I thought that Roman Catholics were strong believers in the doctrine of eternal torment in Hell, and..."

"We're changing," Matt explained. "Oh, the *Catechism of the Catholic Church*—which John Paul II ramrodded through—still refers to 'Hell' as a 'state of definitive self-exclusion from communion with God and the blessed,' and asserts that the punishments of hell are 'eternal fire'; but they *emphasize* it as being 'eternal separation from God,' rather than focusing on it as a place of fiery torment. [1033-1035] But thankfully, the days of the 19th century English Catholic priest John Furniss—who wrote some thoroughly disgusting books for *children*, describing in lurid detail the fiery torments of Hell—and the days of 'Father Arnall,' who preached the sermon on Hell that so terrified the young James Joyce in his *Portrait of the Artist as a Young Man*, are behind us; hopefully, forever."

Eric complimented, "I'm glad to hear that." He thought for a moment, and then asked, "So Catholics no longer believe in Purgatory?"

Matt replied, "We still officially believe in Purgatory: that is, in a post-mortem state of *purification* that is necessary, before we're ready to enter heaven. But the terrifying visions of Purgatory that came from mystics like

Catherine of Genoa are pretty much 'out of fashion' these days. To the extent that anyone still thinks about Purgatory today, it's probably viewed as being more like 'solitary confinement' in a prison, than as a place of torment and punishment."

Eric acknowledged, "Actually, although we Universalists are culturally conditioned by our semi-Protestant background to automatically and strongly *reject* the notion of Purgatory, I have to admit that our own conception of the necessity of post-mortem punishment to make one ready for an eternity in Heaven is probably *very* similar to your idea of Purgatory."

"That's interesting," Matt said. He shrugged, then observed, "I personally think that the notion of something like a 'Purgatory' makes a great deal of *sense;* I mean, how many of us would be able to get along with everyone in Heaven, if we just remained the way that we currently are?"

Eric nodded his agreement, and said, "The fundamentalists and Evangelicals who think we could somehow just be 'Zapped,' and then transferred directly into Heaven in a state of perfection, are dreaming, it seems to me." He thought for a moment as they waited at a stoplight to cross the street, and then asked, "Don't Catholics also believe in a place called 'Limbo,' that's where unbaptized babies are supposed to go to?"

Matt smiled, and said, "Actually, that's one of the very few things that Benedict XVI did that I really liked: he formally abolished the doctrine of Limbo in 2007." He collected his thoughts, and then explained, "Even back when he was a cardinal, Ratzinger had pointed out that Limbo had never been a 'definitive truth' of the Catholic faith, but was only a 'theological hypothesis'—albeit one that was taught to millions of American Catholics via the old *Baltimore Catechism.*"

The light changed, and they began walking across the street toward the Natural Foods Store, as Matt added, "So Catholics are finally allowed now to 'officially' believe that infants who die are taken to Heaven—whether they've received Christian baptism, or not; which is pretty much what most modern Catholics believe *anyway!* So now, Baptism is simply the rite to initiate someone into the Church: it's not an action needed to 'remove the stain of Original Sin' from a sinful human being, who would otherwise be *damned!*"

"That's very interesting," Eric said, as they entered the Natural Foods Store, and headed to the Deli section.

The young African-American woman at the counter said to Eric warmly, "Morning, Eric: want your usual?"

Eric nodded, and handed her some cash. She took out a large cup of fruity beverage from a nearby cooler, and handed it to him, then gave him his change… which he promptly stuffed into the "TIPS" cup next to the cash register.

"Thanks, Eric," she said with a smile. "See you in church on Sunday."

"Thanks, Alyssa," he replied, stepping aside to make way for Matt.

Alyssa smiled at Matt, and said, "Good morning, Father Matt: what's it going to be today?"

He looked at the menu for a moment, then replied, "Better let me have a large 'Liquid Lunch'; I've got a lot of visitations this afternoon."

"You've got it," she replied, then went to a nearby dispenser and filled a cup with a greenish liquid (of "smoothie" texture), which she then put a lid on, and handed to him. When he handed her a prepaid gift card to pay for the purchase, she just shook her head and said, "Forget it; it's on the house, today." Pointing to the two men standing in front of her, she commented, "It looks like you two have got some 'heavy' stuff to talk about!"

Matt smiled, and said gratefully, "Why, thank you, Alyssa." He reached into his pocket and pulled out several dollar bills, which he placed into the "TIPS" cup.

"Thanks, Father Matt," she said. "Have a blessed day!"

"You, too," he replied, and he stepped over to join Eric, who was glancing at a nearby display of magazines.

"Want to sit inside?" Eric asked. "Or outside?"

Matt suggested, "Let's go outside; it's such a nice day." So they sipped their beverages, as they walked through the sliding doors of the entrance, and then headed to the metal chairs and tables on the patio outside.

After they had sat down, and each taken several thirsty swallows of their beverages, Matt asked Eric, "Did I hear Alyssa say she'd see you in church this Sunday?"

Eric nodded, and replied, "Yes, she's a long-term member of our congregation; and she's a *great* singer, too—the altos in our choir would be lost without her." He took another sip from his beverage, and said despondently, "She's also one of the very few African-Americans in our congregation; I wish we could attract more."

Matt nodded, and asked, "Where is your church located?"

"In Riverside Haven Heights," he said quietly, slightly embarrassed.

Matt grinned, and said, "Well, that's the problem," and they both chuckled.

Eric explained sheepishly, "The property was given to us as a bequest, as was our main building; we just can't afford to move anywhere else, and build another church from scratch. So we're pretty much stuck where we're at… even though most of our members now are middle-class, or even lower-middle class." He looked at Matt with curiosity, and asked, "So do you have a regular church congregation? Or…"

Matt replied, "I'm Pastor of the Church of the Redeemer, off Frankport Way."

"Church of the Redeemer?" Eric exclaimed, genuinely surprised. With renewed respect, he said, "Dang, my friend; you're ministering right in the 'hood,' then!" and they both laughed.

Matt said, "I've been there forty years; it was my first parish assignment, so I have a strong sentimental attachment to it: but they also stood right with me after I resigned my priesthood to get married, and then attended the church with my wife—now as lay members—and I was, surprisingly, reassigned there after I was accepted back into the active priesthood, after my wife Maggie had passed. So I feel very much 'among *family*' at Redeemer." He took a slow swallow of his beverage, to quiet the strong emotions that were showing in his voice. He took a deep breath, and then added, "My brother Mark and his husband Brahmvir go there, as well."

"Interesting," Eric commented, then took a sip of his own drink. He observed, "That name 'Brahmvir'; that sounds East Indian."

"Brahm's folks were from India," Matt confirmed. "But he's Sikh, not Hindu—or Christian. But since the nearest Sikh Temple is forty miles from here, he and Mark attend Mass with us on Sundays—but they also go to the Temple when they have festivals, and such."

Eric nodded respectfully, and said, "The world is definitely getting more multicultural—which is great!"

"I agree," Matt replied. They both lifted their beverages in a "toasting" gesture, then drank from them.

Eric looked at Matt, then asked, "If you've been a priest for... what, forty years, you said?" Matt nodded, and Eric shook his head, and noted, "You must have seen a *lot* of changes in that time!"

"I have," Matt admitted. He thought for a moment, then recounted, "I'm from an Irish Catholic family; and we lived in what was originally an almost-exclusively Irish Catholic neighborhood. But those kinds of 'ethnic' neighborhoods exclusively for whites are gone for good; for which I'm very glad! But we still have 'ethnic' neighborhoods for a lot of ethnic minorities—like the 'Little Saigon' area for Vietnamese, just south of downtown; or the 'Delhi Americana' housing development that a lot of upscale local East Indians live in. The neighborhood of my parish church was originally mostly black; but now, Latinos make up about 60% of our congregation, and we say as many Masses in Spanish as we say in English. And these different ethnic groups are all strongly culturally different, as well; about the only thing they all agree on, is that we all *hate* the possibility of Donald Trump becoming President!" and they both laughed.

Eric said with a chuckle, "Well, let's just hope that never happens."

Matt added, "We've got only a handful of traditional Irish or Italian Catholics in our congregation; and almost all of them are my age, or even older." He looked at Eric, and asked, "So what about you? How long have you been a minister?"

"Twelve years; all of it at the same church," he replied. He sighed, and then commented, "The main change I've seen over the years, is that it's getting much harder to convince people to come to a small *church* like ours on Sundays; there's just too much competition from cable TV, movies, the shopping mall, and the sports arena—not to mention the 'seeker-sensitive' *megachurches,* which are siphoning off members and driving small local churches into foreclosure and bankruptcy!"

"Those are definite problems for us, as well," Matt admitted. He shook his head, and recalled, "I remember when I was young, nearly all Catholics not only went to Sunday Mass, but Saturday Confession every week—because it was considered a 'mortal sin' not to! But the only members of our congregation who still feel that way are very recent immigrants from Mexico, or Central and South America!" Eric nodded sympathetically.

Eric said ruefully, "My grandfather Clement's Universalist church was about to 'go under,' when the merger with the Unitarians occurred in 1961. But my Dad told me that Granddad had once confessed to him that the biggest challenge he faced from people was the question, 'If we're all going to go to Heaven anyway, why should we bother to go to church?' No matter how many good reasons Granddad might have given them, many people apparently just felt that question was unanswerable, and they stopped attending."

Matt observed, "Another big change I've noticed is that people expect the Church to be there to support them for all the major 'life events,' like birth, baptism, confirmation, marriage, and death; but the notion that they should ever have to follow any 'directives' or 'teachings' of the Church that they don't already *agree* with, is practically inconceivable to them."

Eric chuckled, and said, "Our congregation is so diverse, that if someone ever tried to impose *any* particular position on them—whether it be about Global Warming, International Terrorism, Animal Rights, Veganism, Transgender Rights, or the Black Lives Matter movement—you'd immediately get a dozen people voicing strong disagreement." He took a sip of his beverage, and added, "About the only things we all agree upon are the modern liberal 'standards': namely, equality for all; diversity; and toleration for different viewpoints." Matt nodded his agreement.

Eric stirred his beverage, then said to Matt, "Say, didn't you tell me earlier that you had some 'sympathy' with the Universalist viewpoint?" Matt nodded again, and Eric asked with interest, "So is that another direction in which the Catholic church is changing?" Grinning, he added, "Or are you just *individually* a 'heretic'?"

Matt replied, "You've probably never heard of the book, *Dare We Hope That All Men Be Saved?* by the Swiss Catholic theologian Hans Urs von Balthasar, but…"

"I've read that book; and I liked it a lot," Eric interjected. He frowned, and then added, "But I got the impression that Balthasar was kind of 'on the outs' within the Catholic church, for taking the position he did in that book."

"It was controversial, to be sure," Matt acknowledged. "But Balthasar was hardly 'on the outs' with the Church; in fact, Pope John Paul II had just named him to become a cardinal—but unfortunately, Balthasar passed away, just two days before his ordination would have taken place."

"That's too bad," Eric observed. He took another swallow of his beverage as he thought, and then said, "I'm trying to remember just what Balthasar said in that book; it was years ago that I read it. One of the things I seem to remember that struck me at the time was the statement that the Catholic church has never actually pronounced that any *specific person* is in Hell. Is that your church's official position?"

"It is," Matt agreed.

Eric looked at him closely, and asked, "Even for someone like Judas? Or Hitler?" Matt nodded, and Eric said, "That's very interesting, because that's nearly always the first objection that people have when they learn that I'm a Universalist: 'You mean you think that *Hitler* is going to be in Heaven? And that *Judas* is going to be spending eternity with the Saviour that he betrayed?'" Matt smiled, and Eric added, "If the person asking about Judas is an Evangelical, I usually ask him or her, 'Well, what if Judas *hadn't* betrayed Jesus, and so the Romans *hadn't* crucified him? What would that do to your theology?'" and Matt laughed.

Matt said, "Those kind of 'hard cases' illustrate where I think Balthasar's first point is well-taken: namely, that none of us can be so certain even about our *own* salvation, that we can be certain about the *damnation* of any other person. Who can know whether or not Judas's repentance after his betrayal of Christ might have been genuine and sincere?"

Eric nodded, and said, "I'm a strong supporter of the idea of the possibility of 'conversion' after death; I simply can't see any justification for the notion that we get this one 'shot' for salvation in our earthly life, and that's it—and it's just tough luck if you happen to die at age fourteen, or to have been born in a Muslim or Hindu or Communist country."

Matt pointed out, "But Balthasar wasn't a 'Universalist' in your sense; he didn't believe that we could advocate what he called 'universal redemption.' In the end, Balthasar simply suggested that we should be allowed to *hope* for the salvation of all persons—including ourselves. Some critics mischaracterized him as arguing that 'Hell exists, but no one is in it,' but that's hardly what Balthasar said. But he did think that we had to allow for the possibility that some might irrevocably refuse God's love; which is a case of man's *self-condemnation*, not of God 'casting someone into Hell.'"

Eric nodded, and conceded, "I certainly admit that there are some persons who are seemingly irreconcilably turned against God at the time of their deaths; but, as for whether that attitude might be 'irrevocable,' well, I would just say… that eternity is a *long time!"* and they both laughed.

Eric said, "Well, it sounds to me like your church has definitely gotten away from the old slogan, 'Outside the Church, there is no salvation'!"

Matt made a face of profound displeasure, then recalled, "A Catholic priest, Leonard Feeney, was actually *excommunicated* more than sixty years ago, for taking a 'hard line' on that particular doctrine!" He took a long swallow from his beverage, then said, "Actually, since Vatican II, the position that has been most influential in the Church is Karl Rahner's concept of the 'Anonymous Christian,' which he expressed in an essay by that name, as well as in a number of the volumes of his *Theological Investigations."*

"Anonymous Christian?" Eric repeated, puzzled. "That sounds intriguing."

Matt explained, "Rahner was very much concerned with the fact that there are persons who have not yet been reached by the Church's missionary efforts; yet such persons may nevertheless be honestly pursuing God and salvation, even though they know nothing of Christianity. Rahner points out that, according to the doctrine of the Church since Vatican II, an individual may already be in possession of sanctifying grace, and can be justified, sanctified, and a child of God, even before he has explicitly embraced a creedal statement of the Christian faith and been baptized. Rahner suggests that such a person might be not only an anonymous *theist,* but also an anonymous *Christian."*

"Really?" Eric exclaimed, pleasantly surprised. Matt nodded, and Eric added, "And this Rahner guy was considered 'okay' by the Catholic church?"

Matt replied, "He was actually one of the most influential Catholic theologians of the 20th century."

"That's fascinating," Eric stated. He was about to ask another question, when Matt's phone began ringing.

Matt rolled his eyes and took it out of his pocket, and said, "Another reason that I hate these damn things; they're so *rude!"* He answered the phone (with a pleasant voice), saying, "Matt O'Sullivan here." He listened for a moment, then looked at his watch, and said, "I should be there in about forty minutes." Then he ended the call.

Eric smiled, and asked, "So it's time to get on to your visitations?"

"Yep," Matt said with a sigh. He looked at Eric, and said earnestly, "I've really enjoyed our conversation, Eric. Maybe we can get together again, some time."

"I'd like that," Eric agreed. He pulled out his wallet, and removed a business card from it, saying, "Here's my card: it's got my office phone number and E-mail address on it, plus my cell phone number, in case you want to text me about a time and place we can meet."

Matt chuckled, and said, "I'm not much for 'texting'; my fingers are too big and stubby to type anything on the tiny keypad my phone has. But I'll definitely keep in touch by E-mail. Maybe we can even go jogging, or you can join my brother and I for a basketball game sometime."

Eric said, "That sounds good; except don't you need an *even* number of people for a basketball game?"

Matt shook his head vigorously, and said, "My two brothers and I played with just the three of us for decades."

"*Two* brothers?" Eric asked, puzzled. "You have another brother?"

"We were triplets," Matt explained. "My brother Luke, who was also a priest, was killed by a drunken driver nine years ago."

"How terrible!" Eric gasped, putting his hand on Matt's shoulder sympathetically.

Matt shrugged, and added, "Luke's definitely the second person I'd want to see, if and when I get to Heaven; the first person would be my mother, who died during our birth. I've always wanted to meet her…"

Eric said eagerly, "I'm dying now to hear the 'rest of the story'; but I'll put it off until we get together again."

The two men stood, embraced, and then warmly shook hands, before parting.

CHAPTER 11

WHAT *DOES* THE BIBLE TEACH?
(Early November, 2016)

The well-dressed middle-aged man said to the television camera, "Hello, and welcome to River City Rumbles. I'm your host, Rick Melville, and the subject of our program today is *Hell;* specifically, does it exist? And who, if anyone, goes there?" He turned to an intense black-haired man (seemingly in his late 30s, who was carefully holding a thick Bible in his lap) sitting in a chair on his right-hand side and said, "I am joined for the program today by Stanley Beechman, Pastor of the Evangelical Community Bible Assembly of River City. Thanks for joining us, Stanley."

"It's my pleasure," the intense man replied.

Rick then added, "I'm also being joined by Eric Swenson, who is the Pastor of the Unitarian Church here in River City; but I'll tell you more about him, a little later in the program." He then turned to Stanley, and said, "I have to say, Stanley, that our Program Director had quite a difficult time finding a local Protestant minister who was willing to publicly *defend* the traditional notion of Hell as a literal place of 'conscious everlasting punishment.' She called mainline Lutheran, Episcopal, Presbyterian, Methodist, United Church of Christ, and even several Baptist churches, before she finally got in touch with you; and you quickly expressed your willingness to appear on the program—so we thank you for that."

Stanley said in an even tone, "I'm always glad to explain the Word of God; the Bible instructs us in First Peter 3:15 to 'be ready always to give an answer to every man that asks you a reason for the hope that is in you.'"

Rick said, "Now, my Program Director told me that, of the ministers who declined to appear on our program, they usually said that the reason they gave was that they and their churches basically *don't teach* the traditional doctrine of a 'fiery Hell,' anymore—which kind of surprised me, since I assume that the doctrine is still found in all of their various Creeds, and…"

Stanley interrupted him, saying firmly, "The so-called 'mainline' denominations have long since sold out their historic beliefs to theological *liberalism*. Frankly, I really don't care what this church or that church teaches, or what is written in some 'Creed' that the Romanist or some other group has written; those churches and denominations also often taught unbiblical doctrines such as salvation by works; infant baptism; the 'perpetual virginity' of Mary; the Eucharist as literally the body and blood of Jesus, and so on. The only thing that matters to me, and all that should matter to any true Christian is, *What does the **Bible** teach?*"

Rick smiled, and then said expansively, "I should explain, that I was raised in an Evangelical church: I went to Youth Group, Sunday School and Sunday worship, and Summer Bible Camps every year; I felt that I got 'saved' when I was twelve, and then after I graduated from high school, I went to a Bible College for two-and-a-half years. But after the 'Rapture' didn't happen by 1988—as Hal Lindsey's bestselling books had convinced most of us it was supposed to—and when Campus Crusade's dreams of 'Reaching the world for Christ *in this generation*' had clearly failed, even as fundamentalist Islam was experiencing a huge resurgence in the Middle East, I dropped out of Bible College. Then I enrolled in the Communications/Journalism program in a regular University, worked extra hard to make up for having wasted five semesters of my life studying the Bible rather than something of any *real* value, and I graduated with honors, then got into my current professional field—and I've never looked back!"

Stanley was about to say something, but Rick continued without interruption, saying, "Now, I explain all this not to *brag,* but just to point out that I'm *very* familiar with the whys and wherefores of fundamentalist churches, such as yours. And as a television journalist, I've tried to keep up over the years with the various issues that grab the attention of evangelical churches, such as abortion, pornography, Feminism, and of course the current 'hot button' issue of Marriage Equality—which I firmly support, by the way." He raised one eyebrow, and asked Stanley bluntly, "I presume that you, like the rest of your cohorts, are rabidly opposed to Gay men and Lesbians having the right to get married?"

Stanley replied calmly, "My own life path was considerably different from yours, Rick; my parents raised me without any religious teaching whatsoever. When I graduated from high school, I attended a secular university for two years as a Finance major; but I felt a real spiritual *void* in my life, and I was increasingly repulsed by all the rampant *materialism* I saw all around me. So, while most of my school peers were commiserating with each other about the *collapse* of the 'Dot-Com Bubble' in the late 1990s, I found myself going forward at a Greg Laurie crusade that was held in my city—and I didn't just 'feel' I had been saved, I *knew,* without a doubt, that I had been saved! So I disenrolled in the secular university, and enrolled in a nondenominational Bible College, where I found out that the Bible had *all* of the answers to the questions I had been asking myself, such as, 'Why am I here?'"

Before Rick could comment, Stanley quickly added, "So to get back to your question about same-sex marriage, Rick, it's really irrelevant what you, or I, or anyone else may *feel* about the issue. The only thing that matters is what the *Bible* says about the issue. And Jesus told us in Mark 10:6-9, 'from the beginning of the creation God made them male and female…What therefore God has joined together, let not man put asunder.' And it's exactly the same with the doctrine of Hell: you and other people may complain that the doctrine of Hell 'doesn't seem *fair* to you,' or that you 'don't *like* the doctrine'; but again, the only thing that's really of any importance is, 'Does the Bible *teach* the doctrine of eternal torment in Hell?' If it does, then there's really nothing to discuss; you and others may *reject* what the Bible teaches, but your lack of belief doesn't have any effect on the *reality* of Hell's existence."

Somewhat taken aback by this smooth and practiced response, Rick said firmly, "Well, that's actually why I wanted to host this program today: because there are increasing numbers of Bible-believing Evangelicals like yourself who aren't theological 'liberals'—such as the ones you quickly dismissed earlier—but who are strongly arguing that the traditional doctrine of hellfire is *not* what the Bible teaches!" He picked up a clipboard from a nearby table, as he said, "I was originally converted in a summer Youth Camp after hearing a terrifying sermon from a Youth Pastor, who convinced me that I was in serious danger of being 'Left Behind' when Jesus returned in a very few years, and that I would then spend all of eternity in literal flames—without so much as a drop of water to ease my thirst and torment!" Looking Stanley directly in the eyes, he asked, "So do *you* preach 'hellfire' sermons like that to the impressionable young people in your own church?"

His voice remaining calm, Stanley replied, "There is no point in *soft-pedaling* the serious realities of life, Rick. I wouldn't think of pretending that international Islamic terrorism is *not* a deadly threat; nor that premarital sex leads to disease, mistreated children, and economic catastrophe for young people. In just the same way, I would be cowardly and negligent of my duty as a Pastor, if I didn't soberly advise *all* the members of my congregation about what the Bible teaches about Hell; and about the endless, conscious torment that awaits those who refuse Jesus' offer of salvation."

Rick countered, "But that's just what I want to discuss: *does* the Bible teach the doctrine of endless conscious torment for everyone who doesn't 'get saved,' in the precise manner that your church prescribes?" He said expansively, "After I 'got saved' at a Youth Summer Camp, they gave me a copy of the book, *Basic Christianity,* by John Stott, who was then probably the most famous and influential Evangelical in England; this book was supposed to give us 'new Christians' a thorough grounding in doctrine. Then when I went to Bible College, I took a yearlong class in Apologetics, and we had three textbooks: Josh McDowell's *Evidence That Demands a Verdict,* F.F. Bruce's *The New Testament Documents: Are They Reliable?,* and Clark Pinnock's *Reason Enough;* I even bought Pinnock's cassette tape set, *Faith and Reason,* to listen to in my car, as I was driving to and from class."

Then he consulted the notes on his clipboard, and continued, "But it turns out that three of those four 'pillars of the faith'—Stott, Bruce, and Pinnock—have actually changed their minds about Hell; and they actively rejected the 'endless conscious torment' approach, in favor of a new doctrine called 'Conditional Immortality'..."

Stanley said sharply, "Pinnock went completely off the deep end in the 1980s, and later; first he rejected Biblical Infallibility—which he had earlier written a short book in *defense* of—and then, since the Bible was no longer his standard, he went further astray and supported the so-called 'Inclusivist' view of salvation, which asserts that followers of non-Christian religions can be saved; next, Pinnock rejected the doctrine of Hell; and finally, he advocated 'Open Theism,' which reduces the infinite God to a *finite* level of..."

Rick cut in sharply, "I understand that you don't *agree* with Pinnock, Stanley; that's why we asked you to be on this program today. But those three, Stott, Bruce, and Pinnock, were like *gods* to us 'born again' types in the seventies and eighties! But now, we see that Pinnock wrote in his chapter in the book *Four Views on Hell,* that 'Everlasting torture is intolerable from a moral point of view because it pictures God acting like a bloodthirsty monster who maintains an everlasting Auschwitz for his enemies whom he does not even allow to die. How can one love a God like that?' And F.F. Bruce wrote a letter to John Stott in 1989 in which he stated, 'Eternal conscious torment is incompatible with the revealed character of God.' And John Stott wrote in the book *Evangelical Essentials* that 'emotionally, I find the concept [of eternal torment in Hell] intolerable and do not understand how people can live with it without either cauterizing their feelings or cracking under the strain.' Then Stott added that 'It would be easier to hold together the awful reality of hell and the universal reign of God if hell means destruction and the impenitent are no more... I also believe that the ultimate annihilation of the wicked should at least be accepted as a legitimate, biblically founded alternative to their eternal conscious torment.' Finally, Stott concludes, 'I have never been able to conjure up ... the appalling vision of the millions who ... will inevitably perish... I cherish the hope that the majority of the human race will be saved. And I have a solid biblical basis for this belief.'"

Stanley began, "Those are simply the opinions of *men,* and are of no more authority than..."

"But it's not just them," Rick interrupted again, looking down at his clipboard notes. "I've since discovered that even C.S. Lewis—who was seemingly Josh McDowell's ultimate authority for useful and literate quotes—had said in his 1940 book *The Problem of Pain* about the doctrine of Hell, that 'There is no doctrine which I would more willingly remove from Christianity than this ... I am not going to try to prove the doctrine tolerable. Let us make no mistake; it is *not* tolerable.' And Lewis tried to minimize hell, when he suggested that 'What is cast (or casts itself) into hell is not a man: it is "remains"... It is... impossible to imagine what the consciousness of such a creature... would be like.' Lewis also notes that Jesus, 'while stressing the terror of hell with unsparing severity, usually emphasizes the idea, not of duration but of *finality*. Consignment to the destroying fire is usually treated as the end of the story—not the beginning of a new story... whether this eternal fixity implies endless duration—or duration at all—we cannot say... I willingly believe ... that the doors of hell are *locked on the inside*.'"

Stanley maintained a stony silence, and Rick continued, "And then Lewis wrote a fictional work, *The Great Divorce,* which allows the inhabitants of Hell to take an occasional bus trip to the outskirts of Heaven—which they *could* enter, if they wanted! In this book, Lewis states that 'Hell is a state of mind... shutting up of the creature within the dungeon of its own mind'; so there's certainly no 'fiery torment' there! And in *Letters to Malcolm,* Lewis admits, 'Of course I pray for the dead. The action is so spontaneous, so all but inevitable, that only the most compulsive theological case against it would deter men... I believe in Purgatory... Our souls *demand* Purgatory, don't they?... I assume that the process of purification will normally involve suffering.' So here, Lewis was even endorsing the Roman Catholic doctrine of Purgatory!" He looked triumphantly at Stanley, who had held his tongue during this onslaught of quotations.

Then (reading from several note cards he had pulled out of his jacket pocket) Stanley pointed out, "But Lewis also said in *The Problem of Pain* that the doctrine of Hell 'has the full support of Scripture and, specially, of Our Lord's own words; it has always been held by Christendom, and it has the support of reason. If a game is played, it must be possible to lose it.' And Lewis added that 'the doctrine can be shown to be moral by a critique of the objections ordinarily made, or felt, against it.' And even in *The Great Divorce,* one of the characters explains, 'There are only two kinds of people in the end: those who say to God, "Thy will be done," and those to whom God says, in the end, "*Thy* will be done."' And Lewis concluded, 'All those that are in Hell, choose it. Without that self-choice, there could be no Hell. No soul that seriously and constantly desires joy will ever miss it. Those who seek find. To those who knock it is opened.'"

Rick was somewhat taken aback by this surprising response, but quickly replied, "Well, I just found it fascinating that so many of the 'great Christian scholars' that I was told to look up to in my youth, had significant objections to the traditional doctrine of Hell. I'm reminded of philosopher Bertrand Russell's famous essay, *Why I am Not a Christian*, in which he wrote, 'There is one very serious defect to my mind in Christ's moral character, and that is that He believed in hell. I do not myself feel that any person who is really profoundly humane can believe in everlasting punishment.'" He shrugged, and then added, "Who knows? Maybe if Stott, Bruce, and Pinnock had expressed these views back when I was in Bible School, I would have stayed within the Christian fold. I mean, the idea of Hell was always a major problem for me; after all, I had some very close friends from high school who weren't Christians—and the notion of them being 'Left Behind' to face the Antichrist, and then to probably endure everlasting fiery torment, was an idea I shuddered to think about."

Stanley insisted, "Again: the fact that you, or atheists like Bertrand Russell, *don't like* the doctrine of Hell, is completely irrelevant to the question of the *truth* of the doctrine..."

Rick went on, saying passionately, "In my research for this program, I found out that even *Billy Graham* has backed away from the Hellfire doctrine he used to preach in his early days! In the late '60s, he asked in a sermon, 'Could it be that the fire Jesus talked about is an eternal search for God that is never quenched?' That's certainly not 'Hell fire'! Then in 1993, *Time* magazine reported him as saying, 'The only thing I could say for sure is that hell means separation from God. We are separated from his light, from his fellowship. That is going to be hell. When it comes to a literal fire, I don't preach it because I'm not sure about it.' And most importantly, he said in a 1997 interview on Robert Schuller's *Hour of Power* television show: 'I think that everybody that loves Christ or knows Christ, whether they're conscious of it or not, they're members of the body of Christ... What God is doing today is calling people out of the world for His name. Whether they come from the Muslim world, or the Buddhist world, or the Christian world, or the non-believing world, they are members of the body of Christ because they've been called by God. They may not even know the name of Jesus, but they know in their hearts they need something that they don't have and they turn to the only light they have and I think they're saved and they're going to be with us in heaven.' Graham also agreed with Schuller that 'There's a *wideness* in God's mercy.'"

Stanley said gravely, "What Billy Graham said in that interview with Robert Schuller was clearly and definitely *heretical*."

"Heretical?" Rick exclaimed, genuinely surprised. "Billy Graham, the most famous evangelist of the 20th century, a heretic?"

Stanley explained patiently, "I said that what he stated *in that interview* with Schuller was heretical. But you need to also be aware that in his final book, which just came out last year, *Where I Am: Heaven, Eternity, and Our Life Beyond*, he's clearly repented of those positions; now he *denies* that Hell is just a resting place, a holding place, or a graveyard, and he states plainly, 'if there is no literal fire in Hell, then God is using symbolic language to indicate something far worse.'"

With a slight smile, Rick suggested, "Well, maybe his Parkinson's Disease is just catching up with him. But at any rate, in my research on this subject, I found out that by far the best book about Conditional Immortality was written by a theologian named Edward Fudge; and his 417-page book, *The Fire That Consumes,* is an exhaustively detailed study of the entire matter of Hell. Fudge deals with all of the biblical passages that claim to 'prove' the doctrine of eternal conscious torment, and shows instead that they have other, better interpretations. And now, there's even a *movie* that's been made about him, called *Hell and Mr. Fudge,* that..."

Stanley interrupted, saying sharply, "Calling Fudge a 'theologian' is a complete misstatement of the facts! He was raised in, and attended colleges of the *Church of Christ,* which is a heretical cultic group—just as much as the Seventh-Day Adventists, or the Jehovah's Witnesses! And for nearly the last thirty years, Fudge has made his living as a *lawyer,* not as a theologian, or a Bible scholar! So he is hardly qualified to properly interpret the Bible passages he cites—although he's unfortunately *misled* a lot of people such as yourself, through his incorrect and biased interpretations, which simply play on and reinforce the *prejudices* that so many people have about this doctrine."

Rick shrugged, and said firmly, "Well, the controversy about this doctrine isn't going away anytime soon. The African-American Pentecostal preacher Carlton Pearson was Pastor of one of the largest churches in Tulsa, Oklahoma, until he began preaching about something that he eventually came to call the 'Gospel of Inclusion,' in which he rejected the traditional notion of Hell, and argued that Hell is simply what we've created here on earth—such as when people are left starving in Africa..."

Stanley said caustically, "In 2004, Pearson was condemned as a heretic by the Joint College of African-American Pentecostal Bishops; he's since been kicked out by his congregation—much of whose membership left as soon as he started espousing these heretical ideas—and now he's become a minister in the ultra-liberal United Church of Christ denomination! And, judging from the two books he's since written his ouster, he's now gone totally over into acceptance of 'New Age' ideas; in fact, I understand that he was even a minister in a New Age 'church' for a while."

Eric Swenson (who had been sitting on Rick's left-hand side, and listening quietly to the animated conversation between the two) unexpectedly interjected, "Pearson actually merged the faithful members of his old congregation into the All Souls Unitarian Church in Tulsa; and he's still listed as being on the ministerial staff there."

"Thanks for that information, Eric," Rick said gratefully, smiling warmly at him. He explained for the benefit of the television audience, "This is probably as good a time as any to more formally introduce Eric Swenson, who is the Pastor of the Unitarian Church here in River City; Eric and his denomination are supporters of the doctrine of *Universalism,* which is why I wanted to have him on the program today—to balance out Stanley's views! So welcome to the show, Eric."

"Thanks, Rick," Eric said graciously, then added apologetically, "But just for the record, I'm not a 'pastor'; we use the term 'minister' in our congregation—which is Unitarian *Universalist,* not just 'Unitarian'; our denomination was formed by a merger in 1961 of the Universalist Church of America and the American Unitarian Association. And we call ourselves the 'Unitarian Universalist *Society* of River City,' rather than a 'church.'"

"I didn't know that," Rick admitted. "Thanks for the clarification." Looking directly at Eric, he asked pointedly, "So how did you get into this line of work? Both Stanley and I have revealed our own backgrounds, so now it's your turn. Did you have a major religious conversion, following a 'Dark Night of the Soul'?"

Eric chuckled, and said, "Actually, I come from a liberal religious background; my grandfather on my father's side was a minister in the old Universalist Church, and he was there at the time of the 1961 merger, and he became a Unitarian Universalist minister after the union. And I was raised in this church; that's where my father and mother met, in fact."

"Interesting," Rick observed. "Now, you've been over there sitting patiently listening to Stanley and I go at it for about five minutes. What do you have to say?"

Eric replied, "I was interested in your discussion of the controversy over Carlton Pearson's 'Gospel of Inclusion.' Of course, the most recent furor over someone expressing Universalist sympathies was the young former megachurch pastor, Rob Bell—whose 2011 book *Love Wins* raised a storm of protest among Evangelical churches, because of his raising doubts as to whether a 'Hell' of eternal torment really existed. He was harshly criticized by Evangelicals and other theologically conservative Christians, and his large church lost about 3,000 members. So, six months later, he voluntarily stepped down as pastor of the Mars Hill Bible Church—which he himself had founded some thirteen years earlier."

Stanley said sharply, "Bell had to resign because he finally went undeniably *too far* in his rejection of Christian doctrines; you can't claim to be leading a professing 'Bible Church' while you are explicitly denying the most fundamental doctrines of the Bible!" He shook his head firmly, and said, "Like a lot of other cocky young people involved in the so-called 'Emerging Church' movement, Bell was constantly rejecting theological soundness in favor of writing shocking and 'trendy' books such as *Sex God, Velvet Elvis, Everything is Spiritual, Jesus Wants to Save Christians,* and other such trash."

Eric shrugged, then replied, "There's nothing wrong with wanting to bring some *fresh air* into traditional religious institutions. After all, that's what got the whole 'nondenominational,' 'Bible Church' movement started back in the 1960s, with groups like Chuck Smith's Calvary Chapel." Before Stanley could reply, Eric quickly added, "But the so-called 'mainstream' churches are coming around more and more to a viewpoint that's *almost* the same as Universalism—even if they don't want to admit it publicly! For example, in 1995 the Church of England's Doctrinal Commission wrote a report called *The Mystery of Salvation,* in which they concluded that 'Hell is not eternal torment, but it is the final and irrevocable choosing of that which is opposed to God so completely and so absolutely that the only end is total non-being,' and that 'Christians have professed appalling theologies which made God into a sadistic monster and left searing psychological scars on many.' The most respected Protestant theologian of the 20th century, Karl Barth, is—judging by several volumes of his *Church Dogmatics,* as well as his smaller book *The Humanity of God*—virtually a Universalist, even though he disclaims that label. And the influential German theologian Wolfhart Pannenberg, in his book *Jesus: God and Man,* endorsed a 'second chance' or 'postmortem evangelization' view. And even some Christian authors who are quite popular with Evangelicals—such as Jacques Ellul, William Barclay, George MacDonald, Hannah Whitall Smith, and Madeleine L'Engle—have admitted that they themselves are Universalists…"

Stanley said contemptuously, "I could care less what some professed 'theologians' and 'Christian authors' believe about Hell, Universalism, and other doctrines. And given that the Church of England has been ordaining practicing *homosexuals* to the ministry for years, this demonstrates their utter lack of regard for the Bible!" Looking directly at Rick, he said sharply, "My only interest in appearing on this program was to explain the *Bible's* teaching on the subject. So if you and your other guest don't wish to discuss the Bible, then there's no need in our continuing with this program."

With a slight smile, Rick replied, "Well, we definitely want to continue with the program…!" Turning to Eric, he asked, "Do you have any objection to discussing the Bible with our other guest?"

"None whatsoever," Eric replied immediately. "Although the Bible isn't 'authoritative' in Unitarian Universalist congregations as it is in Stanley's church, I'm very familiar with what the Bible has to say about life after death."

Rick gave a satisfied smile, and said, "Well, then, it's settled." He turned to Stanley, and said, "We're playing ball in *your* home court, Stanley; so we'll give you the 'first serve.' Take it away."

"Thank you," Stanley replied, picking up the heavy Bible that was lying in his lap, and opening it. He added, "Now, I hope that Eric will utilize *legitimate* translations of the Bible; cults and heretics that don't want to believe what the Bible teaches usually use inaccurate and blatant mistranslations of the Bible, such as the Concordant Version, Young's Literal Translation, the New World Translation, or…"

"I'm using the New International Version, along with the King James Version," Eric explained. "The NIV is the version most popular with Evangelicals today, I understand."

Stanley shrugged, and replied, "I prefer the King James Version myself, since it uses the Textus Receptus. But the NIV is good enough, for our purposes here today." He added smugly, "I can't help but observe that heretical opinions about the doctrine of Hell are primarily held either by outright liberals such as Clark Pinnock, or by cultic groups such as the Seventh-Day Adventists, the Jehovah's Witnesses, Armstrong's Worldwide Church of God, and Church of Christ adherents such as Edward Fudge…"

Eric interrupted, "Early 'Church Fathers' such as Clement of Alexandria, Origen, and Gregory of Nyssa were Universalists; and Ignatius of Antioch, Justin Martyr, Irenaeus, and Arnobius were early supporters of what we now call 'Conditional Immortality.' You can consult Le Roy Edwin Froom's book *The Conditionalist Faith of Our Fathers* for documentation about this, as well as Steven Harmon's book, *Every Knee Should Bow…*"

Stanley interjected, "Froom was a Seventh-Day Adventist, which just goes to reinforce my point—which is that *honest* Christian interpreters of the Bible have always admitted the traditional doctrine of Hell as constituting eternal, conscious torment; while it is primarily members of *cultic* groups who reject the traditional doctrine." Before either Eric or Rick could object, he began explaining, "The doctrine of Hell is strongly related to the doctrine of *Sin;* so if one has an inadequate concept of Sin, one certainly can't come up with a correct conception of the afterlife. And Sin began back in the Garden of Eden, when Adam and Eve disobeyed God's instructions…"

Rick said sharply, "And you take the Adam and Eve story *literally,* I presume?"

"Of course; just as Jesus Christ did," Stanley replied calmly. He continued, "Romans 5:12 tells us that 'by one man sin entered into the world, and death by sin; and so death passed upon all men, for that all have sinned.' Romans 3:23 says, '*all* have sinned, and come short of the glory of God.' Now, Romans 6:23 notes, 'the wages of sin is death'; this tells us clearly that God must *punish* us for our sins. But then Paul adds, 'but the gift of God is *eternal life* through Jesus Christ our Lord.' Now, in order to appropriate this eternal life, we simply need to follow the instructions of Paul and Silas in Acts 16:31: 'Believe on the Lord Jesus Christ, and thou shalt be saved.' Romans 10:9-10 says, 'if you confess with your mouth the Lord Jesus and believe in your heart that God has raised Him from the dead, you will be saved. For with the heart one believes unto righteousness, and with the mouth confession is made unto salvation.' So it's not enough to simply 'study' the Bible as a supposed 'scholar,' or to belong to a so-called 'church'; you clearly must have a *personal relationship* with Jesus. Jesus said in Revelation 3:20, 'Behold, I stand at the door and knock. If anyone hears My voice and opens the door, I will come in to him.'"

Impatiently, Rick objected, "I must have missed the part where any of this entails *eternal conscious torment*."

Stanley continued, undisturbed, "The most well-known verse in the Bible is John 3:16: 'For God so loved the world, that he gave his only begotten Son, that whosoever believes in him should not perish, but have everlasting life.' So God's gift of salvation is available to all, who will humbly follow the path outlined so clearly in the Bible. But Colossians 3:6 testifies that 'the wrath of God comes on the children of disobedience,' And Hebrews 2:3 also cautions us, 'how shall we escape if we neglect so great a salvation'? And just what is it that you are 'escaping' when you get saved? Jesus said in Matthew 25 that the unsaved will go into the 'everlasting fire prepared for the devil and his angels,' while the 'righteous [go] into eternal life.'"

Rick said mockingly, "Yeah, yeah; that's the same old-fashioned kind of 'hellfire' talk that used to terrify me when I was twelve years old. But I thought that the Bible also said that God is *love;* so why are you trying to *scare* people into becoming Christians?"

"Because that's also what the Bible says!" Stanley thundered. "Yes, the Bible does say in places like First John 4:8 that 'God is love.' But Jesus also said in Luke 12:5, 'I will show you whom you should fear: Fear Him who, after He has killed, has power to cast into hell; yes, I say to you, *fear Him!*' And Hebrews 10:31 warns, 'It is a *fearful thing* to fall into the hands of the living God.'" He fell silent, with a satisfied look on his face.

Rick turned to Eric, and invited, "Any comments on our other guest's sermonette, Eric?"

With a slight smile, Eric said, "I'm reminded of the statement in Proverbs 18:17: 'In a lawsuit, the first to speak seems right; until someone comes forward and cross-examines.' I think this is a valid principle to remind our audience of: that they need to refrain from making judgements, or 'taking sides,' until they have had a chance to fairly hear and evaluate *all* sides of a discussion like this one."

"A good point," Rick complimented.

Eric thought for a moment, and then said to Stanley, "Personally, I've always had a problem with that statement in Romans about all of us inheriting the sin of Adam and Eve. After all, you and I weren't in the Garden of Eden—even assuming your quite improbable idea that it ever actually existed—and if it had been *me* in the Garden, maybe I *wouldn't* have disobeyed the Lord's commandment not to eat of the fruit; or if I did, maybe I would have been smarter than Adam, and *first* eaten of the 'Tree of Life,' since it had not been forbidden to him, at that point," and Rick laughed.

Eric continued, "As I recall, the prophet Ezekiel said [18:20], 'The one who sins is the one who will die. The child will not share the guilt of the parent, nor will the parent share the guilt of the child.' And Deuteronomy 24:16 agreed that 'The fathers shall not be put to death for the children, neither shall the children be put to death for the fathers: every man shall be put to death for his own sin.' But if God starts all of us off in life by making us inherit this 'sin nature' from Adam, then we're doomed even before we *start!*"

Stanley was about to respond to this, but Rick motioned for him to remain silent, saying, "We didn't interrupt you while you did your little gospel spiel; so let's give Eric a chance to speak." Stanley remained silent, but stared sullenly at the two of them.

Eric went on, "And your assertion that we all need to have a 'personal relationship with Jesus' seems rather doubtful to me—even on *biblical* grounds! The words 'personal relationship' don't even *appear* in any of the standard scholarly translations of the Bible; certainly *Jesus* never said them! In fact, in Luke 19, when Jesus met with the rich tax collector Zacchaeus, it wasn't until after Zacchaeus had pledged to give half of his possessions to the poor, and to repay fourfold anyone he had cheated, that Jesus announced, 'This day is salvation come to this house.' About Revelation

3:20, where Jesus supposedly said, 'I will come in to him, *and will sup with him, and he with me,*' I would point out that this statement was addressed to the members of a 1ˢᵗ century *church*—albeit a 'lukewarm' one—rather than to unbelievers; so I fail to see its relevance to your evangelistic 'pitch.' And I would also note that the conversion of Saul of Tarsus didn't occur after he responded to Jesus 'knocking on the door of his heart'; in fact, according to Acts 9:1, when he had his conversion experience, Saul was supposedly 'breathing out murderous threats against the Lord's disciples,' and intending to bring any Christians he found back to stand before the High Priest—and presumably be put to death, as the apostle Stephen had been. So he certainly wasn't 'believing on the Lord Jesus' when he 'got saved'…"

Stanley said fiercely, "The fact that the words 'personal relationship with Jesus' aren't in the Bible is of no more importance than the fact that the word 'Trinity' isn't; the *doctrine* is there, and that's all that matters! And Zacchaeus obviously *did* respond 'personally' to Jesus; his later behavior was just proof of his sincere *repentance!* And the fact that Laodicea had a 'church' doesn't mean that they were all *saved;* there are millions of unsaved Christians out there in churches, who…"

Rick held up his hands to silence both his guests; when they both were quiet, he said calmly, "I need to bring the discussion back to the question of Hell; that's supposedly why we're here today, remember?" Looking directly at Stanley, he said, "A real sticking point for me about Hell has always been the *disproportionality* of it. I mean, no matter *how* bad a person has been over the course of a 70-year lifetime, how can it possibly be reasonable for God to impose an *eternal* punishment upon such a person? I mean, I have no problem with Hitler, Stalin, Pol Pot, or anyone like that being punished for thousands, or maybe even millions of years. But 'eternity' means that their punishment will *never end!* After sixty *trillion* years, they will still have an eternity ahead of them!"

Stanley replied calmly, "So what you're objecting to isn't the *principle* of God punishing the sinner; it's just the *length* of the punishment that you don't like: correct?"

Rick hesitated, and then said, "Uhh… well, yeah, basically. I mean, an *eternal* punishment is, by definition, *infinitely* beyond the *finite* number of sins that anyone could commit in a single lifetime. So how is that a 'just' punishment for God to impose?"

Stanley explained patiently, "Deuteronomy 25:2 graphically illustrates the principle that the *punishment* should fit the *crime.* But the seriousness of a crime is measured, in part, by the *stature* of the person against whom the crime was committed. It's more serious to assault the President of the United States or a federal judge, for example, than to assault an ordinary citizen, such as you or me: agreed?"

With uncertainty in his voice, Rick replied reluctantly, "Uhh, yes; I guess so…"

Stanley continued, "But since God is a being of *infinite stature*, by definition any crime committed against him is of *infinite* magnitude; and therefore, it requires an *infinite* response. In other words, since sin is committed against an infinitely holy God, the punishment for this sin must also be infinite; agreed?"

"No, I don't accept that conclusion at all," Rick said, shaking his head firmly.

Eric looked at his notes, and then explained for Rick's benefit, "Stanley is using an argument that derives from the 11th century theologian, Anselm of Canterbury. Anselm argued in his book *Cur Deus Homo*—'Why God became Man'—that 'So heinous is our sin whenever we knowingly oppose the will of God even in the slightest thing… you make no satisfaction unless you restore something greater than the amount of that obligation'; and he further asserted that 'a sinner cannot justify a sinner,' and that 'man's inability to restore what he owes to God… does not excuse him from paying.' So Anselm concluded that 'None but God can make this satisfaction'; therefore, 'It is necessary that the same being should be perfect God and perfect man, in order to make this atonement.'" [Bk.1, XXI, XXIII, XXIV; Bk. 2, VI, VII]

Rick shook his head, and said dismissively, "That's nothing but theological gobbledygook!"

Eric smiled, and then said, "But more to the point, is the fact that Anselm was making a purely *theological* argument, rather than a *biblical* argument. That passage that Stanley mentioned from Deuteronomy 25 was about determining the number of times that a human being should be *whipped;* it doesn't say anything about 'crimes against God being of infinite magnitude.'" Looking directly at Stanley, he asked, "Given your apparent dislike of theologians, is Anselm's argument really one that *you* can utilize?" Stanley flushed slightly, but didn't reply.

Eric continued, "Now, if *every* sin deserves an 'infinite punishment,' how could there *ever* be a way for the sum total of all sins to be atoned for? We're talking about all of the trillions of sins committed by *billions* of humans, throughout all history! How could Jesus hanging on a cross for six hours possibly atone for such a monumental volume of sins? And in order for your argument to work, wouldn't Jesus' punishment have needed to be *ongoing*, since sins are still constantly being committed?"

Stanley began, "Since Jesus was *fully God*, his atonement was therefore *infinite* in its extent, and…"

Eric interrupted, "And why isn't any sin committed by a *finite* being considered infinitely *small*, when compared to an infinite God? If I stole from God's offering plate—as Josh McDowell said he used to do—wouldn't God still be 'infinitely wealthy'? And what about our *good* acts? If they are done to honor God, are these acts '*infinitely* good,' since they are performed for God's glory?" Stanley glowered at him, but remained silent.

Rick said to Stanley in a conciliatory manner, "Let's try and get this discussion back on track; we're supposed to be discussing the Bible, and Hell. Stanley, what does the Bible say, in general terms, about life after death?"

Stanley relaxed, and said in a well-practiced manner, "In Luke 20:34-38, Jesus confirmed to the Sadducees that God 'is not a God of the dead, but of the living: for all live unto him.' Jesus said to the thief on the cross that 'Today shalt thou be with me in paradise.' [Lk 23:43] And the apostle Paul said in Second Corinthians 5:8 that 'to be absent from the body' was 'to be present with the Lord,' and he also said in Philippians 1:23 that he had 'a desire to depart, and to be with Christ.' So for the Christian, immediately after death, we go to be with the Lord—forever!"

Rick pointed out, "But that's only for *Christians;* what about us 'unsaved' folks?"

Stanley turned serious, and said soberly, "Hebrews 9:27 says, 'it is appointed unto men once to die, but after this the judgment.' So *all* of us—Christian and non-Christian—are initially judged immediately after our deaths. But later, there will be a resurrection of the dead, including the justified believers, which is called the 'first resurrection' in Revelation 20:4-6; it's also called the 'resurrection of the just' in Luke 14:14, and the 'resurrection of life' in John 5:29. There will also be a resurrection of *unbelievers* at the end of the Millennium, which is described in Revelation 20:12-15; this happens prior to the Great White Throne judgment, and was called the 'resurrection of damnation' by Jesus in John 5:29."

Rick looked over to Eric, and asked, "So what do you think about all of that, Eric?"

Eric sighed and shook his head, then commented, "In my opinion, Christians arguing about the Rapture, the Great Tribulation, the Millennium, and all this of this stuff, is a colossal waste of time. Even Evangelicals are not all in agreement on questions such as, 'Where did Jesus go during the 40+ days after his crucifixion?'; 'Are *all* Christians raised at the 'first resurrection'?; 'What is the *order* of all the resurrections mentioned in the Bible?'; 'Do we receive our rewards/crowns for our works on earth right after we die, or not until after the Millennium?' and so on. From my perspective, when we die, our eternal soul goes to be with God, and we shouldn't bring in confusing eschatological imagery from the Book of Revelation, and so forth."

Rick nodded his agreement, and observed, "This idea of a 'general judgment' of everyone always seemed silly to me; I mean, just imagine how long it would take to have everyone sitting around while all of the *billions* of people who have lived have all of their sins replayed on a big TV screen, right in front of everyone…"

Stanley interjected, "In *eternity,* they've got plenty of time! But the scenario you're imagining is like something out of a Jack Chick tract, not the Bible; the process described in Revelation 20:12-15 would actually proceed rather *quickly.*"

Rick said stubbornly, "But again, this whole idea of tormenting people *forever* for the sins of an ordinary lifetime seems completely unjust to me; it sounds more like something that *Satan* would do, than what *God* would do! And the notion that the wicked are being kept alive by God eternally just for the purpose of torment them seems completely pointless; that's why this modern concept of Conditional Immortality is so much more attractive to me…"

Stanley asked sharply, "If the Conditionalists—or 'Annihilationists,' as I call them—are right, then there will *never* be any adequate punishment for even the worst sinners! Adolf Hitler, a coward to the end, committed suicide before he could be captured by the Allied forces and brought to justice; but even if he had been captured alive, and had been executed along with the other major war criminals at Nuremberg, how would this have been 'proportional' to the six million Jews he murdered, and the other millions who died in the war that Hitler began?" Rick remained silent, so Stanley went on, "Think of 9/11, and of other Islamic terrorists who blow themselves up with explosives, intentionally killing innocent civilians; think of the madmen who shoot up schoolyards or workplaces, but who then kill themselves, once the police are closing in on them: if these evil people are simply *annihilated,* then they basically 'got away' with their horrible crimes! How can *that* be 'just'?"

Rick flushed crimson, and then shot back, "How is *your* way any better? Throwing a twelve-year-old kid into the very same 'Lake of Fire' that Hitler and terrorists will be burning in forever?"

Stanley explained, "Revelation 20:12 tells us that the dead will be 'judged out of those things which were written in the books, *according to their works.*' And Revelation 21:8 says that various classes of sinners shall 'have their part' in the lake of fire; so these passages clearly state that there are different *areas* in the Lake of Fire. The Bible also indicates that there will be *different degrees* of punishment in Hell. For example, Jesus said in Matthew 10:15 and 11:22-24 that it would be 'more tolerable' for wicked cities such as Sodom and Gomorrha, than for the cities that rejected him. And in the parable of the Faithful Steward in Luke 12:46-48, Jesus said that the servant who *knew* his lord's will but didn't perform it will be 'beaten with *many* stripes'; while the servant who did *not* know his lord's will would be 'beaten with *few* stripes.' Then in Matthew 23:14, Jesus tells the hypocritical scribes and Pharisees that they 'shall receive the *greater* damnation'; so obviously, this implies some forms of damnation must be *lesser* than others."

Before Rick or Eric could respond, he quickly added, "All sins are *not* 'created equal'; with greater revelation and knowledge, comes more responsibility and a stricter judgment. Jesus said in John 9:41, 'If ye were blind, ye should have no sin: but now ye say, We see; therefore your sin remaineth.' Romans 2:12 tells us, 'For as many as have sinned without law shall also perish without law: and as many as have sinned in the law shall be judged by the law.' Hebrews 10:26-29 says that those who sin willfully after having received knowledge of the truth will receive a 'sorer punishment.' And First Peter 4:17 warns us, 'the time is come that judgment must begin at the house of God: and if it first begin at us, what shall the end be of them that obey not the gospel of God?'" He looked from Rick to Eric, and then said gravely, "So the punishment of those who falsely *claim* to be 'Christians' will perhaps be the greatest of all."

Eric pointed out, "Well, this 'different degrees of punishment' idea you're now suggesting is completely inconsistent with what you were just arguing earlier: namely, that *all* sin against an infinite God is of an 'infinite magnitude.' By that standard, even the *tiniest* sin—chewing bubblegum in Sunday School, or giggling during the closing prayer in church, for example—would be deserving of the most *terrible* punishment; so how there ever be a penalty imposed on any sin that was other than the maximum?" Stanley frowned, but remained quiet, so Eric continued, "I also couldn't help noticing that none of the texts you just cited in support of your position are very *literal* in terms of explaining that Hitler and the twelve-year-old kid that Rick just mentioned won't receive exactly the same punishment in Hell. And in those 'more tolerable' passages, remember that Jesus said that it would be more tolerable on the *day of judgment*—not that their fate in *eternity* would be different from…"

Stanley held up his hand to interrupt Eric; after Eric stopped speaking, Stanley admitted, "It's true that the Bible does not *expressly* state that a person's eternal punishment will be different, based on the seriousness of his or her sins. But the passages I just cited provide considerable *inductive* evidence for differing degrees of punishment in Hell." Before Eric could respond, Stanley quickly added, "But let's suppose that we interpreted the Bible to teach that all sinners *were* punished in exactly the same way; how would that do either you, or our host, any good?"

Eric replied sharply, "It would show that your interpretation of the Bible makes God seem like an irrational tyrant!"

Looking directly into Eric's eyes, Stanley said (his voice deadly serious), "I feel led to warn you that those who claim to be *teachers* of Christianity are subject to even *stricter* standards, than others are. James warned in the

3rd chapter of his letter that teachers may receive 'the greater condemnation.' Second Peter 2:20-21 warns of 'teachers' who turn away from the truth, stating that 'it had been better for them not to have known the way of righteousness, than, after they have known it, to turn from the holy commandment delivered unto them.'"

"I don't claim to be a teacher of *Christianity;* I'm a Unitarian Universalist, remember?" Eric replied calmly. He added, "Don't get me wrong; I'm glad that you don't think that a twelve-year-old kid who doesn't respond to his first 'altar call' is deserving of the same punishment as Hitler. The poet Dante was perhaps the first one to suggest this notion of 'degrees of punishment' in Hell, when in his *Inferno* he suggested that there were nine circles in Hell: the first circle being the one containing unbaptized babies, and virtuous pagans; but progressing downward to the ninth level, where Satan is being held, and…"

Stanley waved his hand dismissively, saying, "Dante's interpretation is nothing but a lot of Romanist perversions of Scriptural truth; his acceptance of the doctrine that unbaptized babies go to Hell, for example, is completely contrary to the Bible."

Rick was immediately interested, and asked quickly, "Oh: so you think that babies who die in infancy go to Heaven?"

"Certainly," Stanley replied confidently. "Infants are not only incapable of *believing* the gospel; they are also incapable of *rejecting* Christ! Jesus said in Luke 18:16-17, 'Suffer little children to come unto me, and forbid them not: for of such is the kingdom of God. Verily I say unto you, Whosoever shall not receive the kingdom of God as a little child shall in no wise enter therein.' He said in Matthew 18:3-5, 'Except ye be converted, and become as little children, ye shall not enter into the kingdom of heaven. Whosoever therefore shall humble himself as this little child, the same is greatest in the kingdom of heaven. And whoso shall receive one such little child in my name receiveth me.' And he added in verse 14, 'it is not the will of your Father which is in heaven, that one of these little ones should perish.' Furthermore, David said in Psalm 22:9-10, 'thou art he that took me out of the womb: thou didst make me hope when I was upon my mother's breasts. I was cast upon thee from the womb: thou art my God from my mother's belly.'" He concluded, "Infants and young children below the 'age of accountability' will go to Heaven, because the price of their sins was paid by Jesus on Calvary."

With a slight smile, Eric observed, "Of course, if you were a Calvinist, you might equally well quote David saying in Psalm 58:3, 'the wicked are estranged from the womb; they go astray from birth, speaking lies.' But I certainly agree with you that infants go to Heaven. However, I think that position raises some problems for your theology, and your interpretation of the Bible. For instance, the Bible doesn't define any 'age of accountability'..."

Stanley replied easily, "The Bible doesn't specifically define the term, because it's different for different children; children aren't all ready to learn *Algebra* at the same age, either."

With a sly grin, Rick asked, "Say: if you think that all children are automatically 'saved'—whereas if they grow up, they'll most likely end up going to Hell—do you therefore think it might be a good idea to *kill* all babies? I mean, why take the risk of their eternal damnation?"

"Don't be ridiculous," Stanley said caustically. "God forbids *murder*, you know."

Rick kept probing, "Then what about aborted fetuses? You Evangelicals are usually so strongly opposed to abortion—even calling it 'murder'—but if the fetus is really a 'person' with a *soul,* then under your interpretation, these aborted babies are all going to Heaven!"

Before Stanley could respond, Eric addressed him directly, "I have another question for you. This idea of infants and children prior to some 'age of accountability' going to Heaven: does that apply only to *Western* countries with Christian backgrounds? Or does it apply across the board, to other countries, with no Christian background or history?"

"Of course it applies everywhere," Stanley replied diffidently. "God is no respecter of persons, as we are told in Acts 10:34."

Eric added with pretended casualness, "So therefore, that principle would also apply to predominantly *Muslim* countries, such as Saudi Arabia, Pakistan, Iran, and Iraq: correct?"

Stanley hesitated, but then answered, "That's correct."

Eric then said pointedly, "So let's say we have a boy from one of those countries who is *just below* this 'age of accountability.' However, he's a good kid, and wants to do the right thing, and to obey his parents, and all; and he's starting to think about God, as well. So he begins to say the five daily *Salat* prayers; he attends the local *masjid* with his folks; maybe he even starts to read the Quran. He's not a 'bad kid' in any way; on the contrary, all the adults around him are impressed that he is taking their religion so seriously, at such a young age." Looking directly into Stanley's eyes, he continued, "Now, as long as he's below your 'age of accountability,' he'll still go to Heaven if he happens to get accidentally killed in a drone attack, or something like that, right?" Stanley didn't say anything, so Eric went on, "Whereas if this same kid gets killed a few months or even weeks later—when he's just barely crossed the 'accountability' threshold—he will go to Hell: is that right? Is that what you believe?"

Stanley said contemptuously, "I am content to leave the fate of such persons in the hands of God. But I would point out that the Bible says in Acts 4:12 that 'Neither is there salvation in any other: for there is none other name under heaven given among men, whereby we must be saved.' And Jesus himself said in John 14:6, 'no man comes unto the Father, but by me.' So that's why Jesus is the 'One Way' to Heaven!"

Eric countered, "But Evangelicals who are 'Inclusivists'—such as Clark Pinnock, and John Sanders—believe that Jesus can *still* be the Savior of people in non-Christian parts of the world, although they may never have actually heard his name! Even C. S. Lewis said in *Mere Christianity* that 'God has not told us what His arrangements about the other people are. We do know that no man can be saved except through Christ; we do not know that only those who know Him can be saved through Him.' This is consistent with John 14:2, which says, 'In my Father's house are *many mansions*...'"

"That's an absurd interpretation," Stanley said dismissively. "Jesus was speaking only to his *disciples* in John 14. The Bible clearly states that there is no salvation apart from a saving knowledge of Jesus Christ, and it contains not a single verse suggesting that non-Christians can get to Heaven..."

"Not a single verse?" Eric said, feigning surprise. "You mean that in Heaven, there will be millions of infants and young kids from Muslim, Hindu, and Buddhist countries; but not a single adolescent or adult from the same countries? And they're all going to Hell just because they have never heard the name of Jesus? Even in the parable of the rich man and Lazarus, Father Abraham refused the rich man's request to evangelize his brothers, on the grounds that 'They have Moses and the prophets'—but what about nations that *didn't* have Moses and the prophets? How could they possibly have been saved? Shouldn't the standard be more *lenient* for those nations that didn't have God's revelation to Israel?"

Stanley relented slightly, saying, "Missionaries have sometimes reporting finding people who, before the missionaries arrived, were nevertheless aware of God's righteousness, and of their own sin, as well as their need to seek God's mercy and forgiveness; read Don Richardson's book, *Eternity in Their Hearts,* for some examples of this. But cases like that are fairly rare; and when they occur, it was the earnest desire of such people for God that *led* Him to send missionaries to that particular area, so that those people *can* be saved. But that is precisely why Romans 10:14-15 warns us, 'How then shall they call on him in whom they have not believed? and how shall they believe in him of whom they have not heard? and how shall they hear without a preacher?' That is why missionary work is *essential:* so that people in those countries you mentioned will *not* perish without having had the chance to accept Jesus!"

Before Eric could object, Stanley quickly added, "But your entire argument is incorrect, because no one goes to Hell just 'because they never heard the name of Jesus'; they go to Hell for their *own* sins! As Romans 3:10—quoting Psalm 14:3—said, 'There is none righteous, no, not one.' Romans 1:20 tells us that 'the invisible things of [God] … are clearly seen… so that they are without excuse'! And Romans 2:15 likewise says that all of us 'show the work of the law written in their hearts, their conscience also bearing witness'; so no one can accuse God of 'injustice' or 'favoritism,' when they are quite rightfully sent to Hell!"

Eric said reasonably, "Well, Stanley, I've been patient, and let you explain your position; now may I take a few minutes, uninterrupted, to explain why I disagree with your blanket statement that the Bible 'contains not a single verse suggesting that non-Christians can get to Heaven'?" Stanley hesitated, but (seeing Rick ready to intervene) reluctantly nodded his agreement.

Eric said, "One of the most interesting and yet *mysterious* characters in the Old Testament is Melchizedek. We are told in Genesis 14:18-20 that he was 'the priest of the most high God,' and that he blessed Abraham—who then gave the 10% *tithes* to Melchizedek! And this was *after* Abraham had received his own call from God. Melchizedek was also praised in Hebrews 5-7, where Jesus was said to be a priest 'after the order of Melchisedec'! Or what about Moses' father-in-law Jethro—who, according to Exodus 18, was a Midianite priest, and…"

Stanley couldn't remain silent, and said hotly, "I was referring to people in the *current* Dispensation—not people in Old Testament times! The way of salvation for the Old Testament saints was different, because they were saved through their faith in the *coming* Messiah! But in our *current* Dispensation, the New Testament era, there are no Bible verses supporting salvation outside of Jesus."

Eric suppressed a smile, and then said reasonably, "Okay, so I'll stick to the New Testament. In the fourth Gospel, there are some interesting statements attributed to Jesus. For example, John 9:41 says, 'If you were blind, you would *not be guilty of sin*; but now that you claim you can see, your guilt remains.' Later, in John 15:22, 24, he adds, 'If I had not come and spoken to them, they would *not be guilty of sin*; but now they have no excuse for their sin… If I had not done among them the works no one else did, they would *not be guilty of sin*. As it is, they have seen, and yet they have hated both me and my Father.' So I think those verses suggest that those who haven't heard the Christian message are *not guilty of sin!* And if they aren't guilty of sin, then…"

Stanley countered, "The Bible clearly says that *all* are sinners; you can't just take one single verse out of context, and try to base a whole doctrine on it. You need to put together *all* that the Bible says on a particular subject, to formulate doctrine."

Eric sighed with exasperation, then said, "How about Cornelius the centurion, in Acts 10? We are told in verse 2 that 'He and all his family were devout and God-fearing; he gave generously to those in need and prayed to God regularly'; and verse 22 adds that he was 'of good report among all the nation of the Jews.'"

Stanley said eagerly, "But that proves my point: Cornelius realized his need for God, and God sent Peter to *preach the Gospel* to him!"

Eric explained patiently, "But first, Peter said to Cornelius, 'I now realize how true it is that God does not show favoritism, but *accepts from every nation* the one who fears him and does what is right.'" [v. 34-35] Titus 2:11 also states that 'the grace of God has appeared that *offers salvation to all people.*' Even your Book of Revelation says in 7:9 that 'there before me was a great multitude that no one could count, *from every nation, tribe, people and language,* standing before the throne and before the Lamb.' And those in this multitude were all 'wearing white robes'! Now, if…"

Stanley interrupted again, saying passionately, "And God *does* offer salvation to all people! But that salvation is only brought about by receiving his Son, and accepting what Jesus did for us on the cross! And that multitude you mentioned is saved only because virtually every nation and people *have* been reached with the gospel of Christ."

Eric said sharply, "But in your interpretation, God apparently *doesn't* 'offer salvation to all people'! There are literally *billions* of people who live and die without ever having heard your version of the 'gospel'!"

Stanley replied stubbornly, "If they truly seek God—based on the light that God has given them—then the Gospel will reach them; just as it did for Cornelius."

Suddenly, Rick urgently held up his hand to silence both men, as a woman standing off-camera was frantically waving to him. He turned to Stanley and Rick, and said, "Hold on a minute, gentlemen; my Program Director is trying to get my attention. What is it, Madeline?"

The woman stepped forward, and said quickly, "We've got to wrap this up; we're nearly out of time."

Rick objected, "We can't stop now; the discussion is just starting to get *good!*" He thought for a moment, then said to her, "Let's do *two* shows on this topic; we can just continue taping right now, if my two guests are agreeable." He looked at Stanley and Eric, and they both immediately nodded their agreement. Rick turned back to his Program Director, and said, "I can tape the voiceover intro and closing stuff later. But why don't we just take five, to give the crew a chance to readjust, and then go back and do another half hour?"

She was agreeable, and she informed the camera and administrative crew of the change in schedule; they all relaxed, moved from their stations, stretched, and began to chat among themselves.

Rick looked at his two guests, and said, "Thanks so much for agreeing to extend the program, guys; but I'm really enjoying this discussion—and I'll bet that our audience will enjoy it just as much!"

Eric gave a slight smile, and said, "It's rare to get such detailed discussions on television, these days."

Stanley nodded his agreement, adding, "It's also refreshing to be able to discuss such matters, without being limited to providing only ten-second *sound bites!*" and they all laughed.

Rick got up from this chair, and said to them, "Let's regroup in about five minutes, guys; or, given our crew's usual standards for 'break time,' probably more like ten or fifteen minutes. So go get some coffee or water, stretch, and use the john, and we'll see you back here soon." He removed a pack of cigarettes from his inside jacket pocket, and headed to an exit.

Both Eric and Stanley stood up and stretched, and Stanley admitted, "I can use some coffee."

"Me, too," Eric said, and they both headed to the coffee station that was just offstage.

Stanley poured himself a styrofoam cup of coffee, and then held out the coffee pot to Eric, but Eric shook his head and said, "They don't have decaf, so I think I'll just have a bottle of water, instead; my wife—who's a medical doctor, a pediatric surgeon—is always on my back about cutting down on my intake of caffeine." He took out a bottle of water from a nearby refrigerator.

Stanley chuckled as he set down the coffee pot again, and said, "My wife is always on my case about caffeine, too; but I usually just ignore her." They both laughed, and he added with a smile, "There are times when it's useful to be the 'head of the household.'" Stanley then poured a little cold water from the tap into his cup, so that it would be 'drinkable' immediately.

They both went and sat down on a nearby couch, and took swallows from their respective beverages.

Stanley looked over at Eric, then said with grudging respect, "I must compliment you on your knowledge of the Scriptures! Usually when I have discussions such as this with unbe… uhh, with people who disagree with me, they just want to expound on their subjective *feelings,* and their personal philosophical beliefs. But you have a pretty detailed knowledge of the Bible—although I'm obviously in strong disagreement with you about the *interpretations* you're taking, on nearly all matters."

Eric chuckled, and explained, "Actually, when I was in seminary, I was really into *historical* Universalism—especially from the 19th century; that's what I wrote my Master's thesis on, incidentally. And back then, Universalists defended their positions in books and public debates almost solely from the Bible. So I've absorbed a lot of their knowledge, after reading dozens of books from the 19th century."

Stanley took a large swallow of his coffee, then asked, "So I guess you have to get those kinds of books 'on loan' from a library?"

Eric shook his head, and said, "Actually, since 19th century works aren't protected by copyright, you can order *scanned* versions of practically *any* of them from online booksellers; you can even get .pdf versions of a lot of them for free, online."

"Interesting," Stanley said, taking another swallow of his coffee. He sighed, and said, "That's the one thing I most regret: that I don't have nearly as much time as I would like to just *study!* I study the Bible for ninety minutes a day, but my time for reading *books* is… well, usually somewhat limited."

Eric nodded sympathetically, and said, "Being a 'working' minister, with an active congregation, takes up a *lot* of time."

"You've got that right," Stanley acknowledged.

A young girl wearing a headset approached the two men, and said, "Rick wants you two back on stage. The makeup guy needs to give you both a touchup before you go back on camera, too; both of you were starting to sweat a little bit, at the end."

Eric smiled and said, "From the heat of the battle!"

The two men stood up, and Stanley took a last swallow of his coffee, dropped the cup in a waste can, and said, "Back to the battlefield."

"Yup," Eric agreed, as they headed back to the stage area.

***

Back on the set, the Program Director signaled to Rick that they were "live" again, so Rick said into the camera, "We're returning for the second part of our series on the question of *Hell;* does it exist? And who, if anyone, goes there? Once again, I am joined by Stanley Beechman, Pastor of the Evangelical Community Bible Assembly of River City, and by Eric Swenson, who is the … *minister* of the Unitarian *Universalist*

Society here in River City. Welcome back, gentlemen." They both quickly acknowledged his welcome.

Rick said, "Last week, after some wrangling, we agreed to take a long, hard look at what the Bible itself says on the subject of Hell: does it *really* say that some of God's children are going to spend all of eternity suffering horrible torment? Or, as increasing numbers of theologians and writers are suggesting, does the Bible instead say that the 'bad' people are, in the end, simply going to go out of existence forever? Or, as my new friend Eric would say, are we all ultimately going to end up in Heaven anyway? So let's get right to it, gentlemen: as the saying goes, 'What sayeth the Scriptures?'" He nodded to Stanley, to begin.

Stanley explained, "The creation of man and woman is described in the first three chapters of the Book of Genesis. And yes, I *do* believe in a literal Adam and Eve, who were directly created by God, without the 'benefit' of any kind of *evolutionary* process!" Opening his Bible, he continued, "God told Adam in Genesis 2:16-17, 'Of every tree of the garden thou may freely eat: But of the tree of the knowledge of good and evil, thou shalt not eat of it: for in the day that thou eat thereof thou shalt surely die.' But, as we all know, Eve, and then Adam, *did* eat of the tree of the knowledge of good and evil; thus, our first ancestors committed the first *sin*—the 'Original Sin,' as some call it—by deliberately disobeying God's command. The apostle Paul told us of the disastrous effect of this first sin in Romans 5:12, where he wrote, 'by one man sin entered into the world, and death by sin; and so death passed upon all men, for that all have sinned.'"

Rick interrupted, saying, "That reminds me of something I'd never really thought about before I started my research for this program: God originally told Adam, 'in the *day* that you eat the fruit, you will surely *die!*' But in fact, Adam did *not* die that day—in fact, he's supposed to have gone on to live to a ripe old age! And I also think it's interesting that 'death,' not 'eternal torment,' was the penalty inflicted on Adam and Eve for their actions. And I also think it's very interesting that the text points out that Adam and Eve were *not* immortal in the Garden of Eden; and it was actually the *serpent* who came up with the idea of immortality, when he said in Genesis 3:4-5, '*Ye shall not surely die: For God doth know that in the day ye eat thereof, then your eyes shall be opened, and ye shall be as* gods, knowing good and evil.'" With a grin, he added, "So it looks to me as if the *serpent* is the one who got it right, and not Jehovah!"

Stanley said calmly, "Adam and Eve *did* die that very day: they died *spiritually*—and they also became *subject* to physical death; whereas, if they had obeyed God, they could have lived forever in the garden God had made for them."

Rick pretended to be surprised, saying, "They died 'spiritually'? And not physically? And just how do you claim to know that?"

Stanley explained, "The grammar of the Hebrew text does not necessitate *immediacy* of action—although they *did* immediately die in a *spiritual* sense—but it indicates the certainty of the *consequences* of the action."

Rick rolled his eyes, and complained, "Why is it that whenever you get Christians backed into a corner about the Bible, they always run and hide behind the Greek or Hebrew text, claiming that it doesn't *really* mean what all the English translations say?" He looked over at Eric, and asked, "So what do you think of that interpretation, Eric? Do Unitarian Universalists believe in Original Sin?"

"No, we don't," Eric replied. "Actually, I think all of us UUAs treat the Genesis story of Adam and Eve as a *myth;* as a symbolic story, used for *teaching* purposes. In fact, I'm a lot more in sympathy with the *Jewish* interpretation of the story, than with the traditional, Augustinian version that's found in so many Christian creeds. Jews strongly *reject* the Christian concept of 'Original Sin,' suggesting instead that man enters the world free of sin, with a soul that is untainted. Let's look at what the story says to a Jewish reader: We should first note that the same Hebrew word, *nephesh* or 'soul,' is used of both humans and *animals* in the first chapters of Genesis—although the King James and many other Bible translations inconsistently translate the word as 'creature' in places like Genesis 1:20 and 24, but as 'soul' in Genesis 2:7, when it's referring to Adam. So humans were originally *like the other animals,* even though God gave Adam a quasi-supervisory role of the lesser animals. Furthermore, as male *and* female, we were made 'in the image of God' [1:27]."

He continued, "That's why they were, like the other animals, naked, but not ashamed [2:25]; animals have no sense of 'shame,' after all. But it's significant that, *not* having eaten of the tree of the knowledge of good and evil, we were even more like animals in our mental apparatus: animals don't know 'right' from 'wrong,' for example; they operate by instinct—or, for domestic animals, they generally behave as they've been trained or taught to behave." Looking over at Stanley, he added, "But I think it's also interesting that, since Adam and Eve supposedly *didn't* know what 'good' and 'evil' were before they ate of the tree, that they are considered by traditional Christians to have *sinned*—because animals can't 'sin'!"

He ignored Stanley's indignation, and went on, "Now, I suppose traditional Christians think that Adam and Eve should have just *continued* on, without eating of the tree; but is that really what we humans want? Eternal life, but *without* knowing what 'good' and 'evil' are? Would we truly be happy, just being like a dog or a cat that lived forever? I don't think so. So it was actually a *good* thing, then, that Eve and then Adam ate from the tree, and acquired knowledge. And of course, they then immediately realized that they were naked, and they hid from God. When God realized that they had eaten of the tree, he said, 'The man has now become like one of us, knowing good and evil.' So we were no longer just animals. But then God said, 'He must not be allowed to reach out his hand and take also from the tree of life and eat, and live forever,' so we were banished from the Garden, and cursed to spend our lives in toil." He shrugged, and then summarized, "So I think the whole point of the story is not to detail how we fell into "Original Sin,' but to illustrate how *different* we are from the rest of the animal kingdom—reinforcing the conclusion that we are indeed, made in the 'image of God,' as both Genesis 1:27 and 9:6 say."

Stanley leaped in, saying passionately, "That's a completely erroneous interpretation of the Bible! The 'subtil' or crafty serpent was clearly *Satan,* who was tempting humanity to fall into sin; that's why in Genesis 3:15 God said, 'And I will put enmity between thee and the woman, and between thy seed and her seed; it shall bruise thy head, and thou shalt bruise his heel.' The term 'his heel' was referring to *Christ,* whose sacrificial death on the cross 'bruised' or crippled Satan's work on earth. And this is proved by the fact that this is the only reference in the Bible to the 'seed of a *woman*'— and it clearly referred to Jesus, who was the only person ever born that was not of the seed of a *man!*"

Rick objected, "Now, Stanley, how in the world do you know that the serpent is really good old 'Satan'? I mean, Genesis doesn't *say* that anywhere. It seems to me that this part of the story is just saying that female offspring—the 'seed of woman'—won't *like* snakes; and that *men* will thus have to crush the heads of snakes under their heel."

Stanley explained patiently, "Ezekiel 28:13—and verses 11-19 are clearly referring to Satan—states that the being addressed by Ezekiel had been in Eden, the Garden of God..."

Eric interrupted, "Stanley, Ezekiel 28:11 specifically says that this section is referring to the *King of Tyrus*—not Satan! And the Old Testament refers to the 'seed' of women in several places, such as First Samuel 2:20 and Ruth 4:12. And if this serpent was actually *Satan,* then why were *all* serpents 'condemned' by God to 'crawl on their bellies and eat dust'? [Gen 3:14] They didn't do anything wrong!" He shook his head, and added, "I really have to disagree with Christian interpreters of the Old Testament, who claim to see a 'scarlet thread' pointing to Jesus running all the way through the entire Bible. These Christian interpretations of Old Testament prophecies, for example, are completed rejected by Jewish scholars, as mistranslations and misinterpretations..."

Stanley was about to respond, when Rick held up his hands to silence his two guests. When they were again quiet, and said reasonably, "Once again, we're getting off track; let's see if we can't get back to the subject of Hell, okay?" The two guests reluctantly agreed, and Rick said, "Stanley, since you represent the traditional view, let's let you start off again."

Stanley nodded, and then said confidently, "First of all, we need to acknowledge that the Bible clearly indicates that not only does a state of *salvation* exist, but also a contrasting state of *damnation.* Jesus mentioned damnation in passages such as Matthew 23:14, where he told the scribes and Pharisees that 'ye shall receive the greater damnation.' In Mark 3:29, he said that those who blaspheme against the Holy Ghost are 'in danger of eternal damnation.' In Romans 3:8, Paul speaks of slanderers 'whose damnation is just,' and in First Timothy 5:12 he talks of those who have 'damnation, because they have cast off their first faith.' Heaven is the place for those who are saved, and Hell is the place for those who are damned. The Bible is also crystal clear, from both the Old Testament and the New Testament, that Hell is a condition of everlasting, or *eternal* torment! In the Old Testament, for example, Isaiah 33:14 tells us that sinners and hypocrites 'shall dwell with the devouring fire' and its 'everlasting burnings.' And Daniel 12:2 speaks of the dead being raised either to 'everlasting life,' or to 'everlasting contempt.'"

Rick said energetically, "But those kinds of passages are precisely what people like Edward Fudge are talking about, when they talk about such fires having a 'devouring' or 'destroying' effect! That's what fire does, isn't it? As the title of Fudge's book says, it is a 'fire that *consumes*'! And that passage in Daniel only says that '*many*' shall awake, not that *everyone* will be awakened at some 'Last Judgment.' And the 'shame' and 'everlasting contempt' mentioned in that verse can be fulfilled just as well by sinners having been *annihilated*, yet forever being remembered contemptuously by the 'saved.'"

Stanley argued, "'Many' in that passage just means that not *everyone* needs to be 'awakened,' since a lot of people will still be *living* when the end comes. But your erroneous interpretation clearly illustrates the danger of just plucking isolated verses out of the Bible, as Fudge does; you have to put together *all* that the Bible says on a particular topic. And in terms of Hell, the one who spoke the most about it was none other than Jesus himself! And the one who spoke most clearly and emphatically of Hell being like a *fire* was Christ, as well. He spoke in Matthew 5:22, 18:9, and Mark 9:47 of 'hell fire'; he said in Matthew 7:19 that every tree that didn't bring forth good fruit would be 'hewn down, and cast into the fire'; he said in Matthew 13:42 that at the end of the world, the angels would cast the wicked into 'the furnace of fire.'"

He continued forcefully, "And it's not just Jesus who used the illustration of *fire;* Paul said in Second Thessalonians 1:8 that at the Second Coming, Jesus would be 'in flaming fire taking vengeance on them that know not God.' Hebrews 10:27 speaks of 'judgment and fiery indignation.' James 3:6 refers to the 'fire of hell.' Second Peter 3:7 speaks of the heavens and earth being 'reserved unto fire against the day of judgment and perdition of ungodly men.' And verse 7 of the epistle of Jude speaks of 'suffering the vengeance of eternal fire.' Jesus also referred to this realm in Matthew 8:12, 22:13, and 25:30 as 'outer darkness,' which was a region where there would be 'weeping, and gnashing of teeth'—which is a phrase he repeats over and over, in many different verses. He said in both Matthew 5:29 and 18:9 that it was better to pluck out or cut off an eye or hand that was causing you to sin, because 'it is profitable for thee that one of thy members should perish, and not that thy whole body should be cast into hell'; for in Hell, the 'worm dieth not, and the fire is not quenched.' That's why he solemnly warned us in Matthew 10:28, 'fear not them which kill the body, but are not able to kill the soul: but rather fear him which is able to destroy both soul and body in hell.'"

(Eric was impatiently waiting for an opportunity to respond to this exposition, but Rick signaled for him to wait, and he nodded for Stanley to continue.)

Stanley went on, "But of course, the two most irrefutable teachings which Jesus gave about Hell are found in the account of the rich man and Lazarus in Luke 16:19-31, and his description of the Last Judgment in Matthew 25:31-46. The rich man died, and 'in hell he lift up his eyes, being in torments… And he cried and said, Father Abraham, have mercy on me, and send Lazarus, that he may dip the tip of his finger in water, and cool my tongue; for I am tormented in this flame.' So Jesus said in unmistakable words that Hell was a place of *torment!* And then in Matthew 25:41 and 46, he pronounced, 'Then shall he say also unto them on the left hand, Depart from me, ye cursed, into everlasting fire, prepared for the devil and his angels: And these shall go away into everlasting punishment: but the righteous into life eternal.' And for those 'Conditionalists' or 'Annihilationists,' please note that the same Greek word *Aionios* or 'eternal' is used to describe the state of both the condition of *life*, and that of *punishment!* So you can't believe in eternal life, without also believing in eternal punishment!"

Sounding supremely confident, he added, "But of course, the ultimate description of the fate of the lost is found in the Book of Revelation, which describes in great detail the events of the end of the world, and its aftermath. Revelation 14:9-11 says that the wicked 'shall be tormented with fire and brimstone in the presence of the holy angels, and in the presence of the Lamb: And the smoke of their torment ascendeth up for ever and ever: and they have no rest day nor night.' Then 19:20 says that 'the beast was taken, and with him the false prophet … These both were cast alive into a lake of fire burning with brimstone.' And finally, and most conclusively, 20:10-15 tells us, 'And the devil that deceived them was cast into the lake of fire and brimstone, where the beast and the false prophet are, and shall be tormented day and night for ever and ever… And whosoever was not found written in the book of life was cast into the lake of fire.'" With a triumphant expression on his face, he concluded, "So the Bible is absolutely clear, in describing the fate of the unsaved as *eternal, conscious torment.*"

Rick looked genuinely intimidated by Stanley's barrage of biblical texts, and he turned to Eric and asked hesitantly, "Well, that's Stanley's position; any thoughts, Eric?"

"Lots of them," Eric replied, with a sigh. He thought for a moment, then asked Stanley, "Do you take the 'flames' of this 'hell fire' *literally?* That is, do you think that the wicked are literally cast into a lake of fire? Where their resurrected bodies are capable of feeling pain to an exquisite degree, yet their bodies are somehow never *burned up* by these flames? And where this 'outer darkness' is apparently not *illumined* by the burning flames? And where their bodies can be nibbled on by *worms* for all of eternity, without ever being completely consumed? So that, apparently, God would be constantly and eternally *recreating* their bodies, just so that the torment can go on?"

Stanley replied easily, "Haven't you ever built a campfire on a dark, moonless night? The flames might easily be the *only* source of light. But these flames may well also be *figurative;* the Bible often uses figurative or metaphorical language, to convey its truths. But since most people have had an experience of being burned, and are aware of how stark the pain from this is, God used this illustration to convey the *seriousness* of the punishment."

Eric nodded, then said, "So you're rejecting what the Bible *literally* says about this torment, in favor of... what? What is the torment of Hell *really* consisting of, if not flames and worms?"

Stanley hesitated for a moment, then replied, "We... don't really know. Again, the idea of flame conveys the *horror* of the torment—whatever causes it—and its *intensity;* but precisely *how* God brings this about, we don't know."

Eric observed, "But although you just now admitted that you *don't know* precisely what God has in store for the wicked, you are nevertheless certain that Billy Graham's earlier notion that Hell might just be 'eternal separation from God,' and C.S. Lewis's suggestion that what is in hell 'is not a man: it is *remains*,' are both incorrect: right?"

"That's correct," Stanley replied immediately.

Eric frowned, and then added, "But if you've abandoned the *literal* notion of hellfire, how can you be so certain that such notions are *incorrect?* Your own perspective seems to be just as individualistic and subjective as theirs are."

Irritation came over Stanley's face, and he replied, "Jesus and the New Testament writers would have used *softer* metaphors, if the reality of Hell was as mild as in Lewis's books like *The Great Divorce*."

Eric probed further, "And just how do *you* know what would have been in the mind of Jesus and the New Testament writers?"

Testily, Stanley exploded, "Fine: then let's say for the sake of our discussion that I believe in the *literal* interpretation of Hell! There are literal fires, and literal worms, that torment the bodies of the wicked forever; if God can create the entire universe out of nothing, then He shouldn't have any problem *recreating* such bodies, for all of eternity!"

Eric suppressed a smile, and then said calmly, "Even if we accepted your newly literal interpretation of Revelation 14, by its own terms this passage only applies to someone who 'worships the beast and its image and receives the mark of its name on their forehead or on their hand'; so, since you're apparently what's known as a 'Premillennialist,' these are people who may not even be *here* yet. And Revelation 19 is only referring to the 'beast' and the 'false prophet'; and although Revelation 20:15 says that 'whosoever was not found written in the book of life was cast into the lake of fire,' it doesn't say that *they* are likewise tormented forever and ever. So even the book of Revelation may be reserving *eternal* torments to a special class of demonic beings, as well as to the wicked people who live during the 'Great Tribulation'!"

Stanley snorted, and said contemptuously, "*Now* who's being overly-literal? There's only one lake of fire; and all those who end up in it are tormented forever!"

Eric pressed on, "Revelation 20:14 also says that 'death and Hades were thrown into the lake of fire.' So you're telling us that *they* are going to be 'tormented forever'? Those aren't even *persons!*"

Stanley said impatiently, "That text just means that they will be no more, since they will no longer be needed."

Eric continued his questioning without letup: "There's also a problem with your Old Testament references to 'hell'; the Hebrew word 'Sheol' is translated inconsistently in your preferred King James Version, which translates it as 'hell' 27 times, as 'grave' 35 times, and as 'pit' three times. But trying to read Luke 16 into these references just won't work, because *all* people—good and bad, including patriarchs like Jacob and David— enter Sheol after death; see, for example, Genesis 37:35; Job 14:13 and 17:13; Psalm 49:15 and 89:48; and Hosea 13:14. Even *Jesus* was supposedly in 'hell' or *hades* after his death, according to Acts 2:27 & 31. And the identification of Sheol with Hades is made certain by comparison of Psalm 16:10—which uses 'Sheol'—and Acts 2:27, which quotes this Psalm using the word 'Hades' in place of 'Sheol,' and…"

Stanley countered, "'Sheol' or 'Hades' has *two compartments,* according to Luke 16; one is for the wicked, such as the rich man, and the other is for the righteous, such as Lazarus. Jesus said in John 3:13 that 'no man hath ascended up to heaven, but he that came down from heaven, even the Son of man which is in heaven'; so believers didn't go to Heaven until *after* Jesus' mission. According to Matthew 12:40, 'Paradise' was once in the heart of the earth; but after Jesus rose from the dead, he opened the 'Paradise' section of Hades and emptied it, taking the Old Testament saints into Heaven, so that the Paradise of 'Abraham's Bosom' is now probably the 'third heaven' that Paul spoke of in Second Corinthians 12:2-4. It is only the wicked who go to Hades after death, now."

Eric said wearily, "I find it hard to believe that anyone still thinks that Hell is, or ever was, literally *inside the Earth.* If you take such biblical verses literally, you may as well conclude that Heaven is up in the clouds, since Acts 1:9 says that at Jesus' Ascension, 'a cloud received him out of their sight.' And all this stuff about these 'two compartments,' with one compartment being 'emptied' and moved into Heaven, and so on, are nothing but your own *speculations* about confusing and contradictory teachings in the Bible. But be that as it may, one major objection I have to your habit of 'proof-texting' the words of Jesus is that you completely ignore the *differences* in how Jesus is presented in the various gospels. For example, Matthew is the only gospel to use the 'outer darkness' term; and the 'weeping and gnashing of teeth' illustration also only appears in Matthew, except for a single reference in Luke 13:28. Nearly all of the references to *Gehenna* come from Matthew, whereas Luke uses *Hades* more often. In Luke 8:31 the Gerasene demons ask not to be sent to the 'Abyss,' while Mark 5:10 has them requesting not to be sent 'out of the area'...."

Stanley asserted, "When any of the gospels report Jesus' words, they are reporting them accurately."

"That *can't be*," Eric insisted. "The three synoptic gospels often treat of the same incident, yet there are significant differences in how they report Jesus' words—which suggests that some of the words they are attributing to Jesus may in fact be their own literary 'addition,' or 'embellishment' of the story; only one gospel version of a particular situation may contain a 'hellish' reference. For example, the 'tree and its fruit' story in Matthew 7:18-20 contains a 'cast into the fire' reference that's absent from the parallel account in Luke 6:43-44. The healing of the Roman officer's servant in Matthew 8:5-13 contains an 'outer darkness' reference that isn't found in the parallel in Luke 7:1-10. The parable of the wedding feast in Matthew 22:1-14 has another 'outer darkness' reference not found in the parallel in Luke 14:15-24, and..."

"What is your point?" Stanley said impatiently. "If the gospels say that Jesus said it, then he said it; all of the writers don't have to include every single word that Jesus said on every possible occasion—and in fact, they are often probably reporting *different occasions,* when Jesus used similar, but slightly different words and illustrations."

Eric shook his head, and said, "There were surely not *two* incidents with the Gerasene swine, or two Roman officer's servants..."

Stanley interrupted, saying earnestly, "And the words of Jesus are not found only in the four Gospels! You need to acknowledge that, since the first verse of the Book of Revelation tells us that this is the 'revelation of Jesus Christ,' the words in Revelation are actually *Jesus' own words!* So Jesus was, in fact, the *ultimate* 'hellfire preacher'!"

Eric shook his head, and said, "When you consolidate the synoptic gospel accounts together, there are only about one dozen occasions where Jesus even mentioned 'hell,' 'outer darkness,' 'damnation,' or any related terms; and most of those references are found *only* in the gospel of Matthew, which suggests..."

"So what?" Stanley said dismissively. "He still said it!"

Eric explained patiently, "If the author of the gospel of Luke said in his introduction that he was making an 'orderly account' of all the stories of

Jesus that he knew of, this suggests that at least one version of these stories circulating in his time *didn't* contain all of the 'hellish' references that Matthew's gospel contains; which means that they might have been *added* by Matthew, or—just as bad, from your point of view—deliberately *left out* by Luke. And that closing line in the rich man/Lazarus parable—'If they do not listen to Moses and the Prophets, they will not be convinced even if someone rises from the dead' [Lk 16:31]—was obviously added later by Christians, who were thinking of the resurrection of Jesus!"

He held up his hand to stop Stanley from objecting, and then added, "Since the rich man still has hope for his brothers 'repenting,' the parable is obviously not talking about your 'final,' inescapable Hell, but rather about some kind of 'intermediate state.' Furthermore, the Luke 16 parable refers to *Hades, not Gehenna:* and it's Gehenna that is considered the place of 'fiery punishment' throughout the New Testament."

His voice dripping with sarcasm, Stanley said, "So you think that Jesus was just a limp-wristed, liberal, 'Social Gospel' kind of a teacher?"

Eric shrugged, then replied, "I have little doubt but that Jesus said a few things about *Hades,* and probably even more about *Gehenna*—Gehenna being, not a perpetually burning 'garbage dump,' as some commentators used to think—which was a place outside Jerusalem where some wicked kings had sacrificed children, and so was considered by the Jews to be an accursed place. But trying to base doctrines on fine matters of the precise *language* Jesus used, seems completely futile to me; after all, Jesus spoke Aramaic, not Greek—so we don't know *any* of his actual words! And translating the Greek gospels into English makes his precise words even farther removed from us. And trying to portray Jesus as some kind of 'hellfire preacher' is ridiculous; the only reason that Jesus seems to say more about Hell than anyone else in the New Testament is because there's so *little* about Hell in the rest of the New Testament! Paul never used the word 'Hell' in any of his extensive writings, and James 3:6 is the only reference to 'Gehenna' outside of the synoptic gospels."

Stanley stubbornly insisted, "The gospels accurately report Jesus' words. Naturally, a given author—who was writing for a different audience, and perhaps had different purposes or emphases in his writing—is free to leave out a word or phrase here or there, that another author included."

Eric refused to give up, pointing out, "Even if you accept that 'Luke the physician,' a companion of Paul, was the one who wrote the gospel that now bears his name, Luke was *not an eyewitness of Jesus!* And in the first chapter of this gospel, he admits that 'many' had previously written of the things that took place among Jesus and the early apostles, and that he was simply writing 'an orderly account' of them. So some of the things he includes may have been stories *about* Jesus that were circulating in the early church, and may not be historically reliable as actual…"

Stanley shot back, "Luke said in verse 2 that he *and his companions* 'from the beginning were *eyewitnesses*'; so everything in his gospel *is* historically reliable, as eyewitness testimony."

Growing increasingly frustrated, Eric said, "I have a big problem with the way you were just throwing out so many Bible verses earlier, when we clearly don't have time to go through and discuss them. I could do the same with lots of verses that clearly seem to be teaching Universalism, and Rick could cite a bunch of verses from Edward Fudge's book that seem to support Conditional Immortality. But if we'd just go through them slowly, one by one, I'm sure you'd have different interpretations of our verses; just as Rick and I would have different interpretations of the verses you quoted…"

Stanley said sarcastically, "How can you possibly have a 'different interpretation' of the account of the rich man and Lazarus? Or of the 'sheep and the goats' illustration?"

Eric said firmly, "Because both of those are *parables;* they don't pretend to be an explanation of literal *reality.* And moreover, both of them are reported in only one gospel, which…"

Stanley interrupted, "Which doesn't diminish their *accuracy,* as the virtual words of Jesus! The 'sheep and goats' account is a literal description of the world standing before Jesus on Judgment Day. And the fact that the proper name 'Lazarus' is used in Luke 16 *proves* that it is not a parable, but literal truth—because parables don't use *personal names!*"

Eric countered, "How do *you* know that 'parables don't use personal names'? And what other examples in the gospels do you have where Jesus refers to *real-life events,* and *does* use someone's actual name? And the name 'Lazarus' is just used to simplify the telling of the parable; would you really expect Jesus to have had the rich man say to Abraham, 'Father Abraham, do you remember that poor nameless dude that used to hang out by my front door?' And the name 'Lazarus' was commonly used in Jewish inter-testamental literature; so that lessens even more that argument that he was a historical person. But the rich man and Lazarus is clearly a parable, since it starts out with the phrase, 'there was a...'; which, along with 'a certain man...', are literary forms typically used to begin Jesus' non-'Kingdom of God' parables; see Matthew 21:28 and 21:33; Luke 15:11, 16:1, 18:2, 19:12, 20:9, and so on. It's also part of a *series* of five parables that begin in Luke 15:3; in fact, the parable right before it is also about a rich man!"

Without pausing, he added, "And the sheep/goats parable makes the sole criterion for salvation or damnation whether one did or didn't help out Jesus' 'brothers' while they were on earth; but that kind of 'works salvation' is surely not *your* theology, since there's nothing about having a 'personal relationship with Jesus'! And if there is already a preliminary determination made at one's time of death to decide into which 'compartment' of Hades one goes into, why was it apparently a *surprise* to the 'goats' in this parable that they weren't 'saved'? The rich man in the Lazarus parable certainly would have already known that he was damned!"

Stanley seemed surprised by these questions, so Eric took advantage of the moment, and went on quickly, "Moreover, phrases such as 'fire not quenched' and 'worm shall not die' were used earlier by prophets such as Isaiah [34:10, 66:24], Jeremiah [4:4, 7:20, 17:27], and Ezekiel [20:47-48], in contexts where they were clearly not talking about an *eternal* fire. And a fire that is not 'quenched' may simply be allowed to *burn itself out;* in other words, it's a fire that is not put out or 'quenched' by anyone. Again, it doesn't imply an 'eternal' fire."

Stanley said (somewhat cockily), "The fires that Jesus was speaking about in the gospels, he described in greater detail in the Book of Revelation, which clearly describes the wicked as being tormented day and night, forever and ever!"

Irritated, Eric asked, "How can you possibly take a thoroughly *symbolic* book such as Revelation in such a *literal* fashion? I mean, that book talks about Jesus having 'coming out of his mouth ... a sharp, double-edged sword'; Jesus appears as a 'Lamb, looking as if it had been slain,' which had *seven horns and seven eyes*; there is a woman—presumably representing Jesus' mother Mary—'clothed with the sun, with the moon under her feet and a crown of twelve stars on her head,' pursued by a serpent who 'cast out of his mouth water as a flood after the woman,' but 'the earth opened her mouth, and swallowed up the flood'; there was another woman 'drunken with the blood of the saints,' who had 'MYSTERY, BABYLON THE GREAT' written on her forehead, who was 'sitting on a scarlet beast that was covered with blasphemous names and had seven heads and ten horns'; while the beast or Antichrist 'resembled a leopard, but had feet like those of a bear and a mouth like that of a lion'; there were also 144,000 male *virgins,* 'who had his name and his Father's name written on their foreheads'!" He shook his head, and concluded, "You can't possibly interpret such a book literally!"

Stanley grinned, and replied confidently, "I follow the rule of *literal interpretation,* that is taught in all orthodox Protestant seminaries: 'Where the plain sense of Scripture makes common sense, seek no other sense; take every word at its primary, ordinary, usual, literal meaning unless the immediate context clearly indicates otherwise.' So I *do* interpret most of those things you just cited as *symbols*—although I think the number of 144,000 is literal, just like the 1000-year Millennium in chapter 20 is—because the context of the book indicates that most such symbols should *not* be taken literally."

Eric just shook his head, looked at his notes, and then stated, "Interpreting the Bible isn't that simple, Stanley. For example, in the Bible, the term 'everlasting' doesn't always mean 'eternal' or 'forever.' Canaan is spoken of in Genesis 17:8 as an 'everlasting possession'; circumcision, according to Genesis 17:13, was to be an 'everlasting covenant'; Sprinkling of blood and other ordinances at Passover was to be an 'ordinance forever,' according to Exodus 12:14-24; the Levitical priesthood was to be 'everlasting' [Ex 29:9, 40:15, Lev 3:17, Num 25:13], as was the Temple [1 Ki 8:12-13]; the yearly atonement for sin was to be an 'everlasting statute,' said Leviticus 16:34; Aaron was to burn incense and minister to the Lord 'forever,' says First Chronicles 23:13; First Chronicles 23:25 also said that Israel was to dwell in Jerusalem 'forever.'" Stanley was just waiting for an opening to counter these statements, but Rick emphatically motioned for him to remain quiet, as Eric concluded, "And, directly to the point of Hell, Isaiah 34:8-10 says that the smoke of Edom 'shall go up forever'; but obviously, there is no land of Edom on the earth that is still *burning!*"

Stanley said sarcastically, "What you're doing is no more than 'proof-texting'—flipping through the Bible for a word or phrase here or there, that seems to fit your preconceptions. But true interpreters of the Bible take its entire message, so that it is seen to fit into a glorious, consistent whole!"

Eric shook his head, and explained, "I'm a Unitarian Universalist, not an evangelical Christian; so, unlike the Universalists of the 18th and 19th centuries, I feel no necessity to *prove* everything I believe from the Bible, even though I greatly respect the Bible, as a profound testament of religious faith. And, while all people in our fellowship greatly revere and respect Jesus, if you could prove to me that he thought the world was flat, or that he believed that the planet was only a few thousand years old, or that he thought of Hell as a fiery place somewhere in the center of the earth, it wouldn't disturb my own faith and convictions one iota. Still, I can't help but notice that the texts you rely on most strongly are two *parables*—both of which appear in only one of the four gospels—as well as the extremely symbolic book of Revelation. To me, that suggests building one's house upon the *sand!*"

Rick held up his hand before Stanley could reply, and he said, "I think it's time to switch gears, a little." He looked at both guests, and then suggested, "Eric, you've been interrogating Stanley on his ideas for a while; let's hand the ball back to Stanley: Stan, being mindful of how little time we have left on this program, can you give us a quick summation of why you *don't* consider Eric's position of Universalism to be sound?"

Stanley replied firmly, "Because his position is not *biblically* sound. Universalism suggests that mass murderers like Hitler and Stalin, as well as rapists, child molesters, drug kingpins, and other extremely wicked persons will ultimately end up in *Heaven!* That notion is not only biblically unsound, it's *morally* repugnant! Furthermore, even if Eric thinks that there may be *some* minimal 'punishment' for such people before they get to Heaven—along the lines of the Romanist *Purgatory,* I presume—his ideas fly right in the face of the fact that the Bible contains not a word suggesting that the torments of Hell are *not* 'eternal,' or that there is anything like a 'second chance' for salvation possible after death. The Bible clearly states that we die, and after that, we face the judgment: that's it! Universalism is an unbiblical, cultic teaching that is leading many souls astray—and leading up to their ending up eternally in the very Hell that they claim doesn't exist!"

Rick turned to Eric, and said, "Eric, how would you respond to Stanley?"

With a glint coming into his eyes, Eric said to Stanley, "Stanley, I've noticed that you have a tendency to claim that 'the Bible doesn't say a *word* about such-and-such'; but when I press you on those subjects, it seems like your biblical *evidence* isn't nearly as strong as your *assertions* are. So let me give you some evidence from the Bible that suggests that, One: 'hell' or post-death punishment *isn't* necessarily 'eternal'; and Two: that the Bible *does* suggest that a postmortem change of mind, leading ultimately to salvation, *is* possible."

"That's ridiculous," Stanley asserted flatly.

Eric ignored this comment, and added, "But let me preface my comments by pointing out that, while these biblical passages may not be completely *explicit* about these two issues, neither were the texts you cited about 'different degrees of punishment' in Hell. And I would suggest that my texts are no more 'subjective' in their interpretation than are your decisions about what is 'literal,' and what is 'symbolic,' in the Book of Revelation."

"Sounds good," Rick said, eagerly. "Fire away, my friend."

Eric said confidently, "First, let's turn to the very text that Stanley relied on to prove 'different degrees'; namely, Luke 12:47-48, about being 'beaten with many stripes' versus being 'beaten with few stripes.' I note in passing, however, that the version of this story in Matthew 24:45-51 doesn't contain either phrase; and in fact, the Matthew version has the master ordering the servant to be *cut into pieces*—so this difference just accentuates my argument about the significant differences between the four gospels."

Before Stanley could object, he continued, "Now obviously, if one person is being beaten with *few* stripes, his beating will come to an *end,* before the beating of the other servant does. Yet even one being beaten with 'many stripes' will have his punishment stop, eventually; he's not being beaten with an *infinite* number of stripes! So Stanley's own passage implies an *end* to the punishment."

Stanley eagerly wanted to interrupt, but Rick again signaled for him to remain quiet, then motioned for Eric to continue.

Eric said, "And if we keep reading in Luke 12, verses 58-59 tell us of the person thrown into prison, he 'will not get out *until* you have paid the last penny.' Matthew 5:25-26 has the same saying. So, again, this implies that once you *have* paid this 'last penny,' you will be released from prison."

Stanley was barely able to obey Rick's stern look signaling him to remain silent, as Eric went on, "The parable of the Unmerciful Servant in Matthew 18:21-35 has a similar ending. The master hands the servant over to the jailers to be 'tortured, *until* he should pay back all he owed.' But again, once he has paid back this amount, the 'torture' would presumably stop." He looked Stanley directly in the eyes, then added, "And verse 35 adds, significantly, 'This is how my heavenly Father will treat each of you *unless* you forgive your brother or sister from your heart.' So presumably if you *do* forgive your brother or sister from your heart, you will..."

Stanley could remain silent no longer, and he exclaimed, "But those in Hell *won't* forgive anyone in their hearts; their hearts remain permanently fixed in their resolution against God! And the amount owed by that debtor in Matthew 5 was so great that he could *never* pay it off! The fact remains that the Bible never suggests that anyone gets a 'second chance' after they die, or..."

Eric strongly interrupted, asking, "But Stanley, *how do you know that?* Think of all the people who die without ever even *hearing* your interpretation of the gospel; how can God condemn them to Hell, without presenting them with the gospel at least one time? In Luke 15:3-6, Jesus tells of a shepherd who leaves ninety-nine sheep 'in the wilderness,' in order to pursue the one sheep who is *lost;* this shepherd will 'go after the lost sheep *until he finds it*'! The shepherd doesn't just give up, after some arbitrary time threshold is reached. People are given *numerous* 'second chances' in this life; so why not also in the afterlife? Moreover, if we have free wills, why *wouldn't* we be able to change our minds, and repent, or feel sorrow for our wrongs, in the next life? Does your God somehow 'take away' our free wills once we get to Hell? Even Satan and the rebellious angels apparently had wills, since they used them to *sin,* even while they were in Heaven! And what about infants, and mentally retarded persons?

If there is no 'growth,' 'development,' or *change* allowed in the afterlife, how will such persons ever reach their full potential?"

Stanley said caustically, "Eric, I have no interest in *philosophically* discussing these issues with you. I take the Scriptures unreservedly as my standard, and you clearly don't. You may cleverly twist selected verses here and there, as other cultists do, but you aren't willing to simply let the Scriptures speak to you. But the Bible is crystal clear: in the end, as the final chapter of the last book of the Bible says plainly, 'He that is unjust, let him be unjust still: and he which is filthy, let him be filthy still: and he that is righteous, let him be righteous still: and he that is holy, let him be holy still.'" (Rev 22:11)

Eric said, "Well, let me give you a couple of verses that certainly suggest that at least *some* people may be given a 'second chance' after death. For example, the Apostle Paul in First Corinthians 15:29 mentions approvingly those Christians who are 'baptized for the dead.' Now, if one's state is 'fixed' after death, what would be the purpose of Christians performing a baptism for a dead person?"

Defensively, Stanley replied, "Paul wasn't 'approving' that practice! He was just using that example to say that those who were performing the practice were implicitly endorsing the literal resurrection of the dead, which some of them were apparently denying..."

"Paul also didn't say anything *against* the practice, which suggests at the very least that he wasn't *opposed* to it," Eric countered. "Now let's consider First Peter 3:18-20, which says that when Jesus was made alive after his death, 'he went and made proclamation to the imprisoned spirits—to those who were disobedient long ago when God waited patiently in the days of Noah while the ark was being built.' This verse, along with Ephesians 4:9, is the basis for the statement, 'He descended into hell,' that is part of the Apostles' Creed."

He continued before Stanley could object, "Now, these verses are *not* talking about Jesus preaching to the 'righteous Jews' of the Old Testament, who were supposedly 'looking forward to the *Messiah*,' 3:18-20 specifically says that Jesus preached to those who were *disobedient!* And since it speaks of 'the days of Noah,' it's obviously speaking about people who are now *dead!* And the Greek word *kerusso*—which is translated here as 'proclaimed' or 'preached'—is the same word used throughout the New Testament for the proclamation of the Gospel! So therefore, Jesus is clearly presented as preaching to dead, unrighteous persons." He paused, then added in a reasonable tone, "Now, I don't know why Jesus would proclaim the 'gospel' to only *one specific group* of unrighteous dead—particularly a group that was so evil, that God supposedly destroyed the entire *world* on their account—but I think this passage gives us reason to think that the gospel may likewise be preached to *others* who have not heard the message of Jesus, in this…"

Stanley said sharply, "Those passages are very controversial—and trying to base a doctrine on a controversial text is improper biblical exegesis! We should use the *clear* passages to interpret those that are *less* clear." He added sarcastically, "So are those the only verses you've got?"

"No, they're not," Eric said with a confident smile. "An even clearer passage is First Peter 4:6, which says that 'the gospel was preached even to those who are now dead, so that they might be judged according to human standards in regard to the body, but live according to God in regard to the spirit.' And, since you like the gospel of John, let's look at 5:25-29, which says that 'a time … has now come when the dead will hear the voice of the Son of God and those who hear will live… a time is coming when all who are in their graves will hear his voice and come out— those who have done what is good will rise to live, and those who have done what is evil will rise to be condemned.'"

Before Eric could provide his interpretation, Stanley exclaimed, "The 'dead' in First Peter are those who are *spiritually* dead; or perhaps, it's speaking of people who heard the Gospel, and then died *later!* And those who are 'in the graves' in John 5 are the righteous *and* the unrighteous dead—and you see that it clearly states that the wicked receive a 'resurrection of damnation'!"

Eric replied calmly, "The same Greek word, *nekros,* used for 'dead' in John 5:25 and First Peter 4:6 is the same word used in John chapter 12 to say that Jesus 'raised Lazarus from the dead'! And in that story, Lazarus was certainly not just '*spiritually* dead'!" Rick laughed at this loudly, causing Stanley to blush.

Eric continued, "But my point about John 5:25 is that it says that the *dead* will hear Jesus' voice, 'and those who hear will live.'" He held up his hand to stop Stanley from interrupting, then added quickly, "If the writers of these passages meant 'spiritually dead,' then they surely would have written that; but they didn't, so they obviously meant people who were *physically* dead. Now, I'm sure that you have your own interpretation of these passages; but these are certainly additional passages of the Bible that support the idea that those who are dead *can* hear the gospel; and that they have a chance to respond positively to it."

Stanley scowled, then asked diffidently, "So that's all you have? Those few verses that you're grossly misinterpreting?"

Growing increasingly annoyed by Stanley's attitude, Eric shot back, "Actually, probably my favorite example is the example that *you* like to use: the rich man and Lazarus!" He paused for a moment (enjoying the look of surprise on Stanley's face), and then continued, "The rich man says to Father Abraham, 'I beg you, father, send Lazarus to my family, for I have five brothers. Let him warn them, so that they will not also come to this place of torment.' Then when Abraham demurs, the rich man pleads, 'if someone from the dead goes to them, they will repent.'" He held up his hand to stop Stanley from interrupting, and then explained, "What's interesting here is that Lazarus doesn't argue for himself; no, his attention is on his five brothers, and he wants to save *them* from the same kind of torment he is enduring."

"So what?" Stanley said, with a shrug. "He's just sticking up for his own kind."

Eric replied, "It's also interesting that he says that his brothers would *repent,* if they were able to see a dead Lazarus appearing to them. Now the idea of *repentance* carries the connotation of *sin;* and he's clearly aware that his brothers are in danger of being lost. So this strongly suggests that, since he *can* conceive the idea of repentance, and since he's capable of feeling love and compassion for his family, he *should* likewise be able to regret and repent of his own behavior and attitudes in life; and if he can do that, why shouldn't he be able to achieve salvation, at some point in the future? And since he still obviously has his memory, why would he not be able to recall good, *loving* acts that people did for him? Acts of kindness, that might cause his own heart to want to be grateful, and reciprocate. Once again, why should God arbitrarily impose a 'time limit' on when people can repent, and seek his mercy? Why should everyone's situation be 'frozen' at time of death?"

Stanley said sharply, "Can you show me any place in the *text* where it says that? All you're giving us is your unfounded *speculations* on the passage—which are obviously not Spirit-led!"

Eric sighed, and then said, "First Corinthians 3:15 says of a man's work, 'If it is burned up, the builder will suffer loss but yet will be saved—even though only as one escaping through the flames.' That is basically what we Universalists think about any post-death punishment, which would be *redemptive* in nature, rather than just pointless punishment…"

Stanley snorted contemptuously, and said, "That passage is the one used by Romanists, to try and justify their unbiblical doctrine of Purgatory! So is that what you're defending, also?"

Eric shook his head, and continued, "Now let's consider Matthew 12:31-32: 'every kind of sin and slander can be forgiven, but blasphemy against the Spirit will not be forgiven. Anyone who speaks a word against the Son of Man will be forgiven, but anyone who speaks against the Holy Spirit will not be forgiven, *either in this age or in the age to come.*' Now, the point I want to make is that Jesus didn't just say that anyone who speaks against the Holy Spirit will not be forgiven, period; in fact, that's the way it reads in the parallel versions in Mark 3:28-29 and Luke 12:10. But in Matthew 12:32, Jesus said it would not be forgiven in this age, *or in the age to come;* so why would he make that distinction? Was he suggesting that there were some sins that *could* be forgiven in the 'age to come'?"

Stanley laughed, then said acidly, "That has got to be the most ridiculous excuse for 'exegesis' I've ever heard!"

Eric said pointedly, "But hadn't Jesus just finished saying, '*every kind* of sin and slander can be forgiven'? With this one exception?"

Stanley replied, "The one exception is the rejection of Jesus Christ's offer of salvation, and his forgiveness from sin."

Eric pretended to be shocked, and asked with mock seriousness, "And just where does the text say *that?* What kind of exegesis is that?" Stanley just glowered at him, so Eric asked, "Suppose you were speaking to a man who was depressed, and felt that he was 'beyond being saved,' because years ago, in a moment of youthful rebellion, he blasphemously cursed God, Jesus, and the Holy Spirit. Are you telling me that you wouldn't try to reach such a man with the gospel?"

"Of course I would," Stanley replied immediately. "But I would have to reach him *in this lifetime*—because there are no 'second chance' opportunities! As Hebrews 9:27 says, 'it is appointed unto men once to die, but after this the judgment.'"

Eric responded, "There are surely biblical exceptions to that principle: take Enoch and Elijah, who both supposedly never died. Or what about the Old Testament saints in Matthew 27:52-53 who were resurrected right after Jesus' death—before Jesus' own resurrection?" Before Stanley could respond, he quickly added, "I tend to agree that there is a determination or 'judgment' of sorts that takes place more or less immediately after death—one which separates the Mother Teresas from the Adolf Hitlers, for example—but I fail to see what the purpose is of this supposed mass 'Judgment Day,' in which everyone is assembled before this Great White Throne, and we have to sit and wait as every person who's ever lived is having to 'give account' for 'every idle word' that they ever spoke [Mt 12:36]. I mean, is God likely to *change his mind* about the results of the judgment that was already made at the time of the person's death?"

"The Great White Throne Judgment is only for *unbelievers*," Stanley explained. "Believers appear before the Judgment Seat of Christ, spoken of by Paul in Romans 14:10-12 and Second Corinthians 5:10, which is where we will receive our *crowns* and *rewards*, for what we did on earth." [2 Tim 4:8; 1 Pet 5:2-4; Rev 3:11] Seeing that Eric rolled his eyes about this comment but remained silent, he continued, "I can really summarize the difference between our three positions very simply: I take the Bible as my sole authority, and the two of you don't; it's just that simple. Universalists and Annihilationists refuse to take the Bible 'as is.' Sure, you may spout off a few confusing and superficially glib 'interpretations' of isolated verses, but you are both completely unwilling to submit to the supreme authority of God's inspired and inerrant Word!"

Rick spoke up vigorously, "Well, one of the main reasons I ultimately rejected the Bible is that the usual explanation that Christians like yourself give for all of the evil in the world is the sin of Adam and Eve. But that's a completely ridiculous position; how can you explain and justify all of the wars, terrorism, sickness, and suffering in the world? How can you possibly believe that children born with genetic defects, or who develop horribly painful terminal illnesses, are in that situation because of Adam and Eve eating an apple?"

Stanley began, "Actually, the Bible never says that Adam and Eve ate an *apple;* it only says…"

Eric interrupted, "I think an excellent illustration of why I'm often unwilling to simply 'take the Bible *as is*' is found in the opening chapters of the book of Job. The Bible tells us that Job was 'blameless and upright; he feared God and shunned evil.' [1:1] Even God supposedly admits that 'There is no one on earth like him; he is blameless and upright, a man who fears God and shuns evil.' [1:8] The book also tells us that once, when 'the sons of God came to present themselves before the Lord,' *Satan* was among them. And, interestingly—for those who accept the 'traditional' Christian view of Satan—God doesn't *object* to Satan's presence among the 'sons of God,' but simply asks Satan where he's been. After Satan suggests that Job is only righteous because he's very well-off, God supposedly tells him, 'everything he has is in your power, but on the man himself do not lay a finger.' [1:12] So Satan not only takes away all of Job's property, he even *kills* all of Job's ten children!"

He quickly continued, "Job does not blame God for his misfortune—even though, unbeknownst to him, it *was* God who gave Satan permission to do all those terrible things to him. Anyway, on another day, the angels and Satan came to present themselves before the Lord, and God bragged to Satan, '[Job] still maintains his integrity, though you incited me against him to ruin him *without any reason.*' [2:3] But Satan argues that if Job's body and *health* were attacked, 'he will surely curse you to your face.' [2:4] And, incredibly, God again *agrees* to this test, adding, 'he is in your hands; but you must spare his life.' And thus Job is afflicted so severely, that his wife advises him to 'Curse God and die!' [2:9] But Job refuses to do so. The book then goes on at length, with three of Job's 'friends' giving him some very bad advice. But eventually, God appears to Job [Ch. 38-41], and sharply rebukes him for not knowing about many things that Job would have had no way of knowing. But ultimately, 'the Lord restored his fortunes and gave him twice as much as he had before,' and 'The Lord blessed the latter part of Job's life more than the former part.' [42:10, 12] Job even gets another ten children, and we are told, 'Nowhere in all the land were there found women as beautiful as Job's daughters.' [42:15]

Finally, 'After this, Job lived a hundred and forty years; he saw his children and their children to the fourth generation.'" [42:16]

Eric shook his head vigorously, and said, "To me, this presents a completely *ridiculous* portrait of God: this God is really no better in character than the 'gods' of Egyptian, Greek, and Roman mythology!" Before Stanley could interrupt, he added, "I happen to love the Bible— which is why I've studied it extensively, as you admitted to me when we spoke during the station break. I also often quote the Bible during my sermons to our congregation, and close our Sunday morning services with a quote from the Bible. But I absolutely reject the portrait of an arbitrary, cruel, despotic God such as the Book of Job depicts. If my children had been *murdered* simply to 'prove a point' to Satan, getting another set of children later would hardly repay the grief that had been inflicted upon me!"

"Hear, hear!" Rick praised, clapping his hands in appreciation.

Eric continued, "And for that matter, given the traditional Christian view of Satan and his demons, the mere presence of Satan in the world would be very *puzzling* to me, if I were a Christian. Why is Satan not restrained? Why are demons—like C.S. Lewis's fictional 'Screwtape'— allowed to run around, when their activities are certainly causing some persons to lose their *eternal salvation,* in your interpretation? Sure, you may believe that Satan's going to be restrained during the Millennium, and cast into the lake of fire after that; but why does he have so much 'free rein' *now?*"

Stanley said soberly, "I think you need to be very careful, Eric; remember the wisdom of Job, who said after God directly confronted him, 'I abhor myself, and repent in dust and ashes.'" [42:6] He added, "Job also had the expectation of the other Old Testament saints, who were looking forward to the Messiah; he said in 19:26, 'though … skin worms destroy this body, yet in my flesh shall I see God'! So Job could anticipate seeing his dead children again in the next life."

Eric suddenly asked, "What makes you think we will be reunited with our loved ones in Heaven?" (Stanley looked genuinely surprised, and even Rick seemed puzzled by this unexpected question.)

Stanley finally replied, "First Thessalonians 4:16-17 says, 'For the Lord himself shall descend from heaven with a shout, with the voice of the archangel, and with the trump of God: and the dead in Christ shall rise first: Then we which are alive and remain shall be caught up **together with them** in the clouds, to meet the Lord in the air: and so shall we ever be with the Lord'; so we will be reunited with Christians who have passed on, when Jesus returns. And the Bible does seem to indicate that we will be *recognizable* after death; Peter, James and John didn't have any problem recognizing Moses and Elijah on the mount of Transfiguration, for example. Furthermore, Genesis 25:8 tells us that when Abraham died, he 'was gathered to his people.' Genesis 35:29 says the same about Isaac, as does Genesis 49: 29 about Jacob, and Numbers 20:24 about Aaron. And finally, Revelation 21:4 says that 'God shall wipe away all tears from their eyes; and there shall be no more death, neither sorrow, nor crying, neither shall there be any more pain: for the former things are passed away.' So parents, siblings, spouses, and others who have lost loved ones will certainly find their prayers for reunion answered in Heaven!" He thought for a moment, then cautioned, "Assuming they are all *Christians,* of course."

Eric seemed completely unimpressed by this response, and pointed out, "Those Old Testament references mean only that when you're dead, you join all the others who died before you. And the fact that there may be a lot of people in Heaven, or a 'resurrection of the dead' that occurs for the dead at the same time that living Christians are 'changed,' hardly says that families and friends will be reunited. Christians sitting in a circle around the Trinity—as Dante pictured it, in his *Paradisio*—might be so transfixed by the Beatific Vision that they don't really *care* whether they're sitting with family members, or not." He smiled, and then teased, "And you were just reproaching *me* earlier, for seeming to go *beyond* what the biblical texts literally say."

Stanley said diffidently, "So do you have any biblical evidence that Christian families and friends will *not* be reunited in Heaven?"

Eric replied, "How about Matthew 22:23-33, where Jesus said, 'At the resurrection people will neither marry nor be given in marriage; they will be like the angels in heaven.' That verse is why, when Christians recite their wedding vows, they only pledge to remain together 'Till death do us part.' That's why Christians can remarry after the death of a spouse; because they won't have 'two wives' or 'two husbands' in Heaven. So if the *marital* bond is dissolved at death, why do you think that other, lesser relations will necessarily be continued in Heaven? And for that matter, why do you think there will necessarily even be *gender* in Heaven? Since Genesis 1:27 says 'in the image of God he created them; male and female he created them,' for all we know, Heaven will be *unisex!*"

Stanley snorted, and then replied, "Our relationships will be *changed*, to be sure; but I think the Bible is quite clear that we will see others, and will recognize them. And we will certainly remain as male and female."

Eric kept pressing his point, saying sharply, "But that's not *specifically stated* in the biblical text, is it? You're having to make *logical inferences* from the text, aren't you? Just as I do, for post-death punishments having an end, and for the possibility of post-death salvation."

"The situations are not at all comparable," Stanley said brusquely.

Eric quickly moved on, saying, "Let's take another matter: Does the Bible say that people with physical disabilities will be 'made whole' in Heaven? Will Type 1 diabetics have a working pancreas in heaven? Will quadriplegics still have to use a wheelchair—albeit one that never needs to be recharged?

"Of course everyone with a disability will be made whole," Stanley replied confidently. "Even while Jesus was here on Earth, he told the disciples of John the Baptist, 'Go and show John again those things which ye do hear and see: The blind receive their sight, and the lame walk, the lepers are cleansed, and the deaf hear, the dead are raised up, and the poor have the gospel preached to them.' (Mt 11:4-5) He surely will do the same in Heaven! And Isaiah 35:4-5 says of the millennial kingdom that 'Then the eyes of the blind shall be opened, and the ears of the deaf shall be unstopped.' And Philippians 3:21 says that Jesus 'shall change our vile body, that it may be fashioned like unto his glorious body.'"

Eric commented dryly, "That passage from Isaiah was referring to the situation of the nation Israel; so its application to Christians in Heaven is at least questionable. And Jesus' words to John's disciples were fine for people who Jesus healed while he was here on earth; but there are all kinds of Christians with disabilities—Joni Eareckson Tada, to take one famous example—who were *not* healed by Jesus; then, or now. But to the extent that our bodies are going to be changed to be like Jesus' body, you should remember that the gospels clearly tell us that, after his resurrection, Jesus' body still had wounds in his hands, feet, and side. [Lk 24:39, Jn 20:27]. And Revelation 5:6-12 tells us that the heavenly hosts sing a song to Jesus, who appeared as 'a Lamb as it had been slain'—which certainly implies that he still has the marks of his execution on him."

"You're being ridiculous," Stanley scoffed. "Our heavenly bodies will be *perfect*—free from every kind of limitation and disability; and you don't have even a single verse to prove the contrary!"

Eric replied immediately, "How about Matthew 18:8-9, where Jesus says that 'It is better for you to enter life maimed or crippled than to have two hands or two feet and be thrown into eternal fire… It is better for you to enter life with one eye than to have two eyes and be thrown into the fire of hell.'" With a slight smile, he added, "I'm sure that your rich man of Luke 16 would be more than willing to leave Hades and enter Heaven, even if he was blind and disabled…"

Stanley hissed with unmasked contempt, "I'm not even going to respond to such a ridiculous attempt to twist God's Word…"

Eric said earnestly, "Look, Stanley: I'm not really doubting that we will be reunited with families and friends in the afterlife; quite the contrary, we Universalists strongly believe that parents will also be reunited with their rebellious children who had no interest in religion during earthly life, and that the faithful Christian wife will be reunited with her agnostic but loving husband. I also firmly believe that we will not have any 'disabilities' in Heaven—although I'm not as certain as many people that we will literally have *bodies* that look much the same as ours do now. But the point I'm striving to make, is that you've attempted to portray Rick and myself as simply refusing to 'take the Bible *as it is*.' The plain truth is that the Bible really tells us very little, and almost nothing *specific*, about the afterlife; that's why *all* of us have to speculate about it, and draw inferences." Stanley grimaced, but remained silent.

He thought for a moment, and then said to Stanley, "I'm sure that in your ministry, you've had to deal with objections from people—especially young people—who say that they 'don't want to go to Heaven; it would be *boring*, just sitting around on clouds in white robes all day and playing harps,' right?"

"Dozens of times," Stanley admitted, with a rueful smile on his lips. "They completely misunderstand the glories of what Heaven will be like."

Eric nodded, then continued, "But if you take the Book of Revelation *literally,* there is a real basis for their fears. Revelation 15:2 says that 'those who had been victorious over the beast and its image ... held *harps* given them by God'! In Revelation 11:12, the two witnesses are taken up to heaven in a *cloud;* and in 14:14-16, Jesus is portrayed as sitting on a white *cloud.* 6:11 says that white robes were given to the martyrs, which is presumably the 'standard issue' clothing in Heaven. And 4:8-11 seemingly portrays activity in Heaven as being a constant sequence of people or angelic figures, about whom 'Day and night they never stop saying: "Holy, holy, holy is the Lord God Almighty."' And 21:21 even supports the idea of 'pearly gates' and 'streets of gold' in Heaven! So the youthful fear that 'Heaven will be like an eternal *church service*' is not entirely without foundation... *if* you take the Book of Revelation literally!" Rick laughed loudly at this, and even Stanley had to chuckle.

Eric went on, "Some Christians seem to visualize Heaven as being like an eternal Thomas Kinkade painting—or at least they did, prior to Kinkade's death from Valium and alcohol intoxication—where we will all have our own little cottages, and will have all of infinity to be able to learn to sing, or paint, or study any subject that strikes our curiosity—but how can we know this? How can we be sure that our struggles with sin will be *over,* once we get to Heaven? Traditional Catholics at least believe that we'll have to spend considerable time in Purgatory before we're *ready* for Heaven, but you Protestants don't have that advantage—you just seem to assume that God will somehow *ZAP!* you, and you'll be instantly ready to spend eternity in peaceful harmony... even though Christians like you have *all kinds* of disagreements with your fellow Christians, while you're here on earth! And I'm not aware of even a single verse of the Bible that supports such a view of 'instantaneous transformation,' and..."

Stanley said quickly, "When Jesus healed people, it was instantaneous; so why shouldn't God remove our lustful sin natures just as instantly..."

Eric objected, "Then why doesn't God remove our sin natures *here,* and..."

Rick broke in, saying authoritatively, "Gentlemen, we're starting to run out of time... and I don't think that my producer will let me have a *third* program on this same topic!" and they all laughed. He turned to Eric, and said, "Eric, I still feel like we've given Stanley most of the program, since we've primarily been arguing about traditional and biblical images of Heaven and Hell. But now, please tell us something more about your own beliefs; you don't need to make any arguments: Why are you a Universalist?"

Eric smiled, then replied, "Well, I'm very glad to belong to a 'liberal' or 'progressive' religious tradition, rather than to a rigidly 'biblical' system such as Stanley adheres to—or to a system where you're supposed to believe what your church tells you to believe, such as Catholics have. In our tradition, we don't have any 'creeds' or 'doctrines' that anyone *must* believe in; we have UUAs who consider themselves to be 'Christians' or 'Jews' of a liberal sort, but we also have Buddhists, Hindus, and even agnostics and atheists in our midst! While few if any of us think of Jesus as being the 'Second Person of the Blessed Trinity,' we have a genuine and abiding reverence for the person of Jesus, and his ethical teachings. We think of the essence of Jesus' message as being one of *reconciliation,* and *forgiveness.* This view is found in the Old Testament, as well: Lamentations 3:31-33 states that 'For no one is cast off by the Lord forever. Though he brings grief, he will show compassion, so great is his unfailing love. For he does not willingly bring affliction or grief to anyone.' Ezekiel 33:11 says, 'As surely as I live, declares the Sovereign Lord, I take no pleasure in the death of the wicked, but rather that they turn from their ways and live.'"

Stanley couldn't restrain himself from interjecting, "But then it adds, 'turn ye, turn ye from your evil ways; *for why will ye die,* O house of Israel?'" He added passionately, "God doesn't *want* us to die—he wants us to live with him eternally! But he also imposes firm and unalterable *conditions* for us to come to him. First Corinthians 6:9-11 acknowledges that some Christians at Corinth had been fornicators, adulterers, thieves, drunkards, and more; but then they repented, and became 'washed, sanctified, and justified in the name of the Lord Jesus, by the Spirit of God.'"

Smiling ironically, Eric said quietly, "Thank you for your opinion, Pastor Beechman; but I believe it was supposed to be *my* turn to explain my position." Stanley blushed, and Eric continued, "Well, since earlier in the program you gave a flurry of Bible verses that you feel support your position, let me return the favor, by showing a few of the verses that we feel strongly support the Universalist position."

Consulting his notes, he began explaining, "Second Peter 3:9 says that God 'is patient with you, not wanting anyone to perish, but *everyone* to come to repentance.' Romans 11:32 says that 'God has bound everyone over to disobedience so that he may have mercy on them *all*.' Colossians 1:19-20 says that 'God was pleased … to reconcile to himself *all* things, whether things on earth or things in heaven.' Ephesians 1:9-10 says that God 'purposed in Christ… to bring unity to *all* things in heaven and on earth under Christ.' John 12:32 has Jesus saying that 'when I am lifted up from the earth, [I] will draw all people to myself.' Romans 5:12 says, 'sin entered the world through one man, and death through sin, and in this way death came to all people, because all sinned'; and then verses 15-19 add that 'For if the many died by the trespass of the one man, how much more did God's grace and the gift that came by the grace of the one man, Jesus Christ, overflow to the many! … how much more will those who receive God's abundant provision of grace and of the gift of righteousness reign in life through the one man, Jesus Christ! Consequently, just as one trespass resulted in condemnation for all people, so also one righteous act resulted in justification and life for *all* people. For just as through the disobedience of the one man the many were made sinners, so also through the obedience of the one man the many will be made righteous.'"

Stanley burst out, "That's a *terrible* translation of those passages, and…"

Eric countered, "It's the New International Version; which is the most popular translation among Evangelicals." He went on immediately, "Now, notice the *universal* application of Romans 5: the sin of Adam is not applied just to *some* people; or only to 'those who have heard the gospel and rejected it,' but to *everyone*, worldwide! And thus, similarly, by the act of Jesus, 'all people' will be justified, and receive life."

Stanley insisted, "But salvation doesn't apply to '*all* people'; it applies only to those who believe on the Lord Jesus…"

Eric interrupted, "Didn't you tell us earlier that 'everlasting punishment' and 'everlasting life' in Matthew 25:46 have to be interpreted *consistently*, since the same Greek word is used for both? Well, Paul used the same Greek word, *pas*, for both groups in Romans 5, which is how the NIV translates it!" Stanley grimaced, but remained silent.

Eric continued, "And this same sentiment is repeated in many other places in the New Testament. First Corinthians 15:22 says, 'For as in Adam all die, so in Christ all will be made alive.' Colossians 1:19-20 says that 'God was pleased to have all his fullness dwell in [Jesus], and through him to reconcile to himself all things.' First Timothy 2:4 says that God 'wants all people to be saved and to come to a knowledge of the truth,' and verse 6 adds that Jesus 'gave himself as a ransom for all people.' Paul said in Second Corinthians 5:19 that 'God was reconciling the world to himself in Christ, not counting people's sins against them. And he has committed to us the message of reconciliation.' That's why Philippians 2:9-11 concludes that 'at the name of Jesus every knee should bow, in heaven and on earth and under the earth, and every tongue acknowledge that Jesus Christ is Lord, to the glory of God the Father.' Now, unless you think that God is going to *override* the free wills of men and women in Hell, and *force* them to croak out, 'Jesus Christ is Lord,' they will have to do this *voluntarily!* And how will they be willing to do this, unless they have *changed* after death?"

Stanley said forcefully, "First Timothy 4:10 says, 'For therefore we both labour and suffer reproach, because we trust in the living God, who is the Saviour of all men, *specially of those that believe.'* Jesus said in John 12:32 he 'will *draw* all men unto me,' but he didn't say that they would all *accept* his offer of salvation! And Titus 2:11—even in your New International Version—says that 'the grace of God has appeared that *offers* salvation to all people.' And finally, even those in Hell will certainly have to 'acknowledge' that Jesus is Lord, since that fact will be *obvious* to all!"

Before Eric could reply, Rick suddenly interrupted, saying, "Guys, it's time to wrap up: Let's have a brief closing statement from each of you, starting with Stanley."

Stanley looked directly into the camera, and said earnestly, "We've discussed some subjects in a level of detail that may have been confusing to some of you watching this program. But you must not allow this to blind your eyes to the fact that the fundamental issue is really quite simple, and straightforward. All of us are sinners—and that includes the three of us appearing on this program. And sin against an eternal God, requires an eternal penalty. And that penalty is *eternal, conscious torment* in Hell! Hell is *not* what C.S. Lewis said it is, or what Billy Graham once said that it is. Such misstatements are what Paul warned us of in Colossians 2:4, 'lest any man should beguile you with enticing words.' Sinful man would like to *believe* that 'everyone will be saved in the end,' or that 'at worst, we will just be annihilated'; but do not be deceived: Paul said in Romans 6:23 that 'the wages of sin is death'; but then he added, 'but the gift of God is eternal life through Jesus Christ our Lord.'

"Now, how do we avoid Hell? Jesus told us in Mark 1:15 to 'repent, and believe the gospel.' Paul and Silas said in Acts 16:31, 'Believe on the Lord Jesus Christ, and thou shalt be saved.' To so 'believe,' you must acknowledge your sins before God and ask him to save you, through Jesus' work on the cross. If you do this, then, as Second Corinthians 5:17 assures us, you will be 'a new creature'! Do this, and you will absolutely and assuredly be *saved*—Hallelujah!"

He looked meaningfully over at Eric, and then said solemnly, "Universalism is a false, deadly heresy, originating in the very pits of Hell. Jesus rejected this heresy quite plainly, when he said in Matthew 18:6 of anyone who caused someone who believed in him to turn away, that it would be better for him to be hanged, and drowned in the sea! Jesus said in Matthew 26:24 about the one who had betrayed him, that it would have been better for that man if he had not been born! Now, if all of us are ultimately 'saved,' as Eric has argued, then Jesus spoke *falsely* in those two statements. So the question I have for those of you listening is, 'Who are you going to believe? Those who create false hopes for sinful men? Or those who honestly, and with integrity, teach exactly what the Bible says?" He paused meaningfully, and then added, "I pray that you will make the right choice in this life, because there will be no 'second chances'; your eternal destiny depends entirely upon this decision." He sat back in this chair, satisfied with his summation.

Rick cleared his throat, and said, "Well, thank you for that summation, Stanley... I think. Now let's now hear from Eric."

Eric looked into the camera, and said confidently, "This evening, 'you're heard three different perspectives on life after death: Stanley's 'traditional' view, Rick's 'Conditionalist' view, and my own perspective of Universalism—the perspective of the ultimate, universal reconciliation of all people with God." He shrugged, and then added, "We could go on arguing about whether 'aionios' means 'forever,' and whether or not the Bible really means 'all' or 'the world' in certain passages, and we would

238

probably never agree on a conclusion. In my congregation, and in our larger fellowship of liberal religious believers, we feel no need to justify every detail of our beliefs from the Bible, nor from the words of Jesus; this is the 21st century in America, not the 1st century in Judea. Still, I hope I was able to show you that the biblical support claimed for the 'traditional' interpretation of Hell as a place of eternal, fiery torment has some very considerable problems. That's why, as Rick pointed out, even some prominent Evangelical theologians and ministers are starting to reject that viewpoint—whether they take the Conditionalist viewpoint, or the Universalist one. Personally, although I recognize that there is substantial evidence in the Bible for the Conditionalist view, I'm not a Conditionalist, because I don't see why, after a sinner has been punished by God for whatever period of time is required, and has therefore 'paid' for his transgressions, why God would *destroy* him, rather than let him into Heaven, as we Universalists believe.

"But I nevertheless think that the Conditionalist position is far superior to the 'traditional' view. To both Universalists and Conditionalists, it is simply unreasonable to think that millions—billions, actually—of people who lived and died in non-Christian countries; or young people who just barely passed this supposed 'age of accountability'; or those of us who simply can't agree with the perspective presented by Stanley tonight, are going to spend all of eternity suffering unimaginably horrible torment— with no possibility of *ever* being able to repent, change, or even experience love or hope again! I would ask you, what kind of image of God does this traditional view imply? Could any of us really 'love' a being who might send *us* to Heaven, while just across the way, or outside the gates of the New Jerusalem, our parents, children, family, and friends are hopelessly pleading for even a single drop of water to relieve their torment? And even if we *could* somehow have our memories lobotomized—so that our loved ones' horrible fate didn't cause *us* unutterable grief— would it really be *us* who was in Heaven? Can we truly imagine our feelings of love and compassion for others being thus *neutralized* by God?"

He continued, speaking with great feeling, "When his disciples asked Jesus, 'Who then can be saved?' he replied, 'With man this is impossible, but with God all things are possible.' (Mt 19:16-22) The Bible does speak of the 'anger' and 'wrath' of God; but it also tells us that *God is love*. And that was the point of the message of Jesus. Jesus unhesitatingly sat down with those who were considered the greatest 'sinners' of his time, and he told them that God loved them, forgave them, and wanted to be reconciled with them. With some people, this reconciliation clearly doesn't occur during their lifetimes; but we cannot arbitrarily limit the love of God to the vagaries of this short lifetime. Some babies die in the womb; infant children are killed by disease and accidents; we are all born in completely different social, political, economic, and *religious* circumstances—in this case, one size certainly does *not* fit all! I would strongly encourage all of us to earnestly pursue the love of God in this lifetime; because, frankly, encountering this transcendent love will make your life vastly better, and more fulfilling. But for those who are not reconciled to God here… I would simply suggest that you should continue to *love* them, and to hope and pray for them—because I believe that these hopes will one day be realized, and we will *all* share in the love of God, and each other: *forever!*"

Rick smiled and said warmly, "Thank you, Eric." Looking into the camera, he summarized, "Well, I've been listening to the arguments from both sides for nearly an hour, and quite frankly, I think that I, and the 'Conditionalist' perspective, represent what Aristotle called the 'Golden Mean'! Eric and I strongly agree in rejecting Stanley's 'traditional' view of Hell; I just can't see how even a long lifetime justifies an *eternity* of horrible torture! But I also have some sympathy with Stanley, when he says that people like Hitler don't *deserve* eternal life in Heaven; that's a strong reason why I'm attracted to the Conditionalist position. I'm glad to think that monsters like Hitler and Stalin and Pol Pot, and probably murderous Islamic terrorists, child molesters, and serial murderers and rapists, are not going to be kept alive by God forever—and they're certainly not going to end up in Heaven, with the rest of us! I think the rest of us would enjoy Heaven much more if those kinds of evil people were just … *gone* for good!"

With a thoughtful look on his face, he added, "But despite our obvious differences, the three of us *do* have some commonalities. We all believe there *is* life after death; none of us think that 'death is the *end.*' We all believe that there is some form of punishment or retribution for really *bad* people after death—although we disagree strongly on how *long* it might last—so such bad people aren't just getting off scot-free. And we all believe that there *is* a Heaven—although, again, we have some very serious disagreements about how large its *population* will be! Eric thinks that everyone will eventually make it there; Stanley probably thinks that only a fairly small group from even the two billion living and professing *Christians* will make it there; whereas I would hope that a large majority of the currently living human race will be there—perhaps five or six billion, out of a population of more than seven million; and similar percentages for those persons who have already passed on."

He smiled, and then said expansively, "At any rate, we're glad you joined us for this two-part program; my guests on the program were Stanley Beechman, Pastor of the Evangelical Community Bible Assembly, and Eric Swenson, minister of the local Unitarian Universalist Society. Thanks for joining us, gentlemen. And I hope that all of you watching will tune in next week, when our topic will be, 'Should transgender couples be entitled to the same cosmetic surgery coverage as "traditional" couples get, in government-mandated health coverage? Or should they have higher co-pays?' Tune in next week, for some fascinating discussion of this burning issue. Thanks for watching; Salud!"

The offstage Program Director said, "And… we're *off!* Great job, gang!" There was some scattered applause from the stage crew, as the makeup technicians came forward began removing the stage makeup from the three participants.

Rick then warmly thanked his two guests. Eric (with a smile), said to him, "Just for the record, Rick: if God ends up wanting to annihilate Hitler, Stalin, and similar people, that would actually be fine with me," and they both laughed.

Rick's Program Director then called him aside for a discussion of some issue, so Eric and Stanley were left standing next to each other. They tentatively shook hands, and began walking toward the exit from the stage area.

Stanley complained, "These television programs are so *short,* that we just don't get enough time to go into matters more thoroughly!" He looked over at Eric, and said casually, "My church has a regular radio program, that broadcasts on Saturdays; would you be interested in participating in a series of programs, in which we had adequate time to…"

"I wouldn't be interested in participating in any more 'debates,'" Eric said, shaking his head. "I frankly wouldn't have appeared on this program, if I'd known it was going to be this … confrontational! When the Program Director called me to invite me to be on the program, I had the impression that we were just going to have a nice, civilized discussion of our respective views."

"That's television for you," Stanley said, chuckling. "They always want to focus on controversy; and they just love it when people get into *fights,* because it boosts their ratings!" and they both laughed.

Stanley suddenly turned serious, then said soberly, "Eric, I believe that you are sincere in your beliefs; but I have to reiterate what I said to you earlier, about the severe *dangers* that lie in store for those who turn away from the scriptural truths." Before Eric could object, he quickly added, "Remember what I said about 'different degrees' of punishment in Hell? Well, that also implies not only that some are punished with 'fewer stripes,' but that some will be punished with '*many* stripes'! And certainly, *false teachers* will be punished with the most severe torments, because they are responsible for turning other people away from the truth, and…"

Eric couldn't remain silent, and he countered, "Doesn't your church actively teach that Islam is a *false* religion?"

Stanley stammered, "Yes, of course we do. But I don't see…"

Eric continued, "Aren't you aware of the Quranic promises of horrible torments in the Islamic Hell for those who actively *oppose* Islam? Don't such threats make you want to stop opposing Islam?"

Stanley said proudly, "Of course not. We firmly preach the gospel of Christ, and oppose all forms of untruth! And we…"

Eric interjected, "But you don't fear the Islamic Hell, because you don't think there's any chance at all that you'll end up there, right?" Stanley turned silent, and Eric continued, "Well, your threats of punishment for those 'false teachers' who don't adhere to your particular form of 'Orthodoxy' seem just as unlikely to me. So, while I appreciate your concern, I assure you that it's misplaced."

Stanley said quietly, "I see."

Eric held out his hand, and said, "But, while we don't *agree* on very much, theologically, I hope that we can at least part on friendly terms."

Stanley nodded, and the two men shook hands.

And they went through the exit door, then turned and went their separate ways.

CHAPTER 12

Rest in Peace
(Late November 2016)

Eric was about to say the Benediction at the close of the Sunday morning service in his UUA church. Turning the pages in a well-worn Bible, he said to the congregation (who were all standing), "I'd like to close by reading from Paul's letter to the Philippians, in the King James Bible. This is chapter 4, verse 8." Everyone in the medium-sized church was silent, as he read the following verse:

> *Finally, brethren, whatsoever things are true, whatsoever things are honest, whatsoever things are just, whatsoever things are pure, whatsoever things are lovely, whatsoever things are of good report; if there be any virtue, and if there be any praise, think on these things.*

Then he dismissed the congregation, and they mostly began slowly filing toward the exits; but many of them stopped to chat and hug each other, as they headed to the exit. A number of people also sought out Eric, to thank him, or else make some comment about the service.

One young woman (about Eric's age) asked, "So Christianne couldn't make it this morning?"

He shook his head, and explained, "She's in surgery; it's her second operation on the poor little girl who was in that car accident, and was disfigured."

"Oh, that's right," the woman replied. "Christianne is such a wonderful person; always willing to perform *pro bono* cosmetic surgery on children with birth defects, or facial injuries. Well, give her my love, Eric; hope to see her next week."

"I will," Eric replied. "Thanks, Karin; see you later."

As he shook hands and hugged the other people waiting to greet him, he noticed that there was a couple who he did not recognize standing off to one side; he judged them to be in their mid-30s. He noticed that they kept glancing in his direction, so he assumed they were probably waiting to talk to him after everyone else was gone.

When the last person waiting to greet him had left, he saw the couple still standing off to the side, so he approached them.

Holding out his hand to the man, he said in a friendly tone, "Hi, I'm Eric Swenson; I don't believe we've met…"

"We haven't," the man said, shaking Eric's hand. "I'm Roger Wells, and this is my wife Thea."

"It's nice to meet you," Eric said, shaking Thea's hand. "Is this your first time at a Unitarian Universalist church? Do you have any questions, or can I…"

"Is there someplace we can talk?" Roger asked, urgency in his voice. "Privately?"

"Uhh… sure," Eric said. "We can go to my office; it's just outside the side door over here." He led them to the door, and down the hall, and then over to his office; the couple remained silent the entire time.

Opening the door to his office, he motioned for them to sit down in the chairs in front of his desk; rather than sit behind the desk, he sat down in another chair next to the couple. He said apologetically, "I'm afraid I don't have any coffee, juice, or water here. I can get some from the Fellowship Hall, if you'd…"

"No thanks," Roger said curtly. He looked over at his wife, who nodded slightly to him, and then he said to Eric, "I'll get right to the point, Mr. Swenson. I saw you on television."

"You saw me on television?" Eric repeated, puzzled. "When did you…"

"You were debating a fundamentalist minister," Roger explained.

"Oh, right; *that* incident," Eric said, sheepishly. He began, "I actually wouldn't have participated on that program, if I'd known how…"

"I really liked what you said," Roger blurted out. "I recorded the last two-thirds of the show, and then I showed it to Thea, and she liked it too."

"Oh. Well, uhh… thank you, I guess," Eric stammered, still embarrassed. He explained, "But it was supposed to be more of a *discussion,* than a *debate;* and I have to admit that I even lost my 'cool' a couple of times, and said some things that I wish…"

Thea interrupted, saying quietly, "Our son is dead."

Shocked, Eric said, "Your son? That's *awful!* I'm so sorry to hear that." He moved his chair closer, and grasped both Thea's and Roger's hands. There was a long moment of silence, and Eric could see tears glistening in both parents' eyes.

Eric said softly, "How did…"

"Car accident," Roger replied. "He was riding with an older friend of his… but it wasn't their fault; a drunk driver came over into their lane, and Todd's friend couldn't swerve out of the way in time…"

"They both died," Thea said, her voice shaking with emotion.

"It was just four days ago," Roger added, his own voice quivering with sorrow.

Eric drew even closer to the grieving couple, clutching their hands silently, as they wept. Finally, he asked, "What can I do to help?"

Roger said quickly, "We want you to preach at his funeral."

Eric was surprised. He replied, "I… well, of course, if you wish; I'd be glad to." He thought for a moment, then said, "So you don't have a regular church that you…"

With bitterness in his voice, Roger hissed, "We quit!"

Thea explained, "We both attended a Bible-believing, fundamental church for seven years. But, after the accident… the Pastor told us…" but then her voice broke, and she couldn't continue.

Roger explained apologetically, "David was a good boy, Pastor; he never really got into trouble—no drinking, drugs, or anything like that. But he was… well, he wasn't a church-going kid; he had sports, and video games, and his friends, and he… well, he thought that God and Jesus and church were for…" but he stopped, unable to complete the sentence.

"Pastor James said that David was in Hell!" Thea exploded. "That's why he refused to preach at David's funeral."

Eric shook his head, and said sympathetically, "That's terrible; I can hardly believe it…"

Roger said defensively, "David *was* a good kid, Pastor. Sure, he ran around with his football buddies, and they sometimes got a little loud and rambunctious, but… Shoot, Pastor: *I* used to be just like that! David would have grown out of it, in a few more years…" Silence fell over the three people in the room.

Her eyes brimming with tears, Thea asked Eric, "Pastor Eric, I watched that program with you on TV; do you *really* think there's a chance that our boy could go to Heaven?"

Eric said fervently, "I'm certain of it, Thea. God is love; and that's what Jesus was trying to tell us about. And one day, we're *all* going to be experiencing the love that Jesus told us of: together!"

"That's what you said on TV," Thea whispered, a wan smile coming to her tear-stained face.

Eric said gently, "I'd be glad to speak at your son's funeral."

Roger said, "There's one more thing, Pastor." Eric listened, as he explained, "Since we can't hold the service at our old church, it's just going to be held at the funeral home. But a lot of the people attending his service are going to be… well, friends and other people from our old church. None of them saw your program on TV; and the friends I asked to watch it with us, refused. So I was wondering if you could… well, maybe kind of *explain* to them during the service, why it is you think that David isn't in Hell? Sort of like you did on that TV program?"

"I'll be glad to do whatever you want me to do," Eric replied gently. He suggested, "Why don't we go to the coffee shop just down the street; we can talk in more detail about what you would like me to do. And I'd also like to hear more about David…"

***

The recorded organ music ceased. The Funeral Director then stepped up to the microphone, and in a solemn, practiced tone, introduced Roger Wells (who was sitting in the front row, next to Thea and Eric), who then stepped up to the podium, and took the microphone in hand.

Roger looked out over the assembled people, cleared his throat, then said into the microphone, "Thea and I have asked Eric Swenson, who is the minister of the Unitarian Universalist church here in River City, to deliver a message. What we've asked him to say, you may not entirely agree with—particularly our friends from church. But we would ask that you please extend him the courtesy of listening with an open mind to what he has to say; my wife and I have spoken with Reverend Eric a number of times since David's death, and he has been a great comfort to us. I hope, and pray, that he may be a source of comfort to you, as well." He replaced the microphone on its stand, stepped away from the podium, and shook Eric's hand, before returning to his seat next to Thea.

Eric stepped up to·the podium, placing his notes in front of him, and looked out over the audience. Next to the Wells in the front row were other family members; their closest friends were seated directly behind them. David's many young friends (some wearing their football jerseys) were mostly in the back rows—and often looking uncomfortable, during this service.

Eric cleared his throat softly, then began speaking: "Although it is a sad occasion that brings us here this morning, I hope that all of us will be able to leave this building today, not with a sense of sadness and tragedy, but with a sense of hope. We have already heard several moving testimonies about how David was as a friend; as a teammate; as a coworker; as a fellow student; and as a son. He was, in the common sense of the term, a 'good man'; and it naturally brings all of us a profound sense of grief, to have such a worthwhile young man taken from us at such a young age, and in such an untimely manner. In fact, such grieving thoughts can bring us into a condition of doubt—where we honestly wonder whether there is even any purpose to life; whether our lives, in the end, *mean* anything. Are we, as some scientists and philosophers would argue, nothing more than a collection of organic molecules, that have taken shape according to deterministic and probabilistic laws governing matter? Such that, in the end, our lives are fundamentally meaningless, and with no greater hope than what we can achieve in this lifetime—which may be cut quite short, and entirely without warning, as was the case with David?" He let this statement be pondered by the audience, for a long moment.

But then he smiled reassuringly, and said in a warmer tone, "I would not be here this morning if I believed that. The hope that I wish to leave all of you with today, can be stated very simply: **This life is not the end.** In fact, this life is only the beginning of our existence... which continues on, into the farthest reaches of temporality, and beyond time itself. There is indeed, a better, *greater* life that awaits us, after death."

He then said pensively, "Some of you may be wondering, 'But how can that be? *David was not a Christian!* He actually was, according to what I've heard from his family and friends, strongly *critical* of traditional Christianity; at least, in its Evangelical form." He shrugged, and then continued, "Well, David was not alone in not being a Christian. Only about 2 billion of the 7.4 billion people in the world even profess to be Christians; and the percentage of the world's population that identify themselves as 'Christian' is, moreover, declining over time. If we supposed that *only* born-again, Evangelical Christians have any 'hope' for eternal life, then that means that only about *one-eighth* of the world's current population—at most—will be in Heaven. And that's *without* subtracting out all of the supposedly 'lukewarm' Evangelicals who might get 'left behind' when Jesus returns." There were a few nervous laughs from the listeners.

Eric smiled, and then said easily, "Now, I don't know about you, but that statistic seems… well, completely *improbable* to me. If Jesus came to earth two thousand years ago to redeem the world, and more than 88% of the world is *not* going to be redeemed, then that would make it seem like Jesus' mission was a colossal failure." He added firmly, "But that's not at all what I believe. I strongly believe that not only Christians—*all* Christians, not just any particular subgroup of them—but also Jews, Muslims, Hindus, Buddhists, Sikhs, Bahá'í, Confucians, Jains, Taoists, Shintoists, New Agers, Deists, as well as those with no professed religion at all, have strong reasons to believe in, and hope for, eternal life in God's presence." He again paused, to allow this statement to register with his hearers. He went on, "Now, you may be wondering, how do I arrive at such a belief? Well, two fundamental sources of my belief are the words of Jesus, and other texts of the Bible."

He then pretended to be indignant, saying vigorously, "But how can I say that, you may wonder? Isn't Jesus supposed by many to have been the ultimate 'hellfire preacher'; someone who strongly asserted that the unredeemed will go down into eternal, conscious torment *forever?*" He paused dramatically, and then added in a matter-of-fact tone, "Actually, Jesus only spoke about Hell—which may be called either *Hades* or

Gehenna, in the New Testament—on perhaps ten or so occasions; and for a ministry that many Christians believe lasted for more than three years, that's certainly not very many times. And most of what he *did* say on this subject was given in *parables;* so trying to interpret such parables in strictly literal terms is a very questionable practice. And it's also interesting that, although Jesus often spoke of the 'kingdom of Heaven,' he told us virtually *nothing* about what Heaven is actually like. The common descriptions of Heaven as having 'streets of gold,' 'pearly gates,' and so forth, come mostly from the *very* symbolic Book of Revelation, not from the Jesus of the gospels.

"And what about the Book of Revelation? Well, this book begins by portraying Jesus as one whose hair was 'white like wool, as white as snow, and his eyes were like blazing fire. His feet were like bronze glowing in a furnace, and his voice was like the sound of rushing waters. In his right hand he held seven stars, and coming out of his mouth was a sharp, double-edged sword.'" He paused momentarily, then asked, "Now, is this to be taken *literally?* Can we even imagine what Jesus would look like, with a double-edged sword coming out of his mouth?" This remark produced some hesitant laughter from the attendees, and he went on, "Jesus is also portrayed in this book as a *lamb* that had been slain; now, did Jesus literally look like a sheep? One that had been sacrificed? Or is this simply *symbolic* language?

"And, most importantly, how should we interpret the 'Lake of Fire' in chapters 19 through 21 of the book, that supposedly represents the final fate of the wicked? The book of Revelation is the *only* place in the Bible that talks about such a 'lake of fire,' by the way; and in Revelation 20:14 and 21:8 it specifically says that this 'lake of fire' is the *second death;* some traditional Christians turn this around, and try to interpret the 'second death' as a literal *lake of fire*—but what these passages are actually saying is that this 'lake of fire' is a *symbol* of what it calls 'the second death'—which is the death that has no power over Christians, according to Revelation 2:11 and 20:6. Revelation 20:14 also tells us that 'Death and Hades' are to be 'cast into' this lake of fire. But Death and Hades aren't *people;* and therefore, they can't be 'consciously tormented eternally.' So could it be that the book of Revelation is simply trying to tell us that one day, both death itself, and this 'Hades' or 'Hell,' will be no more?" He let this question hang in the air for a long moment.

He continued, "And even in the Book of Revelation, is there no *hope* expressed for those who were not initially part of the 'saved'? Well, chapter 21 of that book tells us that the 'bad' people are 'consigned to the fiery lake'; but they are also apparently just 'outside' the gates into the eternal city—the New Jerusalem. And 21:24-26 tells us of this city, 'The nations will walk by its light, and the kings of the earth will bring their splendor into it. *On no day will its gates ever be shut,* for there will be no night there. The glory and honor of the nations will be brought into it.' Now, to be sure, verse 27 also says that 'Nothing impure will ever enter it, nor will anyone who does what is shameful or deceitful.'

"But let me ask: what if the status of a person isn't irrevocably 'fixed' at death? What if they are able to *repent,* so that they are no longer murderers, idolaters, and so on? What if the 'Lake of Fire' is telling us of a *corrective,* and *purifying* function—and is not simply representing punishment? C.S. Lewis famously said in his book, *The Problem of Pain,* that 'the doors of hell are locked on the *inside.*' Well, if those people are right outside the heavenly city, and they are eventually purified, why can't they then be welcomed into the open gates of the city, along with all the 'nations' and 'kings of the earth'?" He noticed that a number of his listeners seemed surprised—and even approving—of this statement.

He continued, "What did Jesus say about Hell? Not nearly as much as you might think, if you listen to those evangelists who attempt to portray Jesus as some kind of 1st century 'hellfire preacher.' Certainly, Jesus warned people to avoid Hell, where there is 'weeping and gnashing of teeth,' and 'the worm never dies, and the fire is never put out.' I doubt that most of us would have any really strong objections if people like Hitler or Stalin, or the 9/11 terrorists, were sent to a rather unpleasant place immediately after their deaths. But consider this: If Jesus tells us that the fire is not 'quenched,' or 'extinguished,' does that necessarily mean that it will constitute *eternal,* conscious torment for any people who may be there?" He allowed his hearers ponder this question.

He went on, "The two most frequently-cited examples of Jesus' teaching about Hell are probably the parable of the rich man and Lazarus in Luke 16:19-31, and the parable of the sheep and the goats in Matthew 25:31-46.

Now, some people will argue that the Luke 16 story is not a parable, but it clearly is: Luke places it as the conclusion of a series of five parables starting in chapter 15—including the famous parable of the Prodigal Son. Furthermore, Jesus begins the story with the 'there was a…' preface, that his other parables in Luke typically begin with. It's also interesting that, although most stories that Jesus told appear in several, or even three or four of the gospels, these two parables that I just mentioned each only appear in *one* gospel, which suggests these were not parables that Jesus told and retold on multiple occasions—which doesn't do much for Jesus' reputation as a 'hellfire preacher'!" (Some of those listening laughed lightly.)

He continued, "Matthew 25 is interesting, for a number of reasons—which have nothing whatsoever to do with the 'traditional' interpretation of it. For one thing, when confronted by the judge, the 'righteous' in this parable—represented by the sheep—*all* ask him, 'Lord, when saw we thee…?' So this seems to indicate that they were all *not* consciously aware that they were serving Christ, by their righteous actions; could this apply to persons from non-Christian religions? And, if salvation depends on one having 'received Jesus as your personal Saviour,' why doesn't the judge say that? Why is the only criteria used to separate the two groups at this judgment the *works* they did for the poor, the imprisoned, and the sick? And for that matter, why are both sheep and goats present at the *same* judgment? Aren't unbelievers supposed to appear at a Great White Throne Judgment, while believers appear at the Judgment Seat of Christ, to receive their crowns and rewards?" He judged from the serious expression on the faces of many of his listeners that they were thinking over these points.

He concluded, "So there are some serious questions if we try to take these two parables as literal descriptions of the afterlife. But if instead we simply ask ourselves what is the *point* being made by the parables, it is clear: we need to have compassion for the needy, and to do what we can to help them. And there will be a substantial amount of 'the last shall be first, and the first shall be last' in the world to come. But trying to use Luke 16 to draw a *map* of various supposed 'compartments' in Hades is to miss the point of the parable entirely.

"But then, what *did* Jesus tell us about life after death? Well, in the first place, we know that he *believed* in it! When he was confronted by the Sadducees—who *didn't* believe in life after death, of course—Jesus quoted

Exodus 3:6 to them: 'I am the God of Abraham, and the God of Isaac, and the God of Jacob,' and then Jesus added, 'He is not the God of the dead, but of the living, *for to him all are alive.*' [Lk 20:38] So to Jesus, the Old Testament patriarchs were still alive. Then, do you remember the story of the thief on the cross? The one who began by mocking Jesus, yet ultimately humbly asked Jesus to remember him; and Jesus told him, 'Truly I tell you, *today* you will be with me in paradise.' [Lk 23:43] So I think it's pretty clear that, although Jesus in his earthly ministry didn't describe any pearly gates or streets of gold in Heaven, he clearly believed that there *was* another life after this earthly life.

"Jesus was also very well-known—infamous, even—as someone who often fraternized with disreputable *sinners!* Jesus admitted that some people called him 'a glutton and a drunkard, a friend of tax collectors and sinners'! [Mt 11:18] He even allowed a 'sinful woman' to 'wash his feet with her tears,' kiss them, and then dry his feet with her long hair! [Lk 7:36-50] When Peter asked Jesus whether he had to forgive one who sinned against him as many as seven times, Jesus told him he that had to forgive such a confessed sin *seventy times* seven times; in other words, *every* time—without limit! [Mt 18:21-22] When Jesus was asked what was the greatest commandment—and there are 613 commandments in the Old Testament, incidentally—Jesus replied, 'Love God with all your heart and with all your soul and with all your mind,' and 'Love your neighbor as yourself.' [Mt 22:37-39] He also told us to 'love your enemies, and pray for those who persecute you.' [Mt 5:44]

"Was Jesus constantly, or even frequently, threatening his hearers with eternal fire in Hell, as some would have it? Well, he said in Matthew 11:29-30, 'Take my yoke upon you … and you will find rest for your souls. For my yoke is easy and my burden is light.' Or consider the story in Luke 4:16-21, of Jesus in the local synagogue in Nazareth, reading Isaiah 61:1-2 to the congregation. I find it interesting, that Jesus ends his reading of Isaiah in mid-verse, omitting the next phrase in verse 2, 'and the day of *vengeance* of our God.' If Jesus wanted to remind people about the possibility of eternal conscious torment, wouldn't he have also quoted the last part of this verse from Isaiah? In fact, words like 'vengeance,' 'wrath,' and 'justice' are almost never spoken by Jesus. So I ask you, does this Jesus *really* sound like a 'hellfire preacher'? Or instead, is he someone who primarily wanted to share with us the 'good news'—which is what the word 'gospel' means, by the way—about the love of God?"

He appeared to ponder his next words for a long moment, before he said, "Now, some folks will tell you that you can't just quote Jesus and the New Testament; you need to quote the God of the Old Testament, who is said to be a God of *wrath,* who demands stern *justice!*" He shrugged, and then added, "Admittedly, there are times when the God of the Old Testament is said to have taken such actions as to destroy the cities of Sodom and Gomorrah. But later in the Old Testament, particularly during the time of the prophets, a new spirit and message often came through. Even of Sodom, Ezekiel 16:53 says, 'I will restore the fortunes of Sodom and her daughters and of Samaria and her daughters, and your fortunes along with them.' Even of Gehenna, the valley of Hinnon, Jeremiah says that 'The days are coming... when... The whole valley where dead bodies and ashes are thrown, and all the terraces out to the Kidron Valley on the east as far as the corner of the Horse Gate, will be holy to the Lord.' [Jer 31:38-40] So the prophets spoke eloquently of a future *hope,* of reconciliation and restoration—even for these 'sinful' cities that were 'anathema' to the Jewish people.

"Ezekiel 33:11 also says, 'As surely as I live, declares the Sovereign Lord, I take no pleasure in the death of the wicked, but rather that they turn from their ways and live.' Isaiah 54:9-10 depicts as God saying, 'I have sworn not to be angry with you, never to rebuke you again. Though the mountains be shaken and the hills be removed, yet my unfailing love for you will not be shaken nor my covenant of peace be removed.' Lamentations 3:31-33 states that 'For no one is cast off by the Lord forever. Though he brings grief, he will show compassion, so great is his unfailing love. For he does not willingly bring affliction or grief to anyone.' So even in the Old Testament, it's obviously not just as simple as thinking that 'God demands justice, and this requires eternal, conscious torment.'"

He added in a softer tone, "Actually, the Bible tells us almost nothing *specific* about the afterlife; important questions like 'Will we be reunited with our loved ones?' are never really addressed—much less does the Bible answer smaller, nagging questions such as 'What will we be doing for all eternity? Will we sleep? Will we eat food? Will we be able to drink wine? Will I still be lactose-intolerant? Will we listen to music, or sing? Will my beloved dog or cat be there?' The Bible doesn't specifically answer such questions. Certainly, there are some people writing books—such as Randy Alcorn's popular book *Heaven*—who *claim* to be able to find a biblical verse here and there that might answer such questions; but these claims are nothing more than imagination and speculation."

He shrugged, and then added, "But if the Bible doesn't answer questions such as these, how can anyone be *certain* that a person's status is eternally 'fixed' at death? Or that there is no such thing as change, growth, or development after a person's death? Or that there is no such thing as a 'second chance' ever given to anyone, after their earthly life ends?" He paused for a long moment, and then said, "If the Bible is not going to specifically answer all of our urgent questions, then I would suggest that we put it aside for a moment—and let's just *think* and *talk* reasonably about these matters." The expressions on the faces of most of his listeners seemed agreeable to this proposal.

He asked a rhetorical question, "Can a person even *be* a Christian, without believing in a Hell of fiery, eternal torment? I mean, isn't the doctrine of Hell supposed to be one of the 'fundamentals,' that Christians everywhere must, and have always believed?" He let the audience ponder these questions momentarily, but then answered his own questions, "No, it isn't. In fact, the doctrine of a Hell of eternal torment is not included in either the Apostles Creed, or the Nicene Creed, which are the two earliest 'universal' creeds accepted by the entire Christian church. It wasn't until the Athanasian Creed—written in about the year 500—that the notion of 'everlasting fire' appeared in a Christian Creed. So for nearly five centuries after Jesus' death, people could be Christians, *without* having to profess belief in a Hell of torment and punishment."

He said in an easy, reflective tone, "The fact is that things are not very clear to us about theological matters, in this present life. The apostle Paul said in First Corinthians 13:12, 'For now we see through a glass, darkly'; well, that's putting it *mildly*, I think." (A number of persons in the audience laughed at this.) He went on, "Life often seems to us to be inequitable, and often quite unfair. Some of us, like David, die at young ages, while others live long lives; and there seems to be no particular correlation between a person's age at death, and their moral qualities. 'The good die young,' was an ancient saying of the Greeks, and Wordsworth's poem *The Excursion* agrees with this sentiment. Some babies die during the process of being born, while others may die in early infancy; some die in childhood, or in early youth. Some people have abundant opportunities in this life—for example, what was the likelihood of Billy Graham's son Franklin *not* becoming a Christian?—while literally billions of others live and die without ever even having heard the name of Jesus. If this life is all we have, then we cannot escape the fact that, often, 'Justice' does not seem to have been done; this life just isn't *fair!*

"Now, many Christians would argue that, although things may *seem* to us to be 'unjust' and inequitable in *this* life, things are actually balanced out, and made up for, in the next life. But would that the case if, immediately after our deaths, it is absolutely and irrevocably determined where we shall reside for all of *eternity?* So that young people who just reached the 'Age of Accountability' last weekend, are considered to be just as accountable as a 70-year old lifelong sinner? That the children of a drunken, abusive father get no consideration for the 'extenuating circumstances' of their upbringing, and are judged by the same scale as the children of John Wesley or Charles Spurgeon? Or that a person in an East Asian village who watched Campus Crusade's *Jesus* movie when it was shown there for one night, but didn't 'go forward' at the invitation, is damned forever? That a young man like David, who was somewhat mocking and sarcastic in his relation to religion—which is fairly common among young people his age, of course—is going to spend eternity in the same place that an Adolf Hitler, a Stalin, and a Pol Pot will be in?" He shook his head, and added, "Our sense of justice *rebels* at such a notion!"

He asked rhetorically, "But by speaking of '*our* sense of justice,' are we not committing the fallacy of attempting to 'judge *God*' by our limited, *human* standards? Many people would argue that way. But I would ask them, are we not supposed to have been created in the *image of God?* Are we not supposed to have within us the guiding light of our *consciences?* Since the Garden of Eden, are we not supposed to have 'knowledge of good and evil'? And are our very notions of 'justice,' 'right,' and 'fairness' not in fact guided by the principles found in the Bible—and particularly in the words of Jesus, who told us to 'judge not,' and to 'do *good* to those who persecute us'? First John 4:8 tells us that 'God is love.' If we think and feel emphatically that the notion of an eternal Hell of fiery torment—allowing no possibility of *ever* being able to repent, change, or even feel love again—is a doctrine that is inconsistent with the loving God that Jesus tried to tell us about, may not these very feelings and thoughts of ours be *guided* by God?" (He saw a number of heads among those seated nodding their agreement with this statement.)

He went on, "Most Christians these days believe that infants who die are 'saved,' and that they go to Heaven; even Roman Catholics no longer believe that unbaptized babies go to some shadowy place called 'Limbo'; they now believe that infants may achieve salvation. I certainly agree that infants who perish go to be with God. But how is this possible, given the theology of traditionalists? Infants aren't really capable of 'sinning'; they can't comprehend the 'Gospel,' as it would be presented in an evangelical church; and they can't exercise their free will to 'choose' to follow Jesus. Therefore, they must somehow be allowed to grow and develop *in the afterlife*, in order to ultimately reach their full potential. But if such change and development is possible, why should such possibilities be limited to infants? Will faithful Christians who die as teenagers remain eternal teenagers? Surely not. And if growth and development are possible after death, why can't a *change of heart* also be possible? Why is it not possible for a person—who, after death, now realizes with absolute certainty that God *does* exist, and that there *is* life after death—to turn from their past transgressions, and seek reconciliation with God? Why should the admittedly unequal length of our earthly lives be deemed the *only* time during which God can be sought?"

He shrugged, then admitted, "Of course, at the time when some people die, they may not be particularly *interested* in reconciliation with God. I've spoken with young people who told me bluntly, 'I don't *want* to go to Heaven—I want to go to Hell, so that I can party with my friends forever!' In his *Paradise Lost,* John Milton depicts Satan as saying, 'Better to reign in Hell, than serve in Heaven'; this is also the motto of the Hell's Angels motorcycle club. But such statements are usually just a sign of the 'youthful rebellion,' that many young people go through, and eventually outgrow." He smiled, and added, "That's fine; eternity is a long time," and many of his hearers laughed. He went on, "But if babies can grow up and develop into adults in Heaven, why can't teenagers? Or middle-aged people? Or even senior citizens? Maybe those who die as seniors can even *go back,* to an earlier age, before they became old and gray," and some chuckles were heard from the audience.

He thought for a moment, and then said, "Probably the most common objection to the traditional doctrine of Hell is its *disproportionality:* the notion that whatever amount of sins a person may commit in seventeen, twenty-nine, fifty-five, seventy-six, or even one hundred years, must be punished by *eternal* torment! Think of it: the mean kid who was a 'class bully' in elementary school; the juvenile delinquent teenager; and the young 'thug' who frequently revs up his car at 2:30 in the morning, waking up your family—all of whom you certainly don't want to have living next door to you—will supposedly be tormented *forever!* Now, while I might secretly enjoy the notion of God slapping around the bully, delinquent, and thug for a *while,* would I want this kind of treatment to continue *forever?*

"Cosmologists tell us that the universe is something like 13.7 billion years old, which seems like an *incredibly* long time, to us; actually, even a one-thousand year 'Millennium' seems like a very 'long time' to us, on the time scale that we operate under. But 13.7 billion years isn't even a 'drop in the bucket' of eternity; in fact, even after *400 trillion* years, eternity will still be no closer to an 'end' than it was at the beginning; would I want even the worst of unrepentant class bullies to be tormented for that long? Even taking the most difficult case I can imagine—namely, Adolf Hitler—would even he not have been punished sufficiently after maybe 400 *million* years? Particularly since many or most of the people he ordered killed during the Holocaust are presumably now enjoying eternal bliss in Heaven—and probably don't miss their earthly life at all!"

He paused, and then said gravely, "But to me, the biggest problem with the traditional notion of Hell is it has no *redemptive purpose.* It isn't intended to reform anyone, or to make anyone better, or more loving; and certainly, it isn't intended to encourage anyone to 'repent, and believe the gospel!' It exists purely and solely for the purpose of *tormenting* the lost; it isn't a Betty Ford Clinic, or even a prison, that wants to try to *help* people to become useful, productive members of society; or members of the 'New Jerusalem,' in this case. In the traditional view, we are told that the God who created this marvelous, finely-ordered universe we see all around us has a sense of 'justice' that demands eternal *retribution* for anyone transgressing his laws; and he is somehow 'justified' by keeping billions of people—who 'didn't receive Jesus as their personal Savior' during their brief earthly life—in a tormented state of existence, for all of eternity." He shook his head, and said, "I'm sorry, but I just can't accept that notion; that's certainly not the God that I know of." There were a number of murmurs of agreement from his listeners.

He went on, "But it should be noted that even *Christians* don't believe that anyone is truly 'incorrigible.' If an evangelical Christian had been present when Hitler was hiding in his bunker in 1945, and poised to shoot himself, this Christian would surely have 'preached the gospel' to him—and, according to evangelical theology, if Hitler had accepted this 'gospel,' he would have immediately become a born-again Christian; and would, as soon as he either died or was executed, spend all of eternity in Heaven—notwithstanding that some, or many, of the Jewish people he ordered murdered might be spending their eternity in Hell!" He shook his head, and added, "And if that wouldn't be a supremely ironic and tragic 'ending' to the horrors of the Holocaust, I don't know what is." There was a somber silence in the room, as his hearers pondered this situation,

He continued, "People also have very different *opportunities* to become 'saved,' under the traditional doctrine. Some people may be born into a pious Christian home, and others may be born into a family in which both parents are dogmatic atheists, who raise their children to show nothing but contempt for religion. Some people claim to have witnessed actual *miracles,* while others may have been sexually abused by priests or other religious authorities at a young age. Some people may only convert to Christianity at a fairly 'old' age; which means that if they had died sooner, they *wouldn't* have been saved. Are these different and varied opportunities for salvation all 'fair,' and equitable? Others may be born into a strongly Muslim family in Saudi Arabia—which in itself raises an interesting question: if deceased infants go to Heaven, does that also apply to infants born in non-Christian countries? If so, then are all children born in such countries going to end up in Heaven if they die before the age of, say, ten or twelve? And if that's the case, then are such children actually *fortunate* for having died at such an early age? It would seem so, if their parents, and older peers, are spending eternity in Hell.

"Why should we suppose that it is impossible for someone to *repent*— to change his or her mind—and ultimately find salvation in the afterlife?

God doesn't take away our *free wills* in the afterlife, does he? Remember that even in the parable of the rich man and Lazarus, the rich man clearly felt *concern* for his five brothers, and wanted to send Lazarus to warn them, so that they would '*repent*,' and not end up in Hades, as he had. Isn't this showing love and compassion for his brothers? And aren't such loving feelings thus capable of being broadened and deepened, over time? As I said earlier, eternity is a long time."

He smiled, and then said, "In fact, that's what I, as a Universalist, believe: that, ultimately, *all* of us can, and will, be reconciled to God. It may take some of us much longer than others—Hitler may take far, far longer than anyone else, for example—but who's to say that there is *anyone* who couldn't be reconciled to God in, say, a mere 400 trillion years? I would suggest that there is no reason to think that some souls are going to be 'frozen' at the time of death, so that they can never again seek, or be sought by, God's love. The rich man in the parable in Luke obviously remembered his earthly life; so wouldn't he also remember any incidents of love and goodness that he had experienced, or witnessed on earth? And doesn't the God of the Bible say over and over again that he *wants* people to repent, and turn to him? Who would be forcing God to set an arbitrary 'deadline' of one's time of death?" He paused again, to let these questions be absorbed by the audience.

He went on, "The evangelical author Randy Alcorn, whose bestselling book *Heaven* I mentioned earlier, addressed in this book the difficult question, 'how could we enjoy Heaven knowing that a loved one is in Hell?' His answer was that, 'In Heaven, we will ... fully concur with God's judgment on the wicked... in a sense, none of our loved ones will be in Hell—only some whom we *once* loved.' So apparently Mr. Alcorn thinks that we will no longer *love* our 'unsaved' children, spouses, sisters and brothers, friends, and others who didn't happen to 'make the cut' to get into Heaven." With emotional fire coming into his voice, he said passionately, "To me, that is an absolutely *monstrous* suggestion! What is more 'sacred' than the love of a mother for her child? Or the love of a husband for his wife? Or the fraternal love that brothers and sisters feel for each other? To me, if God somehow 'zaps' us once we get to Heaven, so that we no longer feel love for *all* of our loved ones here on earth, then I submit that not only do we no longer have 'free will,' but that such a 'zapped' being would no longer be **us!** How could we possibly *enjoy* Heaven, if those we love the most were being tormented eternally, just outside the gates of our city? And how could you erase the love of a parent from our memories, without destroying who we truly are, in the most fundamental sense?"

He turned and looked directly at David's parents (whose eyes were gleaming with tears) in the front row, and said gently, "But that's not at *all* what I think will happen, Roger and Thea. I truly believe that God *is* love, and that Jesus wanted to *tell* us of that love. I believe that all of us— Christian and Muslim; New Ager and secularist; agnostic and atheist— *will* continue to live after our earthly lives are over. And I absolutely believe that you *will* see your son again; and it won't be simply by gazing at him across a 'great chasm' in Hades—it will be in a place where love is not only *possible,* but is actually the *goal* of all who are there."

He said in a warm, inviting tone, "Our lives here are not meaningless, nor are they simply a 'probation period' to determine whether we get to move on to Heaven, or not. But we do have the chance here to learn, to grow, to develop; and I'm sure that what we learn here, will be of profound *use* to us in the next life. And, conversely, any lasting *mistakes* we make here—bad habits, hateful attitudes, prejudices, and so on—will be things we will need to *overcome,* and work through in the afterlife. I think that's perhaps the reason why Jesus so strongly warned us to love our neighbor as ourselves. In fact, in the two parables of Jesus that 'traditionalists' about Hell love to quote—the rich man and Lazarus, and the sheep and the goats—those who are condemned are those who failed to provide *materially* for others, during their earthly life; the blessed ones are those who fed the hungry, visited the sick, clothed the poor, and took in the stranger. *That's* the kind of earthly behavior that will pay dividends in the 'kingdom of Heaven,' according to Jesus."

He paused, then said thoughtfully, "But that raises an interesting question: How many of us are really *ready* to be in Heaven—surrounded by all of that perfection?" He smiled, then added, "Traditional Protestants seem to assume that they'll all just 'magically' be free from sin, and get along perfectly with each other, once they're all in Heaven—although their behavior here on Earth doesn't give the rest of us much *confidence* that that will in fact be true!" (This produced a hearty laugh from the audience.) He continued, "And given that such Protestants supposedly already have the assistance of the Holy Spirit while they are down here, it's unclear to me how they are going to behave much differently in Heaven; at least, assuming that God doesn't somehow miraculously change their basic human nature, or take away their free will. But of course, if God can do that in Heaven, why didn't he do that right here, while we were on Earth? The existence of Heaven would seemingly prove that it *is* possible to have a 'perfect world,' without apparently taking away our freedom of will. If that is the case, then the philosophical 'Problem of Evil' is solved—at least, for those in Heaven."

He shrugged, and then explained, "Universalists like myself have historically been of two different opinions about whether there is any actual 'punishment' after death; some Universalists, like Hosea Ballou in the 19th century, think that the 'hells' we go through in this lifetime are sufficient 'punishment'; but the majority opinion—which is also my own—is that there will be some 'punishment' awaiting many or most of us after death, before we are ready for the 'heavenly' state. Now, we strongly reject the old Roman Catholic notion that this preparation involves anything remotely like 'fiery torment.' But I do think that spending some significant time alone on a desert island, or in a bare prison cell—with nothing much to do except review your own life, and see all the mistakes that you made—might very well be just what you need, to be able to progress to the next level!"

Looking directly at David's parents again, he said gently, "So I think it's quite possible that your David may very well need to do some *work*, in order to be ready for Heaven." He smiled encouragingly, and added, "On the other hand, since by the time we die, he will have been there longer than any of us—so that all of *us* may need to 'catch up' to *him,* once we pass on," and this generated a hearty laugh from his listeners.

He said solemnly, "But I would tell you, Roger and Thea, as firmly as I can: *do not despair* about your son; David is surely in a better place, and closer to God, than any of us now are. And I do not doubt that you will see David again, and be able to express your love for him: *forever!*" (A few people in the audience lightly applauded this statement.)

He concluded, "Thank you for your attention. Let us all remember the good that was in our dear departed friend and relative David Wells; and may it inspire us to do even more in our own lives."

He stopped speaking, picked up his notes, and then took his seat again, as the Funeral Director returned to the podium, and introduced a young lady—a friend of David's—who was going to sing a song, in honor of David.

Roger Wells reached over across Thea and grasped Eric's hand, and whispered, "Thanks so much, Eric; that was perfect—exactly what I needed to hear." Thea also took hold of Eric's hand, and squeezed it firmly.

"You're welcome," Eric replied. And they stopped speaking, to listen to the song the young lady was singing...

***

When the funeral service was over, Eric was thanked by a number of people for his kind words about David. "You gave me such encouragement," one lady said, clutching Eric's hand fervently. "I was kind of worried about David; but I feel so much better about him now, and about where he's at!"

When nearly all of the participants had left the room, Roger took Eric aside, and said seriously, "I think that Thea and I might like to join your church."

Eric smiled, and said, "That's fine; we don't really have any 'procedure' for joining our church; but please, just come and worship with us whenever you want to."

Roger suddenly looked worried, and whispered, "But there's just one thing..." Leaning close to Eric's ear, he breathed, "I voted for Donald Trump! But I got the impression that most of your people there voted for Hillary; or even for that crazy Stein lady who was with the Green Party...!"

Eric chuckled, and said reassuringly, "That won't be a problem; we have a very *diverse* congregation..."

THE END

BIBLIOGRAPHY

NOTE: A lot of the "historical" books can be downloaded in .pdf and other formats for free; others are available in scanned/reprinted editions from various Internet booksellers.

UNIVERSALISM, CONDITIONAL IMMORTALITY, NON-TRADITIONAL VIEWS
Modern Publications:

Aldwinckle, Russell: *Death in the Secular City: Study of the Notion of Life After Death in Contemporary Theology and Philosophy*

Alfeyev, Hilarion: *Christ the Conqueror of Hell: The Descent into Hades from an Orthodox Perspective*

Armstrong, Herbert: *Is There a Real Hell Fire?*

Armstrong, Herbert: *What Will You Be Doing in the Next Life?*

Armstrong, Herbert: *What is The Reward of the Saved?*

Associated Bible Students of Central Ohio: 'Where are the Dead?'

Associated Bible Students of Central Ohio: 'Doctrine of Eternal Torment'

Atkinson, Basil Ferris Campbell: *Life and Immortality: An Examination of the Nature and Meaning of Life and Death as They Are Revealed in the Scriptures*

Ayer, Jim: *Judgment & Hell: God May Be Kinder than You Think!*

Bacchiocchi, Samuele: *Immortality Or Resurrection? A Biblical Study on Human Nature and Destiny*

Baer, Jackson: *What the Hell: How Did We Get It So Wrong? Eternity, Grace, and the Message of Love*

Baker, Sharon L.: *Razing Hell: Rethinking Everything You've Been Taught About God's Wrath and Judgment*

Batchelor, Doug: *The Rich Man and Lazarus* (audio)

Balthasar, Hans Urs Von: *Dare We Hope 'That All Men Be Saved'?*

Barclay, William: *Natural Believer: A Spiritual Autobiography*

Barry, Douglas: *Conditional Immortality: Biblical Proof of Annihilation in Hell: The Fate of the Lost from a Messianic, Evangelical Perspective*

Barth, Karl: *Church Dogmatics, Vol. II, Pt. 2*

Barth, Karl: *Church Dogmatics, Vol. IV, 3, II*

Barth, Karl: *The Humanity of God*

Beauchemin, Gerry: *Hope Beyond Hell: The Righteous Purpose of God's Judgment*

Bell, Rob: *Love Wins: A Book About Heaven, Hell, and the Fate of Every Person Who Ever Lived*

Bell, Rob: *Love Wins* (audio)

Blodgett, Ralph: *Hell--Will the Wicked Burn Forever?*

Bonda, Jan: *The One Purpose of God: An Answer to the Doctrine of Eternal Punishment*

Bradley, Heath: *Flames of Love: Hell and Universal Salvation*

Bradshaw, John: *Understanding Hell: Separating Fact from Fiction*

Bruce, F.F.: Foreword to Fudge's *The Fire That Consumes* (1st Edition)

Bruce, F.F.: 1989 letter to John Stott reprinted in *John Stott: A Global Ministry: The Later Years* by Timothy Dudley-Smith

Burnfield, David: *Patristic Universalism: An Alternative to the Traditional View of Divine Judgment*

Campana, Stephen: *The Calvinist Universalist: Is Evil a Distortion of Truth? or Truth Itself?*

Camping, Harold: *The Fig Tree: An Analysis of the Past, Present and Future of National Israel*

Cassara, Ernest: *Universalism in America: A Documentary History of a Liberal Faith*

Chamberlain, Mark T.: *Every Knee Shall Bow: The Case for Christian Universalism*

Christadelphian Magazine and Publishing Association Ltd.: *Heaven and Hell: What Does the Bible Teach?*

Christadelphian Magazine and Publishing Association Ltd.: *After Death, What?*

Church of God, International: *Immortality: God's Gift to the Saints*

Church of God, International: *Hell, You Say?*

Church of God, International: *Lazarus & the Rich Man: Where Are They?*

Church of God, International/Bronson, James: *What Happens When You Die?* (audio)

Church of God, International/Stinson, Vance: *What Happens to Unbelievers?* (audio)

Cook, Jeff: *Everything New: Reimagining Heaven and Hell*

Cox, Steven: *The Rich Man, Lazarus, and Abraham*

Crews, Dennis: *The Rich Man and Lazarus*

Crews, Joe: *Hell-Fire: A Twisted Truth Untangled*

Crews, Joe: *Absent from the Body*

Cullmann, Oscar: *Immortality of the Soul or Resurrection of the Dead?: The Witness of the New Testament*

Date, Christopher M.; Stump, Gregory G.; Anderson, Joshua W. (Eds.): *Rethinking Hell: Readings in Evangelical Conditionalism*

Doctrine Commision of the Church of England: *The Mystery of Salvation: The Story of God's Gift*

Dudley-Smith, Timothy: *John Stott: A Global Ministry: The Later Years*

Eberle, Harold: *Hell: God's Justice, God's Mercy*

Ellul, Jacques: *What I Believe*

Emry, Sheldon: *The Burning Hell: Is It Blasphemy?*

Evangelical Alliance Commission on Unity and Truth Among Evangelicals (ACUTE): *The Nature of Hell*

Evely, Robert: *At the End of the Ages......The Abolition of Hell*

Family Heritage Books: 'What the Bible Says About Hellfire' (tract)

Ferre, Nels F.S.: *The Universal Word: A Theology for a Universal Faith*

Ferwerda, Julie: *Raising Hell: Christianity's Most Controversial Doctrine Put Under Fire*

Flickinger, Eric: *Revelations Hell Fire: Revealing God's Love* (audio)

Fristad, Kalen: *Destined for Salvation: God's Promise to Save Everyone*

Froom, Le Roy Edwin: *The Conditionalist Faith of Our Fathers, The Conflict of the Ages Over the Nature and Destiny of Man*

Fudge, Edward William: *The Fire That Consumes: A Biblical and Historical Study of the Doctrine of Final Punishment* (3rd edition)

Fudge, Edward William: *Hell: A Final Word: The Surprising Truths I Found in the Bible*

Fudge, Edward: *The Divine Rescue: The Gripping Drama of a Lost World and of the Creator Who Will Not Let It Go*

Gillihan, Charles: *Hell No!: A Fundamentalist Preacher Rejects Eternal Torment*

Global Church of God (Norbert Link): *Do We Have An Immortal Soul?*

Goyette, Richard Harold: *Christian Universalism, Maybe God Isn't Such A Bad Guy After All: Surprising Answers to Perplexing Questions People Ask About the God of the Bible*

Grace Communion International (Joseph Tkach): *Hell*

Grace Communion International (Joseph Tkach): *Heaven*

Grace Communion International (Michael Morrison): *The Intermediate State*

Grace Communion International (Michael Morrison): *Between Death and Resurrection*

Grace Communion International (Keith Stump): *The Battle Over Hell*

Grace Communion International (Paul Kroll): *What About the "Intermediate State"?*

Grace Communion International (J. Michael Feazell): *Lazarus and the Rich Man*

Graham, Billy; Schuller, Robert: Interview on Schuller's *Hour of Power* television show (broadcast on May 31, 1997) [available on YouTube]

Graham, Billy: *The Challenge: Sermons from Madison Square Garden*

Graham, Billy: *Time Magazine* article (11/15/93, pg. 74)

Green, Michael: *Evangelism Through the Local Church: A Comprehensive Guide to All Aspects of Evangelisation*

Gregg, Steve: *All You Want to Know About Hell: Three Christian Views of God's Final Solution to the Problem of Sin*

Guillebaud, Harold: *The Righteous Judge: A Study of the Biblical Doctrine of Everlasting Punishment*

Gulley, Philip; Mulholland, James: *If Grace is True: Why God Will Save Every Person*

Harman, James T.: *Beyond the Lake of Fire*

Harmon, Steven R.: *Every Knee Should Bow: Biblical Rationales for Universal Salvation in Early Christian Thought*

Harper, Roger: *The Lie of Hell*

Harwood, Adam: *The Spiritual Condition of Infants: A Biblical-Historical Survey and Systematic Proposal*

Haynes, Carlyle B.: *Life, Death, and Immortality*

Hick, John: *Death and Eternal Life*

Hick, John: *Evil and the God of Love*

Hiett, Peter: *How One Biblical Annihilationist Became a Biblical Universalist* (Rethinking Hell audio)

Howe, Charles A.: *The Larger Faith: A Short History of American Universalism*

Howe, George: *Christ Saves All*

Hughes, Philip Edgcumbe: *The True Image: The Origin and Destiny of Man in Christ*

Humber, Paul G.: *Terminal Hell - Eternal Paradise*

Jacoby, Douglas A.: *What's the Truth About Heaven and Hell?: Sorting Out the Confusion About the Afterlife*

Jersak, Bradley: *Her Gates Will Never Be Shut: Hope, Hell, and the New Jerusalem*

Johnson, Anthony: *The Larger Hope: Scriptural Evidence for the Ultimate Salvation of All People*

Jonathan, Stephen: *Grace beyond the Grave: Is Salvation Possible in the Afterlife? A Biblical, Theological, and Pastoral Evaluation*

Klassen, Randy: *What Does the Bible Really Say About Hell? Wrestling with the Traditional View*

Knauft, Daniel: *Search for The Immortal Soul*

Kronen, John; Reitan, Eric: *A Philosophical Case for Preferring Universalism to Annihilationism* (Rethinking Hell audio)

L'Engle, Madeleine: *The Irrational Season*

Lewis, C.S.: *The Great Divorce*

Lewis, C.S.: *The Problem of Pain*

Lewis, C.S.: *Letters to Malcolm*

Living Church of God (Roderick C. Meredith): *Your Ultimate Destiny*

Living Church of God (Richard Ames): *Is There Life After Death?* (audio)

Living Church of God (Richard Ames): *The Three Resurrections* (audio)

Living Church of God (Wallace Smith): *Are They ALL Lost Forever?* (audio)

Locke, John: *John Locke: Writings on Religion* (Ed. Victor Nuovo)

MacDonald, Gregory (actually "Robin Parry"): *The Evangelical Universalist*

Mansell, Donald E.: *The Mystery of Consciousness: What Happens to the Soul After Death?*

May, Bill: *Are the Dead Really Dead?*

May, Bill: *Is The Devil in Charge of Hell?*

Mealy, Webb J.: *The End of the Unrepentant: A Study of the Biblical Themes of Fire and Being Consumed*

Miller, Russell E.: *The Larger Hope: The First Century of the Universalist Church in America, 1770-1870*

Odom, Robert Leo: *Is Your Soul Immortal?*

Pannenberg, Wolfhart: *Jesus: God and Man*

Papaioannou, Kim: *The Geography of Hell in the Teaching of Jesus: Gehena, Hades, the Abyss, the Outer Darkness Where There Is Weeping and Gnashing of Teeth*

Parachin, Victor: *Life After Death—Your Questions Answered*

Patching, J.: *The Rich Man and Lazarus*

Pearson, Carlton: *The Gospel of Inclusion: Reaching Beyond Religious Fundamentalism to the True Love of God and Self*

Pearson, Carlton: *The Gospel of Inclusion* (audio)

Pearson, Carlton: *God is Not a Christian, Nor a Jew, Muslim, Hindu… God Dwells With Us, In Us, Around Us, as Us*

Peck, M. Scott: *In Heaven As On Earth: A Vision of the Afterlife*

Philadelphia Church of God/Gerald Flurry: 'What Is Hell?' (from the April 2011 *The Trumpet*)

Pinnock, Clark (Ed.): *The Grace of God and the Will of Man*

Pinnock, Clark H.; Brow, Robert C.: *Unbounded Love: A Good News Theology for the 21ˢᵗ Century*

Powys, David: *'Hell': A Hard Look at a Hard Question: The Fate of the Unrighteous in New Testament Thought*

Punt, Neal: *Unconditional Good News: Toward and Understanding of Biblical Universalism*

Punt, Neal: *So Also in Christ: Re-Viewing the Plan of Salvation*

Rahner, Karl: *Theological Investigations, Volume XII: Confrontations 2*

Reagan, David: *Eternity: Heaven or Hell?*

Restored Church of God/David C. Pack: *Is There Life After Death?*

Restored Church of God/David C. Pack: *The Truth About Hell*

Restored Church of God/David C. Pack: *Do the Saved Go to Heaven?*

Restored Church of God/David C. Pack: *What Is Your Reward in the Next Life?*

Rethinking Hell Conference 2015: *Panel Discussion* (Rethinking Hell audio)

Review and Herald Publishing Association: *Seventh-Day Adventists Answer Questions on Doctrine*

Review and Herald Publishing Association: *Seventh-Day Adventist Encyclopedia* [articles 'Death'; 'Eternal Life' 'Hell'; 'Immortality'; 'Resurrection']

Robinson, J.A.T.: *In the End, God: A Study of the Christian Doctrine of the Last Things*

Rogers, Ivan A.: *Dropping Hell and Embracing Grace: Answering Those Questions They Didn't Want Us to Ask Concerning Heaven, Hell and Hope for the Ultimate Salvation of all Humanity*

Scott, Clinton Lee: *The Universalist Church in America: A Short History*

Signs of the Times: 'The Surprising Truth About Hell'

Skinner, Clarence R.: *The Social Implications of Universalism*

Smith, Hannah Whitall: *The Unselfishness of God and How I Discovered It: A Spiritual Autobiography*

Sotak, Max H.: *Damning Assumptions: What Advocates of Endless Torment Take for Granted*

Spiegel, James: *Summing Up the Case for Conditional Immortalism* (Rethinking Hell audio)

Stackhouse, John: *Heaven, Hell, and Everything In-between* (Regent College audio)

Stackhouse, John: *Hell and the Goodness of God* (Recent College audio)

Stetson, Eric: *Christian Universalism: God's Good News For All People*

Stott, John; Edwards, David L.: *Evangelical Essentials: A Liberal-Evangelical Dialogue*

Sweeney, Jon M.: *Inventing Hell: Dante, the Bible and Eternal Torment*

Talbott, Thomas: *The Inescapable Love of God*

Tanksley Jr., William; Date, Chris: *Worth a Thousand Words - A Conditionalist Reading of the Book of Revelation* (Rethinking Hell audio)

The Truth About Hell: 'The Truth about Hades and Hell Fire'; 'What is the Truth about Hell Fire?'

Travis, Stephen (Ed.): *A Consuming Passion: Essays on Hell and Immortality in Honor of Edward Fudge*

Trudeau, Richard: *Universalism 101: An Introduction for Leaders of Unitarian Universalist Congregations*

United Church of God: *Heaven and Hell: What Does the Bible Really Teach?*

United Church of God: *What Happens After Death?*

United Church of God: *What Is Your Destiny?*

Vandeman, George E.: *Life After Death*

Vincent, Ken: *The Golden Thread: God's Promise of Universal Salvation*

Voice of Prophecy (Bibleinfo.com): 'What does the Bible say about Hell?'; 'Soul'; 'What does the Bible say about death?'

Walker, Daniel Pickering: *Decline of Hell: Seventeenth-Century Discussions of Eternal Torment* (1964)

Walls, Jerry L.: *Heaven, Hell, and Purgatory: Rethinking the Things That Matter Most*

Walls, Jerry L.: *Purgatory: The Logic of Total Transformation*

Waren, Dirk: *Hell Know: Eternal Torture or Everlasting Destruction?*

Waren, Dirk: *Sheol Know*

Watchtower Bible and Tract Society: *Insight on the Scriptures*

Watchtower Bible and Tract Society: *Aid to Bible Understanding:* articles 'Death'; 'Gehenna'; 'Grave'; 'Hades'; 'Heaven'; 'Hell'; 'Immortality'; 'Sheol'; 'Tartartus'; 'Enoch'; 'Elijah'

Watchtower Bible and Tract Society: *Is This Life All There Is?*

Watchtower Bible and Tract Society: *Make Sure of All Things; Hold Fast to What is Fine*

Watchtower Bible and Tract Society: *The Truth that Leads to Eternal Life*

Watchtower Bible and Tract Society: *Revelation: Its Grand Climax At Hand*

Watchtower Bible and Tract Society: *You Can Live Forever In Paradise on Earth*

Watchtower Bible and Tract Society: *Insight on the Scriptures, Vol. I ('Hell')*

Watchtower Bible and Tract Society: *Reasoning from the Scriptures*

Watchtower Bible and Tract Society: *What Does the Bible Really Teach?*

Watchtower Bible and Tract Society: 'What Happens When You Die?'

Watchtower Bible and Tract Society: 'What Is Hell? Is It a Place of Eternal Torment?'

Watchtower Bible and Tract Society: 'Who Goes to Hell?'

Watchtower Bible and Tract Society: 'What Is the Soul?'

Watchtower Bible and Tract Society: 'What is the Resurrection?'

Watchtower Bible and Tract Society: 'The Dead Will Live Again!'

Watchtower Bible and Tract Society: 'What Happens After Death?'

Watchtower Bible and Tract Society: *Awake* magazine (No. 3, 2016): 'When a Loved One Dies' [articles 'What Happens After Death?'; 'The Dead Will Live Again']

Watson, David Lowes: *God Does Not Foreclose: The Universal Promise of Salvation*

Weatherhead, Leslie: *Is There More: Heaven, Hell, and the Eternal Life That Begins Now*

Wellman, James K.: *Rob Bell and a New American Christianity*

Wenham, John: *Facing Hell: An Autobiography: 1913-1996*

Wenham, John: *The Goodness of God*

Williams, George Hunston: *American Universalism*

Wisbrock, George: *Death and the Soul After Life*

Wright, Nigel: *The Radical Evangelical*

Wright, N. T.: *Surprised by Hope: Rethinking Heaven, the Resurrection, and the Mission of the Church*

Zender, Martin: *Martin Zender Goes to Hell: A Critical Look at an Un-Criticized Doctrine*

Zender, Martin: *The Really Bad Thing About Free Will*

Zender, Martin; Sheridan, Dan: *Eons and the Invention of Time; Mistranslations of "aion"; We All Arrive at the Same Destination—Eventually; Christ Reclaims the Adamic Race; Death Sucks, But Not For Long; Salvation Murky and Difficult; Mortality; Immortality; Cooperative Salvation...Not* (audio podcasts)

Zens, Jon H.: *Christ Minimized: A Response to Rob Bell's Love Wins*

Historical Publications:

Abbott, Lyman, et al.: *The Problem of Human Destiny as Conditioned by Free Will* (1910)

Abbott, Lyman, et al.: *That Unknown Country: Or, What Living Men Believe Concerning Punishment After Death* (1888)

Adams, John C.: *Universalism and the Universalist Church* (1915)

Allin, Thomas: *The Question of Questions - Is Christ Indeed the Saviour of the World* (1885)

Allin, Thomas: *Universalism Asserted as the Hope of the Gospel On the Authority of Reason, the Fathers, and Holy Scripture* (1895)

Atwood, I.M. (Ed.): *The Latest Word of Universalism - Thirteen Essays by Thirteen Clergymen* (1878)

Ballou, Adin: *Primitive Christianity and Its Corruptions* (1870)

Ballou, Hosea: *A Treatise on Atonement* (1805)

Ballou, Hosea: *An Examination of the Doctrine of Future Retribution* (1834)

Ballou [2d; the great-nephew], Hosea: *Ancient History of Universalism, From the Time of the Apostles to the Fifth General Council* (1872)

Barnum, Phineas T.: *Why I Am a Universalist* (1890)

Betts, F.W.: *Philosophy and Faith of Universalism* (1913)

Biddle, John: *Twofold Scripture Catechism* [Chap. XXIV](1654)

Blackburne, Francis: *A Short Historical View Of The Controversy Concerning An Intermediate State And The Separate Existence Of The Soul* (1765) [Contains appendix documenting Martin Luther's support of "soul sleep"]

Blain, Jacob: *Death Not Life: Or, the Theological Hell and Endless Misery Disproved* (1853)

Bonner, Hypatia Bradlaugh: *The Christian Hell: From the First to the Twentieth Century* (1913)

Brown, Thomas: *A History of the Origin and Progress of the Doctrine of Universal Salvation* (1826)

Bulkley, S.C.; Hutchins, Elias: *A Report of the Discussion Held in Newmarket, N.H.* (1842)

Burnet, Thomas: A *Treatise Concerning the State of Departed Souls* (1739)

Canright, D. M.: *History of the Doctrine of the Immortality of the Soul* (1871)

Chauncey, Charles: *The Mystery Hid from Ages and Generations, Made Manifest by the Gospel-Revelation: or, The Salvation of All Men: The Grand Thing Aimed at in the Scheme of God* (1784)

Clapp, Theodore: *Theological Views (The Teachings of Scripture concerning Punishment, Examination of the Doctrine of Future Retribution* (1859)

Cone, Orello: *Gospel-Criticism and Historical Christianity* (1891)

Constable, Henry: *Hades: Or, the Intermediate State of Man* (1873)

Coppin, Richard: *A Blow at the Serpent; or a Gentle Answer from Maidstone Prison to Appease Wrath* (1656)

Cox, Samuel: *Salvator Mundi: Or, Is Christ the Saviour of All Men?* (1899)

Crispin, William Frost: *Universalism and Problems of the Universalist Church* (1888)

Eddy, Richard: *Universalism in America* (2 volumes) (1886)

Farrar, Frederic William: *Eternal Hope: Five Sermons Preached in Westminster Abbey* (1877)

Fernald, W.M.: *Universalism Against Partialism* (1840)

Flanders, George T.: *Review of Alexander Hall's 'Universalism Against Itself'* (1847)

Fletcher, L.J.; *Universalism: Its Doctrines and Their Foundations* (1864)

Forbes, Darius: *The Universalist's Assistant, or, an Examination of the principal objections commonly urged Against Universalism* (1846)

Guild, E.E.: *The Universalist's Book of Reference Containing all the Principal Facts and Arguments, and Scripture Texts, Pro and Con, on the Great Controversy Between Limitarians and Universalists* (1853)

Hall, D.P.: *Man Not Immortal: The Only Shield Against the Seductions of Modern Spiritualism* (1854)

Hanson, John Wesley: *Bible Proofs of Universal Salvation; Containing the Passages of Scripture that Teach the Final Holiness and Happiness of All Mankind* (1903)

Hanson, John Wesley: *Bible Threatenings Explained; Or, Passages of Scripture Sometimes Quoted to Prove Endless Punishment Shown to Teach Consequences of Limited Duration* (1885)

Hanson, John Wesley: Lozier, John Hogarth: *A Brief Debate on Universal Salvation/Endless Punishment* (1879)

Hanson, John Wesley: *Aion-Aionios: An Excursus on the Greek Word Rendered Everlasting, Eternal, Etc., in the Holy Bible* (1880)

Hanson, John Wesley: *The Bible Hell: The Words Rendered Hell in the Bible, Sheol, Hadees, Tartarus, and Gehenna, Shown to Denote a State of Temporal Duration* (1888)

Hanson, John Wesley: *Universalism the Prevailing Doctrine of the Christian Church During Its First Five Hundred Years; With Authorities and Extracts* (1899)

Huber, Marie: The World Unmask'd: or, The Philosopher the Greatest Cheat:
In Twenty-Four Dialogues (1743)
Hudson, Charles Frederic: Debt and Grace: As Related to the Doctrine of a
Future Life (1857)

Hudson, Charles Frederic: A Series of Letters Addressed to Rev. Hosea Ballou
… Being a Vindication of the Doctrine of a Future Retribution (1827)
Jukes, Andrew: The Second Death and the Restitution of All Things (1867)

Kneeland, Abner: A Series of Lectures on the Doctrine of Universal Benevolence
(1818)
Knox-Little, William John, et al. (Ed.): Immortality, a Clerical Symposium
on What Are the Foundations of the Belief in the Immortality of Man
(1885)
Lead, Jane: The Enochian Walks with God, Found Out by a Spiritual
Traveller (1694)

Livermore, Daniel P.: Proof-Texts of Endless Punishment, Examined and
Explained (1864)
Manford, Erasmus; Franklin, Benjamin: An Oral Debate on the Coming
of the Son of Man, Endless Punishment, and Universal Salvation (1860)
Manford, Erasmus; Sweeney, J.S.: A Discussion on Universal Salvation and
Future Punishment (1870)
Moore, Asher: Universalism, the Doctrine of the Bible (1847)

Moore, Asher: Universalist Belief, or the Doctrinal Views of Universalists
(1841)
Morse, Pitt: Sermons in Vindication of Universalism (1831)
Murray, John: Records of the Life of the Rev. John Murray, Written by Himself
(1816)
Murray, John: Letters and Sketches of Sermons, Volumes I, II, III (1800)
Phan, Peter C.: Living Into Death, Dying Into Life: A Christian Theology of
Life Eternal (audio)
Pétavel, Emmanuel: The Problem of Immortality (1892)

Petitpiere, Ferdinand Oliver: Thoughts on the Divine Goodness (1794 trans.)
Pettingell, John Hancock: The Life Everlasting: What Is It? Whence Is It?
Whose Is It? (1883)
Pingree, E.M.; Rice, N.L.: A Debate on the Doctrine of Universal Salvation
(1845)
Pitrat, John Claudius: Pagan Origin of Partialist Doctrines (1871)

Priestly, Joseph: *Discourses Relating to the Evidences of Revealed Religion* (1796)

Relly, James: *Union: Or a Treatise of the Consanguinity and Affinity Between Christ and His Church* (1759)

Relly, James: *Salvation Completed: and Secured in Christ, as the Covenant of the People* (1753)

Richardson, Samuel: *A Discourse on the Torments of Hell* (1654)

Richardson, Samuel: *The Doctrine of Eternal Hell Torments Overthrown* (1833)

Rogers, George: *The Pro and Con of Universalism, Both as to Its Doctrines and Moral Bearings* (1839)

Sawyer, Thomas J.: *Endless Punishment: In the Very Words of Its Advocates* (1880)

Shehane, C.F.R.: *A Key to Universalism* (1854)

Siegvolck, Paul: *The Everlasting Gospel* (1753)

Skinner, Otis A.: *Universalism Illustrated and* Defended (1839)

Skinner, Otis: *The Doctrine of Endless Misery Not Taught in the Bible* (1842)

Smith, Uriah: *Here and Hereafter* (1897)

Smith, Uriah: *Man's Nature and Destiny: Or, the State of the Dead, the Reward of the Righteous, and the End of the Wicked* (1884)

Smith, Uriah: *Mortal or Immortal? Or, an Inquiry into the Present Constitution and Future Condition of Man* (1860)

Steere, M.J.: *Footprints Heavenward, Or Universalism the More Excellent Way* (1862)

Sterry, Peter: *A Discourse of the Freedom of the Will* (1675)

Stonehouse, James: *Universal Restitution a Scripture Doctrine* (1761)

Swedenborg, Emanuel: *Heaven and Hell* (1758)

Thayer, Thomas: *Theology of Universalism* (1862) [see:

Thayer, Thomas: *The Origin and History of the Doctrine of Endless Punishment* (1855)

White, Edward: *Life in Christ: A Study of the Scripture Doctrine on the Nature of Man, the Object of the Divine Incarnation, and the Conditions of Human Immortality* (1875)

White, Ellen G.: *America in Prophecy* (aka *The Great Controversy*)(1888)

White, Ellen G.: *Early Writings* [available at: http://www.ellenwhite.info/books/books-by-egw-ew.htm]

White, Jeremiah: *The Restoration of All Things* (1712; posthumous)

Whittemore, Thomas: *The Plain Guide to Universalism: Designed to Lead Inquirers to the Belief of that Doctrine, and Believers to the Practice of It*

Whittemore, Thomas: *The Modern History of Universalism, from the Era of the Reformation to the Present Time* (1830)

Williams, Thomas: *Man: His Origin, Nature, and Destiny* (1898)

Williamson, Isaac Dowd: *An Exposition and Defence of Universalism* (1859)

Williamson, Isaac Dowd: *The Philosophy of Universalism, or, Reasons for Our Faith* (1880)

Williamson, Isaac Dowd: *An Examination of the Doctrine of Endless Punishment: Its Claims to Divine Origin Refuted, in a Series of Lectures*

Winchester, Elhanan: *Universal Restoration Exhibited in Four Dialogues Between a Minister and His Friend* (1792)

Young, Joseph: *The Universal Restoration of All Men Proved, by Scripture, Reason, and Common Sense* (1804)

TRADITIONAL VIEW

Modern Publications:

Alcorn, Randy: *Heaven*

Andrews, Edward D.: *What Does the Bible Really Say About Hellfire?: Eternal Torment? Is Hellfire Just? Is Hellfire Part of Divine Justice?*

Bahnsen, Greg: *The Sober News About Hell* (audio set)

Balke, Willem: *Calvin and the Anabaptist Radicals*

Barger, Eric: *Universalism: Is Everyone Already Saved?* (audio)

Bellarmine, Robert: *Hell and Its Torments*

Blamires, Harry: *Knowing the Truth About Heaven and Hell: Our Choices and Where They Lead Us*

Blanchard, John: *Whatever Happened to Hell?*

Boa, Kenneth D.; Bowman Jr., Robert M.: *Sense and Nonsense about Heaven and Hell*

Buis, Harry: *The Doctrine of Eternal Punishment* (1957)

Bunyan, John: *Visions of Heaven & Hell*

Burpo, Todd: *Heaven Is for Real: A Little Boy's Astounding Story of His Trip to Heaven and Back*

Butt, Kyle: *A Loving God and an Eternal Hell* (audio)

Chan, Francis; Sprinkle, Preston: *Erasing Hell: What God Said About Eternity, and the Things We've Made Up*

Conway, Bobby: *Hell, Rob Bell, and What Happens When People Die*

Conway, Bobby: *Hell, Rob Bell, and What Happens When People Die* (audio, from moodyaudio.com)

Cooper, John W.: *Body, Soul and Life Everlasting: Biblical Anthropology and the Monism-Dualism Debate*

Dixon, Larry: *Farewell, Rob Bell: A Biblical Response to 'Love Wins'*

Dixon, Larry: *The Other Side of the Good News*

Dodds, Bill: *Your One-Stop Guide to Heaven, Hell and Purgatory*

D'Souza, Dinesh: *Life after Death: The Evidence*

Erickson, Millard: *How Shall They Be Saved? The Destiny of Those Who Do Not Hear of Jesus*

Esposito, Lenny: *How Can a Loving God Send People to Hell?* (audio)

Fenimore, Angie: *Beyond the Darkness: My Near-Death Journey to the Edge of Hell and Back*

Fernandes, Phil: *Rob Bell is Wrong: Hell is Real* (audio)

Fernando, Ajith: *Crucial Questions About Hell*

Frazier, Gary: *Hell Is for Real: Why it Matters*

Foglein, Stephen A.: *What Do We Know About Our Future? (Heaven, Hell, Purgatory) A Conservative Space-Age Approach*

Galli, Mark: *God Wins: Heaven, Hell, and Why the Good News is Better than 'Love Wins'*

Gerstner, John: *Repent or Perish*

Gerstner, John: *The Doctrine of Hell; Who Is In Danger of Hell?; How to Escape Hell* (audio)

Graham, Billy: *Where I Am: Heaven, Eternity, and Our Life Beyond*

Guardini, Romano: *Eternal Life: What You Need to Know About Death, Judgment, and Life Everlasting*

Hahn, Scott: *Why the Hell?* (audio set)

Hanegraaff, Hank: *AfterLife: What You Really Want to Know About Heaven and the Hereafter*

Herr, Allen H.: *Hell* (audio)

House, Paul R.; Thornbury, Gergory A.: *Who Will Be Saved? Defending the Biblical Understanding of God, Salvation, & Evangelism*

Hyde, Daniel R.: *In Defense of the Descent*
Jackson, Wayne: *The Goodness of God and an Eternal Hell* (audio)
Johnson, Carl G.: *Hell You Say*
Jones, Brian: *Hell Is Real (But I Hate to Admit It)*
Kostenberger, Andreas: *The Doctrines of Heaven and Hell* (audio, from moodyaudio.com)
Koukl, Gregory: *Hell, Yes!: The Terrifying Truth* (audio)
Liguori, St. Alphonse: *What Will Hell Be Like?* (J. Schaefer, Ed.)
Lutzer, Erwin W.: *One Minute After You Die*
Lutzer, Erwin (on John Ankerberg Show): *What Will Happen to You One Minute After You Die?* (audio)
Lutzer, Erwin; Gibson, Gary: *What Happens When You Die?* (audio, from moodyaudio.com)
MacArthur, John: *The Reality of Hell* (audio); *The Furnace of Fire* (audio); *Is Hell a Real Place?* (audio); *A Testimony of One Surprised to be in Hell* (5-part audio)
Martin, Albert N.: *Unspeakable Torment; Body & Soul Shall Suffer; Divine Retribution for Sin; Degrees of Punishment; Conscious, Endless Suffering; False Teaching of Universalism; False Teaching of Annihilationo; Effect This Doctrine Should Have on Believers; Effect This Doctrine Should Have on the Unconverted* (audio)
Martin, Regis: *The Last Things: Death, Judgment, Heaven, Hell*
McGee, J. Vernon: *Hell: Fact or Fantasy?* (audio)
Meister, Chad: *Is the Christian Doctrine of Hell Unconscionable?* (DVD)
Melton, James L.: *Questions and Answers About Hell*
Miller, Dave: *Who Believes in Hell Any More?* (audio)
Milot, Roger A.: *Did Jesus Burn in Hell?*
Moore, David George: *The Battle for Hell: A Survey and Evaluation of Evangelicals' Growing Attraction to the Doctrine of Annihilation*
Moreland, J.P.: *A Case for Life After Death* (audio)
Morey, Robert A.: *Death and the Afterlife*
Morey, Robert: *Hell* (audio)
Morgan, Chris: *Jonathan Edwards and Hell*
Morgan, Christopher W.; Peterson, Robert A.: *What Is Hell?*
Morgan, Christopher W.; Peterson, Robert A. (Eds.): *Is Hell for Real or Does Everyone Go to Heaven?*

Morgan, Christopher W.; Peterson, Robert A. (Eds.): *Hell Under Fire: Modern Scholarship Reinvents Eternal Punishment*

Packer, J.I.: *The Problem of Eternal Punishment* (audio)

Peterson, Robert A.: *Hell on Trial: The Case for Endless Punishment*

Peterson, Robert A.: *Conditionalism: Hell Is Under Fire* (audio)

Petrisko, Thomas W.: *Inside Heaven and Hell: What History, Theology and the Mystics Tell Us About the Afterlife*

Petrisko, Thomas W.: *Inside Purgatory: What History, Theology and the Mystics Tell Us about Purgatory*

Pink, Arthur: *Eternal Punishment*

Piper, Don: *90 Minutes in Heaven: A True Story of Death and Life*

Ramsey, Thor: *The Most Encouraging Book on Hell Ever*

Rhodes, Ron: *What Happens After Life?: 21 Amazing Revelations About Heaven and Hell*

Rhodes, Ron: *Does Hell Really Exist?* (audio, from moodyaudio.com)

Rice, John: *Hell: What The Bible Says About It*

Rice, John: *Predestined for Hell?*

Richardson, Don: *Eternity in Their Hearts*

Robertson, David: *The Horrors of Hell* (audio, from moodyaudio.com)

Ruckman, Peter S.: *Hell Fire and Damnation Sermons Collection* (audio set)

Salza, John: *The Biblical Basis for Purgatory*

Shedd, William G.T.: *The Doctrine of Endless Punishment*

Schouppe, F. X.: *The Dogma of Hell: Illustrated by Facts Taken From Profane and Sacred History*

Schouppe, F. X.: *Purgatory: Explained by the Lives and Legends of the Saints*

Schwertley, Brian: *The Biblical Doctrine of Hell* (audio)

Sproul, R.C.: *Hell* (audio series; includes: *The Place of God's Disfavor; The Great Separation; Degrees of Punishment; The Point of No Return; Questions and Answers*)

Staples, Tim: *Last Call: The Catholic Teaching on Death-Judgment-Heaven-Hell* (audio set)

Sumner, Robert L.: *Hell is No Joke*

Tada, Joni Eareckson: *Heaven: Your Real Home*

Turek, Frank: *Hell? The Truth About Eternity* (audio)

Wales, Seán: *The Last Things: What Catholics Believe About Death, Judgment, Heaven and Hell*

Walls, Jerry L.: *Hell: The Logic of Damnation*

White, James: *Universalism Considered*

Whyte III, Daniel: *Hell: Do We Really Believe It? (A Biblical Response to Rob Bell's Redefining of Hell in his Book, Love Wins)*

Wiese, Bill: *23 Minutes In Hell: One Man's Story About What He Saw, Heard, and Felt in that Place of Torment*

Wiese, Bill: *Hell: Separate Truth from Fiction and Get Your Toughest Questions Answered*

Wilkerson, David: *Judgement Day* (audio)

Wittmer, Michael E.: *Christ Alone: An Evangelical Response to Rob Bell's 'Love Wins'*

Woodcock, Eldon: *Hell: An Exhaustive Look at a Burning Issue*

Younce, Max D.: *A Biblical Examination of Hell*

Historical Publications:

Anonymous: *Universalism Tested by Reason and Revelation* (1848)

Butler, Samuel: *Lectures on Modern Universalism - an Exposure of the System* (1856)

Calvin, John: *Soul Sleep: Psychopannychia*

Catherine of Genoa: *Treatise on Purgatory* [abridged] (16th century)

Cooke, Parsons: *Modern Universalism Exposed in an Examination of the writings of Rev. Walter Balfour* (1834)

Edwards, Jonathan: *Sinners in the Hands of an Angry God*

Edwards, Jonathan: *The End of the Wicked Contemplated by the Righteous*

Empie, Adam: *Remarks on the Distinguishing Doctrine of Modern Universalism Which Teaches that There is No Hell and No Punishment for the Wicked After Death* (1825)

Falconer, Alexander: *Universalism Antiscriptural* (1875)

Furniss, C. Ss.R., Rev. John: *The Sight of Hell* (1874, posthumous)

George, Nathan D.: *An Examination of Universalism, Embracing Its Rise and Progress, and the Means of Its Propagation* (1846)

George, Nathan D.: *Universalism Not of the Bible* (1856)

Hall, A.W.: *Universalism Against Itself* (1883)

Hatfield, Edwin F.: *Text Book of Modern Universalism in America* (1841)

Kinkead, Rev. Thomas L.: *An Explanation of the Baltimore Catechism* (1891)

Kinkead, Rev. Thomas L.: *Baltimore Catechism No. 3* (Ed.) (1885)

M'Calla, W.L.: *Discussion of Universalism or, A Defence of Orthodoxy against the Heresy of Universalism* (1825)

McClure, A.W.: *Lectures on Ultra-Universalism* (1838)

Parker, Joel: *Lectures on Universalism* (1841)

Power, John H.: *An Exposition of Universalism: Or An Investigation of that System of Doctrine* (1847)

Priest, Josiah: *The Anti-Universalist* (1839)

Pusey, E.B.: *What Is of Faith, as to Everlasting Punishment?: In Reply to Dr. Farrar's Challenge in His 'Eternal Hope'* (1879)

Rogers, George; Pingree, E.M.: *A Review of Rev. John H. Power's Exposition of Universalism* (1847)

Royce, Andrew: *Universalism a Modern Invention and Not According to Godliness* (1839)

Shouppe [or Schouppe], Fr. Francois Xavier: *Hell: The Dogma of Hell*

Shouppe [or Schouppe], Fr. Francois Xavier: *Purgatory: Explained by the Lives and Legends of the Saints* (1893)

Smith, Matthew Hale: *Universalism Examined, Renounced, Exposed* (1844)

Softley, Edward: *Modern Universalism and Materialism as Viewed in the Light of Holy Scripture* (1879)

Todd, Lewis C.: *A Defence, Containing the Author's Renunciation of Universalism, Explained and Enlarged; the Notices and Aspersions of Universalist Editors, Answered and Repelled...* (1834)

DISCUSSIONS, DEBATES

Austin, John M.; Holmes, David: *A Debate On the Doctrines of Atonement, Universal Salvation, And Endless Punishment* (1848)

Cameron, Nigel M. de S.: *Universalism and the Doctrine of Hell*

Carpenter, George; Hughes, John: *Debate on the Destiny of the Wicked* (1875)

Craig, William Lane; Bradley, Raymond: *Can a Loving God Send People to Hell?* (audio)

Crockett, William (Ed.): *Four Views On Hell*

Date, Chris; Fernandes, Phil: *Is Hell Forever? Does the Bible Teach that Hell Will Be Annihilation or Eternal Torment?* (audio; available on rethinkinghell.com)

Date, Chris; Richardson, Joel: *The Underground Episode 33: The Case for Rethinking Hell* (video available at: https://vimeo.com/158824480)

Date, Chris; Mohler, Albert: *Should Christians Rethink Hell?* (audio; available on rethinkinghell.com)

Date, Chris; Pettis, Len: *Is Conditional Immortality Biblical?* debate (audio available on rethinkinghell.com; video available on YouTube)

Foster, Benjamin Franklin; Lozier, John Hogarth: *Theological Discussion on Universalism and Endless Punishment* (1867)

Fudge, Edward William; Peterson, Robert A.: *Two Views of Hell*

Hanson, John Wesley: Lozier, John Hogarth: *A Brief Debate on Universal Salvation/Endless Punishment* (1879)

Lavell, J.R.; Harris, G.P.: *Oral Debate on the Doctrines of Universal Salvation and Endless Punishment* (1853)

Manford, Erasmus; Franklin, Benjamin: *An Oral Debate on the Coming of the Son of Man, Endless Punishment, and Universal Salvation* (1860)

Manford, Erasmus; Sweeney, John Steele: *A Discussion on Universal Salvation and Future Punishment* (1870)

Morey, Robert vs. Wisbrock, George: *Soul Sleep and Conditionalism Debate* (audio)

Parry, Robin A.; Partridge, Christopher H. (Eds.): *Universal Salvation? The Current Debate*

Pingree, Enoch Merrill; Rice, Nathan Lewis: *A Debate on the Doctrine of Universal Salvation* (1845)

Sawyer, Thomas Jefferson; Wescott, Isaac: *A Discussion of the Doctrine of Universal Salvation: Question: Do the Scriptures Teach the Final Salvation of all Men?* (1854)

Skinner, Dolphus; Campbell, Alexander: *A Discussion of the Doctrines of Endless Misery and Universal Salvation in an Epistolary Correspondence* (1840)

Sprinkle, Preston (Ed.): *Four Views on Hell* (Second Edition)

White, James; Roger & Faith Forster: *Hell: Two Different Views Debated* (from "Unbelievable" radio show, available on premierchristianradio.com)

White, James; Rutland, Bill: *Is It Possible for Non-Christians to Enter Heaven?* (audio; from aomin.org)

White, James; Sanders, John: *Is Knowing Jesus the Only Way to Be Saved?* (audio; from aomin.org)

Moody Radio also broadcast an "Up for Debate" program with Edward Fudge and Kevin Zuber in 2013.

THOSE WHO "HAVE NOT HEARD"

Crockett, William V.: *Through No Fault of Their Own?: The Fate of Those Who Have Never Heard*

Erickson, Millard J.: *How Shall They Be Saved? The Destiny of Those Who Do Not Hear of Jesus*

Esposito, Lenny: *What About Those Who Have Never Heard?* (audio)

Fackre, Gabriel; Nash, Ronald H.; Sanders, John: *What About Those Who Have Never Heard? Three Views on the Destiny of the Unevangelized*

Hick, John: *God Has Many Names*

House, Paul R.; Thornbury, Gregory A.: *Who Will Be Saved? Defending the Biblical Understanding of God, Salvation, & Evangelism*

Knitter, Paul: *No Other Name?: A Critical Survey of Christian Attitudes Toward the World Religions*

Okholm, Dannis L.; Phillips, Timothy R. (Eds.): *More Than One Way? Four Views on Salvation in a Pluralistic World*

Pinnock, Clark H.: *A Wideness in God's Mercy: The Finality of Jesus Christ in a World of Religions*

Piper, John: *Jesus: The Only Way to God: Must You Hear the Gospel to be Saved?*

Piper, John: *Let the Nations Be Glad!: The Supremacy of God in Missions*

Sanders, John: *No Other Name: An Investigation Into the Destiny of the Unevangelized*

UNITARIAN UNIVERSALISM, LIBERAL RELIGION

Allen, Ethan: *Reason the Only Oracle of Man* (1784)

Bumbaugh, David E.: *Unitarian Universalism: A Narrative History*

Morrison-Reed, Mark D.: *Black Pioneers in a White Denomination*
Parke, David B.: *The Epic of Unitarianism: Original Writings from the History of Liberal Religion*
Robinson, David: *The Unitarians and the Universalists*
Walters, Kerry: *Revolutionary Deists: Early America's Rational Infidels*

WORLDWIDE CHURCH OF GOD/HERBERT ARMSTRONG

The Worldwide Church of God was founded by Herbert Armstrong, and espoused the Conditional Immortality/Annihilationist perspective. Since Armstrong's death, however, the church (now known as "Grace Communion International") has moved somewhat closer to the "traditionalist" perspective. A number of "offshoot" churches still endorse and publish Armstrong's original writings. The evolution of this movement can be traced through the following materials:

Armstrong, Herbert W.: *The Autobiography of Herbert W. Armstrong*
Armstrong, Herbert W.: *This Is the Worldwide Church of God*
Barrett, David V.: *The Fragmentation of a Sect: Schism in the Worldwide Church of God*
Flurry, Stephen: *Raising the Ruins: The Fight to Revive the Legacy of Herbert W. Armstrong*
Nichols, Larry; Mather, George: *Discovering the Plain Truth: How the Worldwide Church of God Encountered the Gospel of Grace*
Tkach, Joseph: *Transformed by Truth*
Tkach, Joseph: *Called to be Free* (DVD)

DVDs

Batchelor, Doug: *Lake of Fire*
Blackwell, Don: *Where Do We Go When We Die?*
Campbell, Charlie H.: *Answers to the Tough Questions About Hell*
DRC Productions: *Escape from Hell* (movie)
Frazier, Gary: Hell *is For Real: Cancel Your Reservation*
Lightbridge Films: *Purgatory: The Forgotten Church*
Meister, Chad: *Is the Christian Doctrine of Hell Unconscionable?*
Miller, Kevin (Dir.): *Hellbound?*

Missler, Chuck: *Heaven and Hell: What Happens When You Die?*
Rethinking Hell: *2015 Conference Presentations*
St. Joseph Communications: *What Every Catholic Needs to Know About Hell*
Wood, Kevin (Dir.): *Hell And Mr. Fudge* (movie)

SOME HELPFUL WEBSITES

Christian Universalism (Universal Reconciliation) and Related Concepts: (http://www.auburn.edu/~allenkc/univart.html) Maintained on (but not affiliated with) Auburn University website; lots of downloadable books (often from 19th century), articles, etc.

Dictionary of Unitarian and Universalist Biography: (http://uudb.org/index.html) contains hundreds of concise biographies of Unitarian and Universalist leaders.

Edward Fudge: (http://edwardfudge.com/) Articles, videos, etc., by the Conditionalist author of *The Fire That Consumes.*

Hell Truth: (http://www.helltruth.com/) Lots of downloadable books, audio, video, articles, etc.; available for purchase, as well.

Internet Archive (archive.org) has a lot of downloadable (free) .pdf books in the public domain, from the 18th and 19th centuries.

Rethinking Hell: (http://rethinkinghell.com/welcome) By far the best site defending an Evangelical Christian perspective on Conditional Immortality. Their website has numerous (free) downloadable podcasts and other materials; they sponsor conferences (available in audio and video formats).

Tentmaker: (http://www.tentmaker.org/) Has many downloadable (free) books (often from 19th century), discussion board, etc.

The Christian Universalist Association: (http://www.christianuniversalist.org/) Blog, some audio/video resources, book reviews, etc.

The Evangelical Universalist: (http://evangelicaluniversalist.blogspot.com/) Blog and discussion forum of Robin Parry ("Gregory MacDonald").

The Evangelical Universalist Association: (http://www.biblicaluniversalism.org/EUA.html) Some articles, links, etc.

The Truth About Hell: (http://www.thetruthabouthell.net/) Articles, links to other websites.

Unitarian Universalist Association: (http://www.uua.org/) Official website of the denomination.

Universal Salvation University: (http://richardwaynegarganta.com/universalsalvation.htm) Downloadable articles, constituting a "course" in Universal Salvation.